ORIGIN
OF HALOES

ORIGIN
OF HALOES

kristen **den hartog**

M&S

LIBRARY AND ARCHIVES CANADA CATALOGUING IN PUBLICATION

Den Hartog, Kristen, 1965-
Origin of haloes / Kristen den Hartog.

ISBN 0-7710-2620-X

I. Title.

PS8557.E537O75 2005   C813'.6   C2004-906092-9

We acknowledge the financial support of the Government of Canada through the Book Publishing Industry Development Program and that of the Government of Ontario through the Ontario Media Development Corporation's Ontario Book Initiative. We further acknowledge the support of the Canada Council for the Arts and the Ontario Arts Council for our publishing program.

Typeset in Fournier by M&S, Toronto
Printed and bound in Canada

This book is printed on acid-free paper
that is 100% ancient-forest friendly (100% post-consumer recycled).

McClelland & Stewart Ltd.
The Canadian Publishers
481 University Avenue
Toronto, Ontario
M5G 2E9
www.mcclelland.com

1 2 3 4 5   09 08 07 06 05

For Jeff

CONTENTS

THE BEGINNING   1

1   ROME 1960, the garden of weeds and roses   19
2   TOKYO 1964, the happy years   69
3   MEXICO CITY 1968, *la lune*   119
4   MUNICH 1972, the invisible eye   171
5   MONTREAL 1976, our lady of the snows   231
6   MOSCOW 1980, saint margaret and the dragon   291

THE END   337

THE BEGINNING

As Kay Clancy told it, one day she was jumping on the high-school trampoline, tumbling up and back down, and instead of landing and bouncing again, as she had done since she was four years old, she fell into Joe LeBlanc's Herculean arms. Happy times followed. There was a child, Estelle, and then another, Louis, but while the third was still inventing herself inside her mother's body, Joe wandered away — which was the part Kay so rarely mentioned. As the baby grew in the womb, the father faded, so together (but not) they formed the sad cliché of ships passing. From the beginning, the child called Margar was shockingly like him. She developed stiltish legs and dangling arms, flat brown hair, and eyes that loomed in her face as though not quite fixed there — too big for the fine bones, too searching.

When he left, just weeks before her birth, it was his second and final disappearance. Where he went is anyone's guess. As

Margar settled into Kay's bony pelvis in preparation for the short but momentous journey, Joe made strides of his own. He entered the garage and pulled out his red scratchless canoe. He put it over his head like a dramatic hat, and he walked with it all the way to the shore of the Ottawa River, as he had done every day for weeks on end. The trees and birds saw him going. The fish saw the boat's red bottom gliding along the river's surface, the glint of a paddle dipping in.

Day in and day out in those final weeks, Joe had paddled over a crack where the riverbed yawned open. Not far from the shore and hidden by water, the black drop-off swallowed the rippled sand, and extended so far down that the river was said to be bottomless. Divers had swum into it, determined to reach or at least glimpse the bottom, but such a feat had never been achieved. People had slipped into the river and never surfaced again. It was the chance one took when entering. No one knew whether that was what had happened to Joe. Or at least, no one said they knew. In one way or another, countless secrets had been thrown into the river for safekeeping, but the river made no promises. It might tell, it might not.

Since the beginning of time, the inhabitants of this valley had looked into the Ottawa River for fish the way Romans looked to the sky for birds. Great emperors based their toughest decisions on the flight and whimsy of birds, so it stood to reason that here, every riddle might be laid bare in the swish of fins or the trout's rainbow pattern. But rather than answers, more questions bubbled up from the river's deepest chasms.

Years before now and years after the birth of Rome, French explorers floated through the Valley in their canoes. So black were the waters into which they dipped their oars, the explorers named the stretch *"la rivière creuse."* Unimpressed, but not oblivious to the change, the creatures who had been there forever continued to wade near the shore – the deer and the raccoons, the bears, the huge moose with their doleful eyes, and, of course, the people. On the land, trees fell and decayed, and new ones grew out of the soft dead trunks, with millions of insects thriving unseen in the patches of moss and lichen. Time rolled forward with no regard for itself.

It wasn't until 1945 that bulldozers thundered through the Valley to make way for a town. Signs that read "Deep River" went up at either end of the place. In hindsight, the signs might have been a warning, but no one heeded, or even understood.

Deep River was a planned community, rather than one that evolved naturally, road by road, store by store, as the population grew. It had the look of a toytown placed – misplaced – in the midst of a jungle. The creatures and the people who had always been there persevered as architect John Bland encouraged streets to curve around them and undulate along the natural slope that led to the river. Nearby, a nuclear-research laboratory rose up, and brainy scientists from all over the world came to work there. Big houses were built for them, "the professionals," and little houses – boxes with windows and doors – were built for everyone else. Or rather, they were brought. As the war came to an end, munitions factories closed in nearby towns in Quebec and Ontario. The "war-fours" and "war-sixes," simple houses with four or six rooms, were sliced in half and brought by rail to the little town-to-be, where they were put back together again by German prisoners of war.

3

The laboratory was constructed at the edge of town, and the scientists who arrived made their homes in what had once been fishing grounds and timber country, a land thick with red and white pines. Wilderness pressed on the town's borders so heavily that it sometimes broke through. Bears padded along the paved streets. They cut across lawns that were now free from weeds, and wondered where the trees had gone, and the berries. Birds swooped overhead to see the tidy devastation.

It was a strange, exciting time. People moved from urban splendour into backwoods Ontario, where they were eaten by black flies and bitten by frost. The respites were spring, when the trilliums emerged and the frogs came back to life; and fall, when everything died again in kaleidoscopic grandeur.

Certainly there was friction between the cosmopolitan newcomers and long-time residents of the Ottawa Valley. The latter were mainly natives and French, who had intermarried for generations, and a mix of Irish, Scottish, and German. They lived in log cabins dotted along the river's edge, but all of these were ignited except one (whose occupants refused to leave), and the families, suddenly outsiders, were relocated to make way for Bland's orderly design. "Here is seventy-five dollars," they were told. "Pack your things and move along, please." And the plumes of smoke dispersed into grey clouds that hung over the Valley as the cabins burned.

After a time, some of the wounds were closed by desire. Families from away began to marry into local clans, and their descendants grew up speaking with a distinct Valley twang. For others, however, the division remained strong. Throughout the sixties, the era of peace and free love, there were those on the outskirts who wouldn't shop in the town, or let their young ones play there. But the scientists, holding fast to that long tradition of the upper crust, remained largely, arrogantly unaware of the hostility. In minds both dim and brilliant, they believed they'd improved – or rather started – a community. They brought their wives and kids, which meant that teachers and schools were needed, as well as shops and people to run them. Soon there was a Bank of Montreal, a tennis court, a hospital, a grocery store. And not long after that, there was everything any little town could hope for: a choral group, four churches, a drama club, a diving club (to investigate the chasm), a chess club, a yacht club, a cinema, a Legion, an arena, a public school, a Catholic school, a high school, Brownies, Girl Guides, Cubs, Scouts, a library, a swimming pool, two beaches, a ski hill, and a dairy that had cows in its backyard. In the altered landscape, the animals grew wary. The fish stayed far from the shore, in the darkest water. Birds squawked messages to each other in the leafy trees, and deep within their feathers, an infestation swarmed. The huge white pines that had not been toppled held fast to the earth. They stretched their arms wide and screamed through the knots in their bark, but few humans heard them. The ragged cedars grew on, and released their scent for the deer, who would now only come at night, aware as they were of some invisible danger, the kind only humans can bring.

The story of Joe and Kay and Margar was a tale of such danger, of secrets kept and revealed, a tale of lies and consequence. It began like the meeting of water and sky, when Joe waded out of the river and in his arms caught Kay as she fell from above. Together, they had three children. In a handful of years Joe would be gone, and his absence would come to define him and the rest of them, too, though the littlest child, Margar, never knew him at all. Yet, because she went looking, it was she who bumped into him most often after he had gone.

One such occasion occurred late in August 1976, in Margar's eleventh year. Kay, Louis, Estelle, Margar, and their neighbour, Ms. Ramona Devlin, piled into the car and drove the three hours from their little town to the city of Ottawa to shop for school clothes. There, they rode through winding streets and stared into leaded-glass windows. The old mansions were made of stone and brick. Lush, sculpted gardens grew upon the wide green lawns of the privileged, and flowers leaned with the breeze.

Margar was in the middle of pretending she belonged in such a place when, stopped at a light, Ms. Devlin gasped and pointed. There was Margaret Trudeau, sparkling wife of Pierre, the debonair prime minister, out walking with her sons. Sacha and Justin ambled one on each side of her and Micha sat in a stroller, gurgling like any regular baby. No one spoke, but every last LeBlanc and Ms. Devlin stared and pressed against each other for a better view. Margar's face was hot and her heart was pounding. She looked around for Pierre, but he was nowhere. And just as she looked back to Margaret and Margaret's twinkling eye met hers, Ms. Devlin honked the horn and began to wave madly.

In her gangling body, Margar shrank with shame. She saw Margaret's lovely mouth spread into a smile that belied all the turmoil to come. She saw her raise a delicate hand and wave at them, and Margar cringed in her seat, squished against the door by Louis and Estelle, who leaned over her, gawking. As if she were looking through Margaret Trudeau's eyes, she saw all five of them grinning and drooling, a car full of nobodies. Ms. Devlin with her brassy hairdo made hard with spray; Kay squealing beside her; Estelle holding up her fingers in the peace sign; and Louis, even Louis embarrassed her by staring with his hound-dog eyes. Margar saw herself, too, her limp hair and her sallow skin, her eyes bigger and gloomier than Louis's, at odds with her rapscallion nature. And having seen herself, she could no longer pretend she lived in the Museum of Man or the Château Laurier Hotel, grand buildings full of windows – not homes, of course, but she wanted a mansion as big. When she was back in her own body, she looked out at Margaret and away again. For years she'd told herself she'd been named for Margaret Sinclair Trudeau, instead of boring old Saint Margaret, but she had not. Margaret Trudeau gave the name a certain pizzazz, while Saint Margaret bogged it down with God and the crucifix. Either way – Louis had shortened her name to Margar, stripping it of dignity. He was three when she was born, and couldn't pronounce Margaret. There were infinite differences between Margar and Margaret. Margar LeBlanc knew she would remember this day forever, and that Margaret Trudeau would have forgotten by nightfall.

As the car pulled away, full of chatters and giggles, only Margar kept watching through the rear window. Only she saw him come alive on the sidewalk: Joe LeBlanc, standing at the base of the stone steps that led up and over a grassy hill. He smiled and nodded at Margaret, and Margar watched him take one end of the stroller that held baby Micha. He helped the young family up the stairs, and Margar held her breath for fear of bursting the moment. His legs, his shoulders, his head of dark hair disappeared over the hill. The car rounded a corner and they, too, were gone.

The LeBlancs and Ms. Devlin had driven to Ottawa, capital of a huge, sparse nation, because the previous week, on August 19, 1976, the Deep River plaza had burned to the ground, and no shopping could be done there. The big trees watched flames lick and gobble the structure much the way fire had eaten the Centre Block of the Parliament Buildings in 1916. Afterwards, charred metal poles had risen out of the rubble, showing where the stores had been.

Only the day before the fire Margar had roamed through the Metropolitan department store that had formed one end of the plaza. While her mother shopped, she scooped hard candies from the bin and then poured them back in – all except five or six, which she pocketed, as was her habit. The layered sound of them showering down was like pebbles, or marbles. Late that night, there must have been a sweet smell along with the acrid when all those candies burned, but Margar had not detected it far away in her bed. She had slept deeply, dreaming of a do-or-die game of croquet against an invisible opponent. The balls were ostrich eggs, and if she smashed one open with her mallet, she'd kill the baby bird inside. A rush of relief came with each unbroken shell, but then there was that other rush – of exhilaration – that came with the risk of breaking the next one.

All that while the plaza blazed and brightened the night sky. In Ottawa, the fire had been fed by dignified stacks of paper and carved, gleaming woodwork, but here it ate candy and whirling plastic windmills. It tore through rows of cheap clothes for children, and it melted vinyl shoes. The wicks of a shelf of candles were lit by a gargantuan match of fire, and inside the flames, the wax liquefied to nothing.

The local paper said the plaza had been razed to the ground, and Margar had never before seen the word. Until then, she had known only of an opposite raise, to put or take into a higher position, to cause to rise or be vertical, to increase the amount or value or strength of, to construct or build up, to cause to be heard or considered, to rouse from sleep or death, or from a lair, and so on.

⬭⬭⬭⬭⬭

Here is a time-lapsed chronology, a little row of consequence, of fallen dominoes:

Kay Clancy, an aspiring teenaged gymnast of uncommon talent, was being coached by a near-Olympian when she met Joséph Patrice Emmanuel François Gabriel LeBlanc, or Joe, in 1960. Both came from families that had dwelled in Valley towns for generations. Joe, of White Pine, Ontario, was descended from a long line of rivermen who sent logs down the Ottawa. His father, Jacques, died doing just that, and Joe grew up without him, under the somewhat shoddy care of his mother, Delphine, which his two great-uncles said was a great tragedy. When the town of White Pine was flooded to make room for a dam, Delphine went south, and Joe, almost but not quite a man, stayed behind. White Pine filled up with water, and the streets Joe had known as a child were washed from the face of the earth, but Kay later said it was a lucky thing, because otherwise he might not have found her when he walked the nine miles to Deep River to live with his uncles, Alphonse and Toussaint.

In Kay's account of the fall and subsequent capture, she claimed, "I don't know myself how it happened. All I can tell you is, one minute I was in a back flip, spinning through the air, and the next, I was in his arms. I don't know where he came from – well, I do. I mean, he came from White Pine, you know that." Here she always laughed, amused with herself, and then became serious. "I mean, I don't know how he came to be in the gym, happening by, right at the moment my spin went wrong. He always said he was just out walking, that he liked walking. He was always out walking, so that's true, I suppose. But I have to tell you" – and her eyes would lift and focus on some distant image – "I think it was more than that. I think he was sent to me."

There were two points in Kay's story at which Margar longed to interrupt. When Kay said, "I don't know where he came from," Margar wanted to ask, "But do you know where he went?" And when Kay said, "I think he was sent to me," Margar wanted to ask, "And away? Do you think he was sent away from you too?" But she said nothing, and continued to pretend that she was just fine without him, for as she'd heard her mother say, how could a child miss what she had never known? But she did miss him. And she looked for him everywhere.

After Joe disappeared for the second time, the myth that surrounded him remained open-ended. He may have tipped his canoe and drowned. What, then, of his body? Even the legendary painter Tom Thomson eventually resurfaced. Eight days after he vanished in this same neck of the woods, he floated up in the placid waters of Canoe Lake, a purple wound at his temple. Which meant the unknown handyman Joe LeBlanc was a man of greater mystery, for he was never seen again. What happened to him was a question around which lives would be sculpted. The possibilities were many, and made the probability misty and easy to ignore. He had been spotted portaging to the river, as usual, but one theory suggested the man with the canoe might not even have been Joe LeBlanc. Admittedly his face was never seen, only his loping, river-bound body, distinct but not singular, making room for the idea that Joe had not run off at all, had perhaps been kidnapped, tied up in the canoe, and carried away by a look-alike stranger.

Margar arose fatherless in the age of the yellow happy face. The flat circle head and eyes, the black half-circle grin, alarmed her brother Louis, but Margar was without fear from her very first moments. Set apart as she was (the last one, and possibly unwanted), she pushed her differences to the extreme, so that before she had all her baby teeth she was a rascal, a mischievous sleepwalker, a pickpocketing imp who needed no one to get by. While Louis quaked in his tiny body, hungry Margar reached out for everything and more. As with a puppy, her big baby feet and hands predicted her stature. By the time she was three, she was as big as six-year-old Louis, who had been a huge toddler but had stopped growing. By the time she was ten, she had surpassed both the teenaged Estelle and their mother Kay. It was obvious she more than resembled her father, but it was rarely mentioned. Without him, Margar was a tall anomaly, a giant in a family of dolls. But she was cunning – no one ever knew she minded.

Nor would they know, years later, how she wept at the death of Pierre Trudeau. It was in September of the year 2000, during the Sydney Olympic Games, that the charismatic former prime minister got old and died. The whole country mourned for both the man and the era in which they had come to know him, but Margar took to her bed, weeping like a schoolgirl who was thirty-five years old. People lined up on Parliament Hill to touch his flag-draped coffin; they lined up again in the tiny towns throughout Ontario and Quebec to watch his funeral train roll by, but Margar, bedridden, was paralyzed with sadness. Transfixed by the images on television, she decided the procession was of a time more romantic than now, and was therefore one that suited him. Two of Trudeau's beautiful sons stood at the window and offered their grief-laden smiles, and when she looked at them, she thought not only of Pierre but of the third son, Micha, who had been swept away in an avalanche just two years before – the little baby she had seen in the stroller long ago. And though Pierre had courted so many women before and since his wife, she thought of Margaret, too, there being something everlasting even about families that don't last.

⬭

A picture of Kay was still hanging in the high school by the time Margar attended. Back arched, flat gymnast's chest thrust out, one leg lifted, she balanced on the beam. Kay Clancy, Female Athlete of the Year 1960. She was sixteen then, the same year she landed in Joe's ropey arms. His muscles had been long and graceful, his skin covered with a fine down.

A year after that – an Olympic year – a very pregnant Kay could still do the splits, though she was advised not to. "Stop it!" yelled her mother. "Stop it right now, Kay! It might come out!" Eventually, of course, it did, and easily, due to the limberness of

12

Kay's young body and perhaps also due to the placid, happy nature of Estelle, who emerged blissfully unaware of her foul beginnings. Joe was gone for her birth too. Out walking. This was his first disappearance.

Kay, bewildered but no longer alone, not ever, named the baby Estelle Huguette LeBlanc, in honour of the phantom French father. She hoped Estelle would be a ballerina. Russian champion Larysa Latynina had been a bit of a ballerina before becoming an Olympic gymnast, and balletic grace showed in her every twirl. Wearing pink furry slippers, with Estelle in her womb, Kay had watched the black-and-white Olympic Games on a brand new television. Larysa Latynina had been pregnant too. She won three gold medals, as well as a silver and a bronze, and stole the All-Around title from veteran Hungarian gymnast Agnes Keleti. Things could have been different had Kay Clancy been in Rome that year. She might have had the talent to compete, but now she was only watching. And even that was a challenge. Time and again Kay's empty gaze drifted away from the screen to the legs below or the antenna above. It was the antenna that brought the world into her living room, but Kay had no idea how, and no particular desire to solve such a large, unwieldy mystery. She believed there were things one was better off not knowing.

⟨⟨⟨⟨⟩⟩⟩⟩

High along the walls of the main hall, among the photographic portraits of Kay and others who'd brought glory to the school, there was for many years a picture of Joe LeBlanc, though he attended the school only sporadically and certainly was no

13

athlete in the common sense of the word. Once, when Margar visited the school to see Estelle in the band, Louis showed her the picture, just as he had once been shown by Estelle.

"Look," said Louis, pointing.

Margar looked up. The photo was of Robbie Hayes, Male Athlete of the Year 1960, son of Margar's piano teacher. Taken from a strange angle, it caused his legs to look very long, his torso very short, and his head very small.

"So?" said Margar.

"Look harder," said Louis.

Margar craned her neck and squinted. There was Joe, passing by in the background, the river and its trees behind him. She could see him only faintly, from the side, but she knew it was he. The extra-long stride of his legs. The hooked nose. Margar touched her own nose and glanced furtively up and down the main hall.

"Boost me," she told Louis.

"*What?* No way!"

But he did. Louis nearly always did what anyone told him. Margar teetered on one foot in Louis's small clasped hands. She lifted the picture from its hook and hopped down, and for a heart-racing moment they stood looking at him, their father, at his shoes and spanned hands, at his far-away crew-cut hair. Footsteps sounded in the distance. Margar slid the picture into her coat and ran with Louis along the hall, down the stairs, and straight outside, leaving a gap in the hall of glory.

⟨⟨⟨⟨⟨⟨⟩⟩⟩⟩⟩⟩

When Joe left the first time, just before Kay's waist began to thicken with Estelle, Kay never expected to see him again. After all, until he'd appeared out of nowhere, she had never seen him before. He had shown up, caught and dazzled her, and disappeared again. Or so the story went.

"Well?" said Kay's mother. "What are you going to do now?"

"I don't know," said Kay.

"This is a fine pickle, Kay, a fine pickle indeed."

The words were repeated so often that Kay herself adopted them. Or, more precisely, she adapted them. Patting her belly, she'd whisper, "How you doing in there, little pickle? Hmmm? My fine tiny pickle?"

But Joe came back. And years later, because he had once before disappeared and reappeared of his own volition, next to no one searched for him when he vanished a second time, on August 25, 1965, weeks before the birth of a third child. "He'll be back," they said. There was no hunt, no official dragging of the river, not yet. He was the boy who cried wolf – if he expected to be looked for, found, forgiven, or even understood, he was mistaken. As soon as she could, Kay resumed work at her parents' restaurant, and took what help could be offered by them and Joe's great-uncles. To her children, she said that Joe would come home. If he had lost his way, he would soon find it again. And then she said it less often. And after a time, not at all.

At first there was a flurry of theories about what had become of Joe LeBlanc. Ramona Devlin, then a new neighbour and soon-to-be family friend, saw him cross the yard that blue summer day and head toward the Ottawa River. In any case she said she saw *someone* – though she swore she would know him, canoe or none, because with his green pants and his Jack-pine legs, his size-thirteen shoes, he was unmistakable. And certainly it was his custom, in those last days, to pace to the river with that canoe on his head. Ramona had been out on her porch, painting her toenails, her dog Olive beside her. Joe passed amid the early morning sounds of summer: the buzz of tree frogs, the birds chirping, a sprinkler hissing in the distance.

"Good morning," called Ramona, but if Joe replied, his voice got lost in the dark hollow of the canoe. Olive yapped and growled as he strode past, but no one understood her warning.

After that, accounts of his whereabouts varied. One man said he saw Joe LeBlanc paddle right across the river to the Quebec side, but he called the canoe aluminum, and said it flashed in the sun and almost blinded him, which a red canoe would not do. Another man said he had seen Joe LeBlanc on land, boarding a bus headed for Montreal, but that he had been wearing yellow pants, not green ones, and Joe LeBlanc did not and would not own a pair of yellow pants, on that everyone who really knew him agreed.

It was a woman who said she saw him thumbing a ride westward on Highway 17. She claimed he got into a red convertible and that his hat, made from straw, had blown off when the car pulled away. What was eerie about this account was that Joe *had* had a straw hat. But such a hat was never found or searched for, not in any formal way, though for years Kay and each of her children would scan the roadside even when they seemed to be looking straight ahead.

Born into a time of pain and sadness, Margar developed her own belief about Joe, secret as a crime, and as chilling: that the thought of her impending arrival was so repugnant to him, he could not remain one moment longer. Something about her that mortified him had emanated from Kay's belly like a poisonous gas or a smelly, jaundiced aura.

Either this, or he had died, never knowing her but loving her just the same.

ROME 1960
the garden of weeds and roses

From August 25 to September 11, 1960, the Olympic Games returned to Rome, where they had ended some 1,500 years before under the reign of the pagan-fearing Christian, Flavius Theodosius. It was perhaps out of respect for him that, all these years later, there was no mascot, no idol to worship, except the athletes themselves. Eighty-three countries participated, bringing 5,338 competitors through the ancient arches and into the Villagio Olympico. Not one of them was Kay Clancy, though she often claimed she'd had what it took. In preparation for the onslaught, tunnels had been burrowed and highways had been built, rejuvenating the saying that all roads lead to Rome.

The contrast of old and new had never been more incongruous: hordes of camera-wielding visitors in snazzy clothes, hats, and sunglasses set against the backdrop of ancient ruined and unruined Rome. Wrestling fans filled the Basilica of Maxentius, as they had two thousand years before, and the Pope, more confident than Flavius Theodosius, watched from his window as rowers traversed the Tiber, the river that swallowed unwanted babies of old and then returned them in the nets of fishermen. Kay didn't know it, but there was a time in Rome when unwanted babies were commonly thrown away, or left on hillsides until they perished or were claimed by someone who could use them later on. *Exposing*, it was called, but Kay was not familiar with that use of the word. To her, *exposing* was showing a part of your body you were meant to keep private, or revealing a doer of nasty deeds. She had done one of these things, but she would never do the other.

Rome was the first Olympic Games to receive full television coverage. It was yet another contrast to see the cobblestones of the Appian Way in one's living room, within the frame of a TV. The marathon was run along this tomb-lined road at night, once the blazing Italian sun had set. The race began on Capitoline Hill, where Rome itself had begun, and it ended, for all intents and purposes, two hours, fifteen minutes, and 15.2 seconds later, when the barefoot Ethiopian son of a shepherd, Abebe Bikila, reached the Arch of Constantine. Worlds were colliding.

This, too, was the year American light heavyweight boxer Cassius Clay beat his Polish rival Zbigniew Pietrzykowski. Once the medal had been placed around Clay's muscular neck, he removed it so rarely that the gold began to wear away, and the dull lead beneath showed through. Later he would claim to have thrown the medal, not into the Tiber, but into the Ohio River in Louisville, Kentucky, when a restaurant in his own hometown would not feed him due to the colour of his skin. Later still he would disclaim that claim, but no one knows — maybe the medal still rests on the riverbed, a relic for a future generation. Volumes could be written on what has disappeared into rivers since the beginning of time – babies, medals, Margar's Malibu Barbie and Ken, and even Kay's wedding band, the hope of eternal love sinking with its circular symbol.

Like the Tiber in Rome and the Ohio in Louisville, the Ottawa River lapped at the shores of Kay Clancy's Valley town. It was a cold river, navy blue, and because of the chasm, as deep as an ocean in places, or deeper. Though the crack in the riverbed made the river's true depth immeasurable, on the surface it looked ordinary enough. Sloshing by the Parliament Buildings in Ottawa, and then on through Arnprior, Constance Bay, and Pembroke, it cut a swath between Ontario and Quebec. But this was the same river that toyed with Jacques the riverman, father of Joe. It spit him into the air again and again, snapping his bones even after he'd succumbed to its wrath and let his eyes fall closed.

When she met Joe LeBlanc, Kay lived in a house on the edge of the river, with her mother and father, who owned a restaurant in which anyone could dine, provided they wore shirts and shoes. She could see the river from her window, the way the Pope could see the Tiber from his, and she could get to it alternately cartwheeling and back-flipping along a path that stemmed from her backyard.

In the years leading up to the Rome Olympics – in the days of footballer Robbie Hayes and the enigmatic Joe LeBlanc, and long before Margar appeared in her father's image – Kay's body was a construct of startling efficiency. Nothing about her was wasted. Her short, muscular legs and arms extended from her torso in exemplary proportion. She was almost breastless, and had a round, tough bottom that served her well in rolls and tumbles, helping to push her through to the other side. She weighed ninety-four pounds. Joe, when he caught her, caught air. As though she was a doll, he held her. So often has Margar conjured that scene, it has become a memory. She sees Joe stretching to six-foot-two in his green pants (she always conjures him in green pants), his arms holding Kay, fresh from a fall and clad in her favourite leotard, vermilion. How the planets must have shifted right then, growing smaller and expanding all at once.

Many questions would be answered in the near or distant future – about Joe and Kay and the unwittingly connected Robbie Hayes – but everything Margar discovered would be out of context, like a tapestry unwoven. The picture could be woven together again, but with strands missing, it would never look quite the same. Perhaps it was just as well that Margar would never know how Kay tried and tried to wrap her tiny self around the hungering body of Joe LeBlanc. Had she been successful in obtaining sex from him, Kay would have changed the course of many lives, but Joe rebuffed her, citing not by any means a lack of desire, but rather an enormous swelling of desire and a fear that he would hurt her.

"I," announced Kay, grinning widely, "am unhurtable. I'm made of elastics! Just watch."

She lifted herself off of him and slid from the pink chesterfield into a headstand, letting her dress fall away from her body. Her panties were purple and blue. She lowered one leg and then the other, arching herself into a bridge. When she climbed back on top of him and he continued to reject her, Kay pleaded, beating his chest and pinching his arms. Finally, she crumpled.

She cried and cried. And then, with her head resting on his chest and her eyes staring at their reflections in the black face of the television, Kay spoke in a flat, clear voice.

"I'm pregnant, Joe. I want the baby to be yours."

(XXXX)

Across town, in a big house on a hill, footballer Robbie Hayes was enjoying a bubble bath. He was not and never would be aware that he had been the seed of such despair and anger, the likes of which he would never know at any point in his tragically short life, ironically void of tragedy.

As he soaked in his coincidentally pink tub, Kay and Joe LeBlanc wrestled and cried on the pink Clancy chesterfield. How could she, Joe wanted to know, and with whom? Why, when, where? What had she been thinking? At the end of every non-answer she gave him, Kay added, "I want it to be yours." But Joe pressed on, craving and dreading answers. He listed boy after boy and she shook her head to all of them. Kay would never know what made him ask about Robbie Hayes, or what made her pause and not answer. She blinked and looked away to convey shame, then bit her lip to convey nervousness. She didn't lie – not yet – but she didn't tell the truth either. And Joe was up and stomping to the door. Her crying eyes couldn't stop him from leaving, which is not to say they had no effect on him. Rather it was the image of Kay's eyes, red and blue, that sent an enraged Joe LeBlanc scissoring all the way across town to the Hayes family home. The rock that smashed the living-room window flew through the space where Robbie's head would have been, had he not been in need of a bath. It landed at the feet of Serge Hayes, mere inches away from his crossed, black-socked feet. His wife Beryl, who had been tinkling the ivories, held her hands above the keys, staring at the rock and the splinters of glass around it.

Almost no one ever knew why or by whom the rock had been thrown, least of all Serge, Beryl, or Robbie.

Joe LeBlanc was gone from town by morning.

⟨⟨⟨⟨⟨⟩⟩⟩⟩⟩

It was not until the fifth month that Kay spoke of her pregnancy to anyone other than Joe. Late one summer evening, after he was gone and showed no sign of returning, she crept along Riverside Drive and slipped unseen into the trees that surrounded Coach Halliwell's blue two-storey. The thick pines and the birches stood behind and around her, and beyond the house ran the river. Pink roses climbed up the blue siding and gave off a sweet perfume that mingled with the smell of wet, hot land. In the moonlit garden, she cried and watched the moths, and waited for Coach Halliwell to appear. But it was the elegant Mrs. Halliwell who came up behind her, having entered the yard from the driveway and seen Kay in a cluster of sunflowers.

"Kay?" she asked. "Is that you?"

Kay could not answer. She stood among the tall, fuzzy stalks, sobbing, and merely nodded when Mrs. Halliwell inquired, "Would you like me to get the coach?"

Mrs. Halliwell stepped lightly along the path toward the house. It was August, but she was carrying a pair of white gloves in her hand, and a white purse dangled from her forearm. Kay cried and watched the empty fingers of the gloves until

24

Mrs. Halliwell entered the house. Before the coach came out, there was a beautiful pause in which the sky turned slate-grey and a moonflower opened. Kay stopped crying. She listened to the river lapping. She envisioned everything unfolding the way it needed to, and smiled. Perhaps she would move in with the Halliwells and they could all raise the baby together.

"Kay?" said the coach.

With his appearance, all of her anxiety returned, and she lunged forward, stretched her arms around his neck, and pressed her tongue into his mouth.

"Stop!" he hissed, grabbing her arms, and in the background, Mrs. Halliwell flipped on the light and spread a large square of bright blue fabric on the kitchen table.

Kay resumed sobbing, and when she finally said it — "I'm pregnant" — her words were so garbled that the coach had to ask her to repeat herself. She told him three times before he accepted what he had heard, and each time he squeezed her arms harder with his strong hands.

After a lengthy silence, she managed, "Coach. I love you," and the dim awareness that she was squandering sacred words made her cry more.

"*Ssshhh*," he hissed. "Get a hold of yourself," though he was the one holding so tightly.

Sweat showed on his forehead, despite the coolish night. Coach Halliwell's breath turned panicky, and the quickness of it reminded Kay of their rendezvous in the gymnasium. The image she preferred of him, the one she thought of whenever other, more disturbing images crowded in, showed him in his green tracksuit, bowing before her, inviting her to dance. He took one of her hands in his and circled her waist with his other arm, and waltzed with her around the gymnasium. That was before they had done anything really wrong, when it was still fun and exciting and seemed like nothing serious would happen, making her wish it would, though she knew it shouldn't. The waltzing went on for weeks before she could stop looking at her feet and the swirling coloured lines on the gym floor. Her laughter echoed in the large room, and the coach held his face to hers with only his finger separating their mouths. Very softly, unlike now, he said, "Ssshhh," because at any time a janitor might go sweeping by in the hall of glory. And then finally, at the end of a waltzing lesson that was supposed to be gymnastics, Coach Halliwell turned out all the lights except one, and spread himself on top of her on the hard floor. She kept thinking it couldn't be, but it was done before she knew how to stop it. Everything changed. Over the top of his head and auburn hair, Kay kept her gaze on the basketball hoop, alternately sick with shame and dizzy with excitement. She had met Joe only days before, not soon enough to slow the momentum of her flirtation with Coach Halliwell.

Now she looked at the sunflowers looming over the coach's head like strangers listening in. "I'm sorry," she said. "To make you mad, I mean."

Coach Halliwell's jaw softened but his eyes remained cold and glittery, as if glass had filled up the two sockets. "It's all right, Kay." He stroked her hair and touched her face with his hand. "Are you sure about this? Your condition, I mean?"

Kay had not previously thought of her pregnancy as a condition, but she supposed it was — a hot disease that in the early days had made her sick at the smell of chicken cooking. By now she had missed four periods. Her rounding stomach was harder to hide.

"Yes," she said, "I'm sure."

Coach Halliwell let his hand slide from her face and looked hard into one eye, then the other. "And – I'm sorry to have to ask this, but it's important – you're sure it's mine?"

It did not occur to Kay to be offended by his question. She thought of Joe on the couch, Joe slamming the door. She wished she wasn't sure, but nodded. "Yes," she said again. "I'm sure."

Coach Halliwell looked away. Under his breath he said, "*Fuck*," which was startling, since he was an adult and a teacher.

Kay followed his glance toward the house and kitchen, where Mrs. Halliwell was cutting the blue fabric. She understood that it would not be possible to live here, but she didn't know what would be possible, or where she would go, or with whom. So she stood and waited. There was a dead worm stuck to the bristly face of a sunflower that rose up behind the coach, and she stared at that as she listened to his breathing escalate once more.

"*Fuck*," he said again, more severely.

"I'm sorry," she repeated. Her tears started again, and the little moans that slipped out of her mouth made him grab her shoulders and shake her, which was so unlike him.

"Stop it," he hissed.

And she even stopped breathing.

Coach Halliwell seemed calm then. He let his arms fall to his sides and surveyed the ground. Slowly he withdrew his wallet and placed several bills in Kay's hand. He leaned forward and kissed her tenderly on one cheek. It was such a mysterious combination – the kiss and the money – that it had to mean two things at once, and so nothing.

"You know what you have to do, Kay." A vein snaked down the middle of his forehead with a pulse that foreshadowed his next words: "And if you say anything, I'll deny it." He turned and walked through the garden, up the steps to the house, and in through the sliding glass door.

She might not have known what he'd meant if a girl hadn't bled to death last summer. The blood had gushed from between her legs, said the rumours, like an empty womb crying. Even if it weren't too late, Kay lacked the courage to risk bleeding to death, and then to miss out on heaven afterwards. Keeping her baby seemed less scary, except for the fact that she would get bigger and bigger, bloated by the awfulness of what she had done, and everyone everywhere would know it. She sank to the soft ground of the garden. The sunflowers looked down at her, and up in the sky, she saw a question mark made out of stars.

⟅⟆⟅⟆⟅⟆

Once he'd pulled the door closed against the garden and the girl lurking there, Russell Halliwell could see only his handsome reflection in the glass, plus that of his wife Marie, and the white stove and fridge behind her.

"It's wonderful," she said to his back, "the way those kids confide in you."

Her husband shrugged, as if it were nothing, when in fact such a comment would be often repeated. In a yearbook printed long after the birth of Estelle, after the reappearance of Joe LeBlanc, after the marriage of Joe and Kay and the birth of

Louis, after the second disappearance of Joe and the arrival of Margar, and in the first year of Pierre Trudeau's reign, the charming Russell Halliwell would still be lauded for his special way with students.

⟨⟨⟨⟨⟨⟩⟩⟩⟩⟩

Three nights later he came to find her.

Kay was walking home from her parents' restaurant when he pulled up beside her in his car.

"Like a ride?" he asked.

Kay climbed in, disconcerting as it was to be in this personal space with him. The car smelled of cigarettes and there were crushed butts in the ashtray, which surprised her, as she hadn't known the coach smoked at all. He lit one now, and his face glowed in the flame of the match. It looked unlike the handsome face from school and the gymnasium – winking, dimpled at the cheek and chin. This face was tired, with puffy circles beneath the eyes, and skin that seemed loose on the bones. She was repulsed to think of it moving close and kissing her as it had done in the past, and as it began to do now, or seemed to. She was queasy, too, from the blue smoke that curled in the air between them. Coach Halliwell's face stopped inches from hers.

"Kay," he said. "I want you to know I'll do anything I can to help you." His expression was soft, coaxing, as it had been in the garden, but his eyes shifted like a cat's. "I'll do anything I can," he repeated, in a whisper this time, and the breath of his words brushed her face.

The car seemed to shrink in on her, turning hot and stuffy and filling with smoke. She wanted to open the window to let the air

29

come through, but there was suddenly something so awful about their secret that she was afraid it would escape on the breeze. Barely visible against the dark sky, bats swooped in silence to the faint song of crickets. Kay looked again at the coach's face in the dim light. She thought about saying "I love you," to somehow make everything kind and romantic, for that was the sort of thing people said when their faces were close like this, but through no apparent will of her own she recoiled. Her back pressed against the passenger door and the metal handle dug into her spine. Coach Halliwell leaned further toward her, and seemed ready to touch her, when the headlights of a passing car illuminated them and he quickly withdrew. He rested his forehead on the steering wheel once the car had gone, and then he said, keeping his head down, "I'll give you more money. You understand what I mean. To get rid of it."

Kay watched the bats. She thought of the dead girl bleeding.

"I hope you will," he said, "but I can't force you. And I can't accompany you either, wherever it is these things are done. It's just too great a risk for me. I'm speaking to you as an adult now, Kay. You're not a child any more. You have to take this in."

He lifted his head and looked at her with his ugly eyes. There was a mark on his forehead where it had laid on the wheel, and she remembered aching to be in his class – all the girls had – because he was good-looking and had glinting teeth and a jokey manner, less a teacher than a boy himself, but bolder. And he was the best of coaches. The students had voted Kay Female Athlete of the Year, but it was Coach Halliwell who'd groomed her for the position. She didn't understand this new revulsion she felt for him, or when and how it had replaced the attraction.

"I'd like to go home now," she said.

Coach Halliwell paused, but he started the engine. He drove in all the wrong directions for quite some time, but neither of them spoke. Kay looked out the window at the distant low mountains, nearly invisible against the night sky, but a steadying sight nonetheless, like a horizon that wards off seasickness.

Not far from Kay's home, he pulled over at a secluded spot near the river.

"I would lose my job, Kay. I would lose everything. And you – well, it would be even worse for you. You'd be a whore, that's the way they would see it."

She glanced at him and saw his bright eyes in his strange plastic face. She looked away.

"A slut, Kay. I'm sorry to say it, but only a certain kind of girl sleeps with her teacher. At least that's what people think. I'm not judging you myself, you know that, I hope."

The smell from the ashtray began to leak into the stagnant air around her, and she thought she would be sick. She reached for the door handle and tried to get out of the car, but as the interior light went on, Coach Halliwell stretched his arm across her body and pulled the door shut. For an instant she saw his desperation in the harsh, artificial light.

"Please think, Kay." His voice dropped low and hoarse. "For your own sake."

"I have to go," she said, and reached again for the door handle.

He cupped his hand around the back of her head and pulled her face close to his.

"It could just as well be someone else's. Have you thought of that?"

Kay struggled away from him and climbed from the car, out into the night where the air barely moved but gave her something fresh to breathe, something cool on her feverish skin. She ran along the path by the river, up through the trees to her house, and though there were a million truths that would not even occur to her, Kay recognized herself and Russell Halliwell as deceivers in tandem, having invented the same paternal solution.

⌒⌒⌒⌒⌒

In the morning, the long yellow fingers of the sun reached into Kay's room and woke her slowly, and as she was rising to consciousness, there were moments of nausea and misgiving, a knot that had to be guilt, but the fingers untied it and a breeze blew the remaining strands away. The child inside was no longer any part of Russell Halliwell.

At breakfast, Kay announced to her parents, "I'm pregnant." Ned and Irene Clancy stared blankly at her, and so she said, more clearly, "I'm going to have Joe's baby."

After that, anyone who was bold enough to ask was told that he was the father of the forthcoming child, a fact there was no reason to dispute. Not even Kay's mother questioned it. Joe had caught and dazzled Kay, after all, and then he had departed. Many boys before him had behaved in exactly the same fashion – not with Kay, of course, but with girls in general. The receptionist at Kay's doctor's office neatly printed his name beneath the word FATHER, and though as yet he was no such thing, a family saga began in his absence.

⌒⌒⌒⌒⌒

Late in the muggy summer, Kay expanded. In Deep River and in the fields of Italy, the sunflowers grew taller. Italians called them *girasoli*, meaning *turn to the sun*, an impossibly beautiful name that Kay would never learn, because all roads do not lead to Rome. Russian gymnast extraordinaire Larysa Latynina was three months pregnant at the Rome Olympics, but Kay Clancy was five months, almost six, and she always said that had the opportunity presented itself, she could not possibly have competed.

To walk back on the trail of the word *gymnasium* is to discover its link to the Greek *gumnazō*, for exercise, which in turn is linked to the Greek *gumnos*, for naked. Unlikely as it seems, Kay knew this. Russell Halliwell, who had very nearly been an Olympian gymnast himself, had told her as he'd stepped out of his green track pants in her presence – and he knew such trivia because his wife had told him. The Greeks did all of their "exercise" naked, he'd said to Kay, wiggling his fingers to convey the laden quotation marks. "You'd never guess what went on in *those* gymnasiums."

What she didn't know, or really care about, was that the same Games that had ended in Rome under Flavius Theodosius had begun in Greece some thousand years before. Those games had been about glory and excellence and every man for himself, as only one man could win. He was crowned with a laurel wreath to mark his victory, while everyone else was branded a loser and ridiculed by the crowd. In modern times, it was less that way, but people still cheered the winners, elevated to larger-than-life status atop little platforms. All eyes were on the Larysas and the Abebes. Sprinter Wilma Rudolph, the Black Gazelle, was once a child riddled with polio, whooping cough, scarlet fever, and double pneumonia. Growing up, she wore a flour-sack dress. But in Rome, she won three gold medals.

Right across the world 1960 was a year of trial and error, gains and losses. No one could have known the twists and turns yet to come. The little girl who would be saved from scandal by Joe LeBlanc was only just developing; her brother Louis was a glimmer in no one's eye; and their giant baby sister Margar was beyond imagining.

In April, the still little-known Pierre Trudeau had tried to canoe from Florida to Cuba, but the wild winds had been against him. Now was not his turn to shine.

(((((((())))))))

After the closing ceremonies of the 1960 Summer Olympics, even the *girasoli* were tired. They turned away from the sun and dropped their yellow petals and their potent seeds on the ground. Every day their brown heads hung lower, as though they were looking for what they'd lost in the earth, and slowly dying from not finding it. Sometimes the seeds disappeared altogether, so looking was a lost cause; no sooner were they dropped than birds and squirrels appeared and gathered them up again, thus there were never as many new flowers the following year as there might have been.

Kay Clancy continued to admire the *girasoli*, despite their silent presence the night she confronted Coach Halliwell in his moonlit garden. She was not the sentimental type. In this way she was flexible in the extreme, and cartwheeled through life in a fluid, forward motion. She had the ability to whirl through any unpleasant event by not slowing enough to examine it closely.

Once she had made up her mind that she was carrying Joe's child rather than Coach Halliwell's, Kay warmed to the idea of motherhood. She soon invited both strangers and friends to place their hands on her stomach and feel the baby moving. She didn't return to high school for her final year, and instead worked as a waitress in her parents' restaurant, situated just outside of town along the Trans-Canada Highway. Most of the clientele was only passing through, and would remain unaware of the town south of there, of its five thousand inhabitants and their criss-crossing lives. If five thousand people each had five secrets, then there were twenty-five thousand secrets, as invisible as germs, skulking around the town. Some overlapped – Coach Halliwell's and Kay's, for instance. But even then there were key differences: the reason for keeping the secret; the people from whom it was being kept; the ramifications of its release; and the perspective of its keeper. So the secret Coach Halliwell and Kay shared was actually two distinct ones. Kay's was like the seed of a *girasole*, one not stolen by a bird or a squirrel. It had slipped into the soft earth to undergo a mysterious transformation, and would soon reappear in the guise of a child.

As that time approached, Coach Halliwell showed up at the restaurant. It was early November. Nearly all the leaves had fallen but the snow had not yet come. Kay had entered her third trimester. The lie inside her was seventeen inches long and weighed just over five pounds. The kicks that had exposed the shapes of feet and knees through Kay's taut belly had changed to squirms and wriggles within the shrinking living quarters. Of course it was not the womb that was shrinking but the baby who was growing. Still, it could not have seemed that way to Estelle, who must have feared the ever-tightening darkness.

Wearing her makeshift maternity waitress uniform, Kay saw Russell Halliwell as soon as she came out of the kitchen. She had not seen him in any significant way since the night of the swooping bats. Once, he had appeared at the corner of Ridge and Huron streets, but Kay, behind him, scurried away, as she did in near encounters at the beach and in the drugstore, and as she believed she could do forever. This time, though, he was seated at the far end of the restaurant, by the window. He was mostly obscured by the other customers, and by a dusty rubber tree, but the left side of his face was visible, and it was staring at her. Kay stared back, and put her hand on her stomach, which had begun to churn. The left side of Coach Halliwell's face grinned. He lifted his hand and waved at her, and at the same moment, Marie Halliwell's pale face craned into view. She, too, waved at Kay, with unconvincing enthusiasm, and as Kay approached the table, she saw that their fat son, Eddie, was with them. Kay's heart raced. Even Estelle's unborn heart, by nature a rapid whir, accelerated to the speed of a hummingbird's.

"We're celebrating Eddie's birthday!" said Marie, but her cheerfulness was brittle, and the smile she sent in her son's direction seemed distant and forlorn.

Kay looked at the boy, who wore a sour expression his thick glasses couldn't hide. She wondered if she would have an equally fat, poor-sighted child, and if that meant everyone would know whose baby it was.

"Happy Birthday, Eddie," she said, but the boy lowered his gaze and ignored her. She passed the menus around, and when her hand accidentally brushed against the coach's hand, Estelle tumbled inside her.

As Kay left the table, she thought she would be sick, and hurried downstairs to the washroom. She looked at her round, pregnant face and her puffy lips in the mirror. Estelle was swimming in Kay's womb, and Kay clutched her stomach with both hands and said quietly, "It's okay, Pickle." She sat on the toilet and breathed until the nausea faded, but it returned when she rose and opened the door of the washroom. Coach Halliwell stood there. He pushed her back and came in with her, locking the door behind them. He pressed her to the wall and held his hands against her shoulders.

"*What the hell are you doing?*" he asked, breathing hard.

Kay didn't answer.

"I thought you were going to take care of this."

Still Kay didn't respond. She didn't look right at him, but she could tell that his face was red and sweaty, like the raw meat upstairs in the kitchen, the layered, fatty bacon, and the patties stacked up.

"Don't try to pin this on me, Kay. You understand?"

She could smell his breath, his hair, his armpits and remembered the odour of his semen. Her insides curdled and she threw up. The toes of the coach's shoes were splattered.

"Go away, please," said Kay, still not looking at him. "This is not your baby."

For a moment he remained where he was, and Kay watched his shoes. His hands were pressing hard against her shoulders, but he loosened his grip upon hearing her speak.

"Good," he said. The edge went out of his voice. He ran his hands down her arms to her fingers and squeezed them. "I'm sorry," he whispered.

Kay winced at his tenderness, so full of shame it reached in and fondled her own shame without asking. She kept her eyes on his shoes, and saw them step back. Coach Halliwell bent down and cleaned them off with toilet paper. His knees cracked. He stood again, and the shoes stayed pointed toward her. Finally they turned and took him out of the room.

And then Kay cried harder than she had cried in the Halliwells' garden, harder than she had cried in Joe LeBlanc's arms, all without making a sound. When she had stopped, she cleaned the floor, washed her face and hands, and returned upstairs. And aside from the fact that coffee cups had gone empty in her absence, there was no clue about the encounter, no sign that she was other than what she appeared to be: a happy, uncomplicated waitress and mother-to-be.

Coach Halliwell was seated with his family when Kay returned to the dining room. In a haze she moved toward them and took their order, and in a haze she brought them two chef's salads, one with Thousand Island dressing, one with Italian, a sirloin steak, liver and onions, a cheeseburger with french fries, two slices of apple pie, and one piece of chocolate cake with a candle in it. Kay lit the wick herself and saw the flame in the boy's glasses. "Happy Birthday" was sung. Travellers – journeying with, toward, and away from their own secrets – joined in. The room came alive with the unified voices of strangers, and their reflections in the restaurant's windows made it sound as though twice as many were singing. Even Kay was singing, though her voice was high and quavery, unfamiliar in her ears.

The Halliwells left as quietly as they had come. Kay emerged from the kitchen, and from her haze, and saw that they were outside, walking toward their car, and that it was snowing. The large flakes fell slowly. Mrs. Halliwell tucked her arm into the crook of her husband's elbow and leaned her head on his shoulder. White snow landed on her lovely black hair, and disappeared again. Fat Eddie trailed behind them.

(00000)

Eddie Halliwell blinked against the snowflakes as they touched his glasses. He turned and looked at Kay, standing at the window. Blink, blink. Without his glasses he would not have been able to see her at all, but with them he could see her clearly. She was small, with a large, round stomach. She was going to have a baby, but she was only a child herself, that was what his mother had said in a tight, clipped voice. Eddie had weak eyes, but he had very strong ears. Sometimes he even heard what wasn't spoken.

He got into the back seat of the car, and his parents climbed into the front. His father was whistling. As they pulled away from the restaurant, Eddie continued to watch Kay through the rear window. She was clearing the dessert dishes and finding the crisp brown bills his mother had slipped beneath her plate when she thought no one was looking. But Eddie had seen. Eddie Halliwell, newly nine, was always watching.

(00000)

39

Kay hid the money – six hundred dollars – in a lavender sachet, where there was already the fifty-two dollars Coach Halliwell had pressed into her palms that night in the garden. She tucked the bulging sachet into her jewellery box, a present the coach himself had given her before their waltzes had culminated in some form of love. The box had been tied with a ribbon, but not wrapped with paper. A *naked* gift, she'd thought as he'd offered it, and just thinking the word had made her too embarrassed to look at him. He'd pulled the ribbon open for her, and lifted the lid of the box. It was beautiful inside, with a pink lining and a ballerina that turned to music.

From bed, Kay looked through her window and watched snow fall in the beam of a streetlamp. She wasn't upset any more, and wouldn't be able to express why she had been. Tears dry faster when you cartwheel through life. While she'd cried in the ladies' room and in Coach Halliwell's garden and on her own pink chesterfield in the arms of Joe LeBlanc, Kay Clancy crying was as rare a sight as a breathing angel. Those who loved her would always be mystified by the sing-song voice and the cartwheels, which camouflaged all she couldn't show and tell.

(((((((

In the official story that summed up this precarious, husbandless time, Kay was more or less happy.

"I knew as soon as he left that he'd be back for us," she'd say, speaking of Joe, of course, and not Coach Halliwell, and speaking of the first time he left, which she did often, and not the second, which she did rarely. "I got bigger and bigger, and I just kept on waiting. I knew he'd come. Not that very night, but sooner or later."

Kay's water broke on a cold afternoon in January. The river was by then covered with ice, and children were skating on its surface while the fish below swam under a swirl-patterned ceiling. Kay was watching the skaters, and she was thinking about the ice breaking and a child falling through, when water gushed from her and landed with a splat on the floor. At first she thought the baby had fallen out, as her mother had predicted, but there was only a puddle, and more water dribbling into it.

"It was the strangest thing," she would later say. "Such watery thoughts, and then my water breaking."

Outside the official story is the dream that came late that night, when Estelle had been released from Kay's body and was lying in a room down the hall with the other vulnerable newborns. In her dream, Kay was spread face down on the ice, but her huge stomach kept her from lying flat and distributing her body weight evenly over the surface. Frantic, she rolled from side to side on her stomach, aware that someone was drowning beneath her. She teetered and reached into the cold water through a hole in the ice that appeared to have been cut for fishing, though it was larger than normal. A man had fallen in, and Kay, in her dream, was searching for him. Her hand splashed in the frigid water, and froze numb, so she couldn't feel the man's skin or his hair if it brushed against her fingers. Cramps flared through her stomach as it pressed against the ice, but she ignored them, because she needed to save the man trapped beneath. With her free hand she scratched at the ice's snowy

41

covering and looked into the water through the spot she had cleared. Instead of a man, a baby floated by. Kay stared at the closed eyes, the luminescent skin, until the baby drifted away. She watched the hole and waited for the child to reappear, so she could grab him as the current carried him along, but no baby came into view. As she dragged herself closer to the hole, in order to reach deeper into the water, she noticed she wasn't rolling any more. Her stomach had flattened. The baby had been hers.

When she woke up, a nurse was standing nearby with Estelle. As Kay fed the baby she kept her eyes fixed on the hungry face and concentrated on erasing the dream of the white, drifting infant. That baby had been a boy, and this was a girl, she thought thankfully, forgetting already. Estelle's lips were a pink rosebud, and while her fuzz of hair had a reddish tinge like the coach's, it could easily grow in as blond as her own or as brown as Joe's. Right now her eyes were a very deep blue, so might turn brown, like Joe's, which would be perfect. There was something gentle about brown eyes, she decided, as she kissed the baby's cheek and let the nurse take her away again. Dogs, cows, otters, horses, chipmunks, monkeys, and deer had brown eyes, whereas house cats, crocodiles, tigers, snakes, lizards, foxes, and lions had green. Joe LeBlanc was a gentle man with gentle eyes, the father of her child. And just as she was thinking of water when her water broke, she was thinking of Joe's eyes when they appeared to her through the hospital-room window.

(00000)

Whole lives are born out of coincidence. No one knew until later, but when Estelle Huguette LeBlanc was inching her way down the birth canal, Joe was on his way back home to Kay and the child she claimed was his. He was hitchhiking with his long thumb exposed in the northern air, and at the instant Estelle slithered out of Kay's body, Joe climbed into the cab of a pickup truck.

"I couldn't get here fast enough," he would say later, according to Kay, and Margar, hearing that story, would long to be able to ask him, "And then when you left again, could you get *away* fast enough?" It seemed to her there were some details missing, and when the answers didn't provide themselves, her grand imagination provided substitutes. *I am not his daughter at all. I am the daughter of Grace Kelly and the King of Morocco, or a czarina with no memory. I have been brought all this way with a blindfold over my eyes to keep me from seeing my captors, and because Joe, my would-be father, refused to raise a girl who wasn't his, he was secreted away and locked up in a windowless tower. In another land far from here, the lampposts are plastered with my photograph on posters that beg for my safe return.*

She confided to her friend Noelle that "I'm not really a LeBlanc," but she left it at that, seeing Noelle's eyes widen, and sensing, early on, the power of mystery. It was more than a white lie, but harmless. Her mother was always telling her to stop making up lies – "Your nose is getting longer than Pinocchio's" – but she also said some lies were justified, though these were mainly Kay's own. When the Jehovah's Witness lady had come to the door, Kay had said, "Sorry, we're on our way out to the kids' lessons," though none of them was taking lessons in anything, not at that time. "It's just a little white lie," Kay had told Margar's dropped jaw once the door had closed. "To spare feelings." But it had to be more wrong to lie to a religious person than to Noelle.

On her own, Margar discovered a spectrum of lies, a spinning colour wheel of primary, secondary, and tertiary lies, each bleeding into the next.

◎◎◎◎◎

It was snowing that January night of Estelle's birth. Kay was tranquilized into a twilight sleep, and had no memory of the labour when she woke. The baby who was placed in her arms wore a tiny cap, like the tip of a sock, and Kay was happy to leave it there, covering the reddish glow.

"My little pickle," Kay whispered. "My fine tiny pickle."

Ned and Irene Clancy had already shown their tight, worried faces, and left again, it being well past midnight when the baby was delivered. For months they had prayed to Joseph, the patron saint of fatherhood, for Joe's safe return, but tonight they were too exhausted for wishes. They were lying back to back and barely awake when a shower of pebbles streamed across Kay's bedroom window. Kay, far from her room, was in the hospital dreaming of ice and a dead baby, so only Ned and Irene heard the pebbles meant for their daughter. They turned to face each other but said nothing. More pebbles rattled the glass. Ned swung his feet from the bed and into his slippers. He glided noiselessly across the bedroom floor and peered out the window.

"Well, well," he said, and turned to face Irene.

Joe LeBlanc had come home.

⦅⦆⦆⦆⦆

"Oh, he couldn't wait to get to you," Kay was fond of telling Estelle. Thus Estelle grew up believing she had been some sort of lucky magnet — just the opposite of what Margar would believe — and that the brightest star had shone above her on the day she was born.

In actuality, Joe returned in seething anger. He really did say, "I couldn't get here fast enough," but after that he said, "when I heard you were saying the kid was mine."

Ned Clancy told Joe LeBlanc Kay had given birth that very night, and Joe stormed across town to the hospital. He circled the building, flying through snowy flowerbeds as he hunted for Kay's room. Since it was late, the rooms were mostly dark, but by luck, by coincidence, or maybe by fate, a light came on over Kay just as Joe was passing. His breath fogged white in the black air as he watched her cradle and feed the baby. The light above the bed formed a halo of sorts over Kay and the tiny child, who after all was a blessedly ordinary baby, without horns or green skin. Joe himself had been green with jealousy when Kay had told him of her pregnancy. Red with rage when he'd thrown the rock through the Hayes's living-room window. Blue with despair when he'd hitchhiked out of town. And now he was back. He stared through the window until a nurse took the baby from Kay's arms. It was then that Kay looked up and saw him. Joe stepped back, and vanished in her reflection.

That glimpse of him was so fleeting she was sure she had dreamed it up, that she was only *wishing* to see him. And he hadn't smiled, so she couldn't tell if he was happy even in her imagination. Certainly the next day, when he showed up during visiting hours, he was nothing but angry. He came empty-handed and stood at the foot of her bed.

"Good timing," said Kay, and grinned.

But Joe didn't smile. "I couldn't get here fast enough when I heard you were saying the kid was mine."

No one other than Kay would ever know how she won him over, or even that she had to. But the power of suggestion is an extraordinary thing. When the nurse brought Estelle for her next feeding, Joe was still standing at the end of Kay's bed. A look of surprise imbued his face when he saw the baby, as though, in his anger, he had forgotten her.

"Look, Joe," said Kay. "Her name is Estelle Huguette LeBlanc. It's French. I did that for you."

Perhaps he'd been unprepared for the gesture, or for the warmth and the smell of a baby. Her skin was soft right down to the soles of her wrinkly feet. The skin was already redder there, in anticipation of life's rough journey. Her bald little head and her utterly toothless mouth foreshadowed old ladyness, as did her curled fingers, which seemed almost boneless and couldn't pull or push away.

Joe LeBlanc had arrived in a rage, and now he was sitting on the edge of the bed with a baby – not his – staring at the tiny perfect hands, and Kay was taking their picture. In the photo-graph, Estelle is barely the length of Joe's forearm. They look only at each other, though as yet, neither one of them is smiling.

Estelle is wrapped in a soft blanket, and Joe is still wearing his coat and scarf, there being no colder time of the year than January. And yet he is so obviously warm all over.

It was too early to search for shared traits, and those that developed would have been purely coincidental. But more than any story, whether true or make-believe, a photograph shapes a memory, which in turn reshapes the moment it has captured. The photo of Kay as Female Athlete of the Year 1960 matched the legend she had spun for herself, and the truth hid inside that legend. And now there was a misrepresentation of greater magnitude. On the back of Joe and Estelle's picture, which years on would go missing under mysterious circumstances, Kay penned the words *Daddy and Estelle, January, 1961.*

◯◯◯◯◯

Kay was still in her teens, but her time as a celebrity was over. Though her picture would hang for years in the high-school hall of glory, to be ignored or observed by strangers of a new generation, by a teenaged Eddie Halliwell, and later by her own children, her quasi-fame had come and gone. But the story of her gymnastic past, or a version thereof, kept growing. "I gave it all up for love," she'd tell her children, sensing that the line between fact and fiction was not a line at all, but a series of dashes. Through the open spaces, one flowed into the other, and over time, the pool became so diluted that each side looked the same. And yet, when she later said of Joe, "I think he was sent to me," she spoke the absolute truth as she knew it. He'd saved her. For years (but not forever), the only angel she ever believed in was Joe.

A month after Estelle's birth, Kay Clancy became Kay LeBlanc in a simple ceremony at Our Lady of the Snows Church. She sighed with relief as Joe slid the gold ring on her finger, not knowing, never imagining how it would one day spin through the air and into the river. She stood on her tiptoes and kissed him. At the party that followed, Estelle smiled her first smile. A Halliwell dimple creased her cheek and went black with shadow.

⬯⬯⬯⬯⬯

The days grew warmer. The ice darkened and cracked and drew back from the shoreline. The snow began to melt into the ground, watering the dry garden of winter. By mid-April, spring had come to the north sides of the streets, which caught the rays of the benevolent sun, but winter still lay on the south sides. The snow that was left at the edges of things – around trees, against fences, and along shady house-front flowerbeds – was of the big-crystal variety, hard, old and dirty. There were new odours in the air, of damp soil and buds on trees. Some of the smells represented not the coming of spring but the slow dying of winter. Leaves that had not been raked before the snow fell were decaying in the season of birth, just as new ones were forming.

Slowly the snow and the ice released imprisoned secrets that fluttered in the cool-warm air until the barren time between seasons had ended, and there were once again safe places to hide. They buried themselves in the ruffled pink blossoms of apple trees, which overnight went from bare grey twig to fuchsia splendour. They stretched themselves thin and hid behind the new blades of grass, and in the heady blooms of lilac.

48

On the forest floor, wood frogs awoke and scrambled out of their mossy winter homes, making their way toward water. Like ducks, they quacked in the river, the sacs in their throats swelling and glowing white as the sound came out. Only their eyes, behind black and yellow masks, appeared above the surface, as they searched for the females with whom they would make tadpoles.

It was right around this time – May 11, 1961, to be precise – that Marie Halliwell was admitted to hospital. Her room, 111, was down the hall from the room where Kay Clancy had nursed the newborn Estelle. Months before, a frenzied Joe LeBlanc had cupped his frostbitten hands against the window of Room 111, looking for Kay, but it had been nighttime then, and now it was day.

Marie Halliwell had been working in the garden of her blue house by the river. She'd had her hair tied back with a green ribbon, and had been wearing a geranium-print dress with deep pockets that could hold tools or the deadheads of flowers. In her garden there was as yet no sign of the tender shoots that would be *girasoli*, but they would come, as always.

In the meantime, Marie Halliwell's tulips were in full bloom. She cut one of every colour and laid them on the counter inside, with the scissors beside them. As she climbed on her stool to fetch an appropriate vase from the top of the china cabinet, she began to sob. She stood crying, with her arm stretched toward the vase, and then she stopped. Patting her eyes with her fingers, wiping her cheeks, she lifted the vase, stepped down, and placed it in the sink to fill it with water. When she put the tulips in the water, the petals burst open as if to soothe her by showing their glowing gold centres, but she went upstairs to the bathroom anyway, leaving the vase in the sink. Ignoring her own reflection, she opened the medicine cabinet and took out a bottle of pills. But when she closed the cabinet, her own face appeared in front of her, and she watched one hand pour all of the little pills into the other hand, and her mouth receive them. She took her hand away from her lips. Her palm showed her heartline and her lifeline, which she couldn't tell apart, and also the lipstick stain of her open mouth, quietly screaming.

◯◯◯◯◯

Eddie Halliwell had found the eleventh of May to be an enchanting spring day. He had walked home from school in his shirtsleeves, arriving late because he'd been dawdling. He had stopped at the creek to see the tadpoles, with their iridescent bellies and yellow spots on their backs. But there was nothing to see except a stream of clear water rushing over the stones. So he waited. He sat and then stood again. Hanging on to a branch, he looked down into the water and just as he caught sight of three tadpoles, the branch split away from the trunk and sent him into the creek. Eddie crouched on his hands and knees and the cold water rushed over him, soaking the legs of his trousers. He could see nothing but a blur of brownish-grey, which was the water, two blurred flesh-toned blobs, which were his hands, and a strip of bright blurry green, which was the grass on the far side of the creek. He groped for his glasses. He dared not move his knees or his feet, and he watched the flesh-toned blobs wander this way and that. He didn't cry, or even breathe until his careful hand landed on the frames, whose curved black arms had stopped them from flowing unreachable downstream. Eddie put the wet glasses on his face. One of the lenses had smashed in the form of a star.

⦅⦅⦅⦅⦅⦆

Marie Halliwell continued to stare into the bathroom mirror. She saw grey eyes from which the brilliant blue had disappeared. She saw black hair and arched black eyebrows against white skin. The skin had just recently begun to wrinkle around the edges of her eyes, but the wrinkles only showed when she smiled, which she did not do often. She smiled now, though, just to see them. Her pale lips curved upwards and her cheeks rounded. Her eyes filled with water. Dizzy, she leaned on the sink and rested her face on the glass of the medicine cabinet. Water streamed out of her eyes but she was not crying with her mouth or her throat or her chest. If she wanted to, she couldn't speak or cry out loud, for the pills had numbed her. But no amount of medication could stop the tears from falling, and though it was a blue sunny day, she thought it was raining. She pressed harder against the sink. It was becoming difficult to hold herself up. Her legs buckled and her arms grew weaker. She fell to the bathroom floor. The water still poured from her eyes, but dripped sideways now, across the bridge of her nose, into her other eye and out the opposite side. Her head was on the bath mat, and she could see hairs woven into the fabric, her own and Eddie's black ones, her husband's auburn ones, though she had washed the rug yesterday. She knew cleanliness was a matter of proximity, and that mites, unseen, bred at the base of eyelashes. She felt her eyes roll back in her head. The tears stopped, but

51

when her eyes rolled forward, they resumed. Pulling herself up onto her hands and knees, she saw that the ribbon had slipped from her hair and fallen on the bath mat. With her hair hanging down at each side of her face, she pushed her fingers into the loop of ribbon and crawled down the hall to the bedroom.

She lay on the bed with water running over to the other side of her face. This was goodbye, coming quickly now. The edges of her vision darkened. She looked at the ribbon through two circles with dark edges, and then the circles became slats, and then the slats became blackness.

◦◦◦◦◦

The sun was shining in the blue May sky and the birds were chirping. The posh black-and-white warblers had returned from the Gulf of Mexico and were singing their rapid *we-see* song. With their narrow beaks they pulled insects from the knots of trees and ate them. Eddie Halliwell knew the knots were eyes or mouths, depending on the tree. Birch trees had eyes, and white pines had mouths, formed when the heavy limbs broke from the groaning trunks. His mother had told him that, but he had noticed on his own already.

Eddie walked home in his wet pants and squeaking shoes. Behind the shattered lens, he kept his eye squeezed shut since looking through the star made him dizzy. One day the star would reappear to him and ironically make everything clearer, but not for a long time to come. For now, with one eye closed, he was more aware of his nose than of anything else, and he could not see to his right (the star side) without turning his head. Still, he managed to find his way along Riverside Drive to the blue two-storey. He ducked through the thick trees that hid the house from the street, and when he entered the yard he saw through one eye that the screen door had been left open, which never happened, because of his father's impatience with insects.

Eddie crossed the yard and stepped through the door, into the loud silence. He walked squeaking to the kitchen and saw the vase of blown tulips in the sink. His right eye opened because his brain now needed to focus on other things, such as the scissors on the counter and the stool that stood in front of the china cabinet, and he recalled a day last year when he had come home to find his mother gone. Eddie had known that time, too, that something was gravely wrong – his mother's bed had been unmade, which meant she had gotten back into it since he had left for school that day, and there'd been a teapot on the bedside table. His mother never drank tea in bed. She never went to bed, as far as he knew, in the daytime. Later he'd learned that his father had come home when she had called and told him of the pain in her side. He had made tea, but the tea had not soothed the pain, and indeed the pain had continued to grow until it had burst open inside her. That had been her appendix. Eddie had an appendix. Everyone did, but no one knew why. His father said it was a remnant, something we used to need, but needed no longer.

Eddie passed the vase and the scissors and the stool in his squeaking shoes. He passed the piano in the white living room, and went upstairs to his parents' bedroom, where he stood in the doorway. His mother was stretched diagonally across the bed in her gardening dress, the one with the flowers.

"Mom?" he said.

He had his geography book under his arm, and he let it fall to the floor as though he was about to rush to her, but he stayed where he was. He looked down at his book. The page about Italy had fluttered out and the long boot drawing he had made rested on the floor in front of him. Rome was halfway up the shin. He had brought it to show her.

"Mom?" he said again.

Eddie squeezed his eye shut. He felt the familiar, hot flare of pain at the back of his neck that meant soon his head would be pounding. He stepped over the book and the drawing and walked toward the bed, looking down at his mother through one eye. Maybe she had a headache too – a splitting migraine, that was what she called them. She said that he got them because she did, that they were the same in that way. Eddie's hands began to open and close rapidly. He leaned forward, continuing to straighten and curl his fingers, and he put his face close to hers, but she was as still as a china doll. Eddie stared. The pain was spreading up the back of his head and knifing into his left temple. He held his breath. And then his glasses fogged, both the starred and the unstarred lens.

Eddie's mother was breathing.

⦿⦿⦿⦿⦿

When Marie Halliwell awoke in her hospital room, there was a hand-drawn map of Italy stuck to her window. It was the first thing she saw when she opened her eyes. Rome was marked with a stick-on gold star. Marie had been there in '50 and '51, two beautiful years. She had studied art history and classical mythology, and afterwards went to find the heart of those worlds. When

54

she met Russell Halliwell in the Sistine Chapel, she fell in love. She returned to North America as half of a radiant couple. The years since 1950 were a blip in Rome's tumultuous history, but for Marie, a million personal lifetimes had passed.

Eddie Halliwell had been conceived in Rome. At the time it seemed impossible that he might turn out to be fat and short-sighted. Marie, twenty-four, lay laughing in the embrace of her new husband. "Husband," she said, again and again. The branches of an olive tree brushed against the window of their room. She stared smiling at the ceiling, thinking of the Sistine ceiling, and how all the angels had watched over them on the day of their meeting.

"I think," she said to Russell, "there must be more angels in Rome than there are anywhere else in the world."

"Mm-hmmm," said Russell.

It was a distracted response, the only one he could manage as he continued to plunge into her, and his exuberance made her forget what she'd been saying and grab on to him. He had a muscular torso, big hands and narrow hips, but it was his face that was most remarkable. Even while he slept, his physical strength was apparent in its tautness, in the wide, angular jaw that always looked firmly clenched, and in the nose, long but not overly broad, with wing-shaped nostrils. His eyes, as she had said then, were green as emeralds, though, being superstitious, she would have chosen a different comparison had she recalled that the foppish, flabby Emperor Nero had watched the gladiator games through an emerald in the years before glasses. In any case, Russell's eyes were not as green as that – they were more the colour of a cat's eyes, with copious yellow in them. His hair was auburn, and curled if it grew longish. Then she had called it his halo, because of their joke that he'd fallen from the chapel's ceiling. She knew about the origin of haloes. Once they'd had nothing to do with the Christian son of God, or even goodness, but appeared radiantly behind the heads of the more mischievous Greek and Roman divinities of her studies. The very first halo appeared over the head of Apollo, who was Zeus's arrogant, beautiful son, and the would-be rapist of the water nymph Daphne. It was not until the fourth century, when he'd been dead for hundreds of years, that Jesus got his halo. Since that day, a pagan tradition had masqueraded as a Christian one. Angels earned haloes in the fifth century, and in the sixth, Mary got hers. From then on they appeared in various shapes and sizes until Titian and Michelangelo, rebels of the Renaissance, abandoned them.

Marie had stood with Russell in the Galleria Borghese, observing Bernini's statue of Daphne and Apollo, which paralyzed both the nymph and the lecherous god in marble. At the moment Apollo touches Daphne's naked waist, her arms stretch high like branches. Leaves sprout from her fingertips and from her flying hair. He's glorious, but something urges her to run. Roots twist up from the ground, braiding with the veins in her feet. Rough bark covers the softest parts of her, forever closing the space between her legs. Soon she will be sealed up, safely buried alive in a laurel tree.

Afterwards, Marie and Russell had walked through Rome at twilight, a handsome couple, his arm around her waist, her head on his shoulder. She had been more in love than she'd thought possible, but then she'd looked at the trees that lined the boulevard and seen, in the evening light, how they bulged and rippled as if they contained human bodies, how they sighed and groaned when the wind blew through their branches. Rome was one of the world's magnificent cities, but it had a wicked past. Nero, the creepy singing emperor of ancient times, was said to have been his mother's boy lover. Maybe it was this that sent him on his hideous path of destruction. When he grew up, he had her murdered, not for passionate reasons but for political ones. Which isn't to say he had no passion. He married three women, one man, and a eunuch. His true love was Poppaea Sabina, who'd been pregnant with his child when he kicked her to death. If the angels had been watching, they'd done nothing to stop him.

In her hospital room, Marie Halliwell turned away from the map of Italy, which Eddie had stuck to the window with bubble gum.

"We went all the way to Rome to make you," she had often told him. "Rome is the most beautiful place in the world."

⟨⟨⟨⟨⟨⟨⟩⟩⟩⟩⟩⟩

On his way home from school, Eddie wanted to see his mother. He should have waited until later, after dinner, when visiting hours resumed. He could have gone with his father, at the expected, appropriate time. But he wanted to go alone. He loved his mother more when his father was not around. In those moments, everything got quieter, and time itself slowed down. His mother seemed smaller, somehow, and softer, as though she had let out a long sigh. Occasionally she cuddled Eddie so close he felt almost babyish. Or sometimes she browsed through her books with him and pointed to the masterpieces she'd seen in Italy, telling him how big they'd been or how surprisingly small, and how she had carried him around inside her so that he could see them himself, before he was even born. He knew she couldn't cuddle with him like that today — she was too sick — but she had been in the hospital all evening, all night, and all day, and he missed her.

He didn't take the road but cut through the woods and followed a trail that led to the back of the hospital, where his mother's room was. He stepped out from the trees and stood on the new spring grass, looking at her window. The four pieces of gum with bits of torn paper stuck to them showed where the map of Italy had been. Eddie did not move closer. He didn't look into her window, as he had planned to do, and so he will never know if either of the images that came to him was real. In one, she kept her back to him, shoulders shaking. In the other, she lay motionless, staring straight through him. Both would stay with him throughout his life, shaping the Eddie to come, just as others had shaped the Eddie who existed already, a boy in his own right but a product of circumstance as well. In all the years ahead, no matter which image he revisited, Italy lay on the floor with torn corners. And so, in memory, it would remain forever.

⁙⁙⁙

As the Halliwell home inwardly crumbled, the LeBlanc family began setting up house. Joe was finished with high school, which he'd attended in a random, disinterested way. He accepted a job with his great-uncles, handymen LeBlanc & LeBlanc, and each week Kay took his paycheque and added it to their house fund.

She had saved the tips she'd earned waitressing over the fall and winter, and of course there was the $652 in the sachet in her jewellery box. It was too big a nest egg for Kay to have saved on her own, so she told Joe that much of it had come from Ned and Irene, and she told Ned and Irene that much of it had come from Joe. They bought a home with money that reeked of lavender, but for Kay, the very word *home* (as well as the pretty green tiles on the kitchen floor) leached the deceit from that fragrance.

They moved from Kay's parents' house to 40 Huron Street, a white bungalow with fading red trim. The porch roof was crooked and coming off at the left side, but Joe, under the guidance of LeBlanc & LeBlanc, would make it good as new. In the meantime, the steps below were very sturdy. The front door opened into the living room, and to the left were two bedrooms, Joe and Kay's plus what Kay happily called "the Estelle suite." Beyond the living room was a kitchen big enough for a table and chairs, and beyond the kitchen was the backyard. The front door and the back door lined up perfectly. You could walk through one and escape through the other and never veer from a straight line.

It was a bare-bones sort of house, a war-four, unlike the Halliwells' stately riverside home, where not long ago she had imagined herself living with the coach, his wife and child, and baby Estelle. Heat escaped through the walls and roof of the bungalow, but Joe promised to fix that. It fled through the windows and doors, and he said that, too, could be remedied, and until summer, he would push more wood into the stove so that more heat could escape.

"You wait," he said to Kay. "Things will change around here."

He couldn't know the full truth of his promise, and meant simply that he was a family man now, and would build a new room made of windows, a log-cabin garage, and a playhouse for the backyard. For though he was just learning his trade, he was learning from masters. Alphonse and Toussaint LeBlanc could whittle a palace from a stick if they so chose. And Joe learned quickly. Days he worked with his uncles, and nights he worked at home, hammering this, planing that. He said that the house had a bad history, that it was tainted from its involvement with war, and that, unchanged, it would invite doom through the peeling, crooked door.

The day the ambulance carrying Marie Halliwell roared by, Kay was painting the Estelle suite robin's egg blue. Marie's heart was barely beating. She slept even more soundly than baby Estelle, who was snuggled in a bassinet in her parents' room. Kay winced, hearing the wailing siren. She pressed her finger to her lips, as though telling the siren, "Ssshhh, don't wake the baby," oblivious to someone else's misfortune speeding by.

Estelle slept on. Her tiny, perfect lips parted just in the middle, where the air went in and out. When the siren faded, her breath was the only sound in the room. She slept beneath a blanket that had been knitted and purled by her grandmother, Irene Clancy. Kay herself didn't knit, and had never understood how "knit" could be the opposite of "purl," without one undoing the other. Using endless combinations of the two stitches, Irene created sweaters, mittens, jumpers, hats, sockettes, slippers, blankets, booties, and bunting bags in all the colours of a pastel rainbow. She liked to say that life was like knitting: every stitch depended on both the last and next until the time came to cast off. She didn't yet have Margar as a grandchild – Margar who, with knitted brows, loved to slide the loops off of the needle, and pull the single, intricate strand undone.

(00000)

When Marie Halliwell had swallowed the pills in front of her bathroom mirror, she'd left the water running. She hadn't been thinking clearly. Eddie, when he found her, did not think clearly either. After her breath fogged his glasses, he detected the sound of the water. He walked in his squeaking shoes to the bathroom, where water poured from the faucet onto an empty pill bottle at the bottom of the sink. The water wasn't filling the sink or sloshing over the edges, as it soon would do, but Eddie should have, in retrospect, turned it off. Perhaps his father was right that sometimes he was very stupid. Instead of turning the taps, he had stared at the water through the star and through the perfect lens of his glasses. And then he had run for the phone.

The water had poured onto the pill bottle and the lid, around and under them into the drain, so relentlessly that the drain hadn't been able to drink the water fast enough, and a swirling pool had risen in the sink. It pulled on the pill bottle and the lid, until the lid found itself sitting in the drain hole, a perfect fit. The water flowed over the edge of the sink and splashed onto the floor. It drenched the mat where Marie Halliwell had rested, and after a time, it seeped through the floor, and then through the ceiling of the family room, though the family rarely gathered there.

Marie's hands flew to her face when she returned home from the hospital and saw the ugly hole.

"Hush," said her husband, though she had not made a sound. "We can fix it," he told her. He put his arm around her shoulder and squeezed.

He had not been so kind to Eddie, who hadn't been the one to turn on the tap in the first place. He had cuffed him – not hard, but his palm had scudded across Eddie's head – and said, "You have to learn to think in a crisis, Eddie. Clear and cool, or you add to the mess of it."

Eddie knew about messes, and who had made them. He glowered at his father, but Russell didn't seem to notice. The days without his mother went on and on, he and his father alone, at odds. Eddie was relieved when she came home, thinking that things would return to normal, and though normal was not good, it was better. He waited for her to smile, or show some sign of encouragement, but when he looked into her face, he found no trace of her.

She stood by the piano, wearing her gardening dress, the one with the geraniums, because that was what she'd had on when she'd gone to the hospital, and her husband hadn't thought to bring her something that didn't hold that day in the weave of its fabric. Russell's hand was on the floral print, rubbing against it. She opened her own hands and peered between her fingers at the plaster hanging down from the ceiling.

"We can fix it," said Russell, but he didn't really mean "we." He meant the contractors. For some jobs, it was important to hire experts. Experts dug and rebuilt and plastered. Once the work had been completed, only the experts and the Halliwells would know where the cracks, stains, and holes had been. To outsiders, all would be good as new.

⟨⟨⟨⟨⟨⟩⟩⟩⟩⟩

The men who came to fix the mess were the same men who'd come to work on the yard years ago, when Eddie was a little boy. Alphonse and Toussaint LeBlanc were the living reasons that the second thing Eddie wanted to be was a gardener. He'd been not quite five when they'd laid the stone path in the yard, and it had been Eddie's job to place seeds in the moist earth between the stones. Every day he watered those seeds. While Alphonse and Toussaint built a fountain, Eddie sat by the path and waited for the seeds to crack open beneath the soil. Like popcorn, he imagined. Soon the seeds would send up fine green shoots that would blossom into flowers, and the flowers would creep low and sneak along the stones.

"But where will we walk?" he asked his mother.

"On the flowers," she said. She brushed a hand through his hair. Her skin was soft and smelled like the pink cream on her dresser.

"Won't it kill them?" he asked.

"These are the kind you can walk on. The more you do, the more flowers will come."

She gave him the calm, private smile she saved for the times they were alone, but it failed to soothe him. He trusted his mother but he believed she was mistaken. And when the flowers came he walked on tiptoe on the path to avoid them. Once they

63

had covered the stones, he stopped using the path altogether, to prevent destroying what he had put in the earth himself, things that were alive and growing. His mother teased him, and called him her little garden gnome, but a gnome was not what he wanted to be. He wanted to be a real gardener (which was not what Alphonse and Toussaint were, but Eddie didn't know that).

He liked the easy manner the men used with each other, and the way, first thing in the morning, they said, "Eddie! We've been waiting for you." Every day they joked in a language he couldn't understand, but he was one of them anyway. They gave him chores and shared their lunch with him — chewy salted beef, crusty bread lumped with butter, and sticky, sugary desserts. He liked their bare brown backs in the sun and their brown eyes winking at him from their wrinkly faces.

The fountain they made had a stone angel as its base and stood inside a circle in the path. The angel's head tipped back the way Eddie's own did when he coiled a spaghetti noodle into his mouth. When the fountain was turned on, water sprayed up from the angel's mouth, then fell in a shower and pooled in her spanned wings. Eddie thought she was as beautiful as any sculpture he had seen in his mother's art books. He had already decided he wanted to be an artist because of those books, but after he'd met Alphonse and Toussaint, he said, "I want to be a gardener too." He announced this at dinner, and looked to his mother and father for their reactions. Both of them smiled, but only his mother looked back at him.

"What brought this on?" asked his father. He was buttering his bread, and looking at Eddie's mother instead of Eddie, and

Eddie waited for his eyes to flutter downward and find him, but they did no such thing. They rolled up and around, two green eyes that rarely saw him. But Eddie loved his father. He still loved him then.

"Alphonse and Toussaint," said Eddie. "They're showing me how."

"Great," said Eddie's father. "He sees two old geezers digging in the dirt and he thinks that's something to emulate."

Eddie didn't know or ponder what *geezers* meant, or *emulate*. Instead it was the little word that stood out for him.

He, thought Eddie. *That's me.*

⟨OOOOO⟩

Some five years after they had laid the stone path and built the angel fountain, LeBlanc & LeBlanc returned to the Halliwell home to fix the floor and the ceiling, as well as the invisible space between. Joe himself restippled the stucco with such painstaking precision that no seam showed where the old ended and the new began.

"*Rien fait, Joséph.* You're a natural," said Alphonse, winking.

He fixed the floor upstairs, too, and when he was finished, his paint-splattered, size-thirteen boots took him down the stairs and through the living room, where Marie Halliwell sat at the piano, not playing but letting her fingers rest on the keys. He passed the china cabinet and crossed into the kitchen, and then stepped outside, where a garden bloomed. A fat boy with thick glasses came through the trees and up the walk, and Joe nodded to the boy, but the boy just stared at him. Joe LeBlanc walked on. His long legs took him up the hill away from the river, and over to 40 Huron, where he joined his wife and baby for dinner.

◌◌◌◌◌

Later in the season Joe was asked to paint the exterior of Robbie Hayes's parents' home.

"No way," he told his uncles. "I'm not setting foot in that place."

Alphonse and Toussaint laughed. "You don't have to go in, eh, Joe?" they teased. "The exterior is on the outside."

Joe neither laughed nor smiled. "In or out, I'm not doing it," he said. "And I'd appreciate you not asking me why."

Because they were his uncles, and because he was a decent, hard-working man, Alphonse and Toussaint didn't insist. If Joe had a reason for not wanting to paint the Hayes family home, they felt it had to be a good one. They let it go at that, and painted the house themselves.

And it was in those days that Robbie Hayes, heading down the narrow path at the side of his house, walked under the ladder instead of trying to go around. Alphonse, above on a high rung, looked down at the top of Robbie's head and called, "Bad luck, my friend! You're tempting fate, you know?"

Robbie paused beneath the ladder's frame just long enough to grin up at Alphonse, the rungs of the ladder like a cage around him.

◌◌◌◌◌

Everything at the Halliwell home was fixed now. The floor and the ceiling and the space between had been repaired, and Eddie

66

had a new pair of glasses. It was summer, the easiest time of year. The baby birds had hatched and matured, at least the ones that were going to, and fretting adults no longer had to feed their crying, open beaks. The babies had become fledglings, and the fledglings had flown or fallen.

Marie Halliwell saw that the birds flew more slowly, now that the grand purpose of the year had been achieved. Soon they would fly south, then return and begin all over again. She knew that it was true that some birds mated forever, but whether or how they might love was a mystery to her. She had heard stories of birds who cried for a mate gone missing, birds who perpetually returned to the place they last saw the other, and she imagined, without encouraging the vision, returning to Rome. She didn't know what was meant by the birds' devotion, but when it came to love, she was only human. She wanted everyone, even birds, to believe in it.

Once a week Marie Halliwell's husband climbed on top of her and made what was called love. Marie opened her legs but she didn't wrap them around his body or even lift her knees from the mattress. She'd stopped hoping for more children. She didn't bother to ponder if it was her own body or her husband's that was failing, and she didn't think, when they made love, of his possibly useless seed spilling into her possibly useless womb, of it swimming around inside of her, or else not swimming at all. Once she had imagined Rome, but these days she thought of the drapes with their blue swirls, of the dust on top of the closet door. Through the window she could see moonflowers blooming, and she remembered that slugs were eating the leaves. Tomorrow she would find them and pour salt on their bodies.

Though Russell was deep inside her, they could not have been farther apart. Wherever her eyes landed, Marie's mind went with them. As of Rome, the fall was not sudden but a slow, inevitable decline. She supposed even the most tenuous kind of love didn't come undone overnight. While theirs had been unravelling, Marie Halliwell had always imagined it would be possible to stitch it back up again, but now that it lay in a tangle around them there seemed to be nothing to do but kick it away, and be careful not to trip on it when coming and going. She went on as she had always gone on, in silence.

Outside, the *girasoli* were stirring. Soon, the yellow petals would unfold to reveal their dark faces, faces made for the sun. Once they had been Marie Halliwell's favourite flower. But unlike Kay Clancy LeBlanc, Marie was sentimental. The *girasoli*, symbols of Rome and the love of her life, would eternally remind Marie of the girl who stood crying in the garden, and how after she'd been in the yard, the weeds had taken over.

TOKYO 1964
the happy years

The 1964 Summer Olympics took place in Tokyo, Japan, from October 10 to October 24. Again there was no official mascot, though in retrospect the Shinkansen bullet train could have served as one. Said to be the world's fastest train, it began its run between Tokyo and Osaka on October 1, 1964, shunting back and forth in an Olympian blur.

Ninety-three countries participated in the XVIII Olympiad, bringing 5,151 athletes to the first Olympics ever held in the land of the rising sun. Emperor Hirohito officiated at the opening ceremonies, and the flame was lit by Yoshinori Sakai, who was in a way a rising sun himself: he had been born the day an atomic bomb was dropped on Hiroshima, a sign of hope on a dark bright day.

The hope brought into the lives of Joe, Kay, and Estelle was named Louis François LeBlanc, born June 17, 1962. His parents had wasted no time. Louis was what was called a long baby until he was able to walk, and then he was called tall. Without doubt, he was Joe's son. He had dark hair and eyes, like his father, but skin that was somewhat sallow, because, unlike Joe, he was sickly. Nasty viruses found their way to him, and he surrendered, letting them course through him and fly away.

Still, these were the happy years. Joe took to fatherhood like a fish to water. Nowhere was Estelle more ecstatic than when she rose to giant stature on top of his broad shoulders. And for nearly a year, Louis was riddled with giggles.

"Gigglesack," hammed Joe. "I'll suck your eye out, you little pipsqueak," he said, grabbing Louis and squeezing him tight.

Delirious, Louis writhed and squealed, and Joe's lips came down again and again on one of the boy's crazed eyes. With a *pop!*, Joe drew backwards. Mock surprise lengthened his long face as a great lump formed like a blackball in his cheek.

"Gulp," said Joe, and the lump disappeared.

Louis screamed and then it all began again – "I'll suck your eye out!"

Throughout this time, Joe continued to work for his uncles, and repair the LeBlanc family home on Huron Street. He straightened the lopsided porch, repainted the fading trim, and added a bedroom to the back of the house, lining it with windows. The only thing that made him unhappy about the room was that he had to cut down a tree to build it. The tree was old and large, an oak, but it was in the way. So it would not die uselessly, Joe used it to make what Kay called the love-bed. He whittled the frame himself, learning tricks of the trade from his uncles, and though the piece was not as exquisitely carved as the work of Alphonse and Toussaint, it was proof enough that gifts ran in families, right in the blood. In a musical-chairs revolution, Joe and Kay moved into the light-filled room with the oak-tree bed, Estelle moved into their old room, and Louis moved into the Estelle suite.

The new room – the love nest, named to go with the bed – sat on the backyard, where years ago, when a different family had lived here, there'd been a garden. All that grew in the somewhat smaller yard now was grass and weeds, and even these had a difficult time beneath the perpetual whir of Estelle's tiny feet. She was a cheerful, sprightly child. Kay, while young and vigorous, could at times not keep up with her, especially once Louis came along. Louis often kept Kay up all night, and in the day she stumbled around with him sleeping on her shoulder, trying not to trip on Estelle, who ran behind and in front of her in fluid figure-eights.

Kay had never been happier, but all over the world people were dying of grief and loneliness. While Joe LeBlanc was building a garage on Huron Street, Marilyn Monroe stopped breathing. No fat myopic boy found and saved her, though she died with the phone in her hand, perhaps summoning someone. Like coroners, biographers cut into her. They opened her up and many secrets flew out. Still others were invented. Ordinary people loved her more than they had before, upon discovering her pain and sadness, which may not have been so had she withered and died like anyone. Some three hundred versions of her life would be penned, though it had lasted only thirty-six years, and she, the object of such relentless desire, wound up in pieces. Every year for the rest of his life, Joe DiMaggio would bring roses to her grave. On the day of her funeral, the sun rose as though it were any old day. Joe DiMaggio wept, and Joe LeBlanc hammered the last nail into his homemade garage. In just three years he would be seen emerging from there, a red canoe on his head. And after that, he would be seen no more.

⟨⟨⟨⟨⟨⟨⟩⟩⟩⟩⟩⟩

Joe LeBlanc bought his canoe in 1964, the year of the Tokyo Summer Olympics. Eddie Halliwell, now twelve, was waiting for his father outside the yacht club when Joe LeBlanc strode past with another man.

"Here she be," said the man when they reached the upside-down canoe. "She's pretty beat up, but you can do 'er over like nob'dy, eh Joe?"

Joe LeBlanc nodded. He reached into his pocket, pulled out several bills, and pressed them into the other man's hand.

"Thanks," said Joe. "Take care."

The man left, and Joe remained. He looked at his canoe, and Eddie, behind him, looked too. Eddie watched Joe stoop and clear the pine needles from his purchase. The surface was green, but it had once been red. Rocks and sand had scratched the bottom, and vandals had engraved messages of love and hate. Joe ran his hand over the letters and Eddie squinted to see the writing. Amid hearts and swear words, he saw *K.C. fucks R.H.* His belly churned, and then he blinked and turned away. He picked at the log he was sitting on and a grey spider crawled out from the bark. Eddie squished the spider with his index finger until its legs stopped moving. When he looked up, he saw that Joe LeBlanc had lifted the canoe onto his head, and that his jacket was draped

72

over the boat, a long merciful sleeve covering the offending letters as he walked to the road.

Eddie picked again at the log. It was the trunk of a cedar, its roots and its crown cut off. Logs like these were strewn here and there around the yacht club. Maybe they had once been deadheads, floating down from the dam, and had been hauled from the river so that boats wouldn't crash into them. Often in summer, motorboats buzzed over the surface of the water as though flying, but birds would never be so noisy. The boats often went to the Quebec side of the river, to places Eddie had heard of but never seen. He surveyed the long strip of foreign land. The leaves were turning there, too. The clusters of orange, yellow, and red shifted while he watched them, growing and shrinking as this leaf coloured and that one fell. The red of the sugar maple looked almost black when it parted from the tree, so in that way it was a red like blood, dry and crumbling.

Just then his father emerged from the yacht club with a couple of men. Eddie watched from a distance and saw how his father talked with his whole body, moving his arms and his shoulders, nodding his head. "There's an art to conversation," he often told Eddie, "even when you're not the one doing the talking. You have to engage people – gesture, and use your eyes," he said, leaning in and locking his green gaze with Eddie's black one. "Even when you aren't really listening, you can look like you are."

Russell turned away from the men and toward Eddie. He jerked his head and whistled, the way a better man beckons his dog, Eddie thought, but still he followed. He fell in line behind his father and observed the back of him, not tall but solid, with broad shoulders and narrow hips. Eddie never forgot that his father had almost competed in the Olympic Games, and that he, his father's son, was a fat disappointment, a kind of slap in the face. He watched his father's calf muscles flex and release as he stepped along. Sturdy shoes, woollen socks, shorts, and a sweater. His father would dress that way until almost November, impervious to the cold. If ever Eddie shook and shivered, his father told him, "Don't be a sissy, the brisk air is good for your lungs," which wasn't true. The brisk air seized them up. It made him wheeze and sputter, and cause his mother to consider the likelihood of asthma.

Nevertheless, he didn't shiver any more in his father's presence, or let on if he was cold. Instead, he trudged along behind him. He thought of the canoe and its letters, and he pushed his glasses down to the tip of his nose as he looked again at the far side of the river. The colours were less distinct this way, but somehow brighter. Since his fall in the creek, he had discovered the superior beauty of a blurred world.

⬤⬤⬤⬤⬤

Under the graffiti was a fine canoe, with bones made from chestnut. Joe spent weeks bringing it back to its former glory, but nothing could convince Kay that it had been a necessary purchase.

"We need a car more than we need a canoe, Joe," she told him. "We're supposed to be saving."

"I don't want a car."

"Well, I do! Everyone has a car. It's not normal to have a canoe instead of a car. Not when you have two children."

Joe grinned. He lifted her hair and kissed her neck to appease her.

"Don't," she said. "I'm angry." But she was already smiling.

"I bought it for you," he said.

Kay scoffed and raised an eyebrow. "Thanks," she said, "but I don't want a canoe."

Joe smiled. "Well, I bought it for you anyway."

He looked more than pleased with himself. In recent weeks he'd been tense and quiet, but now he seemed relieved. And while she was glad he'd returned to his old self, she had no idea what had brought on either mood. She should have linked it to an incident that had occurred weeks earlier, but it had been over so quickly, and seemed so insignificant at the time, that she'd forgotten.

She and Joe had been walking in the cedar grove by the yacht club. Joe carried Estelle on his back, and Kay carried Louis. In one hand Joe held a long branch, which he planned to shape into a walking stick. He tapped on a green canoe with the stick and said, "I can't believe no one steals these."

"Why would anyone want to?"

"To paddle!" said Joe, surprised by her disinterest. "Who wouldn't want a canoe?" He used the stick to brush the leaves from one of the boats and revealed the blistered green paint beneath, defaced by both the elements and crude graffiti.

"I'd steal one. I'd love to own a canoe."

"You wouldn't steal if your life depended on it," said Kay, laughing.

"Okay," he said. "But it's such a waste. Some of these haven't been used in —"

He stopped speaking then, and stared at the canoe, his face gone pale and stern.

"What?" she said. "What is it?"

But Joe didn't answer. He lifted his gaze, and the dead look in his eyes sent a chill all through her. Over his shoulder, Estelle giggled, and Kay became aware of the contrast of those two faces – the man's closed one, hard as granite, and the child's open one, pink and beaming.

"What?" she said again.

But Joe threw his stick back among the pine needles and walked away, Estelle's curls bouncing with each step.

All the way home Kay scurried after him, striving to keep up. She had to let Louis down because she couldn't manage the weight for the whole journey.

"Wait for us!" she called.

And while he did, he didn't speak the rest of the way. Once they arrived at 40 Huron, he stooped to allow Estelle to slide from his back, and then left again immediately. Kay watched him go in great bewilderment.

When he came back, it was as though nothing had happened. He'd picked an armload of black-eyed Susans and given them to her, but he didn't, and wouldn't, explain his curious behaviour.

And though he was working long hours for LeBlanc & LeBlanc, it was shortly after this that Joe began to take odd jobs to earn extra money. One such job was digging new beds in the Halliwell garden. And of course it was *this* rather than his puzzling behaviour near the yacht club that later stood out in Kay's mind. She couldn't tell him how uncomfortable it made her to know he was working for Coach Halliwell and his aloof, sophisticated wife. Over two unbearable weeks Joe was there every evening, digging and replanting, fertilizing the soil. When he arrived home, exhausted and dusty, Kay searched his face for any sign that he had somehow discovered the truth, but in fact he seemed happy. Each night in the love-bed, he loved her with as much vigour as ever, maybe more.

"You know," he said, rolling off of her to lie on his back, "we should have a garden."

Kay didn't care about gardens, but she was glad he wanted to have one with her. She smiled and curled into him.

At the end of the two weeks, he arrived home with a canoe on his head, bought, like a portion of the mortgage on 40 Huron, with Halliwell money.

(((((())))))

Summer in Deep River was over once the '64 Games began, and the weather had turned cool. It was hot in Tokyo, but Abebe Bikila wore shoes. Feet sweating, he ran the race in a record two hours, twelve minutes, 11.2 seconds, winning another gold medal and usurping himself. Only six weeks before his arrival in Japan, he had undergone an appendectomy, so, like Marie Halliwell, he was missing something he had not needed in the first place. He soared to the finish line, but for once, the exemplary performance was not out of the ordinary, as Tokyo was an Olympics of phenomenal triumphs. One hundred and eleven records were toppled at the Tokyo Games, the first for which computers kept track of the scoring. Three billion dollars had been spent to prepare the city, and the athletes thrived in the top-notch facilities. Architect Kenzo Tange had designed a new gymnasium, with a graceful roof that spread like wings over the space beneath. And as in Rome, roads had been widened for the world to come calling.

The American Wilma Rudolph, the Black Gazelle, who had once worn a flour-sack dress, was Wilma Eldridge now, having married her high-school sweetheart. She stayed home from the 1964 Games and gave birth to her second child, Djuanna. Fellow mother and gymnast extraordinaire Larysa Latynina, in her third and last Olympic competition, won six medals for the second Games in a row, two of them gold. But there was someone better than her now: Czechoslovakian champion Vera Caslavska would scoop the All-Around title.

Kay LeBlanc watched and listened from the other side of the world. Coverage was skimpier than it had been from Rome, because of the time difference, but Kay followed it as closely as she could. She knew of the gymnasium, whose curved, graceful shape was as rhythmic as gymnastics itself, and she knew of Larysa's cache of medals. If she felt at all wistful, she didn't say, but once, when the children were in bed and Joe was in the garage painting his canoe, she stepped outside, removed her socks and shoes and did a circle of slow cartwheels around the backyard. In the upside-down right-side-up twilight she twirled, unaware that Estelle had gotten out of bed, and was squatting on the back step, watching her. Estelle crouched in her pink flannel pyjamas, as though that would make her less visible, but she may as well have been made of phosphorous. Kay, in her private cartwheel world, didn't see her, but Joe did. From the side door of his garage, he smiled as he watched her watching her mother. He had a paintbrush in his hand, and red paint dripped on his shoe. The rippling giggles that escaped from Estelle were muffled by her little hand on her mouth, and also by the sound of a car passing on Huron Street. In it was Eddie Halliwell and his mother, Marie. Eddie's round, white face turned toward the passenger window at the moment the car passed the LeBlanc house. The garage shone in the blue evening, and Joe and the wet canoe resembled an actor and his prop. Marie, too, turned her head to the side, but she didn't notice Joe. She was looking at her son, at his black hair, which was his face turned away from her. Lost in disquiet, she failed to brake at the stop sign, and didn't see Robbie Hayes, about to cross the street with his hands in his pockets. As he stepped out he heard the approaching car while Kay cartwheeled and Estelle giggled and Joe smiled and Eddie stared and Marie drove without looking. Robbie stopped and waited until she had gone by, and then he continued on his journey.

In the yard, Kay stopped twirling and spotted her daughter on the steps.

"Hey you, little missy! What are you doing out of bed?"

She ran and scooped her up and Estelle's laughter bubbled out again. "Why are you giggling?" Kay teased. "Are you a squeeze doll, my girl? When I squeeze your belly, do you giggle?"

Estelle screamed with laughter. Kay spun her once around the yard, and then carried her inside.

Joe, unseen and still smiling, returned to his canoe. With his brush he touched a spot he had missed the first time. The "R.H."

and all the other letters were invisible now, having been sanded to nothing and painted again. The rich red glistened on his boat and on his shoe.

⬤⬤⬤⬤⬤

Rowers Roger Jackson and George Hungerford won Canada's only gold medal that year. Most Ottawa Valley residents were in bed when they stood on the podium. The new anthem, "O Canada," was played for them, but the old flag was raised, which was too bad, because the stylish Maple Leaf, red on white, would have looked well alongside the Japanese flag. Some said it was as though Canada, in that moment, had one foot in the past and one in the future.

In some respects, Joe LeBlanc was no different. The canoe was his now. He had obtained and altered it, thereby attaching himself to its dreadful painted message, when he could just as easily have ignored the thing, and left it scattered with pine needles beside the yacht club. After all, there were dozens of other rumours scratched into its body.

Once the canoe had been sanded and painted, he took it the short distance through town to the river. He chose the same path he had used just over a month before, when he had purchased the canoe from the man at the yacht club. He traced his steps in reverse, as though this new trip, with the unscathed red canoe, could erase that old one, with the tarnished green canoe, and thereby destroy the vile truth (so he thought) behind the graffiti it bore. People stopped and asked, "Joe, need a lift?" but Joe mumbled his thanks and portaged onward. He had all he needed to get anywhere now: his long limbs and his canoe.

As rowers Roger Jackson and George Hungerford slept wearing their medals in Tokyo, Joe's paddle dipped into the Ottawa. Certainly if anyone had seen him, they would have said he looked happy, or at least peaceful, though what canoeist does not? In the grey October light, he paddled back and forth along the shoreline. Leaves fell with abandon, and then floated on the water. Soon every deciduous tree would be bare, and then winter would come, as though only the leaves, little sweaters on trees, had been keeping everyone warm.

⟨⟨⟨⟨⟨⟩⟩⟩⟩⟩

Easy Christmas Breakfast Roll

½ c. ground almonds
1 c. seedless raisins
¼ c. sugar
2 egg whites
⅛ tsp. almond extract

Mix these in a small bowl and set aside.

2 c. all-purpose flour
2 tsp. baking powder
½ tsp. salt
½ c. cold butter
¼ c. sugar
2 tsp. grated lemon rind
2 egg yolks, beaten
½ c. milk

Mix flour, baking powder, and salt together in a large bowl. Cut in cold butter finely with a pastry blender or knives. Add sugar, lemon rind, egg yolks, and milk. Blend with a fork. Squeeze the pastry together as much as possible.

Turn out onto a well-floured board or countertop and knead gently about 20 times or until it stays together in a neat ball. Roll into an oval about 12 x 8 inches or larger. Dip your fingers in a little milk and put some around the edges of the pastry so it will stick together when you roll it. Spread with almond mixture but do not go too close to the edges. Roll up like a jelly roll, sealing well by pinching the ends together, having the seam of the roll underneath. Put on greased cookie sheet (grease only the part where the roll will be). Brush the roll with a little milk or cream and sprinkle with sugar.

Bake at 350°F for 40-45 minutes or until well browned. Cool before cutting. The pastry will crack open but it still tastes good.

From the Christmas 1964 edition of a certain Canadian ladies' magazine, both Kay LeBlanc and Marie Halliwell clipped this recipe. Each served the loaf on Christmas morning, and for many a Christmas to come, though neither knew of the shared tradition.

In the year of its inception, Estelle ate only the raisins of the Christmas Breakfast Roll, and Louis tossed his entire helping on the floor. But across town, in the Halliwells' riverside house, in the bright white kitchen where Marie had cut her fabric and later cried over her tulips, Eddie devoured every morsel that was put on his plate, and then asked for more. He spread butter on the already buttery slices and held each bite in his mouth to feel the sugar dissolve. He was fatter than he had been when he was nine. As he ate he eyed the decorated tree in the corner, a spruce whose needles had already begun to drop on the presents below. He had been studying the gifts for some time, and knew which package held the pencils and the watercolour paints and brushes, and which held the sketchbook with its thick white pages. Before it was wrapped, he had sat in his parents' closet smelling the paper. Had sat right on his mother's shoes, crushing the backs down without realizing. The large, upright package was a thinly disguised easel, but he had no intention of using that. A sketchbook he could tuck into his backpack or hold on his knees. It and the pencils and paint set were all he needed or wanted, and all he had asked for, so the easel must have been his father's idea. Even before snooping, he had known of the coming gift of art, having heard a late-night exchange as he lay beneath his covers.

"A treadmill would do him more good."

"Russell!"

"He's fat, Marie. It's not only ugly, it's unhealthy."

"He's a boy. He has lots of time to grow out of it."

"That's a funny way of putting it. Fat children grow into fat adults. I mean, I'm all for art, you know that, but sitting around painting will only make him fatter. If he would *do* something. . . ."

Eddie stopped listening. Though he didn't wish to, he recalled the days when he had admired his father in his tennis clothes, and asked if he could learn to play. Eddie hadn't been completely hopeless then, in his father's eyes, so with great enthusiasm, Russell had Eddie decked out in white shorts and a white shirt, and signed him up for a summer of lessons. What Eddie remembered was a teenaged boy sending a green ball toward him, and the way the ball spun as it flew through the air, and how it seemed to be the only thing in the world that was moving. Sometimes Russell played on the court next to him, and it inhibited Eddie more to watch his father leap and lunge for the ball. He'd come to the fence and holler advice to Eddie. "Look alive, Ed! Show some spunk!" And all the way home he would rave on about Eddie's sloppy demeanour, and the importance of doing anything he tried well, with precision and style, and how it would give him the character he lacked and one day mould him into an admirable man. For Eddie, penned into a small space with his father, breathing the same air, these drives were worse than the lessons themselves. Once he was home, he'd sit on his bed in his white clothes, staring down at his fat white thighs. And a dull pain would form in the nape of his neck and grow up over his brain, squeezing like a rough hand. But it was never that that made him cry.

"What's his problem?" he heard his father say in an unlowered voice.

"Ssshhh."

"Well, what's the matter with him?"

Eddie climbed from his bed and stood at the door to hear his mother's whisper.

"He's not an athlete, Russell. You're too hard on him."

Eddie's cheeks, flushed from crying, flushed further.

"He just wants to play," she said.

"Of course he wants to play, I know he wants to play, but you have to acquire skills, and then finesse for a game like that, you can't just —"

"I mean he just wants to *play*. Have fun. With *you*."

Eddie closed his streaming eyes and put his hands over his hot ears.

That was years before, when Eddie was nine, and now he was thirteen. His wish to spend time with his father had eroded completely, so no one was made uncomfortable by the yearning. What he did want was to open his presents and then repack them into his knapsack, take them farther down the river to the yacht club, where he could sit unnoticed and paint the hoarfrost on the trees, the forgotten upside-down canoes, and the frozen river. And in the afternoon, when the turkey was cooking and his father was resting and his mother was chopping vegetables, Eddie strapped on his pack and headed for the waterfront. The blue house was behind him, posing, but it would be many years before he'd capture it just as it was to him – crumbling from the inside out, and not at all what it appeared to be.

⟨⟨⟨⟨⟨⟩⟩⟩⟩⟩

Christmas came and went like a birthday. Louis LeBlanc received his first pair of bobskates, and Estelle, nearly four, graduated to a pair of tube skates of which she was enormously proud. Because these were the happy years, Joe and Kay tucked their children in, then climbed into their own bed in the room that Joe had built, and made slow, delicious love. Frosted flowers sparkled on the windows, and outside, snow fell white against the black sky. Joe and Kay kissed and collapsed smiling. Though they couldn't yet know it, Margar LeBlanc had just come into being.

⟨⟨⟨⟨⟨⟩⟩⟩⟩⟩

During the final days of that year, Robbie Hayes went skating on the Ottawa, and the ice cracked open beneath him. It was a winter evening, cold but not cold enough. Remnants from an earlier snowfall painted the trees and the hillside that led to the river. A blue-white glow spread over land and water.

Robbie was home for the holidays. Though he was going into his final term of university, that night he wore his old high-school jacket, purple and gold, with the word *Mustangs* curved across its back. Gloved hands in his purple pockets, he skated backwards in circles. The blades of his newly sharpened skates gleamed, but the brown leather was scuffed and well-worn. Alone on the ice, he performed magnificently.

Other than Robbie, two young women had been skating on the river that evening, but now they were leaving. They had removed their skates and pulled on their boots, and were climbing the hill to the road above. Robbie watched them go. He turned and skated forwards, picking up speed, then jumped and spun in the air, landing on one leg with the other stretched cleverly behind him. Perhaps he hoped the women had stopped to watch him. But they had not. No one witnessed his final pirouette. The women turned left when they reached the road, and soon disappeared completely.

The night was quiet in the way that only winter nights can be. Robbie's skates sliced through the silence. When the ice cracked open, it was sometime after 9 p.m. and before 10 p.m., a cumbersome, vague fact determined only by two more distinct ones: the young women who had not turned to watch him later recalled that it had been 9 p.m. when they'd left the river; and it

86

was 10 p.m. when Joe, Kay, Estelle, and Louis LeBlanc passed on the road above and heard the tired screaming.

No one had heard the much louder, wide-awake screaming that had come earlier.

"Help!" Robbie had hollered. "Help!" He'd grabbed the ice but it had broken away in shards each time he touched it.

No one walked by. Five thousand people were in their homes that night. Fires crackled in the warm deaf houses, and dead trees glowed with tinsel and lights. Here and there an ornament twirled slowly, and stopped. Gifts lay beneath the trees in their torn wrappings, and soft music hummed from radios.

The young LeBlanc family had been in such a home the night of the tragedy. They had been visiting Kay's parents at their house on the river, and now were on their way back to 40 Huron Street. Kay hooked her arm in the crook of Joe's elbow, and Joe, with his free hand, pulled Estelle and Louis in a sleigh. The sleigh was a work of art. Presented Christmas Eve, it had been hand-carved and hammered together by Joe's uncles, Alphonse and Toussaint. Kay and Joe had refused the Clancys' offer of a ride tonight, because they wanted to put their children in the sleigh and pull them home.

"See?" said Joe. "Who needs a car?"

The handle had been fashioned from the arm of a shovel, but the uncles had carved birds and twisting vines into the wood. The sleigh itself boasted intricate depictions of toads, wild ferns, chipmunks, and trilliums – a gift of summer in the middle of winter. Nestled behind the high walls of the sleigh, Louis slept bundled in a yellow wool blanket, and Estelle lay awake staring at the stars. Joe had just turned to check on them when he heard the faint cry for help. Estelle blinked at the sound, and when her eyes reopened they were looking into Joe's. Joe stared back at his daughter, at the bits of blonde curl that escaped from her hat. He stopped walking and listened. All of them held still. Their clouds of breath hovered and dispersed.

Joe ran to the edge of the hill that overlooked the river. He saw the ice and the jagged black hole and a figure, barely moving. He ran, slid, ran down the hill and onto the ice, and from here he could see all the cracks emanating from the hole and snapping out at him like snakes. He flopped to his stomach and slid toward the figure, who had begun to move more vigorously at the sight of a possible saviour. The man lifted his arms but as though they were dead weight they fell and splashed in the water. Joe couldn't get close enough to grab him. He unzipped his coat and struggled out of it but not even his own long arm extended by his two long sleeves could reach the sinking man's shaking, outstretched hand.

"Hang on, buddy," Joe called. "I'll get you outta there, guy. Hang on."

He grabbed his coat and hurried back up the hill, where Kay stood with the children. He looked at the beautiful handle on the children's sleigh, but there was nothing to use to loosen it. With his eyes shining and full of tears, he looked at Kay, pulled off her scarf and raced back down the hill, tying the scarf to the sleeve of his coat as he ran. And when he got down on the ice again, ready to send one end of the makeshift lifeline toward the man, he saw who it was: Robbie Hayes. Joe LeBlanc stopped. Kay called out to him but he stayed still, holding the scarf and the coat in a ball in his hands. He stared at Robbie, who, though visibly tiring, reached out to Joe. He groaned and stretched his arms toward Joe's coat and the scarf. But Joe didn't move. He looked down at his bundle and up into Robbie's vacant eyes. A bird cawed, and Joe, as though emerging from a trance, shook his head and sent the lifeline into the air, hanging on to one end. Robbie lifted a limp arm and it fell again as quickly. His eyes appeared heavy and his lips were almost blue.

"Take it," Joe screamed. "Take it!"

Robbie lifted his futile hand once more. When it fell, he smiled, and then moaned.

"Take the scarf! Please — take the scarf!"

But Robbie's eyes were downcast. He looked into the water, where his hand had fallen. His face dropped forward, and he was gone.

◯◯◯◯◯

No one but Robbie himself can know how calm he felt, how warm. After the initial plunge and the freezing, the panic and the frantic treading of water, the yelling for help and the ice that shattered at his every touch — after all that, a glorious heat spread through him. It began somewhere in his centre, and flowed slowly through his torso and limbs, as though a glass of thick, hot liquid had been upturned inside of him. Never had he felt such peace and warmth.

"I'm dying," he thought. "I'm going to die here."

He knew he should not give up, that he should continue to call into the silent night, but he was no longer motivated by cold or fear. Rather, he was warm and he was swimming in warm water. He made some sounds, to see if his voice would still work, and that was when the man came. He seemed to fly down the hill. Down, up again, and down. Robbie smiled and reached out to him. He could not imagine leaving his warm bath, but he would try. He would not die without trying. He stretched his hand toward the man with the shining eyes but the man did not reach to help him. The eyes looked very cold, and the tips of Robbie's fingers, which were pointing at the man, had begun to lose their heat. He let his hand drop in the warm water and he smiled again. The man was throwing things and yelling now but Robbie was tired. He lifted his hand and waved to the stranger, because after all, this was the last person he would ever see.

◌◌◌◌◌

Robbie Hayes's funeral took place on January 2, 1965, a year in which he had not lived. An hour before the service, Serge and Beryl Hayes appeared on the once-crooked porch of 40 Huron Street, their faces puckered with grief.

"We want to thank you," said Serge, looking into Joe's eyes with his own beseeching ones. "We understand you tried to save our son."

He was a brilliant physicist, but today he appeared to be an ordinary man.

His wife stepped forward and clasped Joe's hand. She wore black kid gloves that made her hands softer than a baby's. "We hope you will come to the service," she said, with a face small and pointed like a bird's.

These were people from elsewhere. Unlike the Valley's own Alphonse and Toussaint LeBlanc, or Ned and Irene Clancy, the

Hayes's had lived in Sweden and France. They had come here by choice, Beryl to raise her boy and care for her husband, and Serge to work at the nuclear research laboratories, a scientist's dream. They and their kind had changed the face of the Valley. Even in 1965, some twenty years after they had arrived, there was a great divide between them and the likes of Joe LeBlanc. But as any parent would, they grieved for their son. Joe, too, was raw and aching.

"I'll come," he said, for what else could he say?

He stood with the boy's mother and father as Robbie's eternal soul was blessed and his young body was buried. Joe's head hung low with what could only be guilt and shame, but Beryl and Serge did not blame him or each other or themselves. For the time being, they were protected – also united – by their overwhelming loss. Soon, though, they would begin to analyze what had happened and why, and speculate how it might have turned out differently. But even then they would not blame Joe, who had run in answer to Robbie's screams when no one else had heard him; had lain on the ice with the lifeline while his cold, frightened family looked on. They could see in Joe's eyes – huge, brown, haunted eyes – a sorrow that ran the very length of him, which they assumed had only to do with Robbie. Instead of blaming Joe, they would come to blame each other, which really meant they blamed themselves.

If you had gone with him, the way he asked you to.

You never made time for him any more, not really.

If you had picked him up at eight – it was so dark and cold.

Unbeknownst to Serge and Beryl Hayes, Joe's and Kay's actions complicated the cycle of consequence, which spun round and round like interlocking torture wheels driven by cogs and gears. It circled back to the beginning of time and beyond, linking today with the stories Eddie Halliwell found depicted in his mother's old mythology books – Orestes would never have killed his mother, Clytemnestra, the less lovely sister of Helen of Troy, if she hadn't murdered his father, Agamemnon, a king and a great hero. But she never would have done so if Agamemnon hadn't sacrificed their sweet daughter Iphigenia in exchange for winds that would sail him to Troy. It was his duty to go there and save Helen, even though it was doubtful she'd been kidnapped at all. More likely, she'd run off of her own free will with that seductive Trojan, Paris. Of course Agamemnon suffered as he committed his deed against Iphigenia in the oppressive heat of a windless day – that's why it's called a sacrifice. His pointed blade plunged into her smooth skin, and the gods sent a breeze that lifted off the water and cascaded over the king and his daughter's dead body. The waves swelled. Agamemnon with his band of soldiers set sail for Troy, as any honourable man would. And while he was gone, Clytemnestra waited and grieved and saw red, blood-red, over the unavenged death of her daughter, slaughtered like an animal by her own father. All the while the Greeks and the Trojans killed each other and wept upon the heaps of dead bodies while Helen watched from the palace above, regretting her whims, and then not, as Paris tickled her neck with kisses. The day Agamemnon returned home, his captive Trojan prophetess, Cassandra, saw blood on the walls well before it was shed, but because of a curse that stemmed from her own story of consequence, her words of warning emerged as babble. That night, as they lay in their beds, Clytemnestra – proud and severe in her misery – killed them.

And the gods above, reclining on plush pillows with their ambrosia nightcaps, looked on while their little dolls cried and bled.

◌◌◌◌◌

Gaunt and pale already, Joe grew cadaverous. Out walking, a thing he did even more often than before, he was an eerie sight. His long, thin bones and his sadness evoked the restless shades of the Underworld, doomed to shuffle eternally. Even seated he could not be still, unless Estelle, now four years old, ran and pounced on his lap, sprawling across him. "Daddy, stop jiggling!" she'd say. And Joe would smile, for he could never *not* smile at Estelle. But eventually his legs would resume their rapid shaking. Up and down they'd go, so that, in a sense, even when he was seated he was walking away.

Nights, he tried to sleep and saw the wild eyes of Robbie Hayes. To Kay he confessed, "It's like his eyes are painted on the insides of my eyelids." Side by side, he and Kay stared at the ceiling. Kay knew that right up to Robbie's last moment of life she could have saved him. She had seen her husband run down the hill, back up, and then down again, and she had seen him stop and stare at the man with the outstretched hands. She had looked at the hands and the wet Mustangs jacket, at the faraway face, which she suddenly realized was Robbie's. She understood the reason for Joe's hesitation, but what could she have done? She could have yelled, "Save him, Joe! He's not who you think he is! He hasn't done anything wrong!" Instead she had just yelled "Joe – oh God, Joe," and then fallen silent. But who was to say different words would have made any difference? Even if Joe had thrown the lifeline immediately, maybe Robbie would not have hung on. Or maybe Kay's words would have shocked and confused Joe so much he would have been unable to throw the lifeline at all. *Yes*, she thought. *That was possible.*

So when Joe said, "I killed him," she answered, "No. You tried to save him, Joe. You did your best. You're a hero."

"But I –"

"Stop."

"Do you remember how once I said I could –"

"No, Joe, I don't remember. And anyway, you didn't. Just stop." She kissed his mouth to keep the words from coming out.

But of course she remembered. In the time following his return, when he had fallen in love with Kay all over again, and fallen in love with Estelle for the first time, he had asked her, "Why were you with Robbie Hayes?" Cornered by his clarity and directness, Kay had hedged and wavered and tried to make up a lie. What had come out – "Because he made me" – had seemed despicable only after it was spoken, when it was too late to take it back, for what kind of girl would tell such a lie? But seeing Joe's horror, she'd recognized she'd gone too far – he would forgive *her*, the apparent victim, but he would want to right the wrong she'd claimed had been done to her, and in so doing, her lie would be exposed, along with the dreadful truth behind it, that she'd slept with her teacher.

She'd done everything she could to quell Joe's anger. She'd stammered at first, finding her way through the lie, but as she'd gone on, she'd refined it, and by the end she'd almost believed it herself — that it wasn't as bad as it sounded, because Robbie hadn't realized she didn't want to sleep with him, she'd been too friendly, "You know me," and he had misread her signals, and the next thing you knew, well, perhaps she should have been more forceful herself, but it was horrible and embarrassing, and she wished he wouldn't make her talk about it any more.

"I could kill him," Joe had told her, grinding his teeth.

She'd thought of Robbie Hayes, whom she could barely picture, and of Coach Halliwell's face that night in his car.

"Joe, there's no point any more. Dredging up all that stuff now — what good would it do? What kind of start would that be for Estelle? Look at her. Little pickle. Pudgy little bean."

She'd held the baby out to Joe, and seen she had done so at just the right moment. He'd cradled Estelle in his arms and kissed her, and Kay had taken comfort in the fact that some of the things she'd said were true.

And now there was a third baby coming. Deep in Kay's dark womb, Margar expanded, doubling and tripling in size before anyone knew she existed. By the time Kay realized she was pregnant, it was February. The sky was white and Louis was sick with croup. He barked like a dog and threw up strings of phlegm and looked at her, bewildered. The phlegm was hanging from his mouth, a thing that would not normally have bothered her, since he was her beloved son. But Kay shuddered. She moved Louis out of the way and threw up into the toilet herself. And right away she thought, *I'm pregnant.*

Later she would claim to have been instantly happy. "I couldn't wait to meet you," she told Margar, leaving out an array of details, but Margar had a sixth sense, as unwanted as a sixth toe. She knew the truth when she heard it, and more to the point, she knew a lie.

Joe smiled vaguely when Kay gave him the news.

"Are you happy?" she asked, folding her arms around his neck. She pressed her pert nose to his hooked one and looked into his eyes.

"Of course I'm happy," he said, but when he smiled further, his face appeared sadder than ever.

That night, he woke gasping. He sat up, heaving for air. Roused from a deep sleep, Kay saw that his whole body trembled. She rubbed his back, which was damp with sweat, and kissed his salty skin.

"Hey," she said, to calm him. "You're okay." But her words sounded flat and her voice too sweet, too musical, and neither disguised her uneasiness. Joe continued to wheeze and pant and shake all over. She put her arms around his cold body and held him until his breathing slowed. He curled up beside her, mirroring the baby in her womb.

After that, he began to drift away. Night after night he faded, as his daughter beside him grew more defined. Soon he stopped waking in the night, shaking and crying. Rather, Kay woke. Once she had the disturbing sensation that she was alone in their bed, surrounded by the carved frame Joe himself had built. Afraid to turn and see a hollow where Joe's body had been, she instead lay on her side and ran her hand along the wooden flowers.

"Joe?"

There was no response.

She spoke a little louder: "Joe?"

But Joe did not answer. If he was breathing, he made no sound.

Kay blinked and traced petals. The vine that held the bed together was morning glory, interspersed with oak leaves and acorns. Slowly she rolled over, and more slowly she turned her head to find him. Like a dead man, he lay on his back. He was so still that Kay held her hand in front of his mouth to see if he was breathing. The breath was shallow, but there. She nestled her face into the crook of his neck and stretched her leg over him.

"I love you," she whispered, but Joe slept on. "Everything will be fine," she said. "You'll see."

And surely it would. The truth was as far away as a star, and as harmless, since the chance of Joe confronting Robbie no longer existed. Not for the first time, Kay thought that Robbie Hayes's death, though tragic, was a blessing for her and for Joe and the fragile happiness of their family. Aware of the cruelty of that thought, Kay pushed it away each time it came, so it assumed only the tiniest, darkest space within her.

⟨⟨⟨⟨⟨⟩⟩⟩⟩⟩

Winter ran long and bleak. As the gulf widened between Joe and Kay, others spread wider yet between Russell, Marie, and Eddie. Each in their own oblivion, the Halliwells lived on together in the blue two-storey, gathering around the table in the morning and the evening as families do. Marie played music to drown out the wordlessness, as well as the heartbreaking sound of Eddie eating. She knew his size would make his life more difficult than it needed to be, but he'd been round from the day he was born, and before. Marie had been bursting with him when they'd left Italy, which perhaps they should never have done.

The day she'd encountered Russell in the Sistine Chapel, under the angels, he told her, "*Io sono molto bella.*" I am very beautiful. And though he was — unusually so — what he'd intended to say was that *she* was beautiful. Marie, who was merely pretty and knew it, understood his mistake regardless, and was all the more beguiled by it. She was flattered, too, that he would think she was Italian. She was not, but she could speak the language better than he could, and she liked the idea of pretending to be someone she wasn't. She smiled coyly and answered in her best Italian accent, "*Grazie.*"

The charade continued throughout the evening. Russell struggled on and Marie said next to nothing, but her laugh, he said later, had made him love her from the start. In the years following, she would wonder about love at first sight. She'd taken in his wavy auburn hair and his fresh face, his green eyes and his easy smile, but it was something underneath those that compelled her from the first — a glint in his eyes she'd taken for courage, for humour. Beyond that was the intoxicating sensation that somewhere, sometime, she had already known him, and here he was again, her other. As if, all along, she'd been waiting.

He said, "*Mi Americano*" (though in fact he was Canadian), and she said, faking her accent, "Me too" (because she was), but he seemed to assume she had misunderstood him, and chattered on in his piecemeal Italian as they walked the streets of Rome. At the end of the evening, in the Piazza San Pietro, he kissed her. When their mouths let go of each other, she said, "I'm from Seattle, how about you?"

Marie sent a message to her mother, encapsulating their sweet love story — how he'd appeared like an angel who had fallen from the chapel's ceiling, how she had tricked and teased him with her rolling r's, how they would marry in Rome and honeymoon in Florence – *Firenze*, she said. Her mother's curt reply advised, "Romance that starts on a lie ends on a lie." The harsh words were heard and dismissed, but in the years to come, Marie would have cause to reflect on her mother's little proverb again and again.

At the time, however, she looked only to the future. Russell Halliwell called himself a man with a plan, and said he wanted her to be part of it. His stay in Rome was one stop in an extensive European vacation, which he could only afford because his father had died and left him a modest inheritance.

"Believe me," said Russell with an affable grin and a roll of his eyes, "he would have wanted me to smooth out my rough edges."

Once the money dwindled, he intended to head somewhere entirely different. He'd secured a job in the upstart town of Deep River, a community of scientists that needed teachers for its growing children. The pay was exceptional. She told him she could see him as a teacher. He was confident and gregarious, a show-off with charm. If he'd had his way, though, he would have been a gymnast. He told her he'd made it all the way to the national team some years back, but his father had disapproved of a life devoted to frivolous sports, and pushed him towards teaching. "Never realizing," said Russell, with a smirk, "that I'd end up teaching sports. He'd roll in his grave if he knew."

On the eve of their wedding, Marie dreamed of the ceremony, of Russell's face moving close to hers, so close that she could see his white, perfect teeth were carved from stones, and his green eyes were of cut green glass. He reached his hand to her hair, where a wreath of flowers rested, and at his touch, every petal fell and withered. When she woke, dread washed through her in a hot wave. But then he was there at the door of her room, with cannoli for breakfast, and by three o'clock that blue afternoon, he was her husband. "Until death do us part," they said.

⟨⟨⟨⟨⟨⟩⟩⟩⟩⟩

The following year, in August of 1951, Marie and Russell Halliwell arrived in Canada. They holidayed at Niagara Falls, and in the photographs, Horseshoe Falls sprays its good-luck mist all over a windblown Marie. Unborn, Eddie was huge already, and in each photo Marie has her hands on her stomach, as though holding him up.

Throughout this time, and during the long drive north to Deep River, the feeling of dread revisited her, but each time, she thought of Roman angels and horseshoes, and the fact that Russell himself was good luck. Before he had appeared in the Sistine Chapel, she had not been well. Then Marie Loden, she had travelled alone through Venice and Florence and Rome, plagued by Stendhal's syndrome. While it was her habit to find a syndrome that fit her symptoms and vice versa, this time she believed her diagnosis was right. The symptoms first came over her in a room of maudlin Madonnas. She thought she would faint or be sick. Blotches obscured her vision, and her head grew heavy. Stendhal himself, upon seeing the huge masterpieces of the Renaissance, claimed: "On leaving the Church of Santa Croce, I felt a throbbing in my heart. Life was draining out of me while I walked, and I was afraid I would fall." All through Italy, life drained out of Marie Loden. Melancholy by nature, she became wan and depleted, and the sad faces of the Madonnas appeared before her like reflections in glass. She felt she should not look at them, yet couldn't look away. The thin lips, the lowered eyes, the pale, oval face and the gown, always blue, exuded a strange power. Born to suffer and die, tiny Jesus in her arms seemed almost insignificant, and the glow above their heads not a halo, but a herald of condemnation.

Since there were no Madonnas on the ceiling of the Sistine Chapel, Marie Loden was gazing in uncomplicated wonder at Adam's limp finger and Eve, hiding under God's arm, when Russell Halliwell announced his appreciation of his own beauty. From then on she was with him. The Madonnas still made her swoon, but she couldn't fall down with his muscular arm at her waist. Furthermore, love had distracted her. With him she was less pensive and morose, at least for a time. But she was aware that it was easy to fall in love in Italy, far from home and sipping red wine among the remains of history.

"What is it that makes ruins — something ruined — so beautiful?" she asked him.

"You," he said, which was a short, charming response that both flattered her and turned the conversation back to what interested him at that moment. She leaned across the table and kissed him, because although it was an unsatisfying, dismissive answer to a question she could have ruminated at great length, she preferred to believe it meant he loved her completely.

As they drove to Deep River, Marie Halliwell felt the world close in on her. Her dread was matched by a mounting panic that made her roll down her window and lean her head out into the wind, bringing a moment of such shocking and profound exhilaration that she had to lean in again. Russell was talking and she wanted him to stop. His voice was rattling. He needed to clear his throat but for some reason wouldn't. Marie put her head out the window again. An ocean of wind roared through her ears and obliterated the awful sound of Russell's voice, the awful feeling of finding it awful. For the first time, she thoroughly despised him. Whatever syndrome this was, it had no name she knew of, yet it had to be caused by something other than Russell himself, something other than her, or the two of them together. Soon they would be three, and she would have to try harder than ever to be calm and normal, to be that most vital of people, a mother. As she looked out at the trees and the flat, dead river that ran alongside the highway, she felt a migraine come on. She wished the water would rush and spray, as it had in Niagara, but whenever she glimpsed it beyond the trees, it remained dark and still. Trees, rock, water: that was all there was here. Driving between walls of rock, she tried to imagine the labourers who had blasted through, making a road, and why they might have done such a thing. *Who would ever want to come here?* she wondered, even as they arrived.

The forest thickened, and Marie rubbed her left temple. The pretty, leafy trees that had been so plentiful near the Falls were obscured by enormous pines. They were nowhere near as majestic as the giant redwoods at home, only dark and oppressive, some of them dead but still standing. Even those that had fallen could not fall completely. They leaned over on the living trees, their lifted roots exposed in a massive tangle.

This was a place that swallowed people up — Tom Thomson country, too big and too wild. She had admired his paintings, and here she saw first-hand how well he had captured the bright, new growth alongside the decay. The trees were so heavy with age that they longed to die. Marie shuddered. Tom Thomson had gone fishing and never returned. Rangers had searched for him in the woods and in the lakes and rivers that spilled out across the enormous wilderness of Algonquin Park, and just when they had given up, he surfaced and presented his own dead body as part of the landscape one hot July morning. Rings floated out around him like the rings that show the age of trees. How purple he would have looked, how swollen. This wild place — its trees with eyes, its sky, and its rivers — had witnessed that death.

These were the kinds of thoughts that brought on her headaches, and the nausea that came with them, even this far into her pregnancy. She sometimes summoned them just to see if the sick feeling would come, but it was Russell who'd made her ill today. He'd stopped talking, so she rolled up her window once more and leaned into the headrest. Her head pounded. She looked at the sky. The tall trees pressed on it and the sky pressed back. She felt certain that she, too, could be smothered here, but she rode toward that certainty regardless, the way Cassandra entered the House of Atreus despite the blood on the walls, a prophecy for her eyes only.

"Almost there," said Russell. "How do you like it so far?"

She looked past him to the unmoving river. "It's lovely," she said.

And he smiled, showing his white, even teeth.

⦅⦆⦆⦆⦆

All through the winter of 1965, Eddie Halliwell used his Christmas gift (minus the easel) to practise his drawing. In the riverfront yard of the blue two-storey, he sat in the snow in his snow-pants, and wearing fingerless gloves he himself had de-fingered, he sketched both the barren trees and the coniferous ones. He was good, but he was easily frustrated – he wanted to be more than good.

One Saturday morning as he watched a deer cross the ice, he tried to draw its sinewy body and its long, bony legs, which he noticed were more like arms because of the backwards knees and the slenderness. But the body on paper looked like that of an old horse, and the clumsy head was a dog's. In a rage he tore the sketch to pieces and threw the bits of paper into the cold morning air, but by the time they fluttered down he was already calm. The flash of anger – here and then gone – had made him sweat all over, so he unzipped his snowsuit and let the icy breeze in. He glanced at the pieces of his deer littered on the snow, and then he looked to the river for the real deer, still far from the other side. It was thin, probably starving, but Eddie thought instead of the veins and muscles beneath its tawny hide. His curiosity about the animal's insides grew as the deer moved away from him, and the farther it went, the more Eddie's frustration mounted. He wished he could capture the deer, keep it for himself, until he could draw it so perfectly that it breathed from the pages of his sketchbook. He wanted to draw life rather than the stagnant landscape around him. And even come spring, he found the windblown trees, the budding leaves, and the thawing, rushing river could hold him for only so long. He began to sketch robins and squirrels, who had vibrant eyes and a rapid, nervous manner. He was eager to recreate the pulsating look of them in spring, the hungry season. But like the skinny winter deer, the little creatures would not keep still. The first time he killed a bird it happened by accident. He had just sketched the wrinkled feet and the body, and was about to start on the face when the bird hop-hop-hopped atop a log and turned away from him. There it stood, picking bugs from the bark. Eddie's tantrum rolled in. He hurled a stone and the bird fell sideways, like a trinket knocked over. It happened so suddenly that Eddie laughed – a short, hollow note that fell flat amid the music of early morning. He stood and examined the bird, whose black, glossy eyes were still open. He put his hand on the warm body and saw what he thought was blood on its head, but then he realized it was the bird's own marking, a brownish-red hat made of feathers. Eddie turned the bird over and could see no wound from the stone. The thing was dead, but perfect. He lifted one dusky wing and the other, and marvelled at how easily they unfolded. And then he sketched the bird from all angles, not thinking about the hungry babies waiting in their nest, which had been crafted from grass, roots, and hair collected on a million exhausting journeys.

In years to come he would learn more about Michelangelo Buonarroti, who painted the ceiling from which Russell Halliwell fell. To excel at the task of bringing paintings to life, he stole into the morgue at night and drew dead bodies. Eddie, upon discovering this, would for some time equate himself with genius, until the difference – the fine line of killing – became clear to him.

◯◯◯◯◯

Spring lingered until almost July, and the black flies swarmed. People claimed they'd been eaten alive and showed their bites to each other. As in every other year, pollen from the mammoth white pines travelled in a cloud, like a ghost sauntering down the street. It lifted off the trees in sheets and the humid breeze carried it along. For weeks a thin layer of yellow coated the town and collected at the edges of the river. It drifted through the screens of open windows to cloak the private indoor worlds.

The oppressive summer heat followed, and Eddie sketched on. Once, when he had risen particularly early and gone down to the river, he'd drawn a man in a red canoe, the low morning sun behind him. He'd been transfixed by the man's quick stroke, his easy expertise, and didn't realize until his sketch was almost finished that the man was Joe LeBlanc. He scribbled hard over the drawing with his pencil, and though the sketch was quickly ruined, he kept scribbling until the nib snapped and ripped the paper beneath.

Oblivious to Eddie Halliwell, Joe drifted by. He stirred the water with his handmade paddle, which was carved from black cherry and polished to a high gloss. His straight back and his short, swift stroke showed that he'd been canoeing all his life. If he had travelled through time, he might easily have been mistaken for Jacques, his father, or one of his grandfathers. All had been rivermen of great renown, but in the end only Jacques was remembered – and this for the instant he slipped up and put his foot into the coil of rope that spun him to his needless death. An accident, a cruel trick, or a stupid failure. Like Jacques, Joe had stepped into the centre of something more powerful than he was.

Months after Robbie's drowning, Joe remained tense and withdrawn, consumed with the memory of that young man in the water. Sun glittered on the Ottawa, but as his canoe skimmed the surface, Joe recalled how black the river had been that night, and how blue Robbie's face had looked in the moonlight.

There was not a day he didn't think of Robbie Hayes. Nor was there a day he spoke of him, unless it was to Beryl and Serge, who called on Joe three times over the summer to do odd jobs – shave swollen doors to fit door jambs, paint the trim around windows, change all the metal doorknobs to glass ones. The tasks were easy and they paid him too much for them, though he insisted he didn't want payment at all. He could tell they had linked him to Robbie. Since he had been the last person to see their son alive, they might just find the boy in Joe's eyes if they looked deeply enough. And yes, he was there. He was always there.

Unlike Kay, who'd stashed and perfumed the $652 from the Halliwells, Joe could not keep the money given him by Serge and Beryl Hayes. The bills made his hand hot when they landed in his palm, and when he transferred them to his wallet and tucked his wallet into his pocket, he could feel the skin of his backside burning. He walked along the riverside with the searing sensation, taking the path that led from the yacht club to the place Robbie had drowned, and along that trail, amid the silvery poplars, he lifted a rock and placed the bills, still visible, beneath it, so that the money wouldn't be wasted, and someone else could make a happy discovery. Only the trees watched him, and a squirrel, and two sparrows. A monarch floated by but saw nothing.

()()()()()

With summer, the place on the river where Robbie had drowned turned into a beach, and children swam there, unaffected by the recent traumatic event. To them, it already seemed age-old. The little kids dog-paddled in the shallow parts, and the big kids swam out to the drop-off, climbed onto a raft, and then dove back in. They plunged straight into the water that had taken Robbie. But that was not quite true, because a river is always moving. Still, they treated the spot as though nothing important had happened there, when in fact a life had gone under. In a way, more than one life had gone under that night. Certainly Joe's was down there and would never resurface. He was a different man now. The encounter he had many times craved had changed him. While once he'd been a quiet man, now he was closer to speechless. While once he'd been a happy man, now he was morose and distant.

Every morning he paddled up and down the Ottawa River. Last year he had appeared peaceful on the water, having reformed the green canoe into a red one, and having exorcised the demon that had appeared in the guise of graffiti. But the glow of contentment that had existed in the early days of his canoeing was gone from Joe LeBlanc. The ease with which he'd paddled had been replaced by a different kind of sureness, a tension that drove him back and forth along the Ottawa. A rat in a cage looked calmer.

When the sun rose to a particular place in the sky, Joe steered to shore. He pulled the canoe up under the trees and placed the gleaming paddle inside. He had made the paddle himself, over the winter, under the supervision of Alphonse and Toussaint, and it was this project that saw him through his darkest days. A carved cherry blossom, clumsier than the carvings by Alphonse and Toussaint but well-crafted just the same, graced the handle. He secured the paddle in the canoe, turned the boat upside down, and made his way up the hill, ever oblivious to Eddie Halliwell, who watched him go by.

At home, Joe ate breakfast with Kay and the children, and Louis hung from his leg, repeating, "Daddy! Suck my eye out, Daddy! Pleeease! Suck my eye out!" But those days were over. Even Louis seemed to realize it. His voice finding a new pitch of hysteria, he pleaded until finally Kay spoke.

"Joe!" she said, to pull him out of his trance.

Joe looked up.

Kay raised her eyebrows and nodded in Louis's direction.

Joe smiled at Louis. He scooped him up, but the most he could manage was a kiss on the forehead, the kind any father would give, and Joe had never before been any father. He put Louis on the floor again, stood, and strode out the front door.

For a time, everyone was silent. Kay sat with her fork in her hand, Louis remained where he'd been placed on the floor, and Estelle stopped chewing her cereal. Each of them stared at the door. And then, as though nothing foreboding had happened, as though no one had sensed the gravity of that moment, Kay grinned, clinked her fork against her glass, and announced, "Into your swimsuits, wiggle-bottoms! We're off to the beach."

And the spell of loss was temporarily lifted.

◌◌◌◌◌

Summer unrolled. The damp mornings and the evenings were the most pleasant times, despite the wretched mosquitoes, for in the afternoons a heat so stifling poured out of the sky that any activity was exhausting. On hazy days, the blue sky turned yellow, as though the sun couldn't hold itself together in such heat.

Somewhere around this time, Joe stopped leaving his canoe at the river's edge with all the others, and began to carry it home with him, store it in the garage overnight, and then take it all the way back to the river the following morning. The taunts were plentiful. "Trainin' for the Olympics, eh Joe?" Or, "Joe, you've got it ass-backwards. Canoe's supposed to carry *you*, my lad!" But Joe paid no heed. He took the canoe home with him each day, and walked with a certain side of it facing the trees, for impossibly, the letters that had so disturbed him had begun to show through the bright red paint long after he had sanded them away. K.C., R.H., along with the vulgar word that connected them.

Every summer night that year, once he had returned from his job with LeBlanc & LeBlanc, once he had eaten supper in grim silence, Joe would steal out to the garage to painstakingly refinish one spot on his canoe. Kay stood in the yard and watched through the garage's window, but she could not make sense of Joe's behaviour, nor see a flaw on the area he worked

110

and reworked. She told no one, but she felt certain her husband was losing his mind.

"Joe," she said when he climbed into bed.

Joe didn't answer.

The room filled up with moonlight, and she could see his large open eye and his profile, the high forehead and the hooked nose. "Talk to me, Joe. Everything's gone all crazy."

Joe blinked. She watched him clench and unclench his jaw. "Joe?" she said.

But he closed his eyes and was gone.

⟨⟨⟨⟨⟨⟩⟩⟩⟩⟩

Marie Halliwell's garden had been confused by the wet, overly long spring. In the sudden heat of summer, her perennials shot up, but it was weak growth, and wind snapped the tallest stalks in half. Still, the hostas doubled and tripled in size, and the arching arms of the bleeding hearts stretched and bled, dropping seeds on the rich garden floor. The peonies were so numerous that they leaned out from the blue two-storey and cascaded into the yard. Their odour was everywhere. As a child, Eddie had pressed his nose into a white peony and breathed a ladybug into his nostril. Every summer, Marie Halliwell thought of that, and then of the fact that Eddie had stopped smelling flowers. He wasn't a child any more.

Marie usually worked in her garden at night, because she disliked the heat of the day. By lantern-light, she pulled weeds and deadheaded flowers. Her roses, becoming hips on the vine, had climbed almost to the second storey, but they had powdery mildew, which Marie couldn't see in the dim light, so it spread undetected through her garden and lawn. Every day she walked among it without noticing, bringing in groceries or taking out trash. Days before Joe LeBlanc's disappearance, she saw the destruction. It was widespread, and she wondered where she had been, and what she had been seeing when it happened. The dense white powder covered the magnificent roses, the clematis, the phlox, the rosemary and all the herbs, as well as the blue twining morning glories, the dreadful *girasoli*, and finally the grass. Marie stood looking at her ghostly home and garden, drained of colour and life. The familiar desire to fall down and never stand up washed over her, but the memory of that time brought on such terror that instead of breaking down, she broke up. Up flew her hands and up flew the bags she had been carrying. Up flew bananas and strawberries and ripe red tomatoes. One by one they came down and got tossed up again, at the house, at the windows, at the roses. A bag of bread split open in mid-air and the soft, white slices rained down. Marie laughed and cried. She ran across the littered lawn to the garden and began to pull out plants with her bare hands. She grabbed the roses and wrapped her whole body around them to yank them out of the ground and off of the lattice they climbed on. Thorns opened her skin. The trees that circled her yard kept people from seeing her, but they heard her shouting. They stood at their windows and leaned out their doors. They stopped in the street and watched the wall of trees until, behind them, Marie Halliwell was nothing but a heap on the lawn, sobbing in silence. Almost every plant she destroyed was one she had started herself, from seed.

⟨⟨⟨⟩⟩⟩

The other dramatic event that happened that summer was not in any way dramatic until it was over, and Joe was gone forever. There was no particular warning that this would be the day, and in fact, the days immediately preceding the disappearance had held a glimmer of the old Joe. He'd come home from work one evening pulling a wagon full of lumber. Louis, as always, had run out to the lawn to meet him, and Joe had asked if Louis would like a playhouse.

That night, he began building, and Louis assisted. With scrap cedar left over from a LeBlanc & LeBlanc renovation, a tiny house was constructed. It had a peaked roof, three oval windows, and an arched doorway. Deep into the night, Joe worked on the little house, as though he doubted his ability to complete it, and later, once he was gone, many would say he'd known he was going, that the house was a goodbye present to his children, as compensation for breaking their home. Which was just the opposite of what he told Louis, who stayed up late with him, passing nails and watching him saw and hammer.

"There's no room for you and me any more, Bud, what with the new baby coming. We're moving out here, boys only."

The playhouse came together in a matter of days. And as Joe worked under the night sky, he seemed to regain some of his *joie de vivre*. But once the tools were put away and he came inside, to the real house, his unhappiness returned. This, too, made his ultimate disappearance less surprising.

The last known day of his existence was an otherwise regular day, but the temperature climbed fast and early. Kay woke sweating, with her hair stuck to her neck and forehead. The sun streamed into the room of windows. As usual, Joe breakfasted with Kay and the children, one watching from the womb. He ate toast, two firm poached eggs, fried tomatoes, and a whole orange, cut into wedges. It was not what he had every day, nor was it out of the norm. Much later, Kay would be thankful that his breakfast had been large. She hadn't wanted to cook on such a hot morning, but something had urged her – some subconscious notion that he would need sustenance.

At the precise moment of departure, Kay suspected nothing. She ran to kiss him at the door. In his now common absent-minded way, he leaned forward to receive the kiss, and his failure to return it hurt the way it hurt every other morning – to see him so changed and distant. Undeterred, Kay smiled.

"See you later," she said. A tossed-off, casual phrase. Since the death of Robbie Hayes, Kay had watched Joe more closely than anyone had, and while she knew he was tormented, there was nothing to say that this tormented day was any different from the ones that had gone before, or the many – she was sure – yet to come.

"See you later," she had said.

"Bye," said Joe.

And he was gone.

Usually, she would have been home when he returned with his canoe, but Louis turned red and lethargic in the extreme heat, so she wanted to get him to the beach as early as possible. She did some chores, closed up the house and drew the curtains, then took the children swimming. The water was resplendent and calm. There was no sign of Joe in the distance, nor did they look for him.

In the meantime, Alphonse phoned and phoned, and eventually came knocking at 40 Huron, but by now Kay was in the grocery store. In her flip-flops and a maternity sundress, she filled the cart with food for a family of four, almost five, not knowing the biggest of them was gone. Louis rode in the little seat for children, on a plastic flap that said, DO NOT LEAVE CHILD UNATTENDED, and Estelle hung on to the end of the cart and shouted, "Fast! Push us faster!"

They bought the groceries, loaded the stroller, and began to walk home. Heat radiated off the pavement and turned the houses and trees wavy. Louis said he was melting and began to cry. It was not a great distance, but it took a long time, because there was room in the stroller only for groceries, and not children, whose steps were erratic and small.

When Alphonse found them, they were on Poplar Street, heading uphill. He drove up beside them in the LeBlanc & LeBlanc pickup truck.

"Kay," he said. "Where the hell is Joe?"

Right away, she knew something had happened. In the tremendous heat, she turned cold all over, and lifted her hands to her face. The stroller rolled down the hill backwards. When it reached a plateau, it hit a stone and flipped over, and like a bizarre echo of the event in Marie Halliwell's yard, groceries scattered and spoiled.

◯◯◯◯◯

Marie made a spur-of-the-moment visit to her mother, and Eddie stayed home with Russell. The weeks and then months

115

spread out in the same discomfort that had existed years earlier, when Marie had gone into hospital and left Eddie alone with his father. This time, as her departure approached, he had wanted to run and never come back – he even tried it, but he didn't get far. He came home from the excursion, but no one noticed he had left in the first place. His mother sat in the kitchen with her luggage piled around her, and he stood in front of her, waiting for her to say something to him, but when no words came, he went to his room. They took her to the train station that afternoon, and Eddie pictured her seated in her mannequin pose all the way to Seattle, and although he hated her for going, he was glad she was gone.

No little kid any more, he knew how to gain an advantage with his father. He gobbled his food and smacked his lips, and soon he was allowed to eat in front of the television because, as his father said, "I can't stand watching you wolf it down. Just don't slop food on the sofa."

Eddie sat on the couch and rested the warm plate in his lap, letting the smell of the food flood into him. He put a piece of potato in his mouth and sucked the melted butter out of it. By now he was not just fat but thick-skinned. He welcomed the barbs, and even instigated them, as proof that they could not cut into him. The meals apart, with Eddie in one room, his father in another, dining neatly, lessened the time they had to spend together. The television – filler of silence, food for the eyes – made time itself pass more quickly.

⁂

In Marie Halliwell's absence, in Joe's, in the absence of joy and exhilaration, a baby was born feet first. Kay was tranquilized, but she wept and cried out for Joe during the long labour. Only the doctor and the attending nurses ever knew. And Margar, of course, but she was an alien to this world. She wasn't yet sure what tears signified. Afterwards, even Kay's memory was fuzzy — if she had gone through a twilight sleep when Estelle was born, she'd gone through a twilight nightmare with Margar, her little footling breech who refused to spin into the head-down position. For forty long weeks, Margar had sat upright inside Kay, obstinate and alert already, as though not just waiting but ready for something to happen. She came out with her head squashed on the left side, where Kay's taut uterus had pressed against her soft skull. One eye hung lower than the other, and her hollering mouth was a warped, dark hole in her purple face. But that would sort itself out, a baby's bones being malleable.

During the labour, Irene and Ned Clancy prayed to the patron saint of childbirth, just as they'd prayed to Saint Joseph when Joe left the first time, and when they discovered later how difficult the delivery had been, they urged Kay to name the baby Margaret, after the saint who must have intervened.

When Kay arrived home with the crooked girl in her arms, there was a crib waiting. Like the sleigh, it was built from white oak and trimmed with bird's eye maple. Wild animals chased each other around the border of the crib, blending where a wing touched a tail, where a paw touched an ear, so that there was no beginning or end to the design, no break in the intricate creation. At the top of each post stood a sparrow with its wings expanded.

Kay laid Margar in the crib and admired the uncles' fine workmanship and the bird's eye maple. The uncles had told her that the scudding, freckled pattern on the wood indicated that buds hadn't bloomed on the tree. It was a freak of nature, albeit a beautiful one. Alphonse and Toussaint called it a wood full of eyes, and Kay thought of the woods around the town, the trees of Algonquin Park, and of Joe moving stealthily through them. For the second time since knowing him, she felt he had left her for good, but the announcement that appeared in the *Deep River Chronicle* suggested that any day he might return.

Joseph and Kay LeBlanc are pleased to announce the birth of their Daughter, Margaret Eliza, a beautiful Baby Sister for Estelle and Louis.

The leaves fell early and the snow came. Kay nursed the baby, whose eyes turned a rich, liquid brown. She hoped Joe had made it somewhere safe and warm.

The happy years were over.

MEXICO CITY 1968
la lune

Here, there, and everywhere, life went on.

Shortly before the 1968 Olympics, students gathered in Mexico City's Plaza of Three Cultures to protest their government's funding of fun and games instead of social programs. The Mexican army opened fire. Reports varied, as reports often do, but the general consensus was that 267 people were killed that day, and more than 1,000 were injured.

Ten days later, the world flocked to Mexico City, and from October 12 to 27, flags from 112 countries blew in the thin breeze. The Games would be held at 2,300 metres above sea level, a height that would cause great strain for the athletes competing in endurance events, but IOC president Avery Brundage claimed, when the controversial host city was chosen, that the Olympic Games belonged to all the world, not just the places at sea level.

Mexican president Gustavo Diaz Ordaz and a red jaguar mascot officiated at the opening ceremonies, and Norma Enriqueta Basilio de Sotelo lit the Olympic flame, becoming the first woman ever to hold such an honour. The beloved marathon runner Abebe Bikila was back, but a third gold medal would not be his. A fractured foot would force him to drop out of the race, and while he told himself, *Next time*, that was not to be. One year later, a car accident would paralyze him from the waist down.

On the bright side, the number of female participants was climbing: of the 5,516 athletes involved, 781 were women. The 781st was Czechoslovakian gymnast Vera Caslavska, who, months earlier, had signed the "Manifesto of 2,000 Words," which spoke out against Soviet interference in Czechoslovakia. Forced into hiding when her country was invaded, she'd swung from trees and lifted sacks of potatoes to keep up her strength. At the last, unbelievable moment, she was given permission to attend the Games. The crowd went crazy for her smile and her Mexican Hat Dance floor routine. They loved her so much that their booing lifted her balance-beam score from 9.6 to 9.8. They would accept no less for her, the darling of Mexico City.

Like Kay, Vera Caslavska loved a Joe of sorts. His name was Josef Odlozil, and he was a Czech middle-distance runner. She stood on the podium one day, and married her Josef the next. Ten thousand fans crowded the square where they were united, cheering and wishing them luck, which, like love, is never enough. Just as it was difficult to imagine her elation – having married her Joe, having won sparkling golds and silvers – so it would be difficult to imagine her despair when, years later, their son Martin was convicted of murder. The victim was Josef Odlozil. Martin would be pardoned for his crime, but by then Vera would be broken in countless ways.

Nevertheless, in 1968 she was a star with a bright, joyful future. Kay liked to point out that she was nearly the same age as Vera Caslavska, and might also have been a star had she not chosen love over Rome.

"Why didn't you go?" asked Estelle. "You might've won a gold medal!"

"Well, there was you," Kay answered. "And there was Daddy."

Of the LeBlanc children, only Estelle and Louis were gymnastically gifted. "Look, she can't even touch her toes!" they said of their scowling little sister. She couldn't put her feet behind her head or walk on her knees with her legs folded Indian-style. As a baby, she had never chewed on her toes, and now at three years old, she showed no sign of increased flexibility, not physically, anyway. But mentally she was the most agile of all, and she had already begun to use her wits and imagination (however clumsily) to prove that she was equally, if differently, gifted. "I can fly," she said. "When nobody's looking." Her long eyebrow dipped and wiggled as her eyes flashed at Estelle and Louis, which made them tease her all the more. Estelle, with her backwards somersaults, triggered Margar's greatest wrath, but it was Louis who possessed what could only be called God-given talent when it came to gymnastics. Though he was just six years old at the time of the Mexico City Olympics, Louis studied the spins and leaps of Vera Caslavska and Japan's Sawao Kato like an athlete in training. Kato, five-foot-three and 125 pounds, won the men's All-Around Championship that year, and he would do so again in Munich and Montreal. He was Louis LeBlanc's hero. All through the fall and winter, Louis insisted on being called Sawao instead of Louis.

Kay granted his every wish, since it seemed a miracle that Louis was here at all. After Joe's disappearance, Louis had stopped growing. Kay fed him peanut-butter-raw-egg milkshakes and vitamin cocktails, but nothing worked. No doctor could say what was wrong with him, and therefore no doctor could fix him.

"He's just small," they said, shrugging. "Like you."

Kay didn't understand how the boy had gone from being tall, like Joe, to small, like her, but that appeared to be what had happened. And while Alphonse and Toussaint insisted that his diminutive stature was a direct result of Joe's disappearance, Kay wanted none of it, though inwardly she'd had similar fears.

"Nonsense," she insisted. "Little boys don't shrink from being sad."

He had become a strange, mournful child. It was difficult to reconcile him with the gigglesack who had begged to have his eye sucked out, but this was the same boy. He wore his fine, brown hair neatly parted, and he never spilled food on his clothes. That spring, when Louis was still five, he'd packed all of his stuffed animals into a box and, leaving the lid open for air, had gone into Estelle and Margar's room and unpacked the delivery. Kay stood in the doorway and watched him place each animal in a spot that seemed predetermined.

"What are you doing?" she asked.

Louis looked at the animal he held in his hands, a dog named Blue Blackear, and lifted it up toward Kay. "They don't seem happy to me," he said, as though it was he who had let them down. "I thought they might like it better in here."

Kay observed the dog, which was blue with flopping black ears. It had eyebrows, and also a frozen smile that showed in the lips, not the eyes. She watched until he had placed all of the animals in his sisters' room – on the bed, on the window ledge, on the dresser, peeking out of a dresser drawer. When he finished, he picked up the empty box and stood beside Kay, regarding his work. The animals sat in their chosen spaces, staring blankly into air. After a silent moment, Louis said, with a voice of unsurprised disappointment, "I think all stuffed animals are sad."

Around this time Kay had a dream that Louis was jumping on a trampoline, and she and Joe were spotting. Laughing, Louis bounced so high that, at the height of each leap, the clouds covered him, and in the brief moments that he was hidden, Kay looked desperately to Joe for reassurance, but he seemed unaware she was there. Each time, she held her breath until Louis's feet poked back through the clouds. Her emotions were on a trampoline of their own. The dream went on that way until Louis began to land on his elbow, his knee, his head. He stopped laughing. His eyes widened in his pale face. Kay's panic increased, and her arms flew out toward Louis each time he landed. She could not catch Joe's eye. His face remained expressionless, but finally he stretched out his arms as Louis descended, and in the dream, Louis landed there the way Kay, in real life, had landed years before. But all the air had gone out of the boy, as though he were nothing more than a shaped and painted balloon. Joe held the sagging, deflated body in his arms. His eyes rose to meet Kay's. They were warm, brown, sad eyes, eyes she knew well. At that moment of connection, he vanished, and little Louis went with him.

⟨⟨⟨⟨⟨⟩⟩⟩⟩⟩

Late that very night, while she lay in bed, Kay heard a noise outside: a tap, tap, tap like a hammer and nail. She cupped her hands against the windowpane and looked through the glass. The tapping seemed to come from the backyard, but the noise stopped and she could see only the weedy lawn and the playhouse. When she settled back into bed, the tap, tap, tap started again. It was close, and familiar. She pressed against the glass once more and searched the yard. Again the tapping stopped. He had been gone for three years, but she thought, *Joe*, because of the sound combined with the sight of the playhouse, and also the fog of her dream.

"Silly," she said aloud. "It could be a woodpecker."

Joe, Joe, Joe.

She never stopped thinking of him. Outwardly, Kay LeBlanc was a get-on-with-it sort of woman, but inwardly, the wish that he were here right now, in bed beside her, or there in the morning, eating his cereal with his hand turned backwards, holding the spoon in that awkward way, and then later, fixing the roof or the door hinge, tending to the warping floor, tickling Louis, and swinging Margar to the ceiling and down, Margar, whom he had never met – that wish, along with guilt and shame, filled Kay's whole body. And since the tapping was not a bear, raccoon, or burglar sound, she slipped on her dressing gown and sandals and stepped out onto the porch to look for him, knowing both the hope she would earn from searching and the disappointment that would come from not finding.

The bright stars made the black sky blacker. She could smell the lilies that leaned from Ramona Devlin's yard into hers, necks broken on the fence, the white blossoms hanging in the

124

moonlight. The full moon also shone on the little playhouse, which had weathered to grey. Kay stood in the yard, a ghost in her white dressing gown. The town was quiet except for the humming streetlights and a single car passing. She did a slow cartwheel to extend the moment, and while she was upside down she saw Blue Blackear through the playhouse window. A chill went through her, as though a stuffed dog was somehow scary. She crept closer and peered into the long oval that had been cut with Joe's own saw. Louis had put all of the animals in the playhouse, seated on the handmade bench and chairs. In utter silence, they stared in varying directions. A light breeze blew, and the door of the playhouse knocked against Blue Blackear's chair. Tap, tap, tap. The discovery shrivelled her hope and brought her back to the nasty riddle that whirled on in her mind year after year: if he was dead, then he had not left her; if he was alive, he had chosen to go away.

∞∞∞∞∞

Another Louis sang about what a wonderful world it was, and, true or not, everyone went around whistling that tune. The dashing new prime minister, Pierre Elliott Trudeau, appeared in Ottawa in his Mercedes, and millions of girls and women fell in love with his intelligent, searching eyes, his elegant gait, his mischievous smile, his temper. He had been all over Europe, travelling robed and bearded in the Middle East, and also to China and India, but he knew his way around Ontario rivers in a canoe, so in some ways he was not unlike the unknown Joe LeBlanc, who had never really been anywhere at all, wherever he was.

Since the days of the Greek gods and goddesses, the ordinary have borne an uncanny resemblance to the extraordinary. In the late 1960s, when the latter appeared on television, the screen was like a mirror. One imagined one's self there, crowned and beautiful. Kay saw herself in Vera Caslavska. Like Louis, she studied every leap and spin, though her gymnastics days had ended years ago. People like Vera and Pierre Trudeau spread a word through the air: possibility. Soon a man would walk on the moon. A king named Martin Luther would reign for a tiny time that would seem huge in retrospect. As the blood poured out of him, the world groaned and held its belly, sick with the struggle of change.

It was a crazy, moonstruck era in the Valley as well. Gentle people went haywire, like the man who shot his neighbour's horse, and someone somewhere was killing small animals and depositing their bodies in a dirt hole near the river. At night, wild animals crept out of the bush and appeared in the civilized backyards of Deep River, where vegetables grew in tidy rows. Bears plucked tomatoes and swallowed them whole. A deer jumped through the jewellery store window, and another was killed when it collided with a car on Highway 17. The latter incident had happened late in the night, and by morning, the body had been dragged into the bush, where the meat was carved from the bone by someone who saw no sense in wasting a mound of venison. There seemed no end to the carnage. Ramona Devlin's dog, Olive, had disappeared for an afternoon and returned home bloody and distraught, the pad of one paw missing. Ramona's brother Gus traced the red paw prints down Huron Street, past the school, along Riverside Drive, and into the bushes, but the precise scene of the crime was never ascertained, and the perpetrator remained unknown.

It was in this ominous time that the majority of Louis LeBlanc's travelling stuffed animals were found unstuffed under Margar's bed. Someone had taken the scissors and cut jaggedly along the tummies of the dog, the bear, and so on, and pulled the insides out. When a breeze came in through the window and blew bits of foam out from under the bed, the flat, polyester skins were discovered, their arms and legs splayed and empty.

"It wasn't me," said Margar, before anyone accused her, which only made her guilt more likely. When her mother punished her with no cartoons for a week, Margar bawled so convincingly at the injustice that she convinced herself of her own innocence. "But I didn't *dooo* it!"

No one else believed her. She was not quite three at that time, but precocious. And just the week before, she had cut off the hair of Estelle's Barbie dolls, and snipped a lock of her own hair in the process. The tufts of blonde and brown poked out from the pages of one of Margar's storybooks. She hadn't yet learned about evidence, so all of it pointed toward her. That time, Kay had disallowed ice cream, and Margar had been forced to sit teary-eyed, with her empty bowl in front of her, while Louis and Estelle gobbled their dessert.

Louis was traumatized by the deaths of his stuffed animals, but what affected him more was the fate of the real baby bears who wandered into town every spring. Their mothers had been shot by hunters or hit by cars, and the cubs were lost and hungry. In the moonstruck years, there were many more than usual. They hid in trees and the branches swayed in the cool spring breeze. One day in 1968, they appeared on the grounds of the primary school, and no one noticed until most of the children were inside. It was a fine May morning. Nine teachers and 202 students walked past an apple tree, and none of them saw the two cubs hiding among the pink blossoms. Eight-year-old Estelle LeBlanc was the next to last student to enter the school that day, with Louis, now almost seven, on her heels. Unlike the others, Estelle looked up into the tree, because pink was her favourite colour. Louis looked up because she did. They saw the bears and the bears saw them. All four of them paused and observed each other, and poor Louis turned paler.

"Ohh," he said. The sound was more a moan than an exclamation.

Estelle put her hand over her brother's mouth and gathered him to her. With her arm firmly around his thin shoulders, they marched to the principal's office.

The cubs were soon surrounded by volunteer firemen and the uniformed Deep River Police. Townsfolk stood nearby, guarding the children not yet in school, and the baby bears stared at them. There had always been people who said that bears were invading the town, and that something drastic had better be done before someone was mauled or eaten; and now that bears had appeared on the school grounds, these people were irate.

"Kill them," they said. "Shoot them with real bullets, not tranquilizers, or they'll only be back tomorrow."

There were others, of course, who knew that the town had invaded the bears. The planned, curved streets and crescents (designed by that man named Bland), the tidy houses and the smooth weed-free lawns had once been woods that yielded all the berries a bear could hope for, if indeed bears hoped. Alphonse and Toussaint LeBlanc remembered the town when it was not a town at all. Their home had been one of the few in the beginning, and now it stood, a rustic log cabin, amid the grand houses and the little war-fours and war-sixes.

"Bears lived in our backyard then, uh?" Toussaint often told the LeBlanc children. "You didn't see us fussing for that."

"I wouldn't mind," said Estelle dreamily, "if a bear came to live in our backyard. He could live in the playhouse, and I could feed him through the window."

"You could feed him, all right," said Alphonse. "Your arm, your leg. Your bitty toes and fingers." Roaring, he nibbled one of Margar's toes to demonstrate.

Margar laughed, but Louis's mouth dropped open. "You said bears eat berries!"

"Sure, berries. Bugs and fish too. And meat. You're meat. This little string bean, too," he said, poking Margar. "Bears are like you and me, they eat whatever they feel like. Whatever's around, they eat it if they're hungry. They might think, mmmm, tasty *jambon*, when they see you, eh? Salty meaty children, yum, yum." Alphonse rubbed his stomach, wiggled his big bushy eyebrows, then shrugged. "Or maybe they're gonna pass you by. Not hungry for you that day. You never know with a bear. That's the beauty of him."

"Or her," said Estelle.

"*Oui*, yes. Or her."

This conversation had occurred mere weeks before the cubs appeared in the apple tree, so it was remarkable that Estelle remained as calm as she did when she spotted them. Afterwards, everyone said she took after Joe and the uncles. Even Kay said it – she who best knew it could not be so.

As usual, Alphonse and Toussaint LeBlanc were called to take care of the bears, but they couldn't right away be found. A tense vigil ensued. The onlookers waited, hoping the bears would stay put until the woodsmen arrived. The townsfolk were asked to go home, and reluctantly, over the course of the morning, they dispersed. The children who had not yet arrived at school were granted a holiday, though to them, on this one day, the thrill lay in being *in* the school rather than out of it. Since there were so few in attendance on the other side of the school walls, the students were herded to the gymnasium to sing songs and play games. While they could have been filed out through the fire escape, it seemed safer to keep them where they were, lest the commotion cause the bears to turn violent.

The only way for a child in school to see the bears was to ask to go to the washroom, and then sneak down the speckled corridor into Miss Vaughn's classroom, which overlooked the apple tree. Louis LeBlanc did just so. He hung back by the doorway because he was afraid to get too close, even though glass and brick separated him from the bears. He could see their short, wide feet and their brown bear bodies, but he would have to creep closer to see their heads. He was very frightened, and he didn't yet know that you couldn't be courageous if you weren't scared in the first place. He didn't know, so such wisdom didn't comfort him, but his courage was there anyway. The branches groaned and the little bears, who were really quite big, hung on. Louis could see their thick necks, and the backs of their flat heads. The ears looked as if they'd been attached later, like stiff, stuffed-animal ears. Louis moved closer still. He kneeled on a desk beneath the window, and to those outside, his head showed in the pane's lower corner. Alphonse nudged Toussaint, the two of them newly arrived and assessing the situation, but Louis didn't notice his uncles. He was less afraid of the bears now, and he wished they would turn around. He wanted to see their brown eyes in their brown-fur faces, eyes that were like his own and those of his little sister. He thought of Joe, and the playhouse, and was almost certain he'd slept there beside his father, the rich smell of cedar in his nostrils. He thought he could remember waking up in the night and looking out through the oval window to see a bear raiding the rhubarb patch. Maybe he saw it stand on its back legs and walk through the tall weeds of the yard, but there was no way to know for sure. He'd been very little then, and he could barely recall. He could ask his mother if he had ever slept in the playhouse, and that might answer part of his question, but then again, he might not receive the answer he wanted, so he decided the question, like many others, should remain inside him, allowing the chance of a memory.

Louis tapped on the window and one cub and then the other turned to face him. When he pressed his nose against the glass and blinked, his eyelashes touched the windowpane. He could not imagine the bears eating his toes and fingers, as Alphonse had suggested. There was something familiar about them, and for a moment he had the feeling that they were people dressed up, the way a clown is a person dressed up, and the thought that they might not be what they seemed made them scarier. Pink petals dropped to the ground as the bears shifted in the tree, and before Louis knew what had happened, a branch broke and one of the bears fell, and a shot exploded from Toussaint LeBlanc's gun. Louis looked in shock at the bear on the ground. The tree began waving to and fro as the other bear climbed higher. There was nowhere to go in a tree as little as that. The higher the branch, the weaker it was. Petals twirled down. Just as the bear on the ground closed his eyes, the bear in the tree fell beside him. Toussaint LeBlanc aimed and shot, and Louis rushed from the room.

(((((

Oh, how he cried. He hid in the boys' washroom, in a stall with his feet up, and he sobbed at the death of the bears. He was so upset that he grew violently ill, as was his custom, and turned and threw up into the toilet. A teacher discovered him, and he was sent home, where he stayed for the rest of the week.

"What's wrong?" asked Kay, knowing it wasn't the flu.

But Louis claimed it was. He said he was achy all over, and that his tummy hurt.

Days after the occurrence, Alphonse told Kay about Louis's face in the window, and the expression it had made when the bears had been shot.

"That's it," she said. "He thinks you killed them."

Alphonse and Toussaint entered the sickroom, sat on Louis's mattress, and explained that the bears had not, after all, been killed.

"Those eyes you thought were dying, they were just droopy from the shot, Louis. A shot to make them sleep like babies."

Louis remained small and silent beneath his blanket as they described the events. He looked at the few stuffed animals he had left, poised at significant spots around the room, and he listened as Alphonse and Toussaint told him how the bears' veins had carried the sedative through their big, furry bodies. Asleep, the cubs had been loaded into the LeBlanc & LeBlanc pickup truck and driven deep into the bush.

"Algonquin Park?" asked Louis.

"Algonquin Park," they answered.

Louis smiled a little, and thought the park seemed a nice place for a couple of bears.

Alphonse and Toussaint said they'd sat in the cab of the truck eating peanut brittle until the babies had woken up. It had not taken long. The trick to keeping the bears alive – preventing their hearts from slowing and stopping altogether – was to give them just a tiny amount of the sedative. They could only be driven a short distance from town before they regained roaring consciousness. Which meant, in all likelihood, they'd be back.

"But you'll shoot them to save them again?" he asked.

"*Mais oui*. You bet."

Through the truck's rear window, the uncles had watched the bears stir and look warily around them. They'd peered at Alphonse and Toussaint and then made their way to the open gate of the pickup, where one after the other they'd hopped down to the mossy floor. There had been birds watching, and squirrels. A deer had blinked in the distance and then disappeared. Alphonse and Toussaint had watched the bears smell and touch the trees, and now they told Louis how, like cats, the cubs had rubbed against the bark, and then, without a glance backwards, vanished beneath the canopy of green.

Louis thought about vanishing. "Like my dad," he said finally. A pink spot glowed in the centre of each sallow cheek.

Alphonse and Toussaint paused. Each looked into the other's wrinkled face, and then back into Louis's youthful one. Finally Toussaint spoke.

"Don't say it as though, just like that" – he clicked his fingers – "he went off from you."

"But –"

"No, he would never leave you," said Alphonse, shaking his big head solemnly. "Not on purpose would he ever walk away." He took Louis's face in his rough hands and kissed his forehead. "You remember," he said, staring at Louis with intense, twinkling eyes. "Always remember."

But Louis remembered almost nothing. Even the scraps were slipping away. Joe LeBlanc had disappeared less than three years ago, yet for Louis, a lifetime had passed. He had stayed small, but inside he had grown from toddler to boy. He was a different child than the one who had slept beside his father in the playhouse, if indeed he had. He could hardly remember the man, or even the pipsqueak beside him, though it was Louis himself. Alphonse's command was impossible to obey, since all that remained were the pictures, moments frozen and flattened in time.

Yet an unusual feeling came over him when he looked at photos of Joe. Joe with a string of trout beside him, the fish hanging from a hook in each bottom lip. The mouths were stretched wide and the eyes were open. The speckled skin shimmered but the fish were dead, gutless, ready for frying. He thought he could remember squishing a worm, lengthwise, onto a hook, and the way the worm purpled in places. This in the red canoe with the tawny interior. He thought he could remember casting his line, and the rapid tick-tick-tick of it spinning out from the reel, but he could not be sure. What he knew for certain was that a pleasurable grief came over him when he looked at pictures of Joe – at the tall body, the broad shoulders and the dangling arms, so much the opposite of him. Only Joe's brown eyes showed in Louis. Those, and the dark, fly-away hair. When he looked at the pictures, love and loss mingled for a man he could not remember but, no, would never forget.

⫯⫯⫯⫯⫯

Alphonse and Toussaint LeBlanc had strong beliefs about Joe's disappearance. Never did they suspect Joe had purposefully left his family. They were convinced something untoward had happened to him, and that one day the real story would present itself. Almost no one had looked for Joe when he'd gone missing, but Alphonse and Toussaint LeBlanc had been the exceptions. They had formed a determined two-man team, and combed the town, the forest, and the river, but they had not found him, or any trace of him. What they couldn't understand was how a man, a canoe, and a paddle could be erased in a matter of hours. Though they admitted that Joe had not been himself since the death of Robbie Hayes, they did not accept the logical explanations. If there had been an accident, they insisted, there would have been signs of it left behind. They added that an accident was unlikely, because of Joe's prowess, but they conceded that it was possible. An accident had killed Joe's father, Jacques, for instance. But accidents were messy. There were always clues. And if Joe had left to live elsewhere –

well, Joe LeBlanc would never walk away from his family. No LeBlanc would, they said.

Kay saw in their eyes the perseverance that was so much like Joe's, but reminded them of Joe's mother who had picked up and moved south without him when the town of White Pine was flooded. Since then she hadn't returned for as much as a visit. It was true she was poor, and that she'd resented the sweep of change in the Valley. But although Joe hadn't wanted to leave with her, he was hardly grown up at the time. She could have pushed him to go.

"She didn't treat him like a son," said Kay to Alphonse and Toussaint. "You two were more like parents to him than anyone."

And Alphonse and Toussaint weren't sure whether to beam or glower.

"That was different," they said. "Delphine was no LeBlanc, not in the blood. If Jacques hadn't died, things for Joe would have gone another way, you bet on it. Jacques would not have left the Valley – or his son, for that matter. And Joe – you really think he would pick up and leave? You knew him better than that."

And she thought, yes, I knew him, and wondered if he knew her too, all her secrets and lies. That possibility terrified her, but she didn't let on. She was the brave-faced mistress of whitewash.

For their part, Alphonse and Toussaint knew only that Joe's attempts to save a drowning boy had failed, and that since that night, he had been a miserable man. But no misery was great enough to cause Joe LeBlanc to abandon his wife, his dimpled, curly-mopped daughter, his gigglesack son, and his baby-to-be, now Margar. On this they did not waver. Nearly three years on, Alphonse and Toussaint still hunted for signs of Joe wherever they went. They didn't know it, but a little someone had joined in the search.

CCCCCC

All of Margar's life, which to her was no small amount of time, people had been speaking of "Joe." Where had he gone and why, when would he come back. They spoke of him most often when Louis and Estelle were elsewhere, as though only Margar's ears were not connected to a brain. But ears form before a fetus looks human, and by the end of the second trimester, even the dimmest babies strain to listen to the sounds outside the womb. Margar was two and a half when the death of Blue Blackear and the shooting of the bears traumatized Louis. With her eyes on the television and one ear cocked toward her mother and Ramona Devlin drinking coffee in the kitchen, Margar listened in. The conversation was boring while it was just about Louis, but when Joe's name came up, Margar beetled into the kitchen and sat under the table pulling loose the laces of Ramona's red shoes.

"He didn't use to be like this," said Kay. "When he was little, when Joe was still here, he was a regular boy, you know? And now he's so – sensitive. I don't know what to do."

"Well, you've got to think of something, or that boy'll turn into a noodle of a man," said Ramona. She slurped her coffee and added, "He needs male companionship, Kay. Jesus."

And Margar's mother laughed.

"Jesus would be nice," she said. "But Joe would be better."

CCCCCC

Kay continued to dream about Louis deflating or erupting or disappearing down the drain, and there were many times, in her real awake life, that she searched for him worriedly only to find him in the playhouse or the mostly abandoned garage, doing nothing more than sitting with his hands folded in his lap.

On Ramona's suggestion, she sent Louis for a two-week stay with Alphonse and Toussaint in the summer of 1968, and Louis found himself learning such masculine skills as chopping wood and cleaning fish.

"We'll fix you up, eh? *Tu penses?*" said Toussaint, squeezing Louis's thin white arm. "Soon you'll have Popeye muscles, you wait!"

He was only across town, but Louis felt he'd entered another world. The wood walls of the log cabin were the same inside as they were out, with thick layers of white between. He had moved into a huge multi-layered egg-salad sandwich. His evenings were spent on the dock with a fishing rod, and if Louis had not previously learned to hook his bait and to cast his line, he learned now from the masters.

"This is not the best place to fish," they told him, "but it will do. It will teach you the basics, uh?"

Louis looked at his reflection in the water, and then up at the sky, which was orange and pink. Overnight it would storm.

"What is the best place?" he asked.

"What, to fish?" Toussaint scratched his stubbly chin.

"Green Lake," said Alphonse.

"Or Lynx Lake, in the Park," said Toussaint. "That's a damn pretty spot."

"Joe Lake's good too. Plenty of big trout in Joe Lake."

"Joe?" said Louis with his eyebrows raised. "There's a lake called Joe?"

Alphonse and Toussaint grinned.

"Sure. And so there should be."

Normally, both uncles tucked Louis in and told him tall tales, but that night Toussaint kissed the boy's forehead and left the room, and Alphonse alone told Louis a story. It was a cool summer night so a fire was lit in the wood stove. Louis lay in the flickering light and held fast to every word.

"Me, I know what it's like to lose someone," said Alphonse. "I lost my wife, Clothilde, and *ma petite* Pierrette." With his big thumb, he pointed over his shoulder at a large photographic portrait that hung on the wall. Louis looked at the grey, unsmiling faces. He looked back to the flames in the wood stove's window, for he knew this story was about fire, though he had never heard Alphonse's version.

"My girl was just as little as you. Today she would be an old lady."

"How old?" asked Louis. He squinted at Pierrette, who had a round face and long braids with ribbons at the ends.

Alphonse paused. "Forty-nine," he said, and let out a whistle. "Almost one-half of a century! Your old *oncle* is become an antique himself, Louis." He paused again, then resumed his story.

Louis was afraid it would be sad and fiery, and that afterwards he would not be able to sleep for fear of the flames bursting through the stove's window, smashing the glass and spilling like orange liquid across the floor and upward, melting the egg-salad walls. But it was not that way.

Instead, Alphonse told him about a cool afternoon in early September, when he'd been picking blackberries.

"The berries were dripping on the branch, Louis. So ripe you just touch them with your finger and they fall into your hand. Big as peaches, they were."

Louis listened. He looked from the flames to the portrait.

Alphonse said he had been miles from home that day, but he had smelled the smoke and seen the black cloud in the direction of his home. It rose above the trees, which were only beginning to turn, and stained the blue sky.

"Of course I thought, no, that it couldn't be, but anything can be, Louis, anything can be. I never ran so fast. I never was so thankful for the wide-load bears and those big paths they make through the brambles. I ran through the places that were all crushed over 'til I got to the road and then I got on my bicycle, and you never saw a man pedal so hard as me on that day. I kept saying, no, that it couldn't be, but, as I have said, it always can be, never doubt it. There were not so many houses back then. There was mine and Clothilde's, and a great distance from it, this one, your Oncle Toussaint's. The smoke, unless it was a bush fire, had to come from somewhere."

For a moment, Alphonse didn't speak. Louis wondered if he would cry, and hoped not. He pulled the blankets up over his nose and smelled the woolliness. He looked again at Pierrette, and he watched her unchanging face as Alphonse said that in moments, his family, his home, and all of his belongings were gone. Just he and his bicycle remained. The wind blew the blaze through a swath of trees, so that for years the empty space would remind him. In the middle of a huge wilderness, nothing but tiny shoots grew there, food for raccoons.

"Clothilde and Pierrette were lost to me. I won't ever know why they didn't get out, or how much they suffered in the smoke and the flames. Fire is an animal, Louis, more dangerous than a bear or a whole pack of wolves, with arms and legs too many to count. You have to always be on guard for an animal like that. But why I tell you is not because I want to make you sad or afraid. It's a scary thing when someone goes from you, uh? I know it and you know it too. Like the English hunters say, I was loaded for bear when I lost them. You know what that means, Louis? I was ready. I wanted to kill the whole world, but hey, I could not. I was only me, after all. One man. And then for a long time I was heavy with grief, you ask Toussaint. I couldn't see the good in a sunrise, it's true. But I found out a secret — no one goes from you if you love them enough. That's it, Louis, it's that simple. You're a little boy, too little, even your head is skinny! But you're big enough on the inside to understand many things. It's not what I think, it's what I know. So listen to me — whoever you lose, you can have them back by keeping them in here and in here," he said, pointing to his head and his heart. "You invite them in. Look around and you will see them everywhere." He leaned and kissed Louis's forehead. "Me, it makes me three times the man I might have been."

Afterwards, Louis lay awake in the dying light. He looked at Clothilde and Pierrette, their faces pressed behind glass like flowers. He thought about them coming alive inside him and stared hard into their grey-paper eyes, feeling again the spooky sensation that someone else, disguised, peered out through the eye-holes.

Alphonse had said a dead person stayed alive to you always, if you could be open. Louis unclenched his fists and kept his eyes wide, looking for Joe. He was reluctant to sleep, until he remembered his ears, which would never close, and his mouth, which might fall open while he slept, leading straight through his throat to his heart. His father had lived right in this cabin when his family had gone south without him, but hard as Louis tried, willing Joe through every possible door, Joe did not come. Not all night or the next morning, when Louis awoke. Day after day, Joe was nowhere, unless that was him inside Clothilde or Pierrette. A chill rushed through Louis again at the thought of someone trapped in a picture. A real man, buried alive. He shuddered. For the rest of his stay, Louis tried not to look at the ghostly photograph, but he was so aware of it, it seemed to hum and glow like a living creature. The faces were mean, or sad, he couldn't tell which. Pierrette's mouth was a thin grey line, neither frown nor smile, and Louis could see no trace of her in the kind, wrinkled face of Alphonse LeBlanc, her father, who claimed to keep her in him always.

⟨OOOOO⟩

Once, very late in the night, shortly after his return from Toussaint and Alphonse's cabin, Louis woke and saw a man's hairy arm reaching in through his window. He opened his mouth to scream and the arm was gone. And then he could not say for certain whether it had been there at all, but he could still picture it, white in the moonlight, hairs and a hand ripe with

142

veins, the soft curtains hanging on either side. What the arm might have wanted from him he couldn't guess, but because of Alphonse's story, he connected it with his father. He had begun to associate every mysterious vision, sound, occurrence, with his father, Joe LeBlanc. Most disturbing was that the associations didn't comfort him; he felt more on guard than ever.

He told no one what he'd seen. He checked his screen, which was firmly in place, but the L-shaped rip in the corner (there since he could remember) seemed larger than before. With a ruler, he measured the L, and he continued to do so every evening for the remainder of the summer, recording the numbers in his doodle pad. Sometimes the numbers were bigger than they had been on previous days, and Louis's fear grew in proportion. But other days the numbers were smaller, and he surmised that screens were hard things to measure.

Terrified as he was, he said nothing to his mother or his uncles, and he did not close his window. He was afraid, but beyond that, he was intrigued and hopeful. What could the hairy arm want? Moreover, could it be his father's arm? If it was, did that mean Joe was still alive? Or did it mean there were such things as ghosts? He thought of the hair and veins, and wondered if ghosts could have them.

And then in August he saw legs in the garden. It was evening, and he was sitting alone in his playhouse, looking through the window. From outside, he resembled Clothilde and Pierrette: a solemn, unreadable face in an oval frame. Of this he remained unaware. He was gazing through the window, thinking that he was hungry, when his eyes fell on the fence that divided the LeBlanc property from Ms. Devlin's. Huge leaves spilled over the fence and twined through the slats so that in places it was difficult to see the wood at all. The leaves were dark green and prickly, he knew from experience. The sun was setting and the wind was blowing and the big leaves were lifting and falling, lifting and falling. He thought he saw something underneath the leaves – something large – and then he thought he saw it again, but each time the leaves revealed it, they hid it from him too.

"Louis!" called Kay. "Time for your bath!"

Louis kept watching the leaves. He stared a moment longer, and then he ran, heart racing, across the yard and into the house.

That night, after he had combed and parted his hair and buttoned his pyjamas to the collar, he measured the L with extreme care, but it was more or less the same size as it had been all along. He recorded the number in his book, climbed into bed, and immediately climbed out again, so he could part the curtains and look at the fence. In the blue light of evening the leaves were hard to make out, but they were still moving with the wind. For a second, something showed beneath them: two legs. Two long, green legs were hiding there. He had seen, and now he knew for sure. Trembling, he closed his window and locked it.

◌◌◌◌◌

If Alphonse and Toussaint had known of Louis's vision, they would have shrugged and blamed it on *la lune*, whom they called the Queen of Crazy. But a crazier thing by far happened the day Margar opened the front door of 40 Huron Street and saw Jesus standing there. At first she thought he was Joe, gone straggly from his long journey, for she was always expecting him. But then she recognized the outfit. He was wearing a blue and orange robe and had his arms spread wide like wings. The fabric of his dress – it really was a dress – hung in long pleats like the drapes in her grandmother's living room. He had cascading brown hair and a soft beard that touched his chest and wavered when he smiled. His eyes were startling, so pale they were almost white, and the only thing that looked unlike the picture in her bible for children, a gift from her grandparents. Otherwise it was as if he had lifted himself off of the page and reappeared life-size, alive, on their porch.

"Hello," she said.

"Hello," said he.

His long hands rested on the door jamb and his robe hung down in a hundred folds. He tilted his head, as he'd done in the picture, and smiled benevolently. The sun had to be shining behind him, because rays of it streamed out from his head. He let his hands slide down the door jamb and swung them together in front of his chest, as if praying. His pale eyes closed, and moved beneath his eyelids. His lips moved too, in silence. And then he opened his eyes and said,

"I've been looking for you."

He drew his arms out again, like wings, and Margar watched as he was lifted up into the sky, his bare dirty feet the last to go. She could see the holes in the top and then the bottom, running clear through his skin and bone. When he was entirely gone, the sun that had been behind him shone in and almost blinded her, and she shielded her eyes with her hand, stepped out onto the porch, and looked up, but he was nowhere. There was only the porch roof, without a hole through which he might have made his escape.

He never told her what he wanted, but after he'd gone, she tore his picture from her bible and asked her mother for tape to stick it up over her bed, the first of many pictures to come.

"Oh, sweetie!" said Kay. "You shouldn't have ripped your nice book!"

"But he came to the door. He said he was looking for me."

No one believed her. They said miracles wouldn't happen to a regular girl, so they still didn't know who they were dealing with.

⬤⬤⬤⬤⬤

Had Louis answered the door the day Jesus came, he might have died of stupefaction. As it was, he'd become so tormented by all he thought he'd seen that he approached Kay with clutched hands, his small face pinched in worry. He began to tell her everything, starting with the legs in the garden, and never got as far as the hairy arm, which might have alarmed her more, because she took him outside, parted the leaves that grew on the fence, and pointed to the two fruits dangling there.

"Ms. Devlin calls it the plant that planted itself — neither of us can remember putting it there, but look how big it grew! All it is is squash, Louis. A really big kind of squash. So, we're okay? Is anything else scaring you?"

Louis shook his head, and the pinch of worry dissolved into blank hopelessness. There were no legs in the garden, therefore there was no body attached to them. No eyes watched him day and night from beneath a veil of leaves.

Ms. Devlin made squash loaf and squash soup from the pendulous fruits of the plant that planted itself, and Louis, like the others, was expected to eat them. A beaded film of oil lay on top of the soup as though the soup itself were sweating. Dark, squiggly flecks ran through the loaf like scattered hairs, and one bite was all his sensitive stomach could accept. After two, he threw up. But because Louis was always throwing up, no one thought it was anything out of the ordinary. He remained a tiny nervous wreck until, one day, shortly before the dawn of the Mexico City Olympics, a gift appeared in the backyard, just beyond the playhouse. It was a trampoline.

Alphonse and Toussaint had bought it for all three of the children, recalling how good a gymnast Kay had been, and not knowing the pursuance of that sport could lead the youngest LeBlancs toward the source of so much LeBlanc heartache and ruin.

Louis bounced. He was both terrified and exhilarated. His fine hair lifted as he landed, and rested as he soared. Kay thought of her trampoline dream and in her mind she saw Louis, deflated in Joe's arms. She pushed the ugly thought down, and soon she had buried it so well that at night, when the children were sleeping, she jumped on the trampoline herself and felt nothing more complicated than joy. When the Games began, she saw herself in Vera Caslavska just as Louis saw himself in Sawao Kato. And amazingly, he grew. He was so afraid, but so compelled to jump, that fear clung to the soles of his feet, and desire grabbed the tips of his fingers. Together, they stretched him.

⊙⊙⊙⊙⊙

In a town of five thousand people, one would think that the Halliwells and the LeBlancs — what was left of them — would have happened upon each other regularly, on any given street corner, but they did not. Once they converged accidentally at the mall in nearby Pembroke, and despite Estelle's repeated tugs on Kay's jacket, and her cries of "Mom, Mom, it's the fat boy from home," all the adults managed not to see each other. Eddie, too, looked off in another direction.

Nearly seventeen, he stood five-foot-ten and weighed 203 pounds and counting. Marie cried for him behind a tearless, elegant mask. After her last breakdown, the year Joe disappeared, she'd seen the danger in repetition. Extreme behaviour could become the norm if one practised it often enough. A person could be flipped inside out so that the hidden, crazy part showed, and the dignified part was shut away. Marie's own son had seen her manic side. Twice he had found her in pieces, and he had been – was still – the person she most wished would regard her as a flawless, rational being.

After he'd come upon her in the garden, stretched out on the soil and punctured by thorns, she had gone home to Seattle to recuperate. She'd spent nearly three months away from her husband and son, and in her absence, snow had piled up in the garden. It covered the clawed-up bed and the mildewy roses. When she returned home in December, there was a quiet white-ness about the place that she hoped to absorb. She succeeded. Three years later, she was as subdued as the Renaissance madon-nas who had so disturbed her in Italy. Unwittingly, she exuded as much sadness.

This year, as she waited for the deeper relief that always came with snow, Eddie appeared at the back door with a skull in his hand, his fingers in the eye sockets. It hung at his side, white, with that yellowish tinge typical of bone. Marie was speechless. She looked at Eddie, she looked at the skull, and then at Eddie again.

"I think it's a bear," he said. He held it up sideways and showed her how the bone protruded, snout-like, and where there was a tuft of brown fur near the chin.

"My God," said Marie, her voice tremulous. She put her hand on her chest and closed her eyes. "I don't want to see it. Take it away, please."

"Why should I?" said Eddie. "I'm going to draw it."

"I said take it away. I don't want it here, Eddie. Not in this house, do you hear me?"

Eddie sighed in angry disgust. He stepped back through the door and slammed it closed, and Marie grabbed the counter's edge to steady herself. From the window, she watched him cross the yard, swinging the skull, and vanish into the bushes. She thought of the skeletons she'd come upon in Eddie's room, bones of small animals but animals just the same. And while they upset her, she decided it must be normal to find bones and want to save them, the way she had saved shells and feathers as a child, even though she'd been much younger. But Eddie's casual hold on the skull – something about it felt sinister. She had had a sense of reverence for the things she'd collected, for their origins, whereas Eddie's disregard alarmed her. At various times, she'd tried to discuss her concerns with Russell, but he had laughed her off. "Relax," he'd said. "So he's a bit weird. He takes after his mother. You worry about him too much." At the time his jokey dismissal had insulted her, but now she preferred Russell's version.

She washed her hands in the sink, patted cool water on her flushed face, and went back to her housework as though nothing had happened. If she knew that Eddie soon returned with the skull beneath his jacket, that he kept it in the third drawer of his dresser, under the T-shirts that she herself folded and put away, she never did say. She was not fond of confrontations.

⁣⁣⁣⁣⁣OOOOO

The skull was indeed a bear's. In fact, it was a cub's. Eddie had found it in a pile of leaves, at the very place where the town dissolves into forest. He had come upon money there once, three years earlier. The bills had been spread in a fan that peeked out from under a rock, as though waving, wanting to be found. He hadn't known right away how he would use the money, but his decision had come to him soon afterward in biology, when the class was dissecting frogs. Each pair of students had been given a scalpel that made clean slices through the frogs' anatomy.

Eddie had encouraged his science partner, Duncan Weir, to do most of the dissecting because he found the squishy, almost boneless frog boring. But as he watched Duncan's tentative hand steer the scalpel down the length of the green body, which reeked of formaldehyde, he thought of his old jackknife and the ragged cuts he had made to release delicate skeletons from their fur or feather encasements. When Duncan placed the scalpel on the desk between them, Eddie picked it up and turned it over in his hands. The handle was fine, lightweight. The manufacturer's name, Wisconsin Blade Company, was engraved on the side.

It had taken some doing to obtain all the information he needed, and though Eddie was only fourteen then, he'd always been a tenacious boy, and he knew his way around the library when it suited him. His time was his own during that long autumn, because his mother was gone – recovering in Seattle from her second nervous breakdown – and his father and he rambled the blue two-storey like strangers, barely speaking. Eddie could do what he liked, as long as he accomplished various tasks that had once fallen to his mother. It was his job, for instance, to pick up the mail. Thus he wrote worry-free to the Wisconsin Blade Company, and made his request in the most polished language he could muster.

The scalpel arrived in a black box with plush red lining, like a violin or a precious jewel. It came in November of that year, months after Joe LeBlanc had disappeared and Eddie's mother had left town, and following the birth of Margar LeBlanc, which to Eddie was an event of no significance. He lifted the scalpel from the box and touched the blade to his finger to test its sharpness. A bubble of blood appeared, round, opaque. He burst it with his tongue.

Since the discovery of the money and the gift it had brought him, he always looked in that same spot in the forest for not-so-buried treasure. He found the skull very close to the place where the money had been; a place easy to find again because it was close to a particular tree stump there, wide and hollowed out in the centre like a forest easy chair. He had been sitting in the chair when the skull appeared to him, a flash of white among decaying leaves. At first it startled him, but as he moved closer, he reminded himself that he had seen enough dead things to know that bones were no more frightening than rocks or shells. Remains, they were called, but that was a stupid word, because all the life had gone out of them.

Whether the cub had died of mange or starvation, Eddie didn't know or care. He returned to the scene of discovery time and again, searching for femurs, vertebrae, and curved racks of ribs. The bones would not be huge, he could tell from the skull, but they would be bigger than a bird's or a squirrel's, and that reason alone made his heart beat faster.

Eddie knew that Leonardo da Vinci had once waited at an old man's bedside, wishing he would die, so that he could draw the sinew and veins, and trace the map of a fresh dead body. Bodies were hard to come by. For art's sake, Michelangelo Buonarroti, driven to produce a magnificent Hercules, cut apart the humdrum dead bodies of many to make the superhuman whole. By night, with the help of a monk, he snuck into the morgue of Santo Spirito and dissected the husks of lost souls, paupers, and prostitutes who had died in the care of strangers. He studied the legs and arms and how they joined to the torso. He studied the head, and how the eyes sat in it. From the unworthy he sculpted Hercules, perfect hybrid of the divine and human, a godly man with base urges.

Eddie not only knew the stories behind how the works were created, he knew the stories they depicted as well, since these had been the books he'd gotten lost in as a child, his mother's books, well-thumbed and soft with use. Hercules had married Megara, a king's daughter, but being god and beast in unison, he could never be domesticated. He woke one ordinary night and slaughtered his wife and children. His remorse almost killed him, but eventually he married Deianeira, and tried to carry on. He had an uncontrollable lust for sex and adventure, and once Deianeira followed him when he strayed. In her travels, she was nearly raped by the centaur Nessus, but Hercules appeared, wounding Nessus with his bow. Dying, Nessus whispered his revenge. He told Deianeira she could tame her husband. "Mix his blood with his semen, and smear a bit of the potion on him. I promise – he will love you forever." Maybe she knew what would really happen, for his own potent fluids ate him from the outside in.

Because of the books, and because of Michelangelo, Eddie knew all about Hercules, who (rather than Eddie's near-Olympian father) was the boy's tenuous connection with the Olympic Games. Otherwise he was not interested in sports. He liked to think of his brain filling up with the history of art and its many strange offshoots, the lot of it forming the knotted mass at the back of his head, blue and heavy with knowledge. His pursuit of art had showed him what his brain looked like, and enabled him to feel it in his skull. The brain, not the bone, was the reason for a head's weight. The bear's skull was proof enough of that.

He sat in his room with it now and ran his fingers around the smooth eye sockets. Eddie had never seen a human brain other than in pictures, but he had seen a chipmunk's brain, and those of many birds. He had cut the heads open himself, and drawn them. He had touched the warm insides with his fingers.

He set the bear's skull on his dresser and began to sketch it from every angle, taking pride in his skill. He had read that the greats of the Renaissance had honed their craft so well that viewers stooped to smell a flat, painted rose. Eddie felt he was that good, at only sixteen, and knew he would get better. As yet he had no idea that art was more than duplication, and that all he had mastered was technique: how to copy what was there already, which nowadays a camera could do with the push of a button. But he excelled at what he knew so far – though no one other than he was aware of his skills, except perhaps his mother. He didn't share his sketches with her any more, but she had praised the ones he'd done as a boy, and those were childish scratchings he had long surpassed. When the teachers at school wondered what would become of their students, who would go far and wide and become famous, no one thought of fat Eddie Halliwell, the moody boy with glasses. He was nothing more than the wayward son of the handsome physical education teacher, and only commented on for being so unlike him. Thus far, Eddie had kept his talent secret. He had as many secrets as birds have feathers.

⟨⟨⟨⟨⟨⟩⟩⟩⟩⟩

As Marie Halliwell waited for the snow to come, she looked out at her garden, which really was no longer a garden. Quack grass and pigweed had taken over. Mint sent its suckers down into the earth and back up again, strangling the plants she had once tended. Weeds were the true perennials. The year he'd helped dig the new beds, Joe LeBlanc had asked her what was so bad about weeds. All that work. She remembered him sweating and shirtless, digging so near to the place where Kay Clancy had stood crying. His tanned skin had stretched over his ribs as he'd worked, and Marie had seen each knob of his spine. She had given him lemonade and watched his Adam's apple bob as he guzzled. Pearls of sweat ran down his bony face. Alternately, she'd thought, *he knows, he doesn't know*. It was impossible to tell.

"Does your wife have a garden?" she'd asked, ready to study his face as he responded. But Joe LeBlanc was a man of few words.

"No," he'd said, in a pleasant enough tone. And he'd gone on working.

Marie had laughed, and with her pulse vibrating, she managed to say, "Your wife and my husband have a lot in common. Russell hates yardwork."

Joe had smiled but given nothing away, if there'd been something to give. All Marie could ascertain was that he was a decent man. Like his uncles, he worked hard and carried himself with dignity. Which for some reason had made her sadder — more ashamed — than ever.

At the end of the two weeks, she had given him money and he had turned into a stranger again, slipping by in the distance in a red canoe. Her husband's daughter's father. On his last day of work for her, she'd watched him walk down the path and out through the trees, and she'd recalled that other day, years before, when he had come and fixed the floor and the ceiling in a kind of respectful silence, surely never guessing the seedy story behind the flood, or behind Marie's haggard expression. No, if he knew at all, he had not known then.

Outwardly, she'd recovered by the time he'd come to work in her garden. In those days, though few words had passed between them, Marie had treasured Joe LeBlanc. He'd given no sign that he recognized or returned the affection, and it had been this that had really attracted her: his innate goodness, his devotion to Kay, the girl her own husband had wronged. Marie had not wanted Joe LeBlanc. She'd craved what he'd stood for, and she'd long ago realized that none of it existed in the man she had married. Russell had charmed and wooed her, and had a hold on her still. But he was not, and never would be, a dignified man.

Marie turned away from the window and the river. She closed the curtain on the dying weeds and the sun, sinking, but mostly on the memory of Joe. All that had been ages ago, between the second breakdown and the first, two times she tried hard not to think of. But in her efforts to forget, and to avoid changing into the inner, crazy Marie, she had changed anyway – from cracked bone china, she had manufactured a durable, plastic heart.

⬤⬤⬤⬤⬤

While Eddie sketched the skull in his room and Marie closed the drapes on the garden, Kay, Estelle, Louis, and Margar LeBlanc swept out the garage that had not been used since the days of the red canoe. Beryl and Serge Hayes had given Kay a car.

Since Joe's disappearance, Beryl and Serge had often appeared at 40 Huron Street with some gift or other – a bouquet of peonies from Beryl's garden, a family membership to the new community swimming pool – but the car was the most lavish. Serge stood on the doorstep with the keys in his hand, Beryl at his side.

"We just felt –" he stammered. "Well, we've bought a new one, you see, and we've no need for two. We would have given it to Robbie, so we want you to have it instead. It seems only right, given the chain of misfortunes, that we try to make a chain of fortunes, if you understand my meaning."

Kay looked at his flushed face, the white hair that danced out from his head. She looked at Beryl's black eyes, alive in her bird-like face.

156

"It would please us," Beryl echoed. "We've got no one to give to now."

Kay felt her stomach turn over, and not knowing what else to do, she put her hand out for the keys. She tried to let the children's excitement sweep away her uneasiness, and recalled driving her parents' big Ford, imagining herself behind the wheel of her own one day. She had pushed Joe for a car, and now she had one, but the gift was so tied up in what had happened to Joe, what had happened before Joe, that accepting it felt wrong, even unethical, which somehow felt worse than wrong. And yet, the children were thrilled. And Serge and Beryl had said, "It would please us."

The slick red car sat importantly in the driveway, waiting for them. Someone else's castoff was a luxury to the LeBlancs. There was not a scratch on the paint or a tear in the upholstery. The hubcaps gleamed.

The whole family prepared the garage for the car. Kay pulled out the old horses that had held the canoe, and the children helped her remove lengths of wood and a pile of yellowed newspapers. They took turns sweeping out the cobwebs, but it was Kay who found the largest one, home to a mammoth wolf spider. The web was so big that it was this she'd stooped to see, rather than the scrap of paper hemmed in behind it. She was just about to call the children to look at it with her when she noticed the paper, mostly crumpled but smooth at one corner. *Dear Mrs. Ha* was all she could read. The script was Kay's own. She pushed her hand through the web and opened the note.

Dear Mrs. Halliwell,

I don't quite know how to say this, but I wonder if you could just not hire Joe any more. I know you do it out of the goodness of your heart,

Dear Mrs. Halliwell,

I am writing to ask you not to hire my husband. But please don't tell him I

Dear Mrs. Halliwell,

I don't mean to sound rude

Dear Marie,

Because of the unfortunate connection of our families, I am writing to ask

The children swarmed around her in a dizzying wave that stirred the mustiness of Joe's cooped-up garage. The smell was so strong – of him, of his things decaying – that she could taste it. Regardless, she breathed in through the nose, out through the mouth: Ramona Devlin's cure for everything. She shoved the note in her pocket.

But just an oil-stain away, Margar had seen. She watched her mother's cheeks flush scarlet and then lose colour. She's afraid of spiders, thought Margar. But her mother's hand had reached right through the web and pulled out some wrinkled paper. Her hand had vibrated so badly that Margar thought, *No, she's afraid of paper.* But why would anyone be afraid of a wad of paper? She was about to ask, "What is it?" when Kay chirped, "Come on. Let's have a treat. We'll go up to the restaurant for supper."

And Margar loved the cheeseburger deluxe. As they rode downtown in the new old car, she watched the blurred leaves and the cotton-ball clouds. The sun had not yet gone, but the moon, full and almost blue, peered through the open window and grinned at her. Its white lips squished into an O and blew her hair into a brown tangle.

The day she found the note in the garage, Kay also discovered a new level of misery. She became certain that Joe had seen the note, and put together the pieces of her lie, and that he had left because such deception was unforgivable to him. If she had only explained, he may have understood. If he would only come back, she would explain now.

She went on pretending nothing had changed, but inside a tumourish lump bloomed in her stomach, as if born from anxiety. She tried to ignore it, but her hand, with a will of its own, slid over that spot every night when she got into bed, pushing her further into the memory of the note and all the other memories attached to it. The idea that Joe was still alive, detesting her, was more painful than the idea of him dead, a realization that brought a fresh swell of guilt and expanded the lump in her stomach. She lay in bed and tried to conjure the details of that time. Back then, she had always felt nervous in summer, worried that Joe would again work for Marie, and that eventually the connection might lead to disaster. She tried to recall the day she had written the note, how he might have seen it and when, but three years on, with everything that had happened, it was all a muddle. She remembered writing the note and deciding not to send it because she couldn't take the chance that she had misread the situation, and that Marie Halliwell had no idea about Estelle.

She also remembered burning copy after copy of the note in the sink, and washing the ashes down the drain, so how had this one escaped and made its way into Joe's garage?

She'd proceeded to reread and rewrite the letter several times in the weeks before Joe's final disappearance, when he'd begun his mad refinishing of the canoe. But each time, she'd torn the sheet from the pad and burned it. Or so she'd thought. Somehow she had missed one. He must have concluded not only that Russell Halliwell was the father of Estelle, and that Robbie Hayes was not, but that his own hesitation had killed an innocent man. What kind of woman would that make her in his eyes? She winced and remembered how they'd lain together in the days after Robbie's death, lost in layers of grief. The blankets had been piled heavily on top of them, but Joe was still cold with remorse. She had said he'd done his best. She had called him a hero. She even remembered holding her eyes wide and letting them fill with tears. At the time, it hadn't seemed dishonest that he couldn't know the complicated reason for her sadness. And then he'd gone, without a word, without a question. She should have understood something was wrong – that something was more wrong than before.

Upon her own discovery of the note, she tried to keep going forward. She got up at the same time she always had. She fed the children and sent Louis and Estelle off to school with routine cheerfulness, and then put Margar in front of the television, feeding her cookies to keep her quiet. But every day, Kay despaired. Guilt and loneliness throbbed in the lump in her stomach.

"I miss you," she said aloud to the wall. "I am so, so sorry."

She wondered if she would stay this sad always, and how she would go on hiding it. But maybe the lump was cancer, and she'd die, and wouldn't have to worry any more. Joe might even get news of her death and come back for the children. She suspected he would. He was that decent and kind. And then she thought, *that's crazy*. A man who abandons his children, no matter what his wife has done to betray him, is not decent and kind. Her anger ballooned to the size of her despair, which had not diminished, and her love for him doubled in size. In every way, he took up so much space in her heart there might never be room for another. Still, someone was trying. She had noticed but hadn't let on.

⟨⟨⟨⟨⟨⟩⟩⟩⟩⟩

Margar had also noticed, despite the cookies and the television, which was on all the time, and made her happy. With its contained moving images, it had a structure the rest of the world lacked. As life bulged and sagged and teetered around her, Margar fixed on the pictures in the frame. They were black and white, but Margar saw them in colours more vibrant than the shades of the regular world. The sounds were sharper, with music in between. In the rare times the TV was off, the fridge buzzed, the clock tick-tocked, and the tap dripped, and Margar felt herself being sucked backwards to the dark, watery place she'd come from, where the monotony of her heart beating along with her mother's would have put her to sleep forever had she not kicked and screamed her way out.

To others, it must have seemed that all she did was watch TV, but Margar witnessed more than the screen showed her. It was only she who saw how often her mother's cheeks appeared stained with the juice of berries, then white as *la lune*, and sometimes almost green, the way Louis looked before he threw up. Margar had seen all of that, as well as her mother's hand on her stomach, her mother's face staring down at the table, and her mouth, out loud, saying the words *I miss you* to the wall. With her big Dumbo ears, Margar sat in front of the television, using the right to hear the cartoons and the left to hear Kay, who one day said,

"Listen – I'm not still hoping for Joe."

Margar cocked her head toward the kitchen upon hearing his name. She strained her eyeballs so far to the left that she could feel the whites pulling away, and see her own nose in profile.

"I think you are," said Ramona Devlin.

"That's ridiculous."

"It's all over your face," said Ms. Devlin, and Margar thought of the red, the white, and the green. "You know, my brother was ready to get down on one knee when he met you, and you act like he doesn't even exist."

"Your brother?"

"Don't tell me you don't remember Gus, from Pembroke?"

"Sorry," said Kay.

Whether sorry meant yes or no, Margar was unsure. But *she* remembered Gus Devlin. He had come to the front door, like Jesus. He had knocked, but as with Jesus, Kay hadn't heard him. Margar crept to the door in her toe socks, which were like gloves for the feet. They were knitted with ten different colours and made her silent as a fluff of dust. She looked up at the man through the screen, thinking this might be Joe in disguise. He didn't notice her at first, but perhaps he'd been expecting someone taller. Margar observed him through the zillion squares in the screen. He had on a white T-shirt patterned with blue and yellow spirals that reminded her of the swirled lollipops at the Metropolitan department store, rows of circles on sticks. You had to lick and not bite them, they were that hard, but sweet too. She'd only ever had one, and it had taken ages to eat something so large with her tongue.

"Hello," she said finally. She wiggled her toes and her eyebrow.

"Hello!" said he, looking down through the squares. He had a big head topped with waves of sandy hair. "Is your mom home?"

And then, though she'd returned to the TV when her mother had come to the door, the great flaps that were her ears had listened in as Kay LeBlanc met Gus Devlin of Pembroke, and Margar wished it could be that further-off Pembroke her grandmother had told her about, where there were royals. *Earl of Pembroke*, she thought, and snuck another look at Gus. He told Kay he figured it was only right he introduce himself, since he was Ramona's brother and therefore an almost-neighbour, and he offered to cart away the old lumber in the backyard, which Kay and the children had pulled out of the garage when the car had gone in.

"I've got a truck," he said. "It would be one load, and no trouble, really."

Politely, Kay had refused. The wood still lay warped and greying in a heap next to the garage.

"You know it was his excuse to meet you, right?" asked Ms. Devlin.

Margar's ears twitched, but heard no answer.

"Now he uses any excuse to come to town and visit. Just to catch a glimpse of you. Why wouldn't you take the help? What use have you got for a pile of wood and a couple of horses?"

Hard as she looked, Margar had never seen any horses. From the things people said, she knew they had once held Joe's canoe, but she couldn't imagine it. Egged on, she walked in her toe socks to the bathroom, climbed onto the toilet seat, then the tank, careful not to slip, and looked out the window to the backyard. A squirrel ran across the grass, and then a chipmunk, and next door, Olive the dog barked at each of them. There was not a horse in sight.

⦅⦆

Fall came, and the massive white pine that stood at the base of the LeBlanc backyard began to drop its sticky cones and needles. Its ancient arms reached as far as Ramona's yard, where it scattered more refuse. The tree had almost hidden the hydro wires that ran through it, so the wires seemed to grow from the tree itself, as though technology and nature had mated, and this was the mixed-up child. The long copper needles fell and bled their acidity into the ground, and each year there was less and less grass, and larger patches of weeds and dusty soil. Even if she raked every day at this time of year, Kay couldn't keep up with what dropped from the tree.

"You have to take care of your property," said Alphonse and Toussaint, who had come, on Kay's request, to take the lumber and the horses, and dismantle the trampoline until next summer. "Nothing can grow here if you don't take care."

Which was why, after her initial shock, Kay guessed it had been they who had cleaned the yard for her. Deep in the night, just before the first snow, just before she was to see her doctor about the lump in her stomach, someone had raked the cones and needles into bags – fourteen of them – and taken the bags to the curb before sunrise.

In her room of windows, Kay woke to the yellow light of autumn. She lay in bed, watching the sun discover the trinkets on her dresser – her musical jewellery box, the framed pictures of her children. Estelle beamed out at her from a school portrait in which her two front teeth were missing.

Kay got up and put on her dressing gown. The floor was November-cool so she slid her feet into her slippers, then shuffled to her top drawer, where the note, folded in quarters, was tucked beneath bras and panties. Rather than read it, as she had done every day since the discovery, she began to tear the note along the fold line. And then she stopped. She held the paper in her hands. She was looking out the window and seeing the lawn, bare as a fallow field. She had the sensation of the nearness of Joe, as she'd had the night of the tapping playhouse door, for who but a husband would have tidied the yard?

"Mom," said Margar, invading the silence. She was wearing her rabbit slippers and a pair of fake rabbit ears attached to a hair band. "I'm hungry."

And the moment, to Kay's sorrow, was over. She lifted the lid of her jewellery box, which started the Sugar Plum Fairy song, and she tucked the note into a tear in the lining, and Margar – hopping, feigning rabbity buckteeth, and twirling like a bunny ballerina – followed her from the room.

⬤⬤⬤⬤⬤

During breakfast they all sat at the table, looking out at the bags that lined the curb. Margar said an angel had done it.

"That's dumb," said Louis. "Angels don't rake."

No one noticed, but his face was ashen.

"They do," said Estelle, "but only at night, so no one will see them. And the way they glow," she added, waving her fingers and tracing two half-circles around herself, "it helps them see what they're doing."

"Not *them*," said Margar. "*Him*." She pulled the crust from her toast and stuffed the long snake of it into her mouth. Chewing nonchalantly, she added, "There was only one angel raking."

For once, someone listened. Kay watched the toast pop up from the toaster as the realization came. She looked out at the curb in front of Ramona's place and saw the matching bags lined up there.

So Gus Devlin had been the angel.

⬡⬡⬡⬡⬡

Margar had never slept well. As a baby, she'd nap fifteen minutes and then wake up screaming for milk. As a child, she was wilier, and understood that when she woke in the night, she'd only be tricked back to sleep if her mother knew she was up. So she prowled around in her nightie, leaving her feet bare despite the chilly floor, because slippers made a *ch-ch* sound that might give her away. Last night, she had gone to the window of her room to look at *la lune*, but instead she'd found an angel raking the lawn. And while she'd heard it said that the horses were gone now, that Alphonse and Toussaint had taken them days before when they'd come for the lumber, last night she'd seen them grazing in the yard. The angel had turned toward the neighs and whinnies, and the light from his halo had shone in a beam on the horses. She'd seen them for just seconds before they'd galloped off. They were white with brown blotches. The angel fed them pine cones by hand. She'd never thought of pine cones as food, but she would try them herself now, having seen them eaten. They would be sticky, but so were candyfloss and jam. Pine cones might be as sweet. Clear across town, the last of them were dropping from their branches.

And that day, as she drove with her mother to the doctor's, she watched them swing in the treetops, break loose, and seesaw down. When she got out of the car and followed her mother across the parking lot, she noticed pine cones everywhere. Hundreds of them lay on the pavement, squashed by the fat, black tires of cars. And then a perfect one appeared at her feet. The scalloped edges glistened with stickiness, some of it white and sparkly like sugar. She was squatting to inspect it, hearing but ignoring her mother's "Hurry on, Margar," when a pair of blue high heels stepped into her line of vision. Her eyes travelled up the feet to the ankles and legs, up the blue skirt to the matching jacket, belted at the waist and finished with shining pearl buttons. Up the long neck to the red lips in white skin, and the flashing blue eyes, all topped by a grey hat trimmed with a band of feathers.

The woman smiled, and Margar opened her mouth to ask about the feathers, but it was Kay's voice that sounded.

"Margar! Come on!"

She turned to see her mother hurrying toward her, wearing the same look as when Margar had stuck her fingers in the loose panel on the back of the TV. Nothing had happened then, and there was nothing scary about now either, but Kay grabbed her wrist and yanked her to standing. Her mother nodded hello to the woman but her eyes darted elsewhere. Margar studied the woman's white face, and then her mother's pink one. The pink was getting darker, flooding down through her neck and the V of her chest, and Margar thought, *This is why we're going to the doctor. Mommy's bleeding on the inside.* But then she remembered that blood lived on the inside. It was only when it came out that blood was worrisome.

"How are you?" the woman asked, and at the same moment, Kay said, "Excuse us," and their voices clashed. Kay began to pull Margar across the parking lot so speedily that Margar's feet left the ground and hovered over the pavement. But her mother turned around again before they'd reached the doctors' building.

"Wait!" she called, and they hurried back towards the woman.

She hadn't moved from the spot where they'd left her. She lifted her eyebrows, dark like Margar's, but narrow, each rising in an elegant arc. The woman blinked several times, as when a bug gets in the eye, but it must have flown out again, for her face regained its calm appearance. If not for the eyes and lips, thought Margar, she was almost as white as *la lune*. *La lune* in a hat with feathers. Margar watched the tiny feathers flutter in the breeze. They were mostly grey, but when they moved, flecks of blue and orange showed.

"I'm sorry – I need to ask you," said Kay.

"Yes?" The woman's cheekbones jutted out from her face and made the skin beneath go shadowy, like the dark patches on the white moon. Oncle Toussaint said the moon was a woman and the sun was a man.

"You look like the moon," said Margar, and Kay put her hand over Margar's mouth. She felt her mother's fingers trembling.

"Joe LeBlanc," said Kay, "my husband."

Margar's ears stood at attention. The woman's eyes blink-blinked, and Kay continued.

"Did he —"

"Yes?" Blink-blink.

"Did he come and see you? I mean, did he ask you — did he say — did you tell him about —"

"My goodness, you seem a little upset," said the woman. She touched her hat and smoothed the quivering feathers, then glanced down at Margar. Her blue eyes gleamed. "I'm afraid I don't know what you're talking about."

A wind came up and scattered the pine cones, and Margar stepped on the perfect one just as it began to roll away. The women stood looking at each other, a red face and a white face, until Margar grew bored and tugged her mother's coat.

"Mom," she whined.

"I'm sorry," said Kay. "I'm sorry to have bothered you."

The woman put her hand out then, and laid it on Kay's sleeve. The thin fingers were encased in tan leather, and Margar watched them wrap around her mother's arm, squeezing gently.

"Please don't be sorry," she said in a whisper, and Margar watched her blue eyes turn almost silver, and back to blue again. With that, the woman turned away, and her high heels took her click-clacking across the parking lot.

Kay grabbed Margar's hand and Margar was flying once more, up over the pine cones and into the doctors' building and all the way up the stairs, but not through the door and down the hallway, because suddenly her mother was weeping. They stood on the landing in the dark stairwell, and Kay leaned against the wall with her head tipped back. Margar saw that her mother's coat was buttoned up wrongly, one side hanging lower than the other. She tugged on the hem again, and her mother slid down the wall and hugged her tight, as though Margar were the one who needed comforting.

⦅⦅⦅⦆⦆⦆

The doctor prodded and shrugged, as he'd done when Louis had stopped growing, and announced that there was no discernable lump in Kay's belly. She put her hands on her stomach, searching for the thing that had caused so much worry, but indeed it was gone, which made her surmise that not even she could trust herself if her mind and her body kept tricking each other.

"Whatever it was, all seems well now," said the doctor, who could not have been more wrong. The humiliation she carried was not detectable by touch. Nevertheless, it had reached gargantuan proportions.

And that was why, weeks later, when Gus Devlin appeared on the porch wielding a sumac and winterberry bouquet, Kay stood in the closet until he had gone. Joe's brown eyes blinked up at her in Margar's puzzled face, and Kay pressed her finger to her lips in an urgent plea for silence.

MUNICH 1972
the invisible eye

The 1972 Olympic Summer Games were held in Munich, West Germany, from August 26 to September 11. Abebe Bikila, paralyzed now, was nowhere to be seen. The following year, he would die of a cerebral haemorrhage, and much would be said about the wide swing of his pendulum of luck.

Waldi the Dachshund was Munich's mascot, and a record 121 nations marched in the opening parade. At the start of the Games, the athletes numbered 7,134, but by the end, only 7,123 still breathed. Eleven athletes died at the hands of desperate terrorists, and five terrorists and a policeman (hit by a stray bullet) were killed by desperate police. The world reeled as the bodies lay bleeding, and then the Games went on, as games must.

A little Belarus gymnast named Olga Korbut stunned the audience with her spectacular performance in the team competitions, but the buzz around her was too much. Her scores plummeted in the individual competition, and just when the crowds had almost given up on her, she spun through the apparatus finals with dizzying finesse. In the end, her near failure may have made the spectators love her more. She herself said in her biography that one day, she was nobody, and the next she was a star. The age belonged to such celebrities. Three years earlier, heroes had walked on the moon, leaving footprints behind. The multitudes had gone outside and looked up, then returned inside to watch history unfold on television, where grand things could be made small in close-up, where stars – both the planetary and the celebratory – were contained and almost graspable.

The debonair prime minister appeared on TV often. In 1971, he had married a radiant bride with flowers in her hair, and on Christmas Day of that year, they had a beautiful baby, Justin Pierre James, whose sibling would be born exactly two years later: another boy, on Christmas Day. Of fatherhood, the normally private Pierre confided to the world, "I didn't know about this marvellous feeling. It makes you eternally grateful for the miracle of life and for the mother who bore those children."

By now, Margar had been pulled into the perfumed, childless bosom of Beryl Hayes. Beryl had discovered Margar's musical aptitude by accident, when Margar, age six, had plunked out "Chopsticks" after she was shown once which keys to press. And though the LeBlancs had no piano of their own on which Margar could practise, she was sent off to the Hayes's every Wednesday for formal lessons. Beryl insisted on teaching for free. Margar, caught up in everyone's enthusiasm, decided this might be something to excel at, something rare and beautiful. She thought of Estelle, perched on the edge of her bed with her back held straight, playing the flute. She recalled Estelle's pursed lips, just a hair away from the instrument, and her tiny fingers fluttering over the holes. The music that came out of the flute was distant and airy, an unconnected sort of sound that could be blown away in a breeze. Piano was the opposite. The music came not from pressing on holes but on wood and bone. With a thrilling shiver, Margar conjured hewn black trees and the severed tusks of elephants.

While she loved the music, she was less fond of the rules. Placing her fingers just so seemed silly to her, and much as Mrs. Hayes tried to teach her to read, the new language was nothing but a swarm of dots and lines on paper. She liked the fancy words that came with the music – *crescendo, diminuendo, staccato, pianissimo* – and the sight of her fingers on the keys (though she wasn't supposed to look there), but most of the time the lessons were tiresome, and Mrs. Hayes's breath stunk of coffee. But she always looked forward to going – for the simple reason that a dead boy lived in the large, echoey house.

Twice Margar saw him tiptoe into the kitchen in pyjamas and slippers and steal cookies from the cookie jar. She knew he was stealing because he turned to look at her once he'd lifted the lid, put a finger to his lips, and then dipped his hand into the jar with a conspiratorial grin. She played louder whenever she saw him, to obscure any sound he might make and allow him to mill around undetected, for it was obvious no one else had yet spotted him.

Knowing the story of the boy her father had tried to save, she realized this was Robbie, and she was glad to see he was happy in his afterlife – comfortable in his pyjamas and eating whatever he wanted. What surprised her was that a ghost could lift the lid of a cookie jar, bite into the cookie and have it disappear inside him, just as a living person could do. For some time, she saw him every Wednesday, but the only person she told was Estelle, a lapse she would avoid in future.

Estelle rolled her eyes. "Ghosts don't eat cookies," she said. "And they don't wear pyjamas."

Which only showed how much Estelle knew.

⬤⬤⬤⬤⬤

Eddie Halliwell, by this time, had gone far from the Ottawa Valley. In 1970, he applied to three art schools and was accepted by all of them. He chose the Nova Scotia College of Art and Design in Halifax because it was at the edge of the ocean. The water was all he expected to miss upon leaving Deep River, and living near the ocean would easily fill that loss. He brought his clothing, his most recent sketchbooks, his scalpel, and one complete bird skeleton, but he left a lot behind. As he closed his dresser drawer on old sketches and the fragments of bone he had collected over the years, he thought and truly believed, *I will never come back here again.*

On the day of his departure, he followed his mother and father across the weedy lawn, past the stone-angel fountain and over the obscured path that had been laid many years ago by Alphonse and Toussaint LeBlanc. He stepped without thinking on the snarls of wild mint, long forgetting the little boy he'd been. And when he followed his parents through the arch in the wall of trees at the end of the yard, he did not look back as the trees' branches closed like a door behind him. Russell, Marie, and Eddie climbed into the car as they had often done over the years, and anyone who saw them ride by would have assumed they were a family, which of course they were and were not. Even now, when Eddie was old enough to know how babies were made, when he had experienced and privately sated those physical urges himself, he preferred to believe he had been dropped from the sky, found squawking amid the bulrushes, and that soon his time among strangers would be over. He tried not to think of the past, and only of the fast-approaching future. Once unknowable, now it smelled of rough salt water.

Eddie had been to the ocean once before, but that had been the Pacific, and everyone had been miserable then. During Christmas of 1965, he and his father had gone to Seattle to retrieve his mother months after her second nervous break-down. They had driven together for six days, just the two of them, and Eddie had taken to feigning sleep in the back seat just to escape his father's dissertations on the importance of travel, of posture, of humour; and moreover, to escape the unbearable silence that hung between those speeches. Angry as he'd been with his mother for leaving, Eddie had looked forward to seeing her, and to the black time of her absence being over. He'd believed the drive home would be more tolerable, but he had been wrong. Vacantly, she put her arms in a circle around him, forgetting the squeeze that makes a hug, and Eddie stood in the meaningless embrace, waiting for it to be over.

On the way home, they stopped at oceanside beaches, and the water rushed in and placed shells on the shore. Eddie thought of the river at home, and the dead minnows that washed up on the sand with their eyes open. He looked away from the water, and saw that his mother was like a ghost with the white sky and the white waves behind her. She stood on the sand as the waves lunged for her, and she had the look of someone who would go willingly. Eddie turned his concentration to the shells and stones at his feet, but watched her secretly with the peripheral vision he thought of as his invisible eye. She seemed unaware of her surroundings. She was wearing high heels and a smart jacket and skirt, the grey of which seeped into her complexion. He saw her standing there, and he saw his father appear beside her and fold his arms around her the way he did in the Italian pictures, pre-Eddie, when they were not a mother and a father but two newlyweds gushing with love. And now, after everything that had happened, his mother turned and clung to his father. Eddie felt the salty breeze sting his eyes. It seemed to him that she ceased being his mother in that instant. Later he would understand that she had been going from him slowly, from the very beginning. Eventually he wouldn't remember a time when she had not been engaged in the act of leaving him behind. His invisible eye looked away. There was nothing to see. Or no one. That was who she'd become: no one he knew.

All this passed through his mind with the thought of Nova Scotia salt water, but it passed quickly and he didn't let it alter his mood. They were approaching a different ocean, and today he felt what might be called happy. In fact, there was a version of unspoken happiness among all of them as the car rolled easily forward to whatever would come. The leaves had not yet begun to bleed red into the green but everything was on the brink of change. The burnt look of August had softened, and plants that had been stunted by the sweltering heat gave off their last flourishes before fall, knowing time was running out. His parents rode along in silence. He would have been content if all the way to Halifax they had ridden without speaking, for he felt sure he didn't need them now, except for the driving.

⟨OOOOO⟩

Eddie was right that Marie, too, was happy. She was excited by what the future might hold for him, and remembered embarking on her own early adventures, a time that had ended far too quickly, but she didn't regret it now. She had never gone on to curate exhibitions or teach art history at a university, as she'd thought she might. Instead, she'd put all of her energy into raising her son – and that could never be a sacrifice. Eddie was love, and so life, though she had never specifically told him. The two times she had lost hold of her responsibility to him, it had been Eddie himself who'd appeared to remind her; in the bedroom, as she'd lain trying to die, and in the garden, as she'd clawed at the earth among the strewn, bruised groceries. Today she recalled even these disturbing times with an elation that could not be diminished, not yet. Whatever had happened, Eddie had made it through.

Once, in Sorrento, she and Russell had been walking home from a blissful day in the countryside. It was night, and cool, a cyan blue summer evening. Marie was four months pregnant with the baby who would become Eddie. She had just begun to feel his kicks and kept her hands on her stomach awaiting them. Russell was walking with his arm around her shoulders and there was a kind breeze, not at all foreboding, that stirred the trees' leaves and made them whisper. Until now, the trees of Italy had frightened Marie: olive trees, twisted and lumpy, like the gnarled bodies of old witches; oleander, with its swordlike leaves and its poisonous, tempting blossoms. But the pregnancy had changed her, or Sorrento had. The scent of oranges floated in from the groves, and though the cliffs dropped straight down into the Bay of Naples, she was calm.

The only things that still disturbed her were the madonnas, Bellini's especially, in which – at least to her – something sinister played out in the background. Russell suggested they stop going to galleries and museums. "For your sake," he said, though she knew he had a lukewarm interest in art and was beginning to find the excursions tedious. At first she'd feared losing hold of her passion, but Russell turned out to be right, she did feel better. And that was good for the baby. Anything she could do for the sake of the baby, she would do gladly.

And that night, walking in Sorrento, she was thinking about the growing child when a short, pathetic scream punctured the silence. She and Russell stopped and looked at each other. The scream came again, desperate, raspy, both like and unlike the scream of a baby. Russell took Marie's hand and they continued down the hill more quickly. The sound grew louder the third time it came, and two seagulls swooped overhead, wailing. Gulls' cries were a daytime sound, made eerie by the night sky. The wind picked up, as if it too were on guard.

"Look," said Russell, when they'd reached the foot of the hill.

A baby seagull stood alone in the street. It turned in panicky circles, stretching its spotted fluffy head skyward as if that would lift it into the air. So much noise from something so small.

"It doesn't know to flap its wings," said Marie.

Russell took a step toward it but the two seagulls overhead circled protectively. He glanced at Marie and smiled.

"He has good parents, this little guy."

But the bird wasn't out of danger. It wandered from one side of the street to the other, twice trying to enter a noisy *trattoria*, and twice Russell braved the wrath of the adult birds in order to steer the little one elsewhere.

Marie kept her hands on her stomach all along, thinking the bird had no chance of survival and wishing they had not come upon him at all. She watched Russell chase him to a quieter side street, and as they were about to leave, a flock of gulls descended and sent the two adults into a high-pitched frenzy while the baby squalled below. The other gulls would eat him if they could Marie didn't want to witness that, but she couldn't turn away. The parents flapped and soared, a flurry of white against the deep blue sky, and when the other gulls scattered, they finally resumed their posts on the rooftops nearby. The night fell quiet except for the wind, and the drunken ruckus that came in waves from the *trattoria*.

"Let's go," said Russell. "He's going to be fine."

They walked the rest of the way home in silence, and Marie thought of a baby's vulnerability, and of the burden of being strong for another person, when she was barely strong enough for herself. The first time she'd felt her baby kick, she'd been alarmed by the sensation. Something not part of her was moving inside her, and no matter what she'd read or heard, nothing had prepared her for that feeling. Months after Sorrento, when Eddie was born, and the umbilical cord cut, she worried about how she would protect him now that he had to breathe on his own.

Nearly eighteen years later, Marie marvelled at how far they had come, and how today circled back to the first day of his life.

Hampered by fear and weakness, she had seen him through. He was more ready than most to leave home, and she was happy – *happy* – he was going. She was pleased, too, that he had chosen to study art, as she once had. He would make something of himself, which she had not had the strength or courage to do. He had a vehemence inside him that would serve him well. The greatest artists possessed it. If something good became of him, with the future begun on this day, every awful mistake might be absolved, even if it could not be corrected. She may have been less than ideal as a mother, but he'd managed to find his path regardless, and that was what mattered. She realized, thinking this, that it was his happiness she craved. He had not been happy for a long time, yet now, without looking back at him, she recognized the expression he wore: a barely perceptible smile, a faraway look in his eyes. As a little boy, he had been happy, and what a roundabout journey it had been to bring him back to that place. The difference was that now he was happy alone, and then they had been happy together. She thought she knew the very moment she'd become separate from him, though surely it must have been the culmination of many moments. She had driven the car into the driveway, climbed out, and stepped through the doorway of trees, breathing the sweet smell of flowers in the night air. Kay Clancy had been standing in the garden, and Marie had removed her gloves, finger by finger, aware of her heart souring.

⟨⟨⟨⟨⟨⟩⟩⟩⟩⟩

The truth – a truth no one knew but Eddie and later Marie – was that long before Marie had arrived in the yard, Eddie had watched

180

the hesitant approach of his father's student, Kay Clancy. He was eight years old then, sitting high in a willow at the edge of the Halliwell property. From here he could see both the road and the yard, which was enclosed by trees. Unnoticed, he watched Kay walk by on the street, passing the house slowly, and attempting to peer between the branches. She stopped, but soon resumed walking, and after a time was out of sight.

Eddie stretched out on a branch. The moon was full and bright and it was past his bedtime, but his mother wasn't home and his father hadn't noticed he was still up. Eddie heard steps on the pavement, and when he looked, saw that Kay had returned. She stood at the opening in the trees, looking in at the house. Three times she turned to walk away, and three times she turned back. Eddie leaned into the shadow of the willow's weeping branches. Kay approached the house so silently that Eddie would not have known she had moved had he not been watching. Instead it was she who did not know of his presence. He held his breath as she walked to the house. She kept to the path and passed the stone angel. Her feet moved slowly, like a bride's, pausing at each mid-step, until suddenly she turned, ran back down the path, and darted into a patch of sunflowers. Eddie peered through the leaves to see what had frightened her. He saw his father at the upstairs window, pulling the drapes closed.

It was then that his mother arrived.

⦅⦆⦆⦆⦆

From the car she'd seen his foot dangling, and she'd been about to call up to him, "Come down, you should be in bed," when she'd seen Kay Clancy among the sunflowers. And then

181

every sensible thing had gone from her head and been replaced with the cold brutality of instinct. *My husband has slept with this child*, she thought. She saw the thin arms and shoulders, the girlish sundress, pink with yellow trim, and the hair gathered in a messy ponytail that brushed against Kay's back as she turned to face Marie.

Marie removed her gloves and held herself tall and straight.

"Kay?" she said. "Is that you?"

The girl was crying hard and Marie held herself taller and straighter.

"Would you like me to get the coach?" she said.

The girl nodded, and Marie turned and followed the path to the house. Her vision narrowed and the trees on either side of the lawn pressed in on her. The house before her was warped like a circus funhouse, but Marie's gait remained poised and sure. She took the three steps to the door in her usual refined manner, but it was luck, or habit, that helped her feet land where they should, for the steps undulated like nothing made of wood. He was there, floating before her, warped the way the house had been, despicable. She sent him outside with as few words as possible, and in the dark kitchen, she leaned against the wall with her eyes closed. Finally, with her hand over her open mouth, she turned and looked at them through the glass door. When she saw Kay's lunge and frenzied kiss, Marie flipped on the light in the kitchen and was calmed by her own reflection. She spread a sea of blue fabric on the table and steadied her shaking hands as she pinned down the pattern.

◌◌◌◌◌

Later, as she lay awake beside her husband, she recalled Eddie's dangling foot, which she had forgotten as the nasty truth unfolded. She thought of him resting in the tree, an invisible witness to the words Marie herself had not wanted to contemplate. So he knew. Whatever had been said between Russell and Kay Clancy, Eddie had heard. He must also have seen the girl's eager kiss, which Marie could not erase from her own memory. What would a kiss like that mean to an eight-year-old boy, son of the man who'd received it? And how could she explain when she could not begin to understand? She listened to Russell breathing, disgusted even by that mundane sound, and then without knowing how she had got there, she was in Eddie's room, looking into his sleepy face and whispering *what did you hear, what did they say, tell me everything*. She watched his serious mouth open as the noxious words came out. She made him say it all. The words emerged slowly, matter-of-factly, as she had known they would.

Afterward she knew she had cemented this night in Eddie's memory. Before she had entered his room the chance remained alive that everything he had heard would flutter and disperse and he would be left with the nonsensical remnants – blurred images and snatches of mysterious conversation that he would connect with a bad feeling, nothing more. But she, his own mother, had made that impossible. She'd told him, "Be precise, Eddie. Don't leave anything out."

Coach. I love you.

Marie blinked and looked at the highway. She was so happy now. She focused on the pure simplicity of that emotion, and on the relief she felt that Eddie had grown up and was going off on a wonderful adventure. All sorts of things would happen in his life, pushing out the old memories to make room for new ones. She pulled down her visor and looked at him in the mirror. He didn't return her gaze, but she smiled at him anyway.

⦅⦅⦅⦅⦅⦆

Eddie saw the smile with his invisible eye. It was not the calming smile in which he had basked as a boy, but an artificial smile that said, *Isn't everything nice, isn't everything good?* It interfered with his own musings and revolted him.

⦅⦅⦅⦅⦅⦆

Though he couldn't see the ocean from his room at the college, Eddie could sense its presence. On the first day of school the weather was wet and warm and a thick mist rolled off the roofs of the city. Inexplicably, the sight thrilled him. He felt like weeping with joy, which of course he did not do, for he had two room-mates, Thomas and Nelson, but even if he had been alone he would not have allowed himself the luxury.

He was overwhelmed by a sense of newness. Life would begin now, and he had been waiting a long time. He had already started to plan a series of ocean paintings, though he had no idea what his assignments would be. He could see in his mind that the paintings would need to be enormous in order to swell and spray and hold all of the varying blues, greens, purples, browns that the ocean held, the colours of bruises. He had stared at the ocean just days before with his mother and father, as he had eaten hot battered clams from a bag, and he had told himself that from now on he would eat fried clams every day, with chips.

184

He had not allowed the day to be infected by another day at another ocean years before, because this was miles from there. He faced a different horizon.

Eddie felt a new lightness in his old being as he readied himself for school and breakfasted in the cafeteria among strangers. He did not sit with Thomas and Nelson – in fact, he had barely spoken to them since the initial introductions had been made. He had contemplated making friends with them, but up to now he had done without friends, for the most part, and he didn't know how to begin. He told himself he was here for bigger reasons than camaraderie. Despite his nervous belly, he gobbled his food and made his way to class. He wanted to run his hand along the old stone walls, where there were mosses and vines growing, but he kept his fists in his pockets and pretended to be indifferent even as he breathed in the wet salt smell and the autumn fragrance of things dying. There were no old buildings at home, other than a single log cabin. There was nothing solid, made of stone. The oldest structures were the trees, and even these had ceased to impress him. He knew there were bigger trees elsewhere.

If his happiness was a balloon inside him, lifting him along with a light step and heart, it burst when he sat in class, front row, and was told to forget whatever he thought he knew. Eddie understood the insinuation and was offended.

"Whatever you've learned," said the teacher, St. Clair, "unlearn it."

And just to be certain, just to mock him further, he and the others were made to draw with a long prosthesis. St. Clair gave them sticks with markers attached to the ends and had them

185

make sloppy, childish drawings. The stick rendered every line Eddie drew ugly and meaningless. He felt miles away from what he was creating, and his anger burned so hot he wanted to hurl the stick at St. Clair's smug face. Hurl the stick, tear the paper, storm out. But he stayed.

Day in, day out, he unlearned. He developed a confused fondness for St. Clair, who was not at all friendly, but exuded an unsmiling intensity that Eddie came to admire. He thought of showing St. Clair his portfolio of squirrels and birds and bones – just to prove to him what he could really do – but as he unlearned further, he realized his pictures were immature, however excruciatingly detailed. Art was not birds and squirrels, but a toilet – a real toilet and nothing more – and soup cans stacked up, and paint splattered on canvas. Art was something anyone could do.

"The brilliance," said St. Clair, "is in the idea."

Half of Eddie wanted no part of this nebulous kind of art, and the other half needed to embrace it and be embraced back. So while visibly he rolled his eyes, secretly he took everything in and held on to it as though it were a means for survival.

⬤⬤⬤⬤⬤

On the way home from Halifax, Russell and Marie Halliwell detoured to Quebec City and stayed in an inn with fake Renaissance frescoes on the ceiling. At dinner, they toasted to new beginnings, which was a way of acknowledging, without need for discussion, that Eddie's departure signalled the next phase of their lives. After consuming a bottle of wine, they returned to their room and made love. For the first time in a long time, it felt delicious, as it had in Rome, or perhaps more so, because of the texture that arises when love develops the weathered skin of disappointment. Marie moved out of her mind and into her body to savour the sensations.

Later, as Russell slept, Marie lay awake. Too much red wine made her heart race and gave her insomnia. She looked up at Venus rising from her shell on the hotel ceiling. Marie had seen the real painting, a Botticelli, in Florence. This poor reproduction reminded her of those days and the time she'd asked Russell what made ruins beautiful.

"You," he had said.

She remembered her dissatisfaction, but she thought now that it was a sweet answer, better than any other. Life was easier when it stayed small, when you didn't ask too much from it. She rested her head on Russell's sleeping body and wondered if there was a chance for them to start over. If things could be the way they had been before, at least somewhat. She wondered if they loved each other at all.

The room began to spin, and Venus swam above her, and Marie put her foot on the floor and closed her eyes. The wine would give her a headache soon, and she would question whether the indulgence had been worth it. She realized that whatever emotions had been awakened in her would soon recede, and all that would be left was a hollow space – a reminder of what her life had become. It was better not to taste if she could not eat. Tasting made her miss everything about before. The sharp, clear edges of things and the drama. The heightened sensation of hearing and seeing in detail, even when it was painful, because now she could not hear or see that way if she tried. She had shut down to maintain her sanity, and the price had been dear. She was still paying. She lifted her head and looked at Russell's mouth. Even when she touched his lips with her finger, he slept on.

He was a handsome man, sleeping, but when Russell Halliwell smiled, with his wide mouth and even teeth, his face took on a beatific glow. That Marie first saw him in the Sistine Chapel seemed significant at the time, and later, with the lucidity of distance, highly appropriate. There was a time when art became too beautiful, got up in gold and curlicues. Michelangelo painted his ceiling on the eve of that era, at the cusp of the lure of perfection. In the Renaissance years, the secrets of perspective and light were unlocked and refined by the masters, which led to the Baroque years, when one could look and look but only see beauty, too dependable, the same every time. There was something obscene about such beauty, something not beautiful at all. Mary, who had once been the demure mother of Jesus, wore an orgasmic expression during this phase. Still in her blue gown, her eyes rolled back in her head and her lips lay parted. Gold was everywhere, but you could scratch it off with your fingernail. If Russell belonged to an era other than his own, it was Baroque. Spawn of the Renaissance, full of too much and nothing. She herself belonged to a sparer time and place, though she couldn't say where or when. It was why she was so easily seduced, even undone, by excess – because her own nature was starved and thirsty. These were private theories, compiled over a lifetime. They existed in her mind with the belief that there were bodies in trees, something she knew Russell could not see. She didn't share those thoughts with him any more, for it had been years since he'd found them charming. But in those days, he had shaken his haloed head and opened his wide, laughing mouth. "You're too much," he had told her.

In a way, that was one of the things she had loved most about him in the beginning – how he perceived her. Once he said, in a bungled attempt to be poetic, that she was like someone without skin. "I mean," he said, stumbling, "your skin is amazing, but it's like you've got no protective layer. You really feel things." He blushed, which was rare for him. And then he said: "I've never met anyone like you."

She wanted to be that way again, but Marie Halliwell – Marie Loden – was long dead and buried.

⦅⦆⦆⦆⦆

When the Munich Olympics began, Kay was in her late twenties, still a waitress working for her parents, and the single mother of three children. She had stopped comparing herself to the Larysa Latyninas who came and went in a four-year cycle, but Olga Korbut, the munchkin of Munich, might have been made in Kay's image – a sprightly little human with endearing faults.

Louis LeBlanc, who had inherited his mother's fondness for gymnastics, didn't like Olga Korbut at all. He resented her grin and the show-off manner that proved she didn't take the sport seriously. Louis did. He had grown into a boy who took everything seriously. By now he had stopped measuring the rip in his screen, but he still believed in the hairy arm. Just last winter, he had seen footprints circling the house. They had not been there at night, when he'd gone to bed, but in the morning when he left for school, he saw them. They were big prints, the prints of a man, and they stopped at every window. He stood on the street, sagging beneath the weight of his knapsack, looking back at the house and considering telling his mother about the footprints. He wished he was a man already, and then he would know how to take care of things on his own, but he would not be a man for a long time, and even then, he would be a small one.

"Come on," said Estelle, pulling his arm, and Louis obeyed, as always.

From his desk at school, he watched the snow swirl through the air outside, and paid no attention to his studies. He knew the footprints back at home were being filled in with snow so that, as with the arm, he would never be sure if they had been there at all. But whether they were real tracks or ghost tracks, he decided they belonged to his father. Dead or alive, Joe checked on each of them in the night, as he certainly must have when he'd lived in the house with them. He took big steps through the snow and cupped his hands against the glass to see them sleeping peacefully. The hairy arm had not been his – Louis was certain – but Joe could not have been far behind the arm as it reached in to steal Louis, and he – Joe – could be the only reason for the arm disappearing as rapidly as it had come. These were the things Louis knew in his gut.

By September of 1972, Louis was ten years old and had sprouted to four-foot-three, thanks to Alphonse and Toussaint's trampoline gift, but he was still uncommonly tiny, and no one doubted that he always would be. He remained determined to become an Olympic gymnast like Sawao Kato, and was enrolled in three gymnastics classes a week. He also practised at home on the trampoline, and on a beam Alphonse and Toussaint had constructed in the backyard, next to the playhouse. In 1972, he was most excited about seeing Sawao again. In all this time he had continued to worship the gymnast, and Sawao, in a way, had become Louis's friend.

In Munich, as in Mexico City, Sawao Kato did not disappoint. He won three gold medals and two silver ones, and went down in history as the number-two top athlete at Munich, but in the end, Louis did not feel the unbridled joy or kinship he had experienced four years earlier, because a massacre had been played out on television and turned the Games into a horror movie. He was not allowed to watch horror movies, but he was allowed to watch this. His mother stood beside him and tried to explain what was happening, but her mouth kept falling open before she could finish her sentences. None of it made any sense to him. The Games were on hold and then they were not, except nothing was as it had been before, no matter what anyone pretended. For days afterwards, Louis thought about the men who had hopped the fence to get into the Olympic Village, and how no one had tried to stop them because all athletes hopped fences. They had worn track suits as a kind of camouflage, and carried their weapons in athletic bags. They had blown people apart with those weapons, and then they had been blown apart themselves. He thought about the arm that had tried to get him while he slept. Danger could be anywhere, wearing any disguise.

For the rest of the Games, the many flags of the world flew at half-mast in the Olympic Village, and an invisible poison hung over Munich. It spilled out from television screens and floated all over the world and into the lungs and heart of Louis LeBlanc. He watched the closing ceremonies with the blank face of someone who had been cheated. He was too young to understand the tragedy for what it was – something different from every angle – but he knew that an appalling event had occurred, crashing into a time when the world, despite the high spirit of competition, had come together as one. He had a vague sense that it had been damaging in a way that would be hard to repair.

All this was apparent in the thousands of faces who paraded in the closing ceremonies, and in the faces of the crowd who watched them. It was apparent in Louis's face too, small and sad, paler than a normal boy's. He held a bowl of popcorn in his lap as he watched the countries pour in. He liked to test himself to see if he knew which flag belonged to which country, and he was reaching out to turn the volume down in order to play that game, when he saw Joe LeBlanc among the faces of the athletes. Louis froze. Joe was marching with the team from England. Louis recognized him instantly, though for years his features had been faded and obscure. Head-to-toe, he was dressed in blue. The Union Jack blazed out from his chest. His long legs scissored and hurried him along too quickly. He was moving faster than the others, and faster than the camera too, which meant that soon he would be out of sight, and Louis might never see him again. He could do nothing but hover on his knees with his arm stretched out. He strained to see every detail of Joe's face – the hooked nose, the bony cheeks, what his uncles called a face like a hawk – and just before he stepped off the screen, Joe LeBlanc looked into the camera, right into Louis's eyes, and Louis knew Joe had seen him. His father had seen him.

And just like that, he was gone, and the Games were over.

"Was my father of English descent?" asked Louis that night as Kay tucked him into bed.

"What?" she said, laughing. "No, Louis, he was French. *Joséph LeBlanc*," she said, using an accent.

"But did he have an English background? The way you're Irish, but not?"

"No!" said Kay, tucking his blanket under his chin. "He was French through and through, with maybe a bit of Algonquin thrown in."

Louis wanted to be part Algonquin too, but he showed no sign of high cheekbones or a bony nose. The shape of his face was egg-like and his curved nose was no beak, but maybe it would be one day. Maybe he, too, would resemble a hawk.

"Why are you asking about England?"

Louis shrugged. He thought about telling her how he had seen Joe in the closing ceremonies, and perhaps about the screen and the arm and the way Joe had saved him, and how he had seen Joe's footprints in the snow, but all of it together sounded made-up and foolish, and letting it out might spoil it. He said instead, "Dunno."

His mother kissed him goodnight and left the door open a crack. The trunk and the branches of the tree outside climbed up his wall and stretched all over his ceiling in a spooky maze that moved with the breeze. It was still warm, and his bedroom window was open, and he could hear footsteps on the sidewalk, a sound that grew and diminished. He did not know why he felt so frightened, having seen Joe. He had felt safe when he'd thought about the arm and the footprints, once he'd reasoned it out. Again he experienced the cold feeling that had come over him when Joe had looked into his eyes from inside the television. He remembered the eyes of Clothilde and Pierrette in Alphonse's photograph, and also what Alphonse had said about spirits: "You just invite them in. Look around and you will see them everywhere." And he remembered the bags of garbage that had shown up on the curb just after the last Olympics – had it been Joe or an angel raking the yard? He shivered under his covers and closed his eyes against the black branches on the ceiling.

⬤⬤⬤⬤⬤

Joe LeBlanc was born in White Pine, Ontario, the little village that drowned. Perhaps one day it would be found again, like Pompeii – a place Marie and Russell had visited, from which Russell had pocketed a piece of wall, deep red, enchanting, but Marie had not been able to live with the gift, stolen so boldly, and had thrown it into the River Tiber. If one day it was rediscovered, attempts might be made to restore White Pine to its former glory, but this was unlikely, of course, because the village had never been anything special – at least not in the Roman sense of the word. Some 1,670 years after Mount Vesuvius had smothered it in volcanic debris, Pompeii was found at the end of a paper trail of clues that led the curious back in time. Where was this place that appeared in ancient literature but nowhere at all on earth? A lifeline of words pulled a whole civilization, bones and all, out of the rubble. No such lifeline existed for White Pine, therefore White Pine itself had ceased to exist.

Nevertheless, Joe LeBlanc was born and raised there, on the banks of the Ottawa, and he had remained until the day it was obliterated. The town was flooded in 1959, and a dam went up in its place. Before the water rushed in, all the trees were felled and the houses, containing a mishmash of things left behind by Delphine LeBlanc and others, were burned in a great fire. The smoke could be seen and smelled across the county, across the river, across Algonquin Park and beyond. The dam was named White Pine, after the village that had been desecrated in its honour. Once home to generations of rivermen, now it was buried in water. Most of its stories had gone under too, but the tale of Jacques's death lived on. When Jacques died, Joe had been six years old, raised knowing that the river had a monster's strength. As Alphonse and Toussaint recounted it to Louis, a monster had thrown Jacques into the air again and again, and it had taken more than an hour for the other men to calm the already dead body and bring it solemnly to shore.

White Pine was steeped in the drama of small, simple lives. No history books recorded it, but if a person dove down to the bloated heart of the town, he would see street signs still standing, enduring a watery existence like the gloves of Robbie Hayes, which had stayed behind when he was pulled lifeless from that jagged hole. Something had floated out of his pocket that night, as he'd plunged through the ice: a letter to a girl who would never know he loved her. The words had run on the paper. They'd lifted in a blue cloud, and the ink that had said so much so sparingly had been lost in a river of blue.

The girl had been one of the two who'd left the ice before Robbie had fallen through, and if only he had been more courageous and spoken to her, or given her the letter, he might have unlaced his skates alongside her and gone with her and her friend for hot chocolate or apple cider, and there would have been a beginning, not an end. He would have avoided the weak fault in the ice, and his puzzling encounter with Joe LeBlanc. But Robbie had feared rejection. He had feared the laughter of the other girl, the awkwardness of having someone other than the two of them present as he proclaimed his love, and so he had done nothing but skate vague circles around her, hoping to send out his message in the swish of his blades. She had barely glanced at him, but he had not minded. There were days, weeks, months ahead, an infinity in which to broach the subject of love. Once the holidays were over, he'd return to university, but she would be there too, in accounting, sitting at the desk in front of him as she pencilled numbers into long columns, numbers that swam in front of his eyes amid the heady aroma of her peach shampoo. He'd thought of her fine hand holding her pencil, he thought of the back of her neck and her hair fashioned into a curious twist. He'd thought of the letter tucked into his pocket, not knowing that the words had already escaped and floated down to the riverbed. The blank paper had been down there too, fish nibbling its corners. Before the letter had disintegrated completely, it had drifted along the rippled sand, bumping and twirling, until it had reached the underwater town of White Pine, and the submerged signs marking the streets that went nowhere.

When Joe's mother had moved south, Joe had stayed behind to study carpentry with Alphonse and Toussaint. But what he'd *really* wanted was to move into the Park and live on fish and berries. He'd tried that on and off until the day he met Kay Clancy. Love had shifted his focus, and made him forget what he was doing, and why.

At the time of the Munich Olympics, Estelle, Louis, and Margar didn't know about the quiet scandal born in that time, and the lies that followed, but Kay lived with the knowledge daily. In fact, living with it had become ordinary, as anything does after a while, but there were times when the truth pushed through and looked her square in the eye.

"Was my father of English descent?"

The formal way he'd phrased it put Joe at such a distance that even Kay, who had loved him close up, couldn't picture him clearly. She did her best to answer calmly, and then she kissed him goodnight, pulled his door almost closed, and went to check on Estelle and Margar, who were already sleeping. She stood in the room, listening to them breathe. A moonbeam shone through the window and brightened the little dog-eared snapshot of Joe and Estelle in the hospital. Eleven years, nearly twelve, had passed since that day. Joe had another daughter – his own – whom he had never met, who was starting to ask about him but who seemed unaffected by anything she learned. Her curiosity was more about herself than about Joe, which Kay supposed was normal, for how could a child miss what she had not ever known? Because it seemed so unfair that Margar had never seen Joe, Kay told her she had – that she had been with him in his last happy days, watching from the safe, dark world of Kay's stomach.

"So my eye looked through your belly button?" said Margar.

"Sort of," said Kay. "In a way."

"And it was when I was dead that I saw him?" At this her eyes glittered.

"You weren't dead!"

"Well, I wasn't alive, was I?"

"No, but –"

"So I was dead."

"You weren't dead, Margar. You just weren't born yet."

Margar paused. "But I wasn't alive," she said quietly, and her lips curled into a satisfied grin.

Kay let it go at that. She realized she and Joe had been apart for longer than they had been together, and thinking that, she twisted the ring on her finger. In months she would throw it. Standing at the edge of the river, close to the spot where Robbie Hayes had drowned, she'd fling the gold band through the air and watch it plunk into the water with barely a ripple. She'd feel lighter all over having let him go. That was what he'd wanted, after all – nothing to do with her.

And like so many other discarded things, the ring would see-saw through the water to the bottom. The fish would swim around it, not biting. Nothing startled them these days. They wouldn't bother to watch as the ring drifted to the riverbed and sat round and unblinking, like an eye looking up, looking out beyond the water, awaiting the day of rescue.

⬭⬭⬭

It came as no surprise to Margar that she had seen Joe before she was born. Just as she was arriving, he was heading out, so it made sense that they would pass along the way. Not recognizing each other, they had nodded politely and carried on with their separate journeys. The distance stretched between them. She kept moving, but looked over her shoulder every few steps. He had been *so* familiar. His lanky frame had moved by her and his pained brown eyes had met hers. She'd seen his long face of many angles, and she'd watched it turn in profile. The hooked nose had made her touch her own nose, so recently formed. Before she realized who he was, he'd become a speck in the distance — portaging, carrying all the clues to himself on his back, on his head, in his pockets. She would have yelled, but she hadn't yet been born, so yelling was impossible. Instead she watched him go. He failed to experience a matching revelation. Or if he did, he never turned to confirm it.

⟨⟨⟨⟨⟨⟩⟩⟩⟩⟩

Once more, ice closed over the river and the town turned white. Strings of lights were untangled and draped over trees and houses to liven the monotony brought by the snow. With Christmas came Justin Trudeau's first birthday, and one year later, brother Alexandre would be born. The country basked in the happiness of its leading family.

Before Christmas, Margar had passed the days burrowing a snowy passageway through which she planned to travel vast distances, searching for Joe. She might even make it as far as Montreal, where he had gone, some said, by Voyageur bus. She hoped she would recognize him once she saw him, and thought of the stories on television about siblings who'd been separated since birth, and when they met again, discovered each loved pink, each had big black dogs, each wore her hair in an up-do. Perhaps the same could be true of a father and child — but of course the details would be different: Joe wouldn't wear an up-do. And neither would Margar, really.

She worked for what seemed like hours, pawing at the snow with her mittens, but when she eventually stopped to scoop holes for spying, she saw she'd only made it halfway down the drive. She enlisted Louis to help her, but things had gone awry. She watched him inch along in his snowsuit, wiggling his bum and digging his boots in to push himself through, and though she was grateful for his help, she couldn't resist ever so quietly filling in the opening behind him as he worked away on her tunnel.

"It was selfish and mean," said Kay afterwards, and banished Margar to her room. "And my God, Margar, it was dangerous."

Which Margar couldn't at all understand. In her opinion, it had only been funny. And hadn't she helped dig him out as soon as he called for her? That had been funny too. His words garbled, his voice shrill with fear.

"I don't know what to do with you," Kay told her. "It never stops, Margar. Maybe you shouldn't get any presents this year."

"Noooo!" Margar pleaded. And thinking fast, added, "I didn't even know he was in there!"

"But you asked him to help —"

"No, no, I forgot! I know I asked him, but I didn't mean right then, I meant later, and then I changed my mind and decided I didn't want a stupid tunnel after all, so I thought I better clean up like you're always —"

"Stop," said Kay. "Never mind." She paused, frowning at Margar, and said finally, "No stocking."

"No fair!" cried Margar. "The stocking is almost the best part!" And though she didn't believe in him, she said, "Santa brings that stuff, not you, you can't just —"

"I'll take care of Santa," said Kay, and with that, she left the room.

Margar had thrown herself on her bed, weeping for the Santa she didn't believe in, for the impossibility of the tunnel, and most of all, for Joe. Weeping – but thinking, at the same time, that at least the real presents had been spared.

⬤⬤⬤⬤⬤

On Christmas morning, before the sun came up, she woke to a sound like sleigh rails scraping against crusty snow, and she entertained the idea that Santa existed after all. Ready as she was to accept miracles, she hadn't ever had solid evidence of him. The sound kept repeating, and unless Santa with his sleigh and all his reindeer were spinning and landing giant backflips, this couldn't possibly be him. Margar got out of bed. Quiet as a snowflake, she tiptoed past Estelle, down the hall past Louis's room, and out to the living room, where the tree stood lit up with the presents beneath it, just as it had at midnight when she'd spied on Kay stuffing the stockings – Margar's too, and Margar's heart had swelled with gratitude. She would be good, she promised silently, from this second on. At two o'clock, and at three, when Margar squeezed the stockings to discern their contents, the house still sat idle as a doll's house, waiting for morning. On the coffee table were the cookies Kay herself had nibbled while Margar had watched from the dark hallway. An old rusty bell, apparently from Santa's sleigh, rested beside them. It showed up Christmas after Christmas, with no explanation as to how Santa had retrieved it in order to lose it again the next year.

Margar followed the scraping sound to the kitchen. The daisy-shaped clock on the wall read five-thirty, too early for cartoons, but definitely morning. She parted the green kitchen curtains and looked outside. The streetlights glowed against the dark sky, and the snow appeared pale blue. Near the garage, a man was shovelling. He pushed the big curved blade along and lifted the blue snow, tossing it onto a blue snowbank that was almost as high as the garage window.

The shoveller wore a hat with earflaps and fur boots that came to his knees. He was working quickly, with no breaks, and each time he sent the snow flying up to the snowbank, a matching fog of white puffed from his lips and was gone again. He was moving down the driveway, leaving a clearing behind him, when he glanced up and saw Margar. She gathered the curtains under her chin and imagined how she must look to him – a floating head in the black spooky morning. But at that, she could not help grinning, which she knew ruined the spookiness. The shoveller grinned back, and she recognized him as Ms. Devlin's brother, Gus. She let the curtains fall closed, scurried to the kitchen door, and opened it.

An icy gust rushed in at her, over her bare toes, and up inside her nightie. Sparkles of snow dusted her nose and forehead.

"You should get back inside!" Gus called in a whisper-shout. "It's freezing out here."

"I'm not cold," said Margar.

Gus smiled, but shook his head and turned away from her to resume shovelling. The chill swirled around her and tickled her up and down. The rims of her ears shivered and tiny invisible teeth began biting her long toes. She curled them under. She cupped her hands around her mouth and called quietly to Gus.

"What are you doing?"

But Gus didn't answer. He kept shovelling as though Margar wasn't there. She pushed the door open further and leaned out, and he turned at the sound of it creaking.

"You're a nut!" he said. He sounded serious, but not mean.

Right away she thought of all the nuts in their frustrating shells, and the special nut bowl and the nutcracker that only came out at Christmas.

"A walnut?" she asked.

He tossed a little spray of snow towards her, as if to push her back inside. "I won't have anything to do with you if you keep hanging out the door like that," he said. "Your nose is going to turn blue and fall off if you don't go in."

Margar giggled.

"And your ears, too," he said, pointing. "I can see them coming loose already." And he wiggled one of the flaps on his hat.

"But I —"

Gus held up his hand. "This conversation is over," he told her, turning back to his task.

Margar pulled the creaky door closed with as little sound as possible. She sailed through the sleeping house to the front closet, where she put on her snowsuit and boots, her hat and mittens, all the things she railed against wearing on a regular day, and then she skulked back to the kitchen, moving gingerly to hush the rustle of her snowsuit.

(((((( ))))))

By the time Kay woke, a snowman stood in the yard. He was not a typical snowman, consisting of three balls stacked up, but a sculpted body with arms and legs. He wore Joe's black toque on his head, and his large eyes were spirals of birdseed that stared in through the living-room window with a dead-man's gaze. Two pine cones made his smile, and his nose was a cluster of withered crabapples that had not fallen from the tree in Ramona's yard.

As the cold, white sun emerged, Margar trudged a neat path through the yard to cover the mess of footprints made during the snowman's construction. Her mittens hung from their strings, and her hat lay forgotten in the snow. Her big ears and her cheeks flushed pink, as much from excitement as from cold, Kay knew. She lifted her fist to the window to knock on the glass, but it was then that she saw Gus Devlin. He stood at the bottom of the drive, his hands and his chin resting on his shovel. He nodded once in a slow greeting, and smiled as though he had been watching her for some time. Kay felt her heart expand, just for an instant. She opened her fist and spread her fingers in a wave.

He spoke to Margar then, and put his shovel on his shoulder. In his tall, furry boots, he began walking back to his sister's house, but Kay, before she could stop herself, was rapping on the window and motioning for him to come in. And so it was that Gus Devlin, who lived up the Valley but had come to spend Christmas with Ramona, sat in the LeBlanc kitchen that morning, eating a slice of the traditional Christmas Breakfast Roll and gulping hot, sugary tea like a member of the family. Margar did most of the talking – *How old are you? Do you love root beer? Are your boots made out of dead raccoons? Do you have a colour television?* – but it was Kay who had taken a sudden, inexplicable leap forward. When Louis and Estelle got up and began dumping out the contents of their Christmas stockings, Gus pulled his boots back on and thanked Kay for the breakfast. He tugged Margar's ear and said, "'Take care of that snowman," and he was off. Through the kitchen window, Kay watched him saunter down the newly cleared driveway with his shovel on his shoulder, and through the living-room window, she watched him mosey along the sidewalk, and then through the window in Margar's bedroom, where she pretended to be fluffing pillows, she watched him kick the snow from his boots at Ramona's side door. And just as she clutched the pillow to her chest and had a long gaze at his sturdy form and his broad shoulders, he turned and waved. Red as beetroot, heart clanging, Kay waved back.

Behind her, unseen and soundless, Margar beamed and slipped from the room.

◯◯◯◯◯

In the blue two-storey, a third, uneventful Christmas passed in the absence of Eddie Halliwell. He wrote rarely, and had begun to sign his letters "Edward." Marie Halliwell missed her son, but the longer he stayed away, the more peaceful she felt, and the more hope she had for his uncomplicated future.

She sent him a care package at Christmas, and as always, it included his gifts, a Christmas Breakfast Roll, and an ornament to decorate his room. Just before sealing the box, she thought to include a book of hers he had once loved: Vasari's *Lives of the Artists*. She wondered what he was drawing these days, and how the world of art was unfolding for him. She remembered her own university years, and what an exciting time it had been, and she hoped the same was true for Eddie – but that something more would come of his studies than had of hers. Her education lived in a box in the storage closet, even though, when she graduated, her enthusiasm had sent her sailing across the ocean on a ship called the *Conte Biancamano* – the Count of the White Hand.

She'd had no inkling of what was to come of her life as she pressed against the ship's rail and looked down at the water. She had worn her hair tied up and covered with a hat to keep the wind from snarling it, and every day after an early break-fast, she came out and stood near the prow, leaning into the wind to help the ship move faster. Only once did she arrive on deck too late to assume her favourite spot. A crowd of passen-gers had gathered there, jostling and shoving for a rail-side view. But as Marie drew closer, she realized they were fighting to see something in the water.

"What is it?" she asked, but the woman next to her – baggy-eyed, grey with seasickness – looked past her and didn't answer.

"What is it?" she asked again, but this time a man with a walrus moustache blinked and turned away, as though he hadn't seen her at all.

Marie pushed through the herd of people. She saw something in the water. A body, face down, wearing bright green with a shimmer of gold, like the shot taffeta dress Marie had brought along for formal occasions. And there were the gold buttons, rising up on a whitecap and sinking, and then a foot slipped out of its black shoe, which a wave licked into the ocean. The hat that had kept her hair free of tangles floated off of the body in the water, revealing her own hair, pinned up with its ruby clip. The body sloshed and rolled, and as it turned, her own white face became clear to her before it disappeared. With a last billow, the full, pleated skirt of her dress washed under, and Marie Loden watched herself go with it.

She woke up gasping for breath in her cabin. The dress was hanging on the closet door in front of her, a headless apparition. *It's only a dream*, she told herself. But she never wore the dress again. She rolled it up and buried it in her valise, but shuddered every time she came across it on her travels through Italy. Eventually she left the dress in Sorrento, hanging wrinkled in a closet. It didn't fit her by then anyway. Her waist had thickened with Eddie.

Again she mused about his life away from home. He offered scant information in his letters, but she knew that in the spring he'd be finished his studies. Whatever his plans were, she didn't expect him to come home. He was twenty-one years old, after all. A man. He had begun to make his way in the world.

Once more at Christmas, all she received from him was a card, "Love Edward," which broke her heart, but she said nothing to Russell. In previous years, Russell had called Eddie ungrateful when no presents arrived, and so, aching for all of them, this year she'd bought gifts for Russell and herself in Eddie's name.

The card Eddie sent arrived late, and a hideous storm came with it. Impossibly, the winds brought sleet from every direction at once, colliding and raining down on the Valley, knocking out the power for more than a week. Those who didn't have woodstoves – or wood – gathered in the Catholic church and the high-school gymnasium and were cared for by competent volunteers like Ms. Devlin, who had once been a nurse and always kept her wits during times of adversity.

Those who remained in their homes – such as Alphonse and Toussaint LeBlanc, and also the Halliwells, who had a top-of-the-line woodstove – ate canned beans and potatoes cooked over a fire once the Christmas turkey's carcass had been scraped clean. No other meat could be thawed in such frigid conditions.

The storm brought beauty with its devastation. Marie Halliwell stood at her picture window wrapped in blankets and watched the snow fall on the trees and on the frozen river. Hydro lines hung heavy, and in places, the poles had crashed to the ground. Ice coated the trees and made them shine while it smothered them. It grew on the climbing roses, spreading all over the exterior walls of the house, and Marie had the claustrophobic sensation that it was encasing them too, and that one morning they would awaken unable to breathe because they lived in a box of ice that would never melt and free them.

At the same time, she felt safe and peaceful. When she discovered that the doors would no longer open, that they had been sealed shut by the weather, she realized there was nowhere to go anyway, and she got back under the blankets with Russell and read by firelight, as she had done the day before and the day before that. The snow and the ice covered all the vegetation in her yard. She could see no trace of the weeds or the long-neglected perennials that often poked their heads through the snow.

Several times she contemplated taking people in. It would be the gracious, Christmas thing to do. But she didn't want strangers around, and she was glad when Russell, day after day, didn't raise the issue. She wondered if it even occurred to him. She thought of the time he had taken a chunk of red wall from Pompeii, with no regard for the importance of history, no awe for the ancient place or what was left of it. He had taken the relic for her, she knew, but also for himself, for there was boastfulness in the deed, a kind of pride and arrogance. *He takes what he wants*, she thought. *He does what he wants.* She still couldn't decide if it was an admirable trait or a deplorable one.

And all the while as she questioned his character, she drank up the sound of his voice in the darkness. He told her how the snow formed in the atmosphere and fell as it grew heavy, and how it turned into rain and then snow again as it floated through the varying temperatures in the sky, deciding what to be when it landed. He said it was rare, even here, to have a storm so potent, but Maric didn't believe anything was rare in this place. Or rather, she didn't believe that anything rare should be unexpected. Twenty years on, she had not warmed to the Valley, but she'd developed a reverence for its ruthless, untameable nature.

⬤⬤⬤⬤⬤

Kay kept her family at home for too long during the ice storm. By the time they sought shelter in Our Lady of the Snows Church, the church was already full, and they had no choice but to stay in the high-school gymnasium. The basketball hoops and the coloured stripes on the floor made her anxious. She looked around for the Halliwells, wondering if they had come as well, but she didn't see them in the crowd.

Her parents were staying in the gymnasium too, and had donated food from the restaurant, and Ramona Devlin was bustling around ensuring everyone had a place to sleep. Kay wanted to find a moment to speak to her, and casually drop

Gus into the conversation, but such an exchange seemed trivial under the circumstances, since Ramona, like some sort of tough Florence Nightingale, had barely a free moment. Instead, Kay laid out sleeping bags for herself and her children and watched Margar chase Louis around the gymnasium as though it were a place of no special significance. Of course, for them, that was true.

Across town, Serge and Beryl Hayes lay beneath a very significant ceiling in the basement of Our Lady of the Snows Church. Each was thinking separately of their son's body, carried exactly eight years before, along the aisle above them. They may have found some comfort had they been able to share their private thoughts, and they came close to doing so, but each moved away again, still lost in the sea of memory and blame. Kay, too, may have found some comfort had she ever been able to tell someone her secrets. But she was miles past that point. She had hidden them too long ago, and now they were root-bound inside her.

Once the beds were made, Estelle sat down and said, "Mom, do you realize – next year this will be my school?"

And Kay, sick with dread, said, "Yes, I realize," but smiled when the words came out.

All night, while friends and strangers coughed and muttered in their sleep, Kay lay awake and thought about what had happened here in the gym, this time from the perspective of a woman and mother. She saw Russell Halliwell above her in the dim light. As his pleasure increased, Kay's presence had seemed less related to what he was feeling and why, and she remembered how she'd felt herself disappearing beneath him. All night she thought of that, rather than of her glory days, lived out concurrently in this very room on the balance beam and the mat. She followed the memory through to the Halliwells' garden, where she'd stood in her sundress, her hair caught up in a ponytail. She hadn't been aware of it then, or for a long time afterward, but she'd been a child herself when the child inside her shifted the course of the future. Maybe that changed things. It might even excuse her in part.

She turned in her sleeping bag so she wouldn't be facing the basketball hoop, and instead faced Estelle, sleeping peacefully. Estelle had Russell's dimple, his wide jaw and perfect teeth, and the confidence that enhances good looks. If she'd been a boy, the resemblance would have been obvious. Estelle's mouth came slightly open and her eyes moved under her eyelids, and Kay marvelled at how she could sleep so soundly in a room full of people. But Estelle had always adapted to any situation as if she were meant to be a part of it, as if the situation itself would not exist without her. If Estelle had received any intangible characteristic from the Halliwell bloodline, this was it.

As she looked at the soft curve of Estelle's lashes and her blonde curls on the pillow, Kay couldn't believe Estelle would ever come to do the things she herself had done – not with the coach, of course. He was her father, and he knew it. Or rather, he was her biological father. A real father was full of love and encouragement for his child. More basic than that, he was present. So Estelle had no father at all. Even Joe, in the end, had betrayed her.

Still, she couldn't imagine Estelle growing into a teenager foolish enough to fall for a teacher, a man in his thirties. Estelle would never. And if she did, she certainly couldn't be held responsible. That someone would take advantage of her that way, when she was still new and vulnerable, was disgusting to Kay.

But what was the difference, she thought. *What was the difference with me?*

She wished she could sleep, if only so she wouldn't lie awake, wishing harder for the days when time and experience had not changed her. Once she had been someone who didn't linger in the past, but in recent years something kept pulling her back, urging her to look for what was lost or unfinished. Since the discovery of the note in the garage, she had been cartwheeling backward instead of forward, and she was uncomfortable with her new, reflective nature. For no reason other than to pass time, she told herself, she thought of Ramona's brother in his hat and boots, appearing out of nowhere in her driveway.

⦅⦆⦅⦆⦅⦆

As Kay lay looking at Estelle, Margar's round eyes flashed open behind her. Lying in a gym full of people, the town in a shambles around them, she was more awake than usual. She knew her mother was awake too, and that beyond her, her sister was fast asleep. Estelle always slept easily, with her mouth almost smiling and her fair brow free of worry. Margar's one dark eyebrow striped her face and gave her a mischievous look that Estelle could not possibly have managed, mischief being nowhere in her aspect or her nature. Like mistletoe, which can strangle a tree if it chooses, and hang shining in its branches, the tendrils of mischief needed something to cling to, and Estelle was so smooth, so pure, that they couldn't take hold.

Head to toe, Margar was covered in mischief. When her mother's breathing assumed the deep, even tones of slumber, she wriggled out of her sleeping bag and stepped over bodies as she crept to the gym doors. She was reminded of the secluded beach outside of town, where Alphonse and Toussaint sometimes took them. Long patches of rock rested in the water there, like whales who were sleeping or dead. You had to be careful as you stepped over the sleek grey backs, or you could wake the living ones and they would roar up and eat you. Margar thought about that as she stepped in woolly socks over her mother and sister and brother, over snoring Ms. Devlin, over the man who owned the variety store and his wife, who clicked her tongue while she slept.

She pushed open the heavy door, and if the light from the corridor woke anyone as it streamed into the gymnasium, they were too groggy to see her go. She ran and slid in her socks along the polished hallway of the biggest school in town. All she had planned to do was have a brief snoop around, but when she stopped at the main doors, she saw Gus Devlin brushing snow off a truck with a plough on its front. She stepped into a triangle of the revolving doors, intending to wave, but before she could catch his attention, he dashed to the other side of the parking lot, where some men had gathered by two snowploughs. A streetlight beamed down on them, and in the shadowy brightness, the snowploughs loomed like yellow dinosaurs. While she watched, another man came out of nowhere, ran up the steps to the school and, not seeing her, pushed hard on the door and set it spinning. Margar flew out into the winter night. She braced herself for the whipping wind, the biting cold, the hail that could slash you to ribbons. But there was none of that. The black stillness was broken only by the men across the way, talking with Gus. So there was a calm after, as well as before a storm.

The air was almost warm in comparison to the last few days, but in seconds it was too cold to be outside clad in socks, long johns, and flannel pyjamas. A good girl – Estelle – would have gone straight back inside, but then a good girl – Estelle – would not have snuck out of bed in the first place. Margar glanced around. The truck with the plough on the front was idling, its exhaust drifting up in a smoky plume. The men across the parking lot, Gus included, were deep in conversation, and behind her, no one looked out from the school. With the stealth of a burglar, Margar rushed the few snowy paces to the truck, grabbed the cold door handle, and climbed into the back seat, closing the door behind her. She peeked out the rear window to see if she'd been detected, but the men remained in their huddle, unaware of her infiltration. Settling in among a heap of blankets that seemed placed there just for her, Margar was warm in no time, and more than pleased with herself.

When Gus hopped into the truck and started driving, she got so giddy hiding behind him that she had to stuff her mouth with a corner of blanket to keep from laughing out loud. Together they rode around town without him even suspecting her presence, and it amazed her that there wasn't a smell or a colour spilling out of her to give her away. How could he not sense her, when the near-ness of him bristled the hairs on her scalp? His breathing, and then his humming, brushed against her face where it peered out from the blanket – the breath like a feather tickling, the hum thick like velvet. He was humming Christmas songs. She wanted to tell him which ones she knew on the piano, but she couldn't say a word. As she sat in the rich drone of his voice, the plough scooped snow and the banks grew higher and higher.

◯◯◯◯◯

What she claimed afterwards was that she'd been spun out through the revolving doors, and had landed in the back seat of a jeep. The top was open, despite the cold, and Gus in a safari suit was driving. At first the landscape seemed just like Deep River's, but then she realized the streetlamps were giraffes. Their necks stretched up and then drooped, as though their glowing heads were too heavy, and they stood in two rows saluting her. And in behind were the trees, which were not trees but giant moose whose antlers were silhouetted against the sky. Still as marble they were, just waiting to charge. Their angry breath came out through their nostrils, and floated up to make clouds. And the stars were their eyes glinting – at least, all that was what she invented without a breath when Gus discovered her in the back seat.

"Hey you," he said, nudging her. "What are you doing here?"

Not blinking, Margar stared at the air between them. She made her face go stoney and her eyes blank. Gus shook her arm, and she thought her mouth might twitch, so she pretended to wake up and started babbling about the moose and so on, weaving in a giantess with a mane of feathers, and a bald man in a white suit with white platform shoes, until Gus interrupted and asked her again,

"What are you doing here?"

215

"Oh," said Margar, yawning and rubbing her eyes. "I must have been sleepwalking."

He took her back through the town, into the school, over the sleeping whales in the gymnasium, and shook her mother awake.

"She says she was sleepwalking. Right into the back seat of my truck," he whispered, and Kay, drowsy and confused, muttered, "Oh my God, thank you – oh Margar – yes, well, she does that sometimes."

She opened Margar's sleeping bag and tucked her daughter in, then curled around her to warm her up.

"Thank you," she whispered to Gus, who still crouched above them.

Safe in her mother's embrace, Margar stole one last glance at Gus Devlin, Earl of Pembroke, plougher of roads, shoveller of drives, expert builder of snowmen, and almost as fine a man as Joe. Half smirking, half frowning, Gus looked down at her, and she saw that he was not easily fooled. In spite of herself, she grinned, and fell fast asleep until morning.

⬤⬤⬤⬤⬤

Winter weather was rough in Halifax, but Eddie – Edward – was untouched by the ice storm that raged through the Ottawa Valley. He'd received the package from his mother in the days leading up to Christmas, and when he opened it, he discarded the trinkets, gave the Christmas Breakfast Roll to his roommates without pausing to smell it, and hung the clothes in his closet beside last year's clothes, huge and unworn. He was nowhere near that size now. When he'd first arrived, he'd imagined himself gorging every day on battered clams and chips, but he'd quickly lost his taste for them and all the rich, fat-soaked food that had been one of his few sources of joy. As though to purge his body and his life of its former excesses – disgusting to him now – he moved to the opposite extreme, living on fruit and dry bread, or soup in the freezing winter. His very being assumed a greater intensity as the bulk of him lessened and the bones that held him together showed beneath his skin. He was an attractive young man, but there was a brutality about him that continued to keep everyone at a distance. Which was the way he liked it.

By this time, he had dabbled in most of the programs the college had to offer – sculpture, ceramics, photography. He had even taken a part-time job in what was called "the cage," where the costly photo equipment was kept and signed out to students, and occasionally he used the cameras himself. But painting was still his main area of study. Week in and week out, he painted large abstract canvasses that held no relevance for him beyond the occasional mild amusement he found in their colour and form. He wondered what he was doing, and why, and how long it would take him to know. His anger boiled when he looked around at the other students, for he knew they had to be asking themselves the same thing, which meant that he was no different, and by extension, his ideas were just as dispensable. When he overheard them discussing their meaningless works about meaninglessness, he would have laughed out loud if he hadn't felt such despair inside his fury. All that set him apart from the other students was his growing certainty that the world was no better than this place, only bigger. And so while the others sauntered around campus, got up in smelly, second-hand clothes, their hair hanging in greasy strands, Edward honed his outer differences. He shaved his head, right to the scalp, with a straight razor. And in the process, he felt he'd obliterated "Eddie" from within him.

But when the Christmas box arrived, made beautiful by his mother's delicate penmanship, Edward ripped through the shiny paper and the curled ribbons, disclaiming each gift until he reached the bottom of the box and discovered Vasari's *Lives of the Artists*. The flood of nostalgia felt just like nausea, and he experienced a sudden, grave longing for the boy he had almost been.

As he thumbed through the pages he'd studied years before, he recalled reading by flashlight late into the night, wanting to know everything about every great artist who had lived in the Renaissance. Those books had been his main source of information back then – his mother's school texts from the 1940s about an even more distant time. He had lived in fourteenth-, fifteenth-, sixteenth-century Italy, and in ancient Greece and Rome, while in New York City, Andy Warhol made Marilyn Monroe's face red, blue, green, repeated. Eddie had been so ensconced in the past that he had not been aware of the present, and all the movements between. Now he knew that John Lennon had met Yoko Ono when he'd walked into a white room with a ladder, and that only because he had climbed the ladder had he seen the tiny word *yes* on the ceiling. Edward finally understood the beauty of that; he understood also that not long ago it would have baffled him, because one of the things he'd loved about art was its specificity. Art was a painting that hung on a wall, a world contained within a frame, or it was a sculpture that allowed you to view it from every angle. It was not – at least for him, not until recently — a piece of sky or a grapefruit.

But while Eddie's definition of art had expanded, he couldn't find himself within it any more. He couldn't write *yes* on a ceiling because it had been done before, and if he had learned anything in the last three years, he knew that art would not be found in repetition. "The brilliance," St. Clair had insisted, "is in the idea." But Edward had no ideas. He thought of writing *no* on a ceiling as a clever response to the Ono piece, but as soon as the idea came, he knew it was simple, even pedestrian, and however private the thought had been, he felt the heat of humiliation prickling his skin. Even if it had been a worthy idea, it wasn't the kind he craved. He didn't want to respond, cleverly or otherwise, but to say something — to make something — that was entirely his own.

And now, looking at this old favourite book, he remembered when ideas had poured out of him, and how he had not even thought of them as ideas. They had just come and he had put them down on paper. He had been copying from life, yes, but he had *chosen* what to copy. He had known he wanted the wet black eye of the sparrow to stare up at him — into him — from the page, and that there had to be a way to show it breathing, alive, even though it was already dead.

He wished he could look at those pictures now, alongside the masterpieces in his mother's book, which still impressed him. He felt there was something he had owned then, something he was missing now, that might inspire him if he could reclaim it, and help him feel less empty. But any of the sketches he had brought with him he had thrown away in his first year of study, as part of his own personal renaissance.

It had been years since he'd taken his knife to an animal, and though he didn't like to recall it, he well remembered how it had made him feel. At first he'd killed them quickly, but later he made himself slow down, and watch their faces as they died. The actual moment of death brought relief for the animal, and for Eddie as well. Before and during the suffering, he felt the pressure of his skin tighten around him. From his head to his toes, it shrank and squeezed until his breathing grew laboured and his blood ran hot. He could hear himself wheezing. When the animal finally closed his eyes, Eddie's eyes closed too, and for an instant he felt peace beyond measure. And then his head throbbed and his eyes stung. Every muscle in his neck and back turned to rock, and each ground against the next as he ached his way home.

These memories weighed on him, and drew him to others. The last time he had ever hurt an animal, she had appeared at his special place in the woods, the tags on her collar jingling. She had sought him out in his hiding space, and after sniffing him all over and licking his face, she had climbed up onto his fat legs and basked in the sun with him. Saliva streaked his glasses where her tongue had lapped. Edward – Eddie, then – looked through the wet glasses at the top of the dog's head, her alert, twitching ears, one pointing forward, one pointing back. The dog's hair was longish, somewhat limp like human hair could be, and Eddie leaned forward to smell it. Tenderness fluttered through him, but he mistook it for dizziness, which he sometimes experienced, and closed his eyes until the spell was over. When he opened them, he saw that the little dog had arched her head back and was observing him. A sliver of white appeared at the edge of the dog's eye, like the white of a person's eye. The dog sat so close to him that her breath left a warm, moist circle on his cheek, and against his wishes, something within him absorbed that warmth and allowed it to caress his insides.

And then he removed the scalpel from his pocket and, holding the dog's paw, sliced the thick pink pad from the bottom, quickly and without contemplation. He watched the blood gush over his hand and saw a look of shock cross the dog's mottled face, the kind of look a person would give, which surprised him. He opened his arms and invited the dog to leap off of him, but she sat with her face close to his, panting.

Finally, he pushed her, and she limped into the bushes.

⟨⟨⟨⟨⟨⟩⟩⟩⟩⟩

On Christmas Eve, Edward took a long walk through the streets of Halifax. He wore an old army parka and a woollen hat pulled over his shaved head. His scarf was wrapped high so that only his eyes showed behind round glasses. While the clothes he wore these days were second-hand, Edward purchased them out of necessity rather than bohemian vanity, and chose the plainest, most functional items. He prided himself on that. The night was bitterly cold, but he was appropriately bundled.

The little port city was smaller and quieter now that most of the students had gone home for Christmas. Its silence and its proximity to water reminded Edward of Deep River as he strode along the deserted streets. There was no wind tonight, and no cars drove through the centre of town. He felt he was the sole being on earth until he passed Saint Stephen's Church. The heavy wooden doors and the magnificent stained-glass windows were shut tight against the cold, but Edward could hear a chorus

221

of voices rising and falling in celebration. He stepped through the snow to the sprawling graveyard next to the church, and stood among the tombstones, listening. Through the lighted, arched windows, he saw the shadowy figures of worshippers standing to sing with the choir. He moved up and down the rows of graves, which meant he zigzagged, for the graveyard was so old, with so many burial plots squeezed into it, that its rows twisted and merged. Underneath his boots, under the snow and down in the frozen ground were all the bodies the stones commemorated – Emily Lucy Ingram, who had perished of scarlet fever, and Bertram "Bertie" Winterbottom, who had been taken by scurvy, and two sisters, Matilda and Abigail, who had died at sea, one and then the other, on their way here to the new land. The stone they shared was so worn that the last name was illegible, nearly erased. Edward had a sweeping sense of the smallness of life, which translated, for him, into pointlessness. All these people had been born and then died, and surely the world was no different with or without them. Their petty struggles and anxieties, their tiny accomplishments, had been snuffed out and forgotten. In his mind he saw his own dead face, and what shocked him was not the image itself but its failure to surprise him. He concentrated on the tombstones leaning this way and that until the face left him. Some of the stones had almost toppled but come to rest instead on others, and Edward thought of dominoes, a game he had indulged in often as a child, because it could be played, if necessary, alone.

The big doors of the church swung open and a man emerged into the night. Voices rang out behind him and sank low again when the doors closed, and Edward experienced a rush of shivers along with the burst of song. Convinced he'd simply been standing still for too long, he decided he needed to keep moving on a night like tonight. First he would go inside and warm up, and then he would be on his way. Anyone was welcome in churches – that was what was always said – but he braced himself for stares of reproach as he quietly entered.

His glasses fogged and cleared to reveal a woman in a red dress looking over her shoulder at him. Edward readied his cruel glare as he unwrapped his scarf, but the woman's face smiled at him so warmly, so easily, that he glanced behind to see if another person had come in with him. There was no one. The woman nodded at him and turned back to the service. Edward decided that the red dress and the large green bow in her hair gave her the ridiculous look of a human Christmas present, but his heart was thudding in spite of himself. Even though these were people he would have normally scorned for their foolish beliefs and traditional lifestyles, he moved forward and slipped into one of the rear pews, where he remained until the service was over.

And then as the congregation stood and shared wishes of the season, Edward bolted through the doors, into the cold, and moved in giant steps homeward, breathing hard. He was certain the tightening in his chest was caused by the winter air chilling his lungs. Perhaps after all this time he would get asthma, as his mother had predicted, for she had had the condition as a child and had outgrown it, but had always worried it might reappear in Eddie. He gulped mouthfuls of air and felt his eyes tear from the cold. He thought of Our Lady of the Snows Church in Deep River, where they had gone as a family two or three times a year, since his mother loved the singing. She had told him the story of an Italian church with the same name – a Roman patrician and his wife had lost their son and only heir, and asked the Virgin Mary how they could best use what would have been the boy's inheritance. That night, in the middle of summer, snow fell on the summit of the Esquiline Hill. The man and his wife understood the message. They built a basilica and named it Santa Maria ad Nives. Eddie had always remembered that story because the ending had so surprised him: the boy who died had been forever forgotten.

He returned to his room and waited for Christmas. He kept the window open, which must have been why the tightness stayed in his chest. But it was good to feel something. In the gentle, icy breeze, the big clothes his mother had sent shifted in his closet, and Edward fell asleep watching them sway. They were brand new, but to him they were old skins he had shed – the husk of a boy left behind.

⦅⦆⦅⦆

Not long after the ice storm, when the LeBlancs had settled back in to 40 Huron Street, Margar witnessed the intruder. She had just woken and got up to guzzle water from the bathroom tap, and was headed to her room when the front-door knob clicked. She stopped in the hallway, fighting the fuzz of after-sleep. She couldn't tell if the vision that followed was real or a dream, but the gust of cold air that came in with the man and his big parka seemed ordinary enough. It carried a spray of snow that sparkled and disappeared once the door had closed. Margar stepped unseen into her room. She held her breath and listened hard to determine the direction of his footsteps, but she couldn't hear him going anywhere. She peered out the doorway and squinted at him, careful to show as little of her face as possible. His edges appeared thick and blurry, and she tried to blink him into focus but he wouldn't come.

He was shrugging off his pack and removing another bag that had been strapped around his body. He placed them on the floor with something long, which Margar surmised was a rifle in a cloth sack, and then he stepped out of his boots, unzipped his parka and let it fall to the floor. Margar thought he looked like someone coming home at the end of the day, dumping his things at the door and sauntering in. *Joe*, she thought. *The rifle is for hunting. It's how he's kept himself alive in the woods.*

Watching the dark smear of him disappear into the living room, she strained to hear him sneak through to the kitchen, and wondered if he'd head straight for her mother. She thought of Joe catching Kay in her vermilion leotard, and her heart soared.

Just then she heard his footsteps approaching the hallway. She flew to her bed and waited with her eyes stretched open. He was looking into Louis's room – she knew it – and then he would move down the hall and come in here, for her, and he would recognize her right away because she looked just like him, everyone said so. *If this is a dream*, she thought, *it's the most real dream ever.* And yet the room looked dreamy. Every object had thickened with shadow, like the man himself. The dresser loomed so large and crooked, bigger on the top than it was on the bottom, that it might topple over altogether from the breeze of someone whispering by. The room seemed to have no corners, and the size of the doorway kept changing as she waited for him to appear and walk through it.

He did. His black silhouette stood in her room, spreading right up to the ceiling. *What if it isn't Joe?* she thought, and stretched her mouth wide in a silent gasp. She squeezed her eyes shut in fear and excitement, and wondered if he'd seen the whites of them shining out in the blackness. His presence drew closer. She could kind of see him through her eyelids – but not quite – and though she kept telling herself it was only (finally!) her father, she was still afraid to look. She could sense him standing right over her, leaning closer to get a good look, perhaps even smiling at her. She tried hard to keep her eyelids still. He seemed to watch her for an eternity, but then when he moved away, and the air in front of her changed and cooled, the moment seemed gone too soon. Worried he had left the room, she opened her eyes.

He was sitting on the floor. At first she didn't see him, because she'd been looking up, but the back of his head was right in front of her. She could reach out and touch him if she wanted. He was sitting cross-legged in front of Estelle, and it appeared that he was gazing at her, nothing more. He had his head cocked so that his face was parallel with hers. Unaware of his presence, Estelle slept on. Margar could barely make out her face in the darkness.

Outside the wind howled. It circled the house and tried to uproot it. The windows shook as though someone were knocking. Margar knew the sound, but this man didn't, which made her question whether it was Joe after all. The rattling glass startled him out of his gazing, and his head jerked toward the window and he shot up. His legs were thin, but not as long as she'd expected. She squinted her eyes almost shut and waited for him to turn around and see her again, but he didn't. With the stealth of a deer or a ghost, he left the room, and the hall, and the house. All she heard was his jacket rustling as he slipped on his packs. That and the click of the door, the very sound that had started the scene and now signified it was over.

After he was gone, she lay in the dark listening to the wind. During the ice storm she had been sure that their house would be funnelled up into the sky and rain down later in pieces. She thought they should stay in it in order to weigh it down, but everyone had laughed at that suggestion. She still felt sure that in the spring, when the snow melted, there would be signs of the attempted uprooting: cracks in the cement around the house; mounds of erupted earth. And when the time came she would point them out and say, "See?" But even then they would dismiss her with a roll of the eyes, as usual. She dozed off as the wind knocked on the window and scraped against the house and in her half sleep she thought she saw Joe's shadow made huge as a tree dancing on the wall of her bedroom. She slept and woke and slept and woke, and the wind pulled at the house, but it was Joe who came loose and was lifted into the winter sky, spinning, shrinking to the size of a far-off star, and then fizzling completely.

⬤⬤⬤⬤⬤

By morning, she could not separate that exaggerated part of the night from the mysterious events that had preceded it. She was unsure any of it had happened – and if it had happened, had it been Joe?

She wouldn't have revealed anything had Estelle not stormed into the kitchen, demanding to know where the photograph had gone, the one of Joe and herself as a baby. She didn't name names, but her eyes accused Margar.

"I don't know what you're talking about," said Margar. Inside, her blood sped up. Who other than Joe would have come in the night and stolen that, and nothing more?

A hunt ensued, but nobody found the picture. Estelle's white cheeks turned hot pink as she accused Margar of stealing it, but Margar swore she hadn't.

"It must have been the man," she said cautiously. "He came in the middle of the night, and —"

"Oh, stop it," said Kay. "That's enough out of both of you."

And Margar took her mother's hand and pulled her to the front hall, where she pointed to the dried salty puddles his boots had left, but all Kay did was lift up Margar's boots, and Estelle's, and Louis's too, and say, "So?"

Until that moment, Margar had been on the verge of naming the prowler as Joe. But that was pointless. It was useless. They were blind to the truth, and ruined it whenever she blurted it out. They didn't deserve to know. Crushed as she was by his choice of memento, she hung on to the thought of him lingering over her as she pretended to sleep. *He came to see me*, she thought. *And he'll be back again, too. It's only a matter of waiting.*

⬤⬤⬤⬤⬤

Winter moved on. The ice storm had left fallen trees and hydro wires, and pipes had frozen and burst. A house caved in when a red pine fell on it, and although the family inside made it out safely, their old cat died in the rubble. Well into spring, much of the mess remained.

The Halliwells' experienced a burglary early in the new year. Nothing of significance was taken, not that they could see, anyway, but Marie's gift to Russell was gone: a camera and tripod, which had been expensive but would be covered by insurance. Marie tried not to read too much into the theft, but couldn't help thinking it meant something. She'd given Russell a present and he'd left it under the tree while a crystallized, photogenic world lay sparkling around him. During all of the days of the storm, and later, when the frozen scene was at its most spectacular, Russell had not thought to take one picture. And now the camera was gone. He had said it was something he wanted — "to fool around with a camera," those had been his words — but he had been less than enthusiastic when presented with the opportunity to do so.

Worse than the crime itself was that it had occurred while they were sleeping. Someone had come through the archway of trees, up the path to the house, and entered through the sliding glass door, so recently thawed. No one locked their doors then. That was part of the beauty of living in the wilderness — that and the trees and the animals. But just as hydro lines ran through the branches of age-old white pines, thieves moved through the forest.

In the spring, signs of the storm's devastation showed amid the new leaves and the flowers and the backdrop of rushing water. The Halliwells' dock, little used since Eddie's childhood, had cracked in two, and half of it threatened to float downriver. Since Russell Halliwell was a man who liked things in their place and appreciated perfection, he called the experts to repair it, and so it was that Alphonse and Toussaint LeBlanc began work, in

May of 1973, replacing a broken dock that was never used with a new dock that would never be used. As the last piece of warped, faded wood broke away, something floated to the surface. Covered in silt and algae, it rose vigorously as though rinsing itself off. Toussaint reached for it while Alphonse held the last piece of the dock in his hand. Toussaint lifted the thing out of the water and together the uncles saw that it was a paddle, and that one clumsy, hand-carved cherry blossom graced the handle.

"*Mon dieu*," said Toussaint, turning the paddle in his hands.

Alphonse threw aside the old wood he was holding and dove in.

MONTREAL 1976
our lady of the snows

The Montreal Olympics took place in 1976, between July 17 and August 1, the dog days of summer. A staggering $100 million was spent to build and protect the Olympic Village, and to avoid the kind of bloodshed that had occurred in Munich. Cranes littered the skyline of one of Canada's finest cities, sad proof that Montreal's eyes were bigger than its stomach. All the work undertaken to prepare Montreal for the onslaught of athletes and tourists had not been completed by the time they arrived, and the city had to host the party half-dressed and embarrassed.

Longing for shade and water, Amik the Beaver led participants from ninety-two countries through the newest Olympic Village. Of the 6,084 athletes, 1,260 were women, so the disparity was steadily closing. And yet, the total number had dropped since Munich. Fear of terrorism wasn't the reason. Participation at the Montreal Olympics would have set a record had thirty-two nations not pulled out, protesting New Zealand's presence because that country's national rugby team had toured apartheid South Africa. And Taiwan didn't come because Canada wouldn't let them in under the moniker "The Republic of China," and Taiwan refused, on principal, to compete under a vague banner that boasted only the linked Olympic rings. Some said Canada simply didn't want to offend China, largest buyer of Canadian wheat, by allowing Taiwan a title China disapproved of. Whatever the politics – squabbles on a global scale – if the sixteen thousand police and soldiers who worked this particular Games could have been counted among the participants, the numbers would have swelled beyond compare.

Amid the feuds and rumours, the stalled cranes and the roving security, Queen Elizabeth appeared in a pink suit and hat and presided over the opening ceremonies. Her daughter, Anne, was entered in the equestrian competition, and the whole royal family, suddenly like any family, had come to cheer her on. It was the first time the six of them had visited Canada together.

Despite their regal presence, a serious girl from Romania stole the show. Nadia Comaneci was fourteen years old when she arrived, hidden in the charming shadow of Olga Korbut. Her first performance was so striking that the sun changed position and the shadow was cast elsewhere. Once she had their attention, Nadia announced to the press that while Olga had come to Canada to smile, *she* had come to win medals. And win she did. She took home three gold medals, one silver, and one bronze. In the culling of them, young Nadia Comaneci scored seven perfect tens, a feat never before achieved by an Olympian.

Watching her, Louis LeBlanc nearly lost all hope for himself.

He was just her age and had not yet competed outside the Valley, whereas she had travelled through the sky across an ocean, to a place that was only three hours by car from Louis's home. Dejected, but also riveted, he hooked his feet behind his head as he watched her so he wouldn't feel he was accomplishing nothing while she accomplished everything and more. He saw how the strength of her upper body was like his own, and how all the tiny muscles in her legs and arms worked to push her off with ease and speed. She was supple, like he was. One leg in the air, she balanced without a waver, and Louis knew that he, too, had that skill. He even saw his seriousness reflected in her large brown eyes, but what he didn't see there was something he had in spades: fear. Louis LeBlanc was afraid of failing. He was afraid of falling. He was even afraid of trying.

But try he did. He was not conscious of it, but deep in the recesses of his memory, Joe beckoned from the opening ceremonies in Munich, and Kay from the hall of glory. He was more directly inspired by his teacher and coach, a muscular, compact man who aped the moves of the champions as though he were a champ himself. Louis knew – as everyone did – that Coach Halliwell had almost competed in the Olympics years before. Rumour had it that he would have won gold had his parents let him attend, and Louis was fond of repeating that story.

"That might be a bit of a tall tale, Louis," his mother told him.

But Louis didn't see why. He liked to believe it, tall or not, because even though the coach hadn't gone, he had almost gone, which rendered the torch and the medals and the five interlocking rings treasures an ordinary boy could reach for. All this made the breath of possibility expand in Louis's chest. He felt the pull of destiny leading him to no other path than this one, if only he could find the courage to follow it through.

The year before, when Louis first started high school and extracurricular gymnastics, his heart had hammered away as Coach Halliwell observed him on the balance beam. He knew high school was his big opportunity. Gymnastics would no longer be taught to him by the flabby-armed Ms. Rubens, who doubled as the French teacher and treated the sport like a hobby, no more important than macramé.

"So," said Coach Halliwell. "Show me what you can do."

And Louis had watched his own feet, as he went through his steps and tumbles. He sent his body through the air with his chin tucked neatly into his chest, ever aware of Coach Halliwell, who leaned against the wall with his arms folded. Louis landed with his arms spread wide, his chest thrust out, and his head held high and proud.

"You're good," said the coach. "You could go places."

Those words came back to him now, and as he sat with his feet behind his head watching Nadia Comaneci, the optimism that had withered mere moments before spread through him with a new vitality. That was Louis's way, to swing from despair to hopefulness. He had inherited his flexibility from his mother, but he realized he would need more complex abilities if he wanted to get anywhere near a podium. The new school year would soon begin, and Louis promised himself that he would ask the coach to groom him for bigger things. He would not just try but strive. He would give himself over to the sport. And then if he failed he would know what he was, or at least what he wasn't, and he would not have to spend his years wondering. For he had already discovered that life was brimming enough with unknowns.

⟨◌◌◌◌◌⟩

To Louis's great chagrin, Margar was at the Olympic Games as he sat stretching and ruminating. A child of ten, and clumsy, she possessed no passion or aptitude for any sport at all, but there she was in the hastily constructed Olympic Village, blasé about the history made, the medallists lauded right under her nose. In the melting heat, she licked an ice cream cone and watched Wilt Chamberlain walk by. Margar was extraordinarily tall for a ten-year-old girl, but Wilt Chamberlain was much, much taller. She saw his hips passing in white pants, and she looked up, way up, into his face to see who could own such long legs and travel around on them so casually.

"Look it's Wilt Chamberlain," whispered Noelle, pointing, and touching Margar's hair with the tip of her ice cream cone. "Don't you think Wilt is a funny name for such a big man?"

Noelle giggled, and mimicked a man wilting, but Margar continued licking her ice cream and studying the long legs in their white pants. Sometimes she found Noelle annoying – a tiny gnat of a girl, rising to Margar's shoulder, laughing giddily at things that weren't all that funny, and snuffling, always sniffling from allergies. But Noelle was the reason Margar was here. Noelle's parents, sports fans, had invited her along as company for Noelle so that they could engross themselves in the competitions. Margar didn't care much about sports, and Noelle, who was wheezy and generally unhealthy, cared less, but both found

235

celebrities impressive. In three days they had seen the Queen, Prince Philip, Nadia Comaneci, and now, Wilt Chamberlain. They had eaten pizza for supper every night, and Noelle's parents bought them any delicious junk they wanted. Which should have been heaven. Margar with her sweet tooth gobbled candy floss and gooey caramel apples. Nevertheless, by this third day, she was sick of food and crowds and puny Noelle. She had ice cream in her hair now, because of Noelle, and she tried to lick it out, but she knew it would stink and become sticky anyway. All of her was sticky under the hot sun – though even she understood that if she'd been enjoying herself the stickiness and the hot sun would be nothing she'd notice.

At times the crowd was so thick that she was squished against the backs of people all around her. She was not tall enough, yet, to see over the heads of most adults, but one day she would be, that was obvious now. She watched Wilt Chamberlain disappear, heads above the rest, and imagined the great distances he could see and the lengths he could travel just by putting one long foot in front of the other. She was happy she had seen him, not because she cared about basketball, but because she would have one more thing to tell when she arrived home and everyone asked about Montreal.

I saw Wilt Chamberlain, she imagined herself saying. Or else, *I met Wilt Chamberlain*. Yes, that was definitely better. *I met Wilt Chamberlain and the Queen*.

The cone of her ice cream was soggy, so she tossed it on the ground and stepped on it. Noelle opened her mouth in delighted shock and gasped wheezily.

"This is boring," said Margar. "Let's find some pop."

And she began to make her way through the crowd with gnatty Noelle behind her. She pushed against the sweaty people and laid her hand on the back of a man who stood in the way. When he stepped aside, a Deep River face appeared in profile. It was the coach from the high school, his eyes fixed on the medal podium. His wife stood beside him in a black straw hat that shaded her pale face from the sun. Margar had seen that hat before. It made her feel odd, and dizzy. Montreal was not far from Deep River, so it wasn't unusual that other people from the Ottawa Valley would show up at the Games. But Margar felt cold all over, in spite of the hot day, when the woman turned and met her stare.

In her mournful hat, she nodded demurely, and looked away.

(((((((( )))))))

By the time of the Montreal Olympics, Pierre and Margaret Trudeau had had a third baby, also a boy. Instead of being born on Christmas Day like the others, Michel Charles-Emile, or Micha, had been born on October 2, 1975, which was Mahatma Gandhi's birthday, and also the Archangel's Feast Day. His mother believed he was an angel.

Yet despite his presence, cracks had begun to show in the image of the perfect family. The man, Pierre, looked old and tired. At times his face wore an exasperated expression that showed he believed everyone other than he was stupid. His wife, who had been beautiful, looked sad and stiff, holding her arms at her sides and facing straight forward as if trying not to be distracted by the world fluttering by. The little boys grew and became gorgeous, ruddy-cheeked elves who had every advantage but must surely have anticipated, as children do, the trouble that was to come. The country watched a black cloud gather over the family at 24 Sussex Drive, and the boys must have sensed not only that cloud, but the watching.

The cloud that had formed over the LeBlanc family at 40 Huron Street had long ago burst with the disappearance of Joe LeBlanc, but it kept re-forming. The discovery of Joe's paddle near the Halliwell home, some three years before, had caused a rumble of thunder, but after that there was only confusion as Alphonse emerged, wet and shivering, and claimed that he could see no trace of the canoe, or of Joe himself, or any of his belongings.

The uncles, who had never been convinced that Joe had simply left home, marched toward the blue two-storey with the battered paddle, and asked Russell Halliwell if he knew anything about it, or why it might have been lodged beneath his dilapidated dock.

"Search me," said Russell, obviously surprised. "Nobody's used that dock in ages. Our boy Eddie used to fish from there years back, but that was when he was – what, Marie? – ten, eleven?"

Marie Halliwell appeared by her husband's side and answered, "Yes. Since then, no one uses it."

"We must go to the police," said Toussaint gravely. "This paddle, it belongs to our nephew, the missing Joe LeBlanc."

Though they had never before left a job in a mess, Alphonse and Toussaint headed off in their truck to the police station. The warped, faded wood that had once been the Halliwell dock floated out into the river, and the new lumber sat piled on the shore.

After that, a flurry of activity ensued. Yellow tape went up around the area, and divers plunged into the river, searching for days on end. At first they found just what Alphonse had found – nothing.

The LeBlanc household hummed with tension in those days, as everyone awaited further evidence of Joe's demise. Estelle cried herself to sleep each night, and Louis slept in the big bed with his mother, refusing to discuss either his worries or his sorrow. Margar slept even less than usual, one moment imagining the body popping up in the river, and the next, imagining Joe coming back to find her, just when everyone else had stopped believing in him. Those words, *believing in him*, made her think about Jesus standing on the porch when she was little. She wished she could remember his face more clearly, or that she could remember Joe's, because maybe it had been him. "I have something to tell you," he'd said, but then he hadn't told her anything – so he still had something to tell her, and no silly paddle could stop that from being true. He had come again in the wake of the ice storm. If only she'd had the courage to open her eyes when he'd stood over her, she might have convinced him to stay.

"I don't think he drowned," she announced at breakfast.

"Not now, Margar," said Kay as she poured juice into plastic tumblers.

Margar sipped her drink and glanced around the table – at Louis looking wan, Estelle pink-eyed, and Kay with her hair gone tatty. She tried not to say anything more, and guzzled her juice to keep the words down. When the juice was gone, she sucked the tumbler to her face, but it popped off and she blurted, in spite of her efforts, "I know he didn't drown. I've seen him."

It should have been a moment of shocking revelation, and Margar braced herself for the response, the flood of questions, but there was only Kay's hand slamming down on the table, Estelle's bloodshot eyes tearing, and Louis pushing back his chair and leaving the room without eating a morsel.

"Not one more word," said Kay quietly. "Not now."

And it was then that Margar noticed the gold band gone from her mother's finger.

⦅⦅⦅⦅⦆

She wasn't permitted to go near the investigation, but Margar rode by on her bicycle every day after school anyway. She stood to one side of the Halliwell house, spying from a distance through the trees to the river. She couldn't see anything good from so far away, or hear a word that was spoken, so on the third day, her terrier determination took her, bicycle and all, into the thicket of trees surrounding the big blue house. She leaned her bike against the scarred trunk of a birch tree, and crept closer to the river.

Later, she was certain that luck – good, bad, or mischievous – had pushed her to the spot on that particular day, because with her own eyes she saw a diver surface, waving a narrow piece of wood at the officers on shore. Margar pricked her ears to try to hear what was being said, but the spring wind was roaring and the leaves overhead were shooshing against each other, and under her big feet, twigs popped and snapped. She glanced back at another noise behind her, and though it was only a nervous chipmunk, it saved her hide, for Margar saw in that glance Mrs. Halliwell peering out at the river from behind a curtain. In her bright red jacket, with her bright red bike, Margar moved not a muscle lest her presence be detected. And not for the first time she was faced with the challenge of sending each eye in a different direction, needing to watch the river and Mrs. Halliwell at the same time.

Soon the woman disappeared from the window, and since the day was drawing to a close, the police and the divers began to pack up their things. Margar moved ever so slowly through the trees and out to the road, willing herself as small and insignificant as a bird – a red cardinal – and not turning to look in case the tingling at the back of her head meant someone's stare was boring into her.

⬤⬤⬤⬤⬤

The slender piece of wood, bleached of its rich chestnut stain, sat on the kitchen table when Margar arrived home from school. Kay, Alphonse, and Toussaint had gathered to hear the latest meagre detail delivered by the chief officer on the case. Kay motioned to Margar to go into the living room, but Margar took her chances. She stayed put, and waited to be told again.

The officer had a googly, wayward eye that seemed to stare straight at Margar as the other one shifted neatly around, meeting the various gazes. It was just what Margar's eyes had tried to do back at the Halliwells', and she marvelled at the coincidence that somehow made the recent events eerier still.

The wood that was found was a thwart, the officer told them, a sort of bar that crosses the canoe like a seat belt. It had come loose from a canoe, but the canoe itself was nowhere to be found.

"*A* canoe?" said Alphonse, "or Joe's canoe?"

"Well," said the officer, "there's no way to know for sure, not without the rest of the boat. But what with the paddle, I think we can assume."

Margar peeked between Alphonse and Toussaint to have a better look at the clue, but it was no more meaningful to her than the paddle had been, with its funny knot at the top that everyone called a cherry blossom.

"What can all this mean?" asked Toussaint. "Can it be what you call foul play?"

The officer shook his head. "There's no doubt it was an accident, plain and simple." He said it would be futile to continue the search, as no other signs of Joe had surfaced. "It's a big river. We could search it for years and never come out wiser. This was just luck."

"Luck, you call it – and all in a breath you tell us he's dead?" said Alphonse, his voice gruff, his whiskers twitching. "Easy for you, if you don't mind, but we know Joe paddled since he was so high. You think he just fell overboard on a calm day's fishing? Just like that, you give up when a man goes missing?"

"Hang on a minute," said the officer, and both his eyes widened as he went on about the thoroughness of the police and their various experts. They'd examined the currents of the river, he said, and whether and where such currents might carry a paddle or a thwart or a man gone overboard. *A body*, was how he put it, with his bad eye still fixed on Margar. It was possible Joe had met his misfortune much further upriver, he added. The paddle and the thwart might have been carried homeward without him, snagging themselves on the old Halliwell dock in the process. "Who knows?" said the officer.

"But what about the canoe?" said Alphonse. "What about 'the body,' as you call it? The body of our Joe. You say you don't know what happened to him and yet you call it Case Closed?"

"Look," said the officer. He pointed to some harsh grooves on the thwart, and said they must have been caused by Joe's fishing line, of which, unfortunately, there was no sign. "And no, there's no sign of Joe or his canoe either. But this is more evidence than we've ever had. I know it must be painful for you. I'm sorry." And turning to Kay, who had remained silent throughout, the officer nodded, put on his hat, and was gone.

Margar could see that Alphonse and Toussaint were furious, and that her mother was only sad. She herself felt what might be called sadness for the man she had never known – or perhaps, more accurately, for her own convictions, dwindling and flying off like bits of ash from a fire. She had a vision of Joe, her father, wearing the huge shoes and painted face of a clown. His own serious face showed beneath the makeup. He was juggling with rocks, and then he put the rocks into the pockets of his green pants and plunged into the water. The weight took him down to the deepest part of the river, where there was a crack in the floor, and Margar saw him – still breathing, still awake, with his brown eyes open in his clown-white face – slip through that crack and down into the bottomless heart of the earth.

If not Joe, she didn't know who had come into their house that night after the ice storm. And the man who'd stood robed on her doorstep must have only been Jesus after all.

○○○○○

That night, Kay woke with a start. Estelle stood over the bed, her pretty face twisted into sorrow.

"So he's dead then, right? He's really dead."

Kay opened the covers and Estelle climbed in, and along with Louis they stayed like spoons until morning. But Kay didn't sleep. She touched the carving on the headboard Joe had built years before. She pictured the pained faces of Alphonse and Toussaint at her kitchen table. They had been old a long time, but a new haggardness had worked itself into their features. They looked worn out and beaten.

In the days after the wedding, when Joe had recently returned from his first disappearance, Alphonse and Toussaint had made a feast to celebrate what they called "*l'amour magnifique*." There had been wine and pork hocks and a thick soup that was almost like gravy. The light from the fire painted them all in shadows, and Kay had thought then of how old the uncles were, and how they couldn't live forever. And she had looked at Joe's youthful face, never guessing that he, of all of them, would go first. In the quiet months before his second and final disappearance, he would even come to resemble a dying man.

At the end of the evening, Alphonse, impassioned by wine and lost love, had held Joe's face in his big, calloused hands. "You did the right thing, coming back," he said fervently. "You're a family man now, eh? You said 'I do' to this girl. *Alors*, do, *Joséph*, do."

And Joe had done so, for a time.

⬡

In '73, weeks before the paddle surfaced, not long after the ice had cracked and melted, Kay stood on the riverbank and threw her wedding ring into the river. It was a cold day in early spring, and the water was dark and choppy. She was wearing the same scarf that had stretched snakelike across the ice to Robbie Hayes, the scarf he had not grasped in the moments before he went under, and now it whipped around her in the bitter wind, a striped scarf with tassels, knitted by her mother. Twisting the ring from her finger, she held it up and looked through the circle to the dense forest across the river. The horizon was dark, oppressive, conifer green, unbroken by snow, or by the bright new leaves yet to come. She turned the ring and looked along the inside of the band, where the word *forever* had been engraved. The letters had been placed to span the entire circle, so the word itself had no beginning or end, but that had been the jeweller's idea, not theirs. They had been so young. She put the ring back on her finger and looked at it on her hand.

The day before, standing on the step outside the kitchen, Gus Devlin had kissed her. He had appeared with bulbs for her garden, and when she saw him outside, planting them, she opened the door and leaned out.

"I meant to do this for you in the fall," he said, "but it went by so quickly and the ground froze before I got a chance."

Kay smiled, but was embarrassed by his strange persistence – which couldn't really be called persistence, because though he kept appearing, he maintained his distance too. She pushed the door open further and came out onto the step.

"Why are you doing these things?" she asked.

"It's what I do," said Gus.

In a way that was true – Kay knew from Ramona that Gus worked in a greenhouse in the nearby town of Pembroke, and that once a week he did a tour of the Valley, selling wholesale plants and flowers to florists. But that was different than this. She said, "Not quite. I mean, this is a bit above and beyond –"

But before she could finish, Gus Devlin dug his spade into the earth, removed his gardening gloves, took the three porch steps in one big one, and kissed her.

"Oh," she said.

He walked down the steps and crouched at the flowerbed, and Kay waited for him to look up at her, but he was putting on his gloves and placing the bulbs into the earth, patting soil around them. When he'd finished planting, he stood and nodded at her, and moved off down the driveway, whistling.

And all day she thought of the softness of his mouth as it had pressed against hers – brief but unforgettable. She had not been kissed that way in years, so long that she thought her libido had died, so it surprised her to realize she wanted more. Doing the dishes, taking her bath, standing aimlessly in the hallway, she closed her eyes and lifted her head toward the imaginary head of Gus Devlin, a strong head, bigger than Joe's, but with gentle eyes the colour of honey, sweet, limpid eyes, full lips, and a wet, roaming tongue, a hand so large it seemed to cover her whole back when it pressed her to him. But then, in the middle of her delicious fantasy, Joe would appear. Long and angular, he hung over her, taking the space where Gus had been the moment before. He opened his mouth and all his teeth loosened and fell clattering to the floor.

She didn't know that in ancient times Penelope had waited twenty years for Odysseus to return home from the war in Troy. While he fought off cannibals and a crazed one-eyed

246

monster, while he resisted the tantalizing songs of sirens, while he lolled against his will on an island, under the spell of the wily sex goddess Calypso, Penelope, certain of his return, spent the years weaving a funeral shroud for his father. To her anxious suitors, who believed Odysseus dead and gone, she said that she would remarry only when the shroud was completed. By day she wove the strands together, and by night she undid her progress. And finally he found his way. In the guise of an old beggar, Odysseus appeared in the hall of his own home and slew the lecherous, greedy suitors with bow and arrow. Afterwards he lay with Penelope in a bed he had carved himself from an olive tree still growing. The tree's trunk reached down through the floor and into the earth, where its roots held fast.

Kay was not familiar with the story. She didn't know that it was Penelope's faith combined with Odysseus's cunning that allowed for his safe return. She only knew that whatever she'd been waiting for would not happen. Whoever she'd been waiting for was never coming home. But she dreamed that night of Joe's long legs and his torso made of fish scales, the head of Gus Devlin on its shoulders – Gus Devlin's head kissing her and Joe's legs wrapped around her. The dry scales of his fish chest flaked off when he rubbed against her. They stuck to her skin like tattered flecks of gold leaf, evidence she could not brush away.

That morning she got the children off to school and donned a coat over her nightgown. She wrapped the scarf around her neck for extra warmth, and paused on the step, because the sun was shining there, and also because Gus Devlin might appear out of nowhere and the sight of him might give her the longed-for sign that, yes, this was the right thing to do. But Gus didn't come. His truck was gone from Ramona's driveway, which meant he must have returned home to Pembroke, and who knew when he would come again.

Wearing rubber boots, with the frill of her nightgown sticking out the bottom of her coat, Kay passed the car in the driveway and made her way to the river. It was only a short walk, but the extra time might allow her to change her mind. She wasn't crying yet, and knew she might not cry at all, which made Joe seem farther away than ever.

The ring circled in the air when she threw it, and made more rings in the water when it landed, but in no time the river was calm as glass. Her bare hand looked the way it had looked years ago, only older. It occurred to her, walking home, that if hope were remotely tied to reality, she had thrown away any chance of Joe's return. She had flung it into the water.

And weeks later, when Joe's paddle floated up into the hands of Alphonse and Toussaint, when a diver retrieved a piece of his canoe from under Russell Halliwell's dock, of all places, it was as if the ring had gone in and told Joe just what she'd done. What surfaced was his message – that he could never forgive her, and that it was time, finally, to say goodbye.

◌◌◌◌◌

Creeping up on eight years after his disappearance, a funeral was held for Joe at Our Lady of the Snows Church, where he'd married Kay more than twelve years before. For the wedding, Alphonse and Toussaint had had their old suits cleaned and pressed, and worn fat red carnations in their lapels. Then they'd stood as proud, dual best men, but now, outraged, they refused to attend the funeral, or stand by a grave in which there was no body. They had pleaded with Kay not to bury Joe's essence until his death could be proven and understood, but she had gone ahead with the mock funeral anyway.

"I need to," she'd said. "As much as you need to find him, I need to let him go now."

And in unison they'd shaken their heads and let the fight drift out of them. "We cannot support you in this," they'd told her. "We will not."

Instead they went fishing, as a sort of tribute to Joe. They sat with their backs to each other and watched their lures sink into the cool water. Unified in their silence, they spoke not a word. They thought of Joe and the paddle, and also of Jacques, and how history had a mean way of repeating itself. They thought of Joe's mother, Delphine, who had been told of the funeral but wouldn't be coming. Couldn't, she had said, but they knew better. Her reasons were different than theirs. They lamented the death of Jacques, whose life — whose presence — might have made all the difference in his child's life, and in the lives of his child's children. In what way, they were uncertain, but they remained resolute. All of this they spoke back to back, without need for words. They fished until the sky blackened, then made their way sadly home.

⬤⬤⬤⬤⬤

Aside from Kay and her children, there were fewer than twenty people in the church for the funeral, and the sound of them coughing and whispering and scuffing their feet somehow underscored the poor attendance. Beryl Hayes clung to her husband's arm and wept as though she had lost Robbie a second time. Serge, with white hair more dishevelled than ever, kept his head high and his sturdy jaw clenched, but tears poured down the creases in his face the way rivers flow through valleys.

Marie Halliwell found their obvious devastation garish and puzzling. She recalled that Joe had tried and failed to save Robbie Hayes, but beyond that, she couldn't comprehend the bond between the two families. For her, Serge and Beryl had no place on the trail of consequence. Even so, she was glad of their presence, which muted her own. She had hoped for more people than this. She had hoped her attendance could go undetected. The best she could do was stand quietly at the back of the church.

The Madonna and child rose larger than life behind the altar, and Mary, maudlin as ever, gazed down at the sacrificial baby with her eyes heavy, her mouth down-turned. She held her hands in front of her chest in prayer, but her curved, limp fingers barely touched each other, as though she had no energy for praying, and so the prayer, void of hope, laden with resignation, was not an entreaty at all. The baby lay cadaverously in front of her on a platform, his sleeping head resting on a cushion made of plaster.

Marie watched the Madonna and child throughout the service, yet she was aware at all times of Beryl Hayes weeping, and further up, of the small, dark-haired head that repeatedly turned to eye the back of the church, where Marie was standing. Though she didn't look at the little face directly, she could see in her peripheral vision the dark hair turn to pale skin, and back again.

As the service came to a close, that disconcerting figure sat down at the piano and played a child's song so bright and cheerful that Marie almost sobbed out loud. When she was finished, the girl stood and bowed to the little crowd of mourners. She returned to the first pew and squeezed in between her mother and her brother, and then Beryl Hayes took her place at the piano and began to play the most tender of dirges. Marie marvelled at how Beryl composed herself, sitting at the bench with the veil of her hat pulled back and her bird's face full of ardour. Kay and her children came down the aisle of the church in that cloud of music, and Marie remained aware of the dark head and the pale face, which lifted toward her in passing. At the last possible moment, Marie looked down. It was a riddle of a face, more impish than girlish. The large ears that poked out from the fine hair were like pink magnolia blossoms, or seashells. But the doleful eyes were replicas of Joe LeBlanc's.

((((((()))))))

After the funeral, Marie returned home. Russell was on the chesterfield with sections of the newspaper spread around him, and she tried to sit for a time in the same room with him, but she could not do it. He knew where she'd been, but he said nothing. He turned the pages of his paper and looked as relaxed as he did any Sunday, with his feet crossed on the coffee table and a pillow propping his head. Her old anxiety, tinged with hysteria, woke up and tickled her insides. Long masked by time and little blue pills, it had stayed as quiet as the blood that travelled through her.

Marie went upstairs to their bedroom to be away from Russell, but his socks were on the floor, and his inside-out pants hung vulgarly from the bedpost. He thought of himself as tidy but really it was she who cleaned up after him. She experienced a fast, hot surge of disgust, and when it passed she sat on the bed and looked out the window. She thought of Kay at the funeral with a line of children beside her, two dark heads and a blonde one. Marie had not looked at her husband's daughter. She had looked at the other girl, and seen Joe LeBlanc's eyes shining out at her. If she had looked at the eldest, would she have seen Russell's? Something heavier than jealousy pressed on her chest. If there had been anyone else for Russell since Kay, Marie had done her best to remain oblivious. She never wanted to know anything like that again. Knowing the details had been her undoing.

Over the course of their marriage, she had often suspected Russell of cheating. There'd even been a time when she'd confronted him, losing every fibre of her dignity as she screamed into his calm expression. He had actually smiled. He had held her and soothed her and said he would never understand her paranoia. Which she had believed, for she didn't understand it herself. After that, every time her doubts arose, she'd rummage both insanely and methodically through his wallet, all of his pockets, his desk drawers, with her heart knocking so hard she thought it would push through her chest wall and smash on the floor – and then, finding no proof of his infidelity, she'd remind herself of what he had said. *You get yourself so worked up. But don't worry, I'll keep you anyway.* Once, on his sweater, there had been three blonde hairs woven into the wool. One by one she had freed them and watched them twirl and shine in the light. She'd imagined a mass of blonde curls on her husband's shoulder, a woman laughing or crying in his arms. She had never imagined a girl.

Marie stripped out of her clothes and laid down on the bed but it smelled of sleeping bodies, so she sat up again. She wanted to rest, and close her eyes and mind to everything. She draped her robe over her shoulders and crossed the hall to Eddie's room, where she hadn't been since well before Christmas. Right away she saw it was different. The closet door was ajar and two dresser drawers were open – only a crack, but she knew they had not been that way before. His room had been immaculate; she had cleaned it herself following his departure, inspecting all that was left as thoroughly as she had her husband's things. She thought of calling downstairs for Russell, but instead she just stood in the doorway. She told herself that perhaps it had been Russell who'd been in the room, but she didn't believe it. He didn't care enough to be that curious about Eddie any more. Maybe he never had. Her eyes scanned the room, looking for other changes, or signs that whoever had been there was still lurking in the closet or under the bed. She pushed the door open hard to be sure no one hid behind it. The harsh spring sun shone in through the curtains and illuminated the dust motes, which twirled through the air like the smallest flakes of snow. Sunlight fell also on Eddie's bed, and as she stepped into the room, she saw the imprint of a person on the mussed blanket, the indentation of someone's head on the pillow. A faint, salty boot tread stained the quilt. Marie walked to the closet and wrenched open the doors. The few shirts he'd left hanging there swayed and slowed. She turned and pulled open the dresser drawers and found Eddie's sketchbooks missing. There had been three left behind when he'd gone to Nova Scotia. She sat on the bed and ran her hand over the place his boots had been. Of course it had been he. The thief who had come in the night months before had been her own son – so close and she'd not sensed him at all. Yet when he was a baby, she'd always woken seconds before he cried. Only she had been able to soothe him, rocking him back and forth, back and forth. He had stared up at her and gripped at her skin with the strongest, tiniest fingers.

◎◎◎◎

Eddie – Edward – had indeed come in the wake of the storm. It had taken two buses and two days to get to Deep River from Halifax, a foul existence in foul weather, and Edward had been unable to sleep for most of the journey.

Bundled in his old army parka, he arrived in his hometown at 3 a.m., and walked from the highway through town toward the river. He passed the house that had been shattered by the red pine, and saw by moonlight many other fallen trees and toppled fences that would take some time to repair. The town was deathly silent. It was only sleeping, he knew, but even the trees seemed empty of the spirits that had pulsed through them when he was a child. Those were spirits his mother had showed him, and he had tried hard to capture that vitality on paper.

He told himself he had come home – though he didn't use the word – to retrieve his sketchbooks, rather than to see his mother and father, his old house by the frozen river, the deer and the wolves gingerly crossing the ice, the blue jays, the winding streets banked by walls of snow, all the things a normal boy might miss. He would see those things, yes, but he had

254

come for his sketchbooks, that was all. Nevertheless a picture crept into his mind, of himself, grown and slender, sitting at the table with his parents as he mimicked St. Clair and his other teachers, and he imagined his mother, even his father, amused, impressed, grateful to have him home.

Edward continued to Riverside Drive, past the school and the Clancy house and the other homes that stood tall and proud along the waterfront. Of his own house, all he could see were the trees that surrounded it, black in the moonlit night, and as he trudged toward them, he tried again to conjure the scene around the dining-room table, but what came were the real times – his father in his tidy tennis clothes, his cruel pink face watching Eddie help himself to more spaghetti, the noodles wiggling as he sucked them into his mouth, the orange sauce splattering his glasses, his face, his shirt. He saw his mother's vacant eyes, and the fine bones of her wrists moving beneath her skin as she twirled pasta onto her fork. She used a fork and spoon, the way they do, she told him, in Italy.

Eddie had sat at that table for seventeen years and watched the river thaw and freeze, thaw and freeze. The world had moved in a loop around him, and he had grown bigger while everything else stayed the same. For seventeen years he'd sat in the thick silence of his parents' misery. It couldn't have always been so, but that was how he remembered it. Had he once been small, and ticklish? Someone, his father, tickled his summer-black feet until he wanted to scream from the torture, if only he could stop laughing.

And now he stood in front of the trees that barricaded the house. He saw himself grab his mother by the arms and say,

Please. But he pushed the image away and thought instead of turning around and walking back up to the highway in the freezing darkness. Through his wool scarf, he breathed steadily in and out. And then he parted the snow-laden branches and entered the yard.

He stepped into the house and smelled the same old smells, along with the bitter pine of the Christmas tree. The tree's lights had been left on, and gave the room an artificial glow of contentment. The glow illuminated the opened presents beneath the tree, and Edward stuffed his hat into his pocket, unwound his scarf, and knelt to inspect the gifts. His mother had given his father an expensive camera, complete with light metre, zoom, and wide-angle lens. Edward traced the rim of the case with his finger. He bent to smell the leather. It was then that he noticed his own name. *Merry Christmas Mom, Love Eddie.* The card, written in his mother's hand, sat nestled in a blue flannel nightgown. Beside it was a box that held plaid pyjamas, and a card that read *Merry Christmas Dad, Love Eddie*, though he had given nothing to either of them. Something like guilt turned in his stomach, but he laughed and covered his mouth with his hand to muffle the sound. He stood and crossed to the couch, and laid down with his boots on.

After that, he must have slept, for when he opened his eyes he felt disoriented. Blinking, studying the room as he sat up, he noticed his boots had sullied the couch. He flipped the cushion and hid the spot where his feet had been. He knew he had slept for some time, for his boots were almost dry.

He didn't bother to remove them as he climbed the stairs to the second floor, and the spongy soles landed without a sound.

He passed his parents' room and heard them breathing steadily. Exhilarated by the idea of himself as an intruder in his own home, Edward pushed open the door to his old room. One window overlooked the yard where the manicured garden had been, the other overlooked the river, a ribbon of ice barely visible in the darkness. He touched the curtains, then held them to his nose and smelled only the stale odour of dust. He had been gone a long time.

Exhausted from his near sleepless journey, Edward dozed again on the bed, but was jolted awake by the sudden memory of his mother's face in front of his, her voice hoarse and urgent. *What did you hear, what did they say, tell me everything.* The hollows of her eyes had been black with shadow. He had been lying right here, a little boy sleeping.

Edward got up and opened the drawers of his dresser to retrieve his sketchbooks. Reaching in, he caught the glint of his old glasses. He pulled them out, along with his sketchbooks, and saw that each piece of the shattered lens was still in place. He tucked the glasses into his shirt pocket and put the books in his backpack. On the top shelf of his closet, he found the bear's skull, which he wrapped in a big shirt he had worn in high school. Putting the bundle, too, in his bag, Edward left his room, and moved silently along the hall, past the steady breathing, and down the stairs, where he paused in front of the tree. The camera had been given with film and fancy lenses and a tripod, and though Christmas was over, it had not yet been put to use. Settling the lenses and the camera back into their appropriate spaces, he closed the case, and strapped it over his body. He put on his pack, tucked the tripod under his arm, and strode silently through the back door, down the path, and out through the trees.

And just as he had done once before, Edward vowed he would not return here in the future.

⟨⟨⟨⟨⟨⟨⟩⟩⟩⟩⟩⟩

Louis LeBlanc wore a spring jacket and tie to his father's funeral, and pants that he'd pressed himself, taking pride in the tidy creases that would in some small way honour his father. After the investigation, he thought he didn't believe in the death, but Margar's proclamations made him waver. Her outlandish lies rendered his own hopes ridiculous. But whether or not Joe was dead, Louis had been craving some sort of formal commemoration of the man he adored but could hardly envision. Today was that day. He shined his shoes, and since there was still time before the ceremony, he shined Estelle's shoes, and then Kay's, but not Margar's because he was mad at her and, besides, they were sparkly already. He checked the kitchen clock against the three bedroom clocks, worrying they'd miss the funeral, and then he waited outside on the driveway, standing, so as not to wrinkle his pants.

When they arrived at the church, the first person Louis noticed was Gus Devlin, who had come with his sister, Ramona. Had there been a bigger gathering, Louis may not have found Gus's presence suspect, or even noticed him at all, but as it was, he could not help seeing Gus, and the flash of wrist protruding from his suit jacket, as well as the golden hairs that curled upon it. Almost five years had passed since the hairy arm had reached through the rip in Louis's screen, but Louis had not forgotten. He thought the hairs had been brown, but he might have been wrong. He also remembered what had seemed to be a man's legs hiding by the fence that divided their yard from Ms. Devlin's. It had been such a long time that he once more doubted the eventual explanation: the squash that they had eaten as soup and bread. Who was to say there had not been someone looking, someone spying from the same place the squash had grown? And if it had not been Joe, if none of it had been Joe, as a funeral implied, who was to say it had not been Gus Devlin? The same year, fourteen bags of needles and cones had appeared on the curb in the dead of night. And later still, footprints in the snow had surrounded the house. He glanced again at Gus's wrist. No, he did not like Gus Devlin. He did not trust Gus Devlin.

As he tried to concentrate on the priest's words about Joe, his stare travelled up Gus's arm to his face, and found eyes that were neither green nor brown, but almost amber. Louis thought of marbles or candy, something hard and artificial. He looked at the eyes a long while, in his distant, observing way, before he realized that the eyes were looking back at him. The whole face and being of Gus Devlin took shape around the amber eyes, and just as Louis, startled, began to turn away, one of the eyes squeezed closed and popped open again. Nearly eleven at the time of the funeral, Louis believed he was too old to be winked at. He faced front and slipped his hand into Kay's. He had not witnessed the kiss amid tulip bulbs, or his mother's subsequent daze as she'd imagined more and more kisses. And he knew nothing of the throwing of the ring that had bound his parents in a circular eternity. But he sensed big changes when it came to Gus Devlin. And among them he perceived disaster.

◯◯◯◯◯

Beside Louis, Margar craned her head in the opposite direction and stared at the pretty woman at the back of the church. It was a dim memory, but Margar remembered Mrs. Halliwell from the parking lot the day her mother had cried, and of course, more recently she'd spied her in the window of the blue house by the river. For a moment, when she faced front, Margar felt a tingling at the back of her scalp. She zipped her head around again, to catch the woman staring, but Mrs. Halliwell was looking past her. She wore a broad-brimmed black hat, and beneath it was the same white skin that shone so brightly. *Moon Woman*, thought Margar. She had eyes of such brilliant blue that Margar could see them all these rows away, and she was transfixed backwards instead of forwards, where there were only dead people – Jesus, Mary, her father. Her father wasn't there, of course. No one could say for sure that he was dead, but they were pretending he was, so that his spirit could be locked in the ground once and for all. For more than seven years, Margar had grown up in the shadow of his absence, so this new official absence was meaningless to her. But out of all of them, she was the one chosen – the only one capable of playing a song for Joe on the piano beside his shrine.

Once the priest had spoken, she walked to the front of the church, past the picture of Joe with his string of trout, past the vase of wilting daisies, and such a puff of pride inflated inside of her that she forgot, temporarily, about the woman in the black hat, about Gus Devlin, and even her mother. She thought about Joe and her fingers hammering out a tune for him, and only at the end of the song – which she cleverly looped back to the beginning so she could play it over again – only then, the second time, did she want to turn and see if Mrs. Hayes was watching, but taking her eyes from her fingers might cause her to falter, and she would not do that, not at her first real performance. Anyway, she knew Beryl would be annoyed to see she was looking at her fingers, and she didn't want that annoyance to ruin the recital. Once she had finished, she stood and curtsied. All the sorrowful faces looked back at her, and she was on the verge of smiling when she noticed, again, Mrs. Halliwell in her sombre black hat. The tips of her fingers tingled with an exciting, bewildering burst of fear.

When Margar sat down, Beryl Hayes took her place at the piano, and played a melody of such ringing beauty that Margar saw the stained-glass windows shimmer. Our Lady of the Snows bowed her head more deeply over her sleeping baby. As Margar watched, the Lady lifted her face and looked into some vague distance, her eyes pooled with tears. No one else seemed to have seen it, which meant they would say it hadn't happened if she told them it had. But she'd been a witness. She would always believe it. That was what faith was: believing, no matter what anyone said. That was how Grandma Clancy had described it, and though she'd been talking about God and Jesus, she probably meant Mary too.

As the music swelled, Margar's mother urged her down the aisle, and together all of them left the church the way a bridal party does, with everyone watching in respect and admiration.

Margar had never felt so important. *I am the daughter of the man who disappeared. I am the pianist.* She kept her head down to temper her jubilation, and discovered the opulent sight of her white shoes on the red carpet. *If only everyone would look,* she thought. *If only everyone would see me.* She glanced up and noticed she was approaching Mrs. Halliwell. The music was so loud that Margar felt it swim around her and find its way inside of her. She moved down the aisle and kept her eyes on Mrs. Halliwell's eyes as the song coursed through her. The piano music combed her hair like fingers.

Look. Look at me. See me.

The eyes stared into the distance the way Our Lady's had, but at the last possible moment, they looked down to find Margar. As though she had willed it to happen.

⫟⫟⫟

That week, when Margar entered the Hayes's house for her Wednesday piano lesson, she knew in an instant that Robbie was gone. The air had turned stale, unlike when Robbie's ghost had inhabited the place and a clement breeze had travelled through every room. Mrs. Hayes seemed just the same without him. If she sensed a change, she gave no sign. Her black eyes danced like musical notes as she tapped out the rhythm to every tune. Margar had never felt so sorry for anyone. Her son had died a second time, and she didn't even know it.

Walking home, Margar worried that Robbie's absence might somehow mean Joe really had died – that the two of them were so connected in life and in death that Robbie could only find rest once Joe had been bidden goodbye. Margar had been waiting to meet Joe all her life. Not waiting was something hard to imagine. It made the sky widen and the land and river spread out around her, turning her into an ant-sized Margar, or a puff of pollen flying by. What would she do without him? She cut across the front lawn and mounted the porch steps and thought of Jesus standing there. If faith could apply to God and to Jesus and to Mary, why couldn't it apply to Joe? If she believed with enough conviction that Joe was alive, maybe her wish would find its way to him, and tap him on the shoulder as he loped through Montreal, or through the bushes across the river, and he'd dig his heel into the ground, spin around, and start the journey homeward.

⟨⟨⟨⟨⟨⟩⟩⟩⟩⟩

Not long after that day, Louis boosted Margar in the hall of glory, and she unhooked the photograph of Robbie Hayes with Joe skulking by in the background.

⟨⟨⟨⟨⟨⟩⟩⟩⟩⟩

In the years between '73 and '76, the slow-as-molasses flirtation between Gus Devlin and Kay LeBlanc began to spread into romance. Of the children, only Margar was pleased about love flowing under Joe's leaky roof, but the pleasure was marred by her persistent belief that Joe lived, and that one day he'd come back to them. With a rush, she wondered who Kay would choose. And what would she, Margar, do in such a dramatic, double-father situation, when all her life she'd never had even one?

Since the day of the snowman, Margar had adored Gus. His was the only real-person photograph that had made it onto her

263

bedroom wall, where clippings of royalty formed a messy collage. She continued to call him the Earl of Pembroke, so in a way he fit in with the others. The photo captured him stepping out of his truck in Ms. Devlin's driveway on the occasion of his first official date with Kay, which was not until May of 1974 because Kay kept declining. Margar had lain in wait for hours that day, crouching by the fence. Blooms of lilac from Ms. Devlin's tree hung down over her. Heavy, sickly sweet, their purpleness would quickly deepen into rancid, shrivelled brown, but for the time being, bees floated through the pungent branches, and zigzagged away, drunk on nectar. Margar had never been afraid of bees. Once she'd declared she wouldn't scream if stung, as Estelle had, or fuss after the stinger came out and the skin began to redden and swell.

"You don't know that," Estelle had said. "You've never been stung."

Margar could have argued, but chose to shrug and lift the left side of her long eyebrow as if to say, *I don't care what you think.* Bee stings could not be worse than needles. During every shot she could remember having, Margar had been advised to look away from the needle piercing the vein, from the red-wine blood spilling backwards into the vial, but she had gawked, fearless.

"Why are veins that bluey-green when blood is so red?"

Nurse after nurse couldn't answer.

Under the lilac bush, she decided Gus would know.

He arrived pulling a spring storm behind him. The sky was a patchwork of bright blue and black, and thunder was just starting to rumble when he pulled into his sister's driveway. Margar sat up and aimed the camera over the fence. Like a private detective, she snapped the picture without him knowing.

An hour later he was on their doorstep wielding a small bouquet of daffodils and a large, striped umbrella. The rain teemed down behind him. Margar ushered him in and seated him on the sofa, grinning from big ear to big ear. She skidded out of the room and across the kitchen to her mother's bedroom, where Kay, with shaking hands, was choosing a necklace from her jewellery box.

"This one?" she asked Margar, holding up a gold chain with a tiny gold cross.

"No," said Margar. She stepped forward and fished with her big hand into the mess of trinkets. "This one," she said, pulling out a tarnished silver locket.

Her mother watched the locket spin as the chain untwisted. "No," she said firmly, and put on the cross.

Margar had rarely seen her mother so finely dressed. Gussied up, Kay called it, and said she felt ridiculous, but she looked more pleased than anything. She had her hair pinned up and wore a sleek new dress of fire-orange, which she felt at the last minute was too showy, but Margar grabbed her mother's hand and pulled her down the hall, past Louis and Estelle, who kept to their rooms rather than witness the occasion of their mother's first date.

In the living room, Gus Devlin offered Kay his daffodils, and together they stepped out into the pouring rain.

⬤⬤⬤⬤⬤

Kay watched the raindrops fall and ruin her new pink shoes. She tried not to step on the fat, slithery worms that scattered the walk as she hurried with Gus to his truck, but she knew smushed bits of them stuck to the soles of her shoes, and that it was no way to start an evening or a lifelong romance. And she had already decided, *I don't want to fall in love, I'm not going to fall in love.* But Gus's nearness was running shivers up her back and neck, like fingers tickling. And when he started the engine and turned the heat full blast, the shivers stayed and spread.

Kay touched the cross at her neck and watched the wipers slide back and forth across the windshield. As Gus pulled out of Ramona's driveway, she saw Margar waving from the window, and pictured her holding the twirling locket. Kay had almost chosen to wear it, as a way of bringing Joe with her. Even now, after all this time. But out of guilt, or out of love? Years ago, before they were married, the locket had held a picture of Joe, but she had cut the picture too small and it had fallen out and been lost. Careless to the bone – rotten and lazy – she had never bothered to replace it. The locket lingered unworn in her jewellery box, an empty talisman, tarnished black with neglect.

Still – two glasses of wine and she forgot all about him. Gus, amber eyes in the amber light, suggested a meal of shared appetizers, and all the pretty snacks came fanned out on blue plates with twirls of carrot and orange for garnish – orange like her dress.

"You look so pretty," he said, and she curled her toes in her stained shoes and told him she hadn't been on a date in fourteen years. She told him too many things during the evening, as their faces got closer and closer. Loose-lipped, she felt giddy as an adolescent. She wanted to gobble him up like buttery escargots, wash him down with more wine and a hot, boozy blueberry tea, give in to the spell of attraction.

At the end of the evening they drove home the way they had come. It was still raining, but in the dark, with only the headlights brightening the road, the raindrops seemed to be popping out of the pavement rather than falling onto it. The night that had unfolded was folding up again. They would pull into the driveway and rush to the house under the striped umbrella, just as they had rushed away from it, and then Gus would go back out alone, and in her room she'd see herself in the mirror, made-up face smudged from the decadent evening, and it would be obvious that she was not so pretty after all. She'd step out of the ruined shoes, strip off the orange dress, remove the cross from around her neck and place it back in her jewellery box beside the locket where Joe was not. Every day was like the sweep of the windshield wipers sliding back and forth, like a bed being made, mussed, and made again. The food that had been so delicious, and the wine, had already turned her mouth sour.

Despite all of this, she stood on the porch and let Gus Devlin kiss her goodnight, she who had not been touched in so long that she could almost lay claim to her virginity again. She closed her eyes in the sweet embrace and felt herself spinning.

⦅⦅⦅⦆⦆⦆

Two steps forward, one step back. It seemed the romance would die on the vine, but Gus kept planting seeds, and by spring of 1976, when the sun began to grow hotter and the apple trees made pink clouds of themselves, the green sprouts in the patchy

LeBlanc yard promised a floral paradise. Gus had taken his thumbs outside of the greenhouse to grow gardens in the real world. Summer brought a sea of wildflowers that swayed in the humid breeze. Alphonse and Toussaint grudgingly admired the transformation. They remembered how it had looked when pine needles had burned the soil and not even grass would grow. They admitted – at least to themselves and each other – that their beloved Joe would never have achieved such a garden. But only Kay realized just how long Gus had tilled the soil, and that years ago, when Margar said she'd seen a haloed angel raking, it had actually been Gus, in pale cotton clothes, with a headlight strapped on.

The flowers he had planted would reseed themselves and spread through the neighbouring lawns. Soon cosmos would sprout in back lanes. The almost weightless poppy seeds would be blown as far as the beach, where new blooms would rise out of the sand. Up to the highway, cornflowers would float at the roadsides like small blue feathers.

The offspring of the original seeds already covered the LeBlanc-Devlin fence where the startling squash had once grown – a squash Gus himself had planted. The two properties had merged into one expanse of garden. Passersby stopped to gawk at what had long been two nondescript houses, and over the next couple of years Gus was called upon to put his talents to use in yards throughout the town. He became known locally as "the gardener."

"I could give up my job," he said to Kay. "I could move here and find enough work to keep me going most of the year. We could get –"

"No," said Kay. "Not yet."

Still, the dusty yellow pollen tripled and quadrupled. Estelle said the yard looked messy with so many colours in it, and why didn't *he* — for she never used his name — plant something low and tidy, that wouldn't be yanked and twisted by the wind. Some stems grew higher than the playhouse, which was not played in any longer, and though a respectful path was cleared around it, Louis resented the dwarfing of his father's old landmark, and the petals that littered his trampoline. His eyes and nose ran and itched with new-found allergies. His cough was a bark that time and again fooled Olive in the yard next door, who ran in circles, yapping at a dog she couldn't see.

But Margar loved the flowers. She stretched out on her back and watched the tall stalks lean this way and that around her, like a crowd pressing to see a queen drift by. There was a photo like that in the burgeoning collage on her bedroom wall — the backs of heads and bodies leaning towards a gold carriage in the distance, Elizabeth II inside, draped in purple splendour. The Wall of Royalty was just part of what made the room she shared with Estelle resemble two rooms from which the dividing wall had eroded. Estelle's side was kept tidy and mostly free from mementoes, while on Margar's side, tattered streamers left over from New Year's Eve hung from the ceiling, snacks she had not quite finished transformed under the bed, and all the clothes she had worn in previous days lay balled on the floor, stained with mustard or grass, and smelly.

By the time of the Montreal Olympics, Estelle's bedside photograph of Joe and herself as a baby had been missing for years. Estelle still believed that Margar had stolen it, but Margar had not. No one accepted the story she gave – that an intruder had pinched it in the black of night – which only proved to Margar that no one would have accepted the real story either: that the intruder had been Joe.

Estelle had filled the empty space with the snapshot used at the funeral, depicting Joe and a string of trout, but it was a far cry from the photo of a father gazing at his new baby. And even though it had been Joe himself who had stolen it, coming and going without a word, Margar was glad that old picture was gone. She wouldn't have minded, either, if the new garden covered up the playhouse that had existed since the summer before her birth. For she knew, and had always known, that Joe had returned for Estelle – that she had been the lucky charm who'd once drawn him back home – and that he had built the playhouse as a home for himself and Louis in anticipation of the new baby taking up space. "Boys only," he'd told Louis, and Louis had told Margar a hundred times or more. For Margar, there were no such stories. She loved Joe LeBlanc, but she hated him for that.

The famous people on her wall were not the regular idols of an almost eleven-year-old girl. Alongside Earl Gus climbing out of his truck was the Queen of England, whom Margar now claimed to have met, though no one believed her, Princess Grace of Monaco, who by marriage was a cut above ordinary stardom, horsey Princess Anne in her equestrian outfit, and Margaret Trudeau, who was only a princess in a very small way, because she was married to the king, so to speak, of Canada. He too gazed out into the room, unfazed by the mess and the dirty underwear.

There were three pictures of Pierre Trudeau on Margar's wall. In one he is still a boy, with pigeons resting on his arms and shoulders. In another he is a grown man, riding a smiling camel who flares one nostril and looks into the camera with lethargic eyes. Pierre wears a jumble of flowers around his neck, and a mark on his forehead that resembles a feather or a burst of fire. In the background, behind all of the people who accompany him, is a sagging clay roof ready to give way and cave in on the house beneath. Everyone faces away from the house, so there is no danger of anyone witnessing such a catastrophe. Pierre looks down on the people and smiles. In the third picture he is dancing nose to nose with Margaret and for once seems unaware of the camera at all. His hand looks big and strong as it holds hers, and the ring of their union is on his finger. This is a gala event, a ball perhaps. He's in a tuxedo with a rose in his lapel, and she's in a glittering dress that exposes her shoulders. Her bare skin glows.

Margar belonged among these people. She could feel it when she looked at them. She did not belong here, at 40 Huron Street, where there was no spiral staircase leading to a second, third, fourth storey, where there was not even a basement, and where the dining room consisted of a plain old kitchen table. It was perhaps why Jesus had come – to take her elsewhere – but she had failed to grasp his hand, and he had floated up and away like a lost balloon.

Shortly after she returned from the Montreal Games, full of embellished stories about whom she had met and how she had spent the sweltering days (which had quickly become boring), Margar had an elaborate dream. She was wearing a pink chiffon gown and a tiara with pink twinkling jewels in it – though in real life she didn't like pink and owned nothing but underpants in that colour, gifts from Grandma Clancy. She had long blonde hair in the dream and actually looked nothing like herself, but it was she just the same, swinging a pink croquet mallet at a large pink egg – an ostrich egg – in an effort to send it through an array of pink hoops that went on into a green eternity. A rolling meadow spread lush around her. It dipped and rose again, so that the trail of hoops vanished and reappeared, and it was impossible to know whether it was a trail to follow or one she had already mastered. She was the only one there, but she had the sense that somewhere, someone else was playing. She couldn't say who was in the lead, only that the invisibility of the opponent suggested a gap too great to be closed. While she was aware of these things – the confusion, the opponent, the gap – none of them bothered her. She worried only about the egg, and if it would crack when she struck it with the mallet, and what would come out if it did, and if the game would then be over. She could see herself from afar, and she watched herself steady the mallet and survey the egg, which rose and fell as though breathing. She could see little beads of sweat on her forehead, and she could feel them too. The tiara was heavy but too lovely to remove, so she played on in discomfort. She sent the egg safely through six hoops, but on the seventh turn, she smashed the shell to pieces. The sound was like a wall of glass shattering. People appeared on every hilltop masquerading as flowers. The only ones who looked human were Wilt Chamberlain and the Queen. The Queen in her pink suit and hat rose to Wilt's hip, and each of them stood shading their eyes from the sun and staring at Margar to see what had happened and why. The flowers craned their green necks. Margar looked back at the egg. There was indeed an ostrich inside, and even though she had never before seen a baby ostrich, she recognized it, just as she recognized herself looking like another person. The baby ostrich was not moving. Fragments of the shell were stuck to its yellow, featherless body, and scattered around it in sad disarray. She remembered how the shell had breathed just moments before, and knew that that meant it was the stroke of the mallet – in short, her own hand – that had killed the bird inside.

◌◌◌◌◌

As the shell smashed like glass, Louis dreamed of the hairy arm coming to get him. It punched through not just his screen but his window, which, in his dream, he had closed and locked against it. Glass flew in fine splinters and landed, pointing up, in the cracks of the floor. The arm reached in and pulled him by his hair out of bed and across the floor, and the little splinters ate into him all up the side of his body, as though a series of knives were slicing him open. The arm pulled him up over his night table, through the window and outside, and it dragged him at an astonishing pace along the grass to the street, and then down the pavement, and though in the lamplit darkness he could see the familiar town going by, he could not see the owner of the arm, which held him in such a way as to cause his face to stare in the opposite direction. He could hear the owner of the arm breathing in the steady manner of an athlete, and though Louis recognized that breath as an athlete himself, it also sounded to him like scary-movie breath, breathed when

273

the killer is perilously close. The arm took him through town and down along the river and up past the yacht club and tennis courts, and not once did Louis see anyone anywhere, because – as in real life – it was night and everyone was sleeping. He did not shout but simply closed his eyes and tried to tell himself he was dreaming. He could not believe there was anything left of his body, but of course there was – which was why it continued to hurt as the arm hauled him over the roads and the rough dry grass. Louis played dead but he kept on living. And then the running halted, and the breathing slowed, and the hand let go of his hair. His head flopped down onto the ground, but he did not open his eyes until he heard the owner of the arm retreat and fade into the distance. There was an orange light behind his eyelids before he opened them, so he knew it was daytime. He could smell flowers and rich soil and the spice of cedar trees, and also a cinnamon fragrance that made him think of red-heart candies. When he opened his eyes, he was in an unknown tangled garden, and pungent roses and blackberry were stretching their thorny arms out to him. The berries dripped black juice and the roses opened so wide that he could see their seedy centres. His relief at the sight was as big as his dismay. He could only believe he had died and gone on to heaven.

⬤⬤⬤⬤⬤

In real life, glass had smashed. Fire grew in the walls of the little plaza downtown, spreading through the floorboards and up the corners of the rooms. The wildlife that prowled the town at night stopped and listened to the sparks snapping. Their ears and noses twitched. In the contained heat of the stores, plastic objects sagged and melted before the flames touched them. The heat pressed on the walls and windows, and in the black night – an August night, and hot enough already – every pane of glass in the plaza exploded in unison. It might have been a miracle, but no human saw it. A brigade of sleepy volunteer firemen arrived too late to control a blaze of such massive proportions, the likes of which they'd never seen before and never would see again, once they went back to stopping chimney fires in winter. Everything was ruined. In the morning, townspeople came to observe the rubble. Within a night's sleep, the shops they had frequented were gone, and all the things they had wanted but had not yet bought were unavailable to them.

Louis thought of Pierrette and Clothilde, and Alphonse pushing through the bushes on his bicycle. Alphonse spoke of death as though it were a person, so maybe Death had a hairy arm, and last night, they had all escaped the grasp of its fingers. He had not dreamed of the arm in a very long time, and he was aware, suddenly, of growing older. Four years had passed since Louis had spotted Joe in the closing ceremonies of the Munich Olympics, and only now did he realize that during the ceremony for the Montreal Olympics, he had not thought to look for Joe at all. He had been too busy imagining himself in future parades, himself as gold medallist, as torchbearer, carrier of the Canadian flag. *One day*, he swore, but he did not know how or when. There had been no room for Joe in those images, but with the realization that he'd forgotten him, the sight of Joe in his British athlete's uniform returned. He saw Joe meet his gaze and disappear from the edge of the TV screen. He tried to hang on to the memory even once the image had faded, but it floated out of his mind and into the black smoke that filled the sky above Deep River. He was no longer a boy in a playhouse, carefully placing his puzzled stuffed animals. He could hardly picture the father who'd promised to move into the playhouse with him only to disappear forever. In four years, Louis had become a man, however little, instead of the son of someone who had ceased to exist.

So in the wake of the fire, no matter how he tried, he thought mostly of the one thing he'd wanted and not bought before the store burned down: a large and lofty book about men's gymnastics. The pages he had thumbed in the bookstore must have burned in a heartbeat, as every heroic medallist transformed to ash.

⟨⟨⟨⟨⟨⟨⟩⟩⟩⟩⟩⟩

By contrast, Margar thought of the candies through which she had run her hands the day before, and of the fact that she had been saving for Barbie's camper, yellow with wavy pink stripes along the side, but a camper made of plastic must have been one of the first things to melt to nothing, along with the rows of Barbies and Kens. She pictured their faces sagging from the heat, and then caving into their hollow heads.

Later that grey, smoky day, she was hot from the fire and the sun. She tucked her own Ken and Barbie into each pocket of her shorts and took the footpath to the river. She had no way of knowing that her mother had stood in nearly the same place three years before when she had thrown her wedding band, or that this was also the place where Robbie Hayes's love note had lost its words and floated blankly along the riverbed, soon dissolving to nothing. Robbie Hayes had died before Margar's time – or at least when no one had known she existed.

She squatted at the river's edge and let the water lap over her sandals. Taking the dolls from her pockets, she made them kiss. She wondered if Gus Devlin would ever marry her mother, and if he did, would she automatically become Margar Devlin, Earl-ess? She laid the dolls on their backs in the water, painted smiles facing the hazy sky. Barbie's hair spread out in a bright blonde circle that made Margar recall her dream and the tiara she had worn for her croquet game. She remembered the distinct sensation that someone was somewhere in the distance, playing the game with her, and now, as she looked down into the river, her own reflection turned into Joe's face. He stared up at her, pressing his hands on the underside of the water's surface, and then he opened his mouth, but her own face returned before he could say why he'd come.

Margar looked up and saw Mrs. Halliwell walking along the riverbank toward her. She still thought of her as the Moon Woman because of her bright white face beneath her night-sky hair. There had been something creepy about that day in Montreal, when the crowd had parted and Mrs. Halliwell had looked at her, and only now did Margar recall that the hat she'd had on, black and wide-brimmed, had also been worn at Joe's funeral years before. She thought she remembered looking up into the bright blue eyes and discovering that the woman was crying. But that had been Our Lady, dropping tears on the baby Jesus.

Mrs. Halliwell had no hat on today, despite the sun. Her black hair was pulled back from her face, revealing streaks of grey near the temples. Wearing a blue cotton dress with a red sash at the waist, she oozed elegance. Of everyone Margar knew (or almost knew), this woman was most like royalty. She knelt beside Margar and gestured toward the water.

"You're sending them on a cruise, I see?"

Margar turned to see Barbie and Ken floating from shore. She lunged and grabbed the dolls. She was shaking the water off of them when Mrs. Halliwell said, "That was some fire, wasn't it?"

Margar nodded.

"I could smell it in my sleep," said Mrs. Halliwell, fanning herself with a paperback. "It woke me up – I honestly thought my own house was burning."

Margar glanced at Mrs. Halliwell, who gazed across the river in the vacant way that Barbie looked at things. Margar looked there too, to see what she was seeing, but there was nothing but trees and more trees, on the verge of turning. A long silence ensued, and Margar felt pressured to fill it.

"I didn't wake up," she said. "I heard the windows breaking right in my dream. They exploded at the same time as this big egg – well, it's too hard to explain."

Mrs. Halliwell's plum lips spread slowly, revealing white Margaret Trudeau teeth. The smile was somehow scary, and a little thrill buzzed through Margar. She liked to be scared.

"Tell me," said Mrs. Halliwell. "I'm interested in dreams."

And Margar's words rushed out in a silly, nervous torrent. "I looked like me but not, and I had on a pink dress, and everything was pink except this huge green field, well not a field, but a prairie or something, all open, and I was playing croquet . . ." and she sat and told the entire dream to this woman she didn't know.

"My," said Mrs. Halliwell. "Quite a dreamer, you are." Her eyes turned even bluer in her white face, and Margar remembered how vibrant they'd been on the day of the funeral. She had an image of the woman in a blue suit and a feathery hat, but there was no story attached to the picture, so it flitted off unexplained. Margar swished Barbie's toes, then Ken's, in the river.

"Do you think dreams mean anything?" she asked.

"I suppose," said Mrs. Halliwell.

"Do you think sleeping is like being dead?"

Mrs. Halliwell laughed. "I doubt it. I think being dead must be much quieter than sleeping. Sleeping can be very – busy."

"I always say that the things that happened before I was born happened when I was dead, because I wasn't alive yet."

Mrs. Halliwell smiled in a strange way, but didn't respond. She let her eyes roam over Margar's face in a manner that seemed too personal, too intimate, and caused Margar to look away. She saw that Barbie and Ken were at sea again – she must have let go a second time without realizing. They rose and dipped with the waves and drifted past the raft toward the drop-off. Barbie's synthetic Malibu hair gleamed in the sun. She smiled up at the sky, and then her legs and torso were submerged, and her blonde happy head sank into the water. Ken followed. The water entered the little holes in the soles of their feet, which were like Jesus' stigmata.

Margar looked back at the Moon Woman, who was still staring at her in that searching, intimate way. She lifted her hand and pressed it to Margar's forearm. Margar flushed at the contact.

She looked away from Mrs. Halliwell's eyes, to her neck, and the hollow between her collarbones. A sapphire pendant sparkled in the light.

"You know," she said softly, too closely. "You look so much like your father."

⦅⦆⦆⦆

That afternoon Margar went home and stood in her mother's bedroom, where there was a three-way mirror that allowed her to view herself from all angles. Her nose – said Estelle and Louis – grew at an even faster rate than the rest of her. It might already be bigger than Joe's had been, the cheekbones higher and pointier. It was one thing for a man to look like a hawk – said Estelle and Louis – and another thing altogether for a girl. She had to admit she did not look like any other girl she knew. And she towered over the boys her age, gazing down on the tops of their heads the way a bird would, or a Martian.

Margar put her face closer to the mirror and pinched her cheeks hard, as if the squeezing could change her face into a soft apple-cheek face, like Estelle's, square-jawed, but squishy enough to make a dimple. Estelle's dimple was in her right cheek. All she had to do was curve her mouth the tiniest bit and it appeared, a little stamp of beauty. No matter how Margar contorted her face, no dimples appeared. Joe had had none either. There was no room left for dimples in the tight skin of their faces. Perhaps she would continue to look more and more like him. She would turn into him, a man, and leave her old self behind.

She lifted the lid of Kay's jewellery box, intending to try on earrings and necklaces, the cross and the tarnished locket. She

280

was thinking of Mrs. Halliwell and her sapphire pendant, but in pulling the case toward her, she dropped it on the floor, and all the jewellery landed in a pile with the box on top of it. The mechanical ballerina inside, which had never worked as far as Margar knew, started up again, turning slowly and emitting the tinkling song of the Sugar Plum Fairy. For a reason just out of reach, but nagging, the music reminded Margar of her old bunny slippers and the ears to match, and the way she used to twitch her nose when she wore them. Margar stooped and turned the box upright. The jewellery lay in a knotted mass beneath it, and something white – a piece of paper – poked out from a tear in the lining. Margar sat cross-legged with the box in her lap. She pulled the note from its hiding spot and began to read the words written in her mother's hand. She didn't understand what the words implied, but she knew it was something big, something that made the whole world different. She reread the line, *the unfortunate connection of our families*, and knew she had stumbled on something she wasn't supposed to know, and that her mother, of all people, had a secret. Her mother and Mrs. Halliwell. All of them whirled through her mind like a sped-up movie – Mrs. Halliwell and the short, muscly coach, their fat son who was a faceless blob to Margar, and her own mother, her brother, her sister, and Joe. What could they possibly have in common?

Margar folded the letter along its worn creases. The paper was smooth and floppy like fabric, vulnerable as an ancient artifact. She tucked it back into the lining of the jewellery box, and as she ran her finger along the rip, the velvet closed together so seamlessly, she couldn't see the tear at all. With unusual care and patience, she began to untangle the necklaces, ensuring no one would know what she'd discovered, whatever that was. All the while her mind raced. She was fond of secrets, but this one made her uneasy. As she placed the box back on the dresser, she looked at their dusty, framed school pictures. She closed the lid of the box and the only sign that she had been prying at all came from the ballerina. As though making up for lost time, she kept spinning, and her music kept playing the Sugar Plum song. Margar opened the lid and held the little figure between her thumb and finger, which stopped the movement and muffled the sound, but she could feel the ballerina struggling to keep on. The rhythm of her mechanics was like a heartbeat, until, with a click, it stopped, and the doll broke off in Margar's hand. Margar gasped. She laid the body on top of the jewels, closed the lid, and whisked from the room.

(((((())))))

Disparate worlds were spinning toward each other while Edward's progressed steadily away. He had not veered off course since his nocturnal visit to the blue two-storey in the winter of '73. True to his word, he had never returned home again. When he left that night with his father's new camera and tripod, his half-shattered glasses in his pocket, Edward embarked on a career he had not previously imagined.

In the brutal cold, he thumbed his way to Ottawa, then curled up on a bench in the depot until his bus arrived. A migraine was starting at the base of his skull and up high, around his temple. The arms of his glasses felt like vice grips. He took the glasses off and slept a while, but it was restless sleep, worse than his earlier dozes, because his head pounded throughout. When he woke in a fog, the last of the passengers were boarding the bus and the driver was loading the luggage into the undercarriage compartments. Edward clambered on unseen, and found a seat in the back. He hoped the driver wouldn't take his ticket, so he could trade it in for cash when he got back to Halifax.

He didn't wake again until a long time later. A different driver shook him by the shoulder, and unfolded the crumpled ticket Edward produced. The driver grimaced.

"You trying to pull a fast one, or did you get on the wrong bus?"

Edward looked blearily out the window at a generic black sky and snowy ground. "Where are we?" he asked, and fumbled for his glasses.

"You serious? We're in Syracuse, in New York state," the driver said, and waited for Edward's response, but Edward was dumbfounded. "I don't know how we missed you at the border, but you're getting off here, kid. Come on, I got a schedule to keep."

It was 4 a.m. Bright stars scattered the sky like chunks of exploded ice, and Edward shivered beneath them. He must have slept for hours while the wrong bus hurtled along to a foreign land. His headache had passed, but he was dazed and bewildered, having woken so suddenly. He entered the depot and found a map on the wall, and tried to make sense of the route he had taken. The names of the towns dotted throughout the state swam before his eyes, then settled and made themselves clear to him. Syracuse. Ithaca. Attica. Rome. Greece.

Troy. Corinth. Athens. Edward almost laughed. He let his bags fall in a pile around him.

⬭⬭⬭⬭⬭

Edward never returned to Halifax, or to art school. Instead, with eight dollars and a packet of nuts in his pocket, he hitch-hiked to New York City. It took him five rides to get there, and in between there were long cold stretches during which he thought he might die of exposure, despite his parka and his fur-lined boots. Once, when no cars had appeared for hours, Edward took shelter in an abandoned house along the side of the road. The door was unlocked, as his parents' had been. Inside was barely warmer than outside, but there was no wind, at least, and a roof to shelter him from the snow that had begun to fall. He sat on the floor with his arms around his knees as though to hold himself in place. In a heartbeat, he had made a tremendous decision, and now he felt weightless, aimless, like an astronaut who leaps out into space. Suddenly life had no parameters.

Come dawn, shafts of light poured in through the torn curtains, and Edward opened the window and watched the curtains move in the light. Invigorated by the fresh blast of cold air, he set up the stolen tripod and put the camera on top of it. He took ten shots of nothing but the moving curtains, which were blue with yellow flowers, and grubby along the centre hems, where too many hands had touched them.

When the light changed, he looked around the room to see where it had gone, and became aware of the cracked green tiles in the kitchen, the worn floorboards, the mildew that blackened the baseboards and the corners of the room. Paw prints – possibly a

284

raccoon's – trailed across the kitchen floor, up to the counter, and down again. Grime plumed around light switches and door jambs, and mouse droppings littered the shelves of the open cupboards. On the ceiling, there was a brown stain with a hole at its centre. It gaped down at him like an eye not blinking, like a dead eye that had failed to close.

The things that had been left behind surprised him. In the kitchen there was a pot on the filthy stove, with charred black residue stuck to the bottom. A spoon rested on the counter, and it was that – the spoon – that gave a feeling of stopped time to the room and the house beyond it. Stickers decorated the bottom drawer of the stove, the lower part of the fridge door, the wall beneath the kitchen window – anywhere a child could reach. Edward could see that there had been a half-hearted attempt to scrub or peel them away, but it had been too big a job, too fiddly, and so the ridiculous cartoon faces remained, some torn in half, grinning out at him. There were what looked like two plates on the floor, but they had been smashed to pieces, and Edward pictured them being thrown down within the violent clamour of shouting, the child sitting amidst all that, playing with his stickers.

As he mounted the stairs to the second floor, something moved in the wall next to him. He froze and listened, but the sound stopped. *A squirrel*, he told himself, *or a family of mice*. He continued on. The carpet that covered the steps was thin and brittle and peeled up at the edges, straining against the tacks that held it in place. He put his hand on the banister, which came loose and fell onto the stairs. Grit and dust puffed out of the holes it left behind, like Edward's breath clouding in the chilly air.

The layout of the upper floor resembled that of the blue two-storey: the master bedroom, and across from it, a smaller room, with the bathroom at the end of the hall between them. Edward looked into the room that was like his own. It had been a boy's room too. Rippled posters of cars hung crookedly from the walls. The narrow bed had been stripped bare but a pillow – stained yellow, never washed – remained at the head.

Edward set up his camera and took more photographs, and then he stepped across the hall to the master bedroom. Again, the bed had been left behind. It was a double, and though the sheets were gone, a garish turquoise spread remained. The fringe had been cut from the bottom and lay in a coil on the floor. Not far off were the scissors that had done the mysterious deed, rusted and spread wide.

Edward turned back to the bed. Two exotic painted birds loomed out from the headboard. The paint was faded and chipped, and had been hand-done, improperly, but Edward was strangely touched by the birds' long graceful tails, which curved out and then in again, meeting at the centre like the point of a feathered heart. He crossed the creaking floor. Some of the boards were missing, and he could see through to the room below. The hair on his arms stood up in a way that had nothing to do with cold. He heard something scurry across the floor in the room downstairs, and peered through the gaps in the floorboards. There was a small shadow, and then nothing. The sounds diminished, and he resumed his slow investigation. He wondered what he would do if he came upon someone, or if someone came upon him. Despite his fear, he sat on the edge of the bed and brushed his fingers over the birds. The paint, a creamy, opaque pink, flaked beneath his hand and fell like hail to the mattress.

Edward lay back on the bed and looked at the closet, where the doors were flung wide. Bent hangers hung naked from the rod and scattered the floor beneath. A pair of gold shoes sat sparkling in the sunlight. The shoes were cheap high heels but glamorous. They looked like prize possessions, barely worn, kept only for special occasions, and yet they remained, along with the cans of soup and boxes of macaroni and cheese that sat on the top shelf of the closet. Why such things would be needed in a bedroom, Edward couldn't guess. He knew the answers to these questions had left as thoroughly, as irrevocably, as the inhabitants of this decaying house, once a home, and it was this, in part, that stirred him. More than ever, he, too, was a member of the leaving kind.

⬤⬤⬤⬤⬤

Edward made it all the way to New York City. It was weeks before he called his mother for money, and told her he had left school, had left everything behind, unfinished, and had no plan of returning. She sobbed into the receiver, but the wet sounds of her crying failed to move him. Only after they hung up did he think about how close he had been to her, how he had stood in the hallway and listened to her sleeping, how he had almost stayed to surprise her at the breakfast table – a new son, a better son, smaller and bigger all at once. He paused with his hand on the phone and let that memory – the possibility of a memory – fall away.

He rarely thought about his little room in Halifax, or the stone walls of the art college, or the sea that crashed nearby. His world had changed, utterly and completely. The streets of New York teemed with every kind of person imaginable. It seemed impossible to him that any one type could be called "a New Yorker," a fact that put him at ease and allowed him to move comfortably among the rest.

For a time he lived in an old warehouse, squatting with a handful of other transients and sleeping with his equipment strapped around him. He could bear anything because he knew it was temporary, and that he would rise. He was so unlike the other squatters that the distance between them seemed like a physical thing in itself, a presence that hung in the air. Which was usual for him. It would have disturbed him, after all this time, to feel a sense of belonging.

The money from his mother sufficed for a short time, but he'd promised himself he wouldn't ask again. In the day, he panhandled, and used the cash to eat and buy film. He photographed the faces of the squatters close up, and the building itself, with its rats, its broken windows, its smashed-in walls. Time and again, he was amazed by how light alone could turn the place beautiful. It occurred to him that he might be approaching happiness, as when he'd first left home, but it was a dark, precarious emotion, and like raw film exposed to the light, at any time it could leave him with nothing.

Within three months he had a job at a lab. As a resume, he took in his own work – the few pieces he could afford to develop – and while the pay was poor it soon allowed him the very basic luxuries of a room with a cot and a lock on the door. The lab gave him privileges too, and he spent many of his off-hours there, turning his film into photos. His work grew stronger. He loved to watch the images come slowly into being – the blank paper floating in its chemical pool and the features of a face, or a room, taking shape in that poison.

Sometimes he thought of his photography professor, who had boasted that only the photograph could duplicate reality so precisely – or not, he said, for it could deceive and obscure as well as it could capture. Edward had bridled at that, as much as or more than he'd bridled at St. Clair's every word, in the beginning. Mostly he'd recoiled from the idea that photography could be art, could have the same power, the same worth, as something that had been painted by hand. He remembered how he had laboured over his realistic depictions, needing to perfect every detail. His sole aim, his greatest need, had been to painstakingly recreate life with pencil and paper. It seemed, in his early years at school, that he was being taught the pointlessness of such work, which had been so important to him. He was being asked to leave the core of himself behind, and he'd bitterly resisted at every turn.

Back then he would never have guessed he'd be here, on the precipice of happiness, imprisoning moments inside the body of a camera and releasing them later, in the privacy of a darkroom. He saw the irony. With the click of a shutter, every detail was perfect already. But despite the precision of his instrument, he never quite knew what he had captured until afterwards, when the image stared up at him from the liquid. And every time, it included things he had not seen through the viewfinder. In the bedroom with the birds, for instance, he saw a strand of pearls lying just beneath the bed. Straight across the room, near the

289

closet, a loose pearl rested beside the sparkly shoes. It seemed so obvious now, in the photograph, that he couldn't fathom having missed it at the time. It made him think about perspective and distance and focus, and how even a moment caught and held in the hands as paper changed before one's very eyes. But which was true? The moment as he'd lived it, or the one he understood long after it had passed?

MOSCOW 1980
saint margaret and the dragon

In 1980, for the first time ever, a socialist country hosted the Olympic Games. Next to no one was there to see it, but it happened just the same. The only other bidder had been Los Angeles, and some said that losing to Moscow was the real reason the Americans boycotted the Games. But President Jimmy Carter insisted it was because of Afghanistan, and the Soviet invasion that had taken place in December of 1979, and announced that the United States could not condone such behaviour. Though not everyone trusted his earnestness, sixty-five countries, some with twisted arms, declined to participate, which meant that only eighty countries took part. Canada was not among them.

Between July 19 and August 3, with Misha the Bear as the official mascot, President Leonid Brezhnev presiding over the opening ceremonies, and Sergei Belov lighting the Olympic flame, 5,179 athletes entered the Olympic Village, 1,115 of them women. There were so few competitors that the Soviet Union found itself without an opponent in the sport of field hockey. Five weeks before the Games, Zimbabwe was invited to put a team together and play against the host, just so the host could play, and wonder of wonders, Zimbabwe won.

But mostly, the USSR gobbled medals. The Soviet team received eighty gold, sixty-nine silver, and forty-six bronze, for an astounding total of 195. Eight of them belonged to gymnast Aleksandr Dityatin, who won six medals in one day. There was no way to tell what might have happened had Louis LeBlanc been among the contenders, but those days were long gone for him. Years had passed, and taken so many lives in different directions.

His mother had once had grand Olympic dreams, but while Kay had relished personal glory, Louis had longed to achieve, in the biggest sense of the word. While it still seemed a possibility, he'd tended to his career as a gymnast in the same careful way that he parted his hair and made his bed every morning, wiping the wrinkles away with a gentle hand.

Following the previous Summer Olympics, when Louis returned to high school, he'd kept his promise to give himself over to gymnastics. In spite of his mother's baffling protestations, Louis sweated five nights a week in the high-school gymnasium, and within the single school year of '76–'77, he advanced all the way to the provincial championships.

In the early days, Louis was overjoyed and also terrified to have Coach Halliwell as his trainer. At first the coach gave him almost no encouragement, which bruised Louis to such an extent that he nearly lost faith in the idea of destiny – but then, by fluke, by fate, his old uncles gave him his Christmas present. He tore off the wrapping and found the book he had coveted – or rather, a new copy, but Louis imagined it as the same one, having survived the fire to bring him stories of athletes who had once been ordinary boys from ordinary places. Louis was inspired anew.

He still worried about failing, but those very worries spurred him on too. He trained relentlessly to force his body into peak physical condition. The pressure of competing drew dark circles under his eyes. It crept into his sleep and gave him dreams of struggling uphill. He was pulling bags of stones so heavy that the rope handles twisted and frayed until nothing but single threads held him to his load. But the threads would not break. Instead his arms snapped off like a doll's, and Louis lurched forward and fell to the mossy ground. Turning to watch his burdens hurtling away from him, he saw how his fingers still gripped the shredded rope and would not let go even though the journey had been utterly reversed.

Rundown as he was, his adrenalin pumped on. His skills hollered out amid the mediocrity in his gymnastics' class, and Coach Halliwell finally acknowledged him.

"You're good, kid," he told Louis, one day after practice. "If you can keep doing that in competition, we'll have lots to talk about."

And Louis's soul hummed.

More than once – more than three or five times – Coach Halliwell gripped Louis's shoulder with his firm, muscular hand, and told him, "I like you, Louis. You're willing to really work. That's what'll give you a shot in the big leagues. More than a shot."

More than a shot, Louis told himself repeatedly. Suddenly he could not recall a day when he hadn't suspected there was something special about him, something he must achieve, a magical force drawing him toward his very purpose for being. Before every meet, anxiety scraped his insides, but he had never felt more alive, more potent, more sure he could win. He wished his mother would be proud of him, and jump and cheer at his meets, the way other parents did, but she stood in the crowd and clapped politely, as interested as a stranger. He thought if he tried harder – but nothing moved her. Once she had loved gymnastics right along with him, and had taught him his earliest positions. He didn't know why her enthusiasm had waned, but he wavered between two beliefs: either he was disappointing to watch, and would never be as good as she'd been, or he was better. And that meant he wavered between two forms of shame.

His greatest joy came wrapped up in Coach Halliwell's approval. The coach tempered his praise with criticism, which was the way Louis preferred it, because criticism told him he could always improve, and if he kept improving, there would always be more praise. Louis dreamed of making it to the Moscow Olympics, which at that time was a few years away. Until then he needed to compete regionally, provincially, and nationally, but beyond that, he wasn't sure what was required of him – and he was too timid to ask, in case he jinxed himself, for the more successes he accumulated, the more precarious they seemed.

Alphonse and Toussaint had made a shelf for his trophies, but no one foresaw that there would be so many. The little strip of wood bowed under the weight. If it collapsed, and landed on Louis as he slept, he would certainly die, and never make it to the ultimate podium. These were the thoughts that ate away at him and also urged him forward.

When Louis had run himself absolutely ragged in his pursuit, when his fingernails were chewed raw and he could barely eat for nervousness over the biggest competition so far – the provincial championships – only then did Coach Halliwell say to him, moments before he competed, "I don't know why you work yourself up over these nothing meets, Louis. Just relax. Have fun with it."

"But if I don't win –"

"So you don't win. It doesn't mean anything. It's not like you'll make it to the Olympics," he said, cuffing the back of Louis's head. "Hey, there's always basketball." He laughed with his mouth wide open, and what Louis thought might be a tonsil wiggled at the back of the coach's throat.

Louis's baffled heart snapped into fragments. The bitten skin around his nails stung. A little parasite of humiliation fluttered inside him, but when his turn came to compete, Louis stepped onto the mat with the same fragile poise he had always exhibited. He stood on his hands and pointed his toes at the ceiling, wishing there was a way for him to be pulled up through the roof or down through the floor without anyone seeing him go. He was aware of his mother somewhere in the audience, and of the coach behind him. Until now, Louis's eagerness to please, his fear of letting everyone down, had pushed him to excel, but he had been misguided. He'd never guessed that he didn't have the power to disappoint, since no one believed in him anyway. In spite of this revelation, he executed every move brilliantly, and when he finished, he held his head high and spread his arms like the wings of an eagle. Closing his eyes to the thunderous applause, he wondered what he would do now, and who he would be, for his days of competing were over.

⦿⦿⦿⦿⦿

He packed his newest trophy into a box with the rest, and stored the lot in the crawlspace, with all the other things no one wanted or needed, but couldn't possibly throw away.

⦿⦿⦿⦿⦿

Days before Louis's heartbreak, Kay LeBlanc had happened upon Russell Halliwell in the lobby of the post office. As they looked through their mail, discarding the flyers, the room emptied and they were alone. At first it seemed neither would speak. And then Kay said,

"Stay away from Louis."

Even her mouth was shaking.

"How can I possibly do that," said Russell. "I'm his gym teacher. And I'm not the one who signed him up for extracurricular gymnastics."

"It's going too far," said Kay. "Put an end to it."

"But you must know how good he is. I think he could –"

"Don't," said Kay. "Just end it."

The door pushed open and a woman entered, and Kay and Russell looked away from each other. Their first exchange since before Estelle's birth was over. Side by side, they gathered their mail in silence, and one after the other, they exited in the congenial manner of strangers.

(00000)

Not even snoopy Margar had witnessed the exchange. If her big ears had been listening in on that tiny span of time, the note she had found in the jewellery box might have begun to spell itself out. As it was, her unanswered questions evolved into an obsession. Taking the chance she might be caught by the coach or the eerily compelling Mrs. Halliwell, she poked around their property throughout the fall, and even occasionally in the chilly winter, peering through the mess of trees to the garden. She knew that at one time her father had tended the flowerbeds here, and that there had been a stone path and an angel fountain created by her uncles, Alphonse and Toussaint. She squinted through the branches, but the yard was thick with weeds, and if it contained a stone path and a fountain, both were covered by vines.

It was the sight of Mrs. Halliwell through the windows that drew Margar to the blue two-storey again and again. She watched her wash and dry dishes and place them in neat stacks in the cupboards. She watched her play the piano and polish the silverware and dust the photos that decorated the white walls. Margar had never seen such a tidy house, or such a composed, elegant person. At home, her mother slopped around in worn slippers and a paint-splotched T-shirt, but Mrs. Halliwell dressed for the day, and put her hair up, and wore lipstick and earrings whether she went out or not. Only once did Margar see a break in the pristine monotony, an outburst so shocking that it pimpled her skin right down to the ankles. She had just arrived at the house, and was watching the space between the open curtains, when a stack of plates flew by, one white disc after another, like china Frisbees that must have crashed on the floor. But as the windows were closed, Margar heard nothing. Mrs. Halliwell followed with a red face, her mouth hollering, the tendons in her neck taut with rage. She passed as quickly as the plates had, as silently, though she must have been screaming her lungs out. Margar crouched among the leaves and waited, eyeing the space the curtains framed, but no one appeared, nothing hurtled past, and soon she backed away, feeling dirty for seeing what she'd seen, but already deciding she'd be back tomorrow.

And so, right into the winter, Margar came and went. She left footprints in the snow the way Joe had when he'd gone to the hospital to look for Kay and Estelle, and the way an unknown someone had when he'd prowled around the edge of 40 Huron Street during the moonstruck season. She itched to step into the yard and spy up close through the windows, but she was warier than that, especially after seeing Mrs. Halliwell turn crazy. So intent was Margar on remaining invisible to the Halliwells that she sometimes forgot she might easily be seen by whoever drove past on Riverside Drive. And that disregard – not watching her back – meant that once, she was caught by her mother.

Kay rolled down her window, eyes bright with disbelief. She hissed to Margar to *get in the car right now!*

"My God, what were you doing?" she yelled, once Margar was inside the car, the windows and doors shut tight.

Margar tried to think of some reason she might have been hanging around the Halliwell home. She was as startled as Kay was that they'd encountered each other, but hiding her reaction came naturally. She opened her mouth and a lie popped out even before she summoned it.

"I was looking for holes in trees – the kind squirrels nest in."

Kay glanced at her suspiciously but said nothing.

"A project for school."

Red patches had formed on Kay's cheeks, and now they began to fade. "You shouldn't get so close to people's properties. You should look in the woods, or in our own yard."

"We only have one tree," said Margar, "and there aren't any squirrels living in it. I already looked."

"In the woods, then. Or ask Ms. Devlin." Kay released a sigh and opened her window a crack, letting in an icy breeze. "It's not good to hang around peoples' houses like that, that's all."

Margar shrugged, but her insides pitched and rolled. Sick with knowing more than she should – with not knowing enough – she kept returning to the big, quiet house by the river, and the woman who lived within.

⬤⬤⬤⬤⬤

It was spring when Marie Halliwell noticed she was being watched. Over a period of weeks, she became aware of something red moving amid the trees, and then she saw the whole girl, frightfully skinny, tall as a scarecrow, and as obvious. Marie stepped out onto the porch.

"Would you like to come in?" she asked.

And Margar nodded.

⬤⬤⬤⬤⬤

The interior of the Halliwell home was white and spacious, with cut flowers in every room as in soap-opera homes. There were white curtains, white furniture, and white rugs – plush but not inviting – and a picture window that ran the length of the dining and living rooms, and looked out over the river. A piano had been oddly placed in the centre of the room, with a vase of lilies and a number of framed photographs on top of it. Awkward in the silence, Margar said, "I play the piano," and Mrs. Halliwell smiled her ambiguous lipstick smile, and said, "I know." Margar thought of the funeral, her first recital. She looked away from the woman's very blue eyes.

Mrs. Halliwell opened the lid of the piano bench and showed Margar the music inside. "Play something if you like." And then: "I could make you some hot chocolate."

Margar nodded, and watched Mrs. Halliwell disappear into the kitchen, recalling the plates flying. Mrs. Halliwell's shoes clacked on the floor, and Margar thought how weird it was – how uncomfortable – that a person would wear shoes in her own home, as if she were just visiting herself. Margar looked down at the hole in her sock, at her somewhat dirty toe. She drew the toe back in, like a turtle pulling its head into its shell.

The photographs on top of the piano and on the walls around her were black-and-white images taken somewhere far from here, where there were old buildings and statues much larger than Our Lady of the Snows. A young Mrs. Halliwell smiled out at her, and Margar was so caught up in examining that face that she almost failed to notice the man next to her – Coach Halliwell – but in an instant his easy smile, his dimples, his deep-set eyes became clear to her. Estelle's face rose out of his and settled on his skin the way Margar's face had done on the few photographs of Joe LeBlanc. Margar gasped. She squeezed her eyes shut and opened them again, and Estelle was still there. She looked along the wall at the rest of the pictures and saw that Estelle looked more like this man than did the child who had to be his son, a fat boy with glasses and a fringe of dark hair surrounding his round, sour face. Margar didn't know Eddie Halliwell, being some fourteen years younger than he, but she could see his morose character in the pictures that remained of him, pictures that traced his life from boyhood to late teens and then ended abruptly.

"Here you are, Margaret."

Mrs. Halliwell had returned with the hot chocolate, and Margar sat in a big white chair and sipped her drink. Confused and panicky, she wanted to run from the house, but she wanted to stay too, so that she could figure out what had happened, and how everything pieced together. *Mom and Louis's coach had a baby*, she kept thinking. *Estelle*. There was a concrete reason, now, for all of their differences. Her mind flew from Estelle to the coach, to her mother, to the fat boy, to Mrs. Halliwell, and of course, to Joe. *You were the one he came back for*, she thought, picturing Estelle's face crumpling. *But me, I'm his daughter. You aren't even related.* And then she thought, *I'm sorry.* She remembered the story she had told Noelle – that she was a kidnapped czarina whose real father wasn't Joe – and though she had had it all wrong, the tall tale held a glimmer of truth that she hadn't anticipated. In her smug, sad, bewildering turmoil, she lost track of what Mrs. Halliwell was saying, and caught only the nonsense of,

"up by a dragon but miraculously survived."

Margar gulped and her hot chocolate scalded her throat. "What?" she asked. "I mean, pardon?"

Mrs. Halliwell's lips curved. "Saint Margaret of Antioch," she said. "Your namesake."

Mrs. Halliwell pulled out a big book from a careful pile on the coffee table, and flipped through the colourful pages until she came to a painting of a couple holding hands. The pale man was dressed in a black and brown cape, his face thin and serious beneath his broad hat. The woman's face was pink and round. She wore a white veil and a green gown with blue sleeves poking out from fur-lined armholes. One hand reached to her husband, and the other rested on her round tummy. Their slippers were made of wood, and lay on the floor near their feet, where there was also a scraggy dog who looked like Olive. In behind, luxurious red drapes hung from the ceiling around a red, pillowy bed.

Marie Halliwell pointed to a barely discernable figure on the bedpost.

"Saint Margaret," said Mrs. Halliwell. "Her story is carved along the headboard. She was swallowed by a dragon but came out of its belly alive, which is why she's the patron saint of childbirth."

Margar started at the word, but said nothing.

"Wait," said Mrs. Halliwell. "I'll show you another one."

She flipped through the pages until she came to a picture of Margaret, beautiful in her blue and red robes, golden hair cascading over her shoulders. Her delicate, naked foot rested on the dragon's wing. The conquered beast seethed beneath her, his pink mouth stretched open as if she had emerged from there only moments ago, victorious. His red, awful eyes and his nose

302

seemed almost human, but Margaret herself was so fine as to be otherworldly. Margar remembered her croquet dream, and how she'd had long blonde tresses and a pink gown, which was sort of like red.

"See?" said Mrs. Halliwell, pointing to the text. "Read it out, why don't you."

And Margar read: "'Margaret is the patron saint of dying people, exiles, the falsely accused, martyrs, nurses, peasants, sufferers of kidney disease, childbirth, and anyone fleeing from devils.'"

Birth, thought Margar. *My sister is half a sister.*

"Sound like you?" asked Mrs. Halliwell, smiling.

Margar paused, and said, "I have to go now."

"Okay, dear. That's fine."

Mrs. Halliwell walked her to the door, and Margar stepped out of the spare, white decor into the yard, where twisted vines and weeds poked up through the last bits of snow. She had the feeling that if she didn't run, even fly over the yard, the vines would slither like snakes around her arms and legs and neck, then suck her down into the earth and keep her there. She dashed across the yard, only stopping to part the branches of the raggedy hedge. Over her shoulder, Margar stole a last look at the house and saw a boy in the second-floor window, a fat boy with dark, bowl-cut hair. He lifted his head and looked at her with his dead, sad eyes, and then he faded from view. It scared her – fearless Margar – to learn that this was not a happy boy, like the cookie stealer Robbie Hayes. This was a suffering, miserable boy. And it scared her more to know that though the boy had grown up and moved away, as evidenced by the photos, she'd seen him standing in the window without even using her imagination to coax him into place.

Chilled, enthralled, stunned by her visit, Margar sped homeward. The sun and the moon loomed simultaneously in the darkening sky, and the saint she'd been named for flared to life inside of her.

⚬⚬⚬⚬⚬

Margar was greatly disturbed by the knowledge about Estelle's parentage, a secret that seemed both an illicit treasure and an unbearable burden. She wished she could tell someone, but she couldn't decide who that someone should be. If Kay, she couldn't imagine how to say it, or what would come afterwards. Would the truth come out to all of the family, and would Gus be mad and go away? Would Estelle? And more importantly – would Joe stay away? At least she understood, now, why he had gone in the first place. He, too, had discovered the truth. But if he'd wanted it known, he would have let it out then, and left Kay to suffer the ramifications. Instead he had kept the secret, so maybe that meant he would be back, just as Margar had always believed, when he was ready to forgive and forget. Margar thought a lot about forgiveness and what it meant to have faith in faith. She thought of her namesake, Saint Margaret, and how they had loads in common. They believed, against the greatest odds, and withstood the ugliest punishments.

Though she had never been a studious girl, Margar frequented the library after her encounter with Mrs. Halliwell, and read every scrap she could find about Saint Margaret of Antioch, who

304

had eventually been sentenced to death for spouting her belief in Jesus. When the dragon gobbled her down, her cross tickled his throat, and he threw her up again. (Which should really make her the patron saint of barfing, Margar couldn't help thinking.) When Margaret shot out of the dragon, babbling, her persecutors nailed her to a cross and set her on fire. But Margaret didn't burn. They submerged her in the river, but Margaret didn't drown. Only when they lopped off her beautiful head did she finally rise to heaven – which was not to say she was silenced. You could receive a perpetual crown in heaven if you spread Margaret's story on earth. And if you called on her from your deathbed, she would save you. This was the part Margar didn't understand, and that the books didn't bother to explain. Were we not meant to *want* to die, so that we could rise to heaven?

One early summer Wednesday, she was contemplating just that as she walked to the Hayes's for her piano lesson. She was wearing a black slip on her head so she'd appear more saintly, and while she would have preferred blonde, slips didn't come in that shade, and anyway, the fairness would have drawn attention to her eyebrow. She cradled her books in her arm and wondered if she resembled goodness personified. That morning, Estelle had asked why she was wearing underwear on her head, and for a moment, the outer Margar had itched to lash back. But Saint Margaret had glowed inside her like a sacred heart, red and throbbing, encircled with light. Surely she was visible through bones and clothes, for those with the will to see. Margar pitied Estelle for not having that ability – and, of course, for other things too. *Will Estelle go to heaven?*, she asked herself as she climbed the steps to the Hayes's house. *Are bastards allowed in?* She straight-ened her slip, knocked, waited, and knocked again. But strangely, no one answered.

⟨⟨⟨⟨⟨⟩⟩

Earlier that day, the radio in Serge and Beryl Hayes's car was playing sports news, and Beryl reached out a skinny finger and changed the station. Violin and cello music swirled from the speakers. She had no interest in sports, and neither did her husband. Even when their son had been alive, they hadn't gone to his football games or rooted for him when he'd competed (and won) in track and field. He had played hockey every season from the time he was seven years old, but they had only attended the games until he was old enough to be there alone, to lace his own skates tightly, to don his bulky equipment with no help from them. They wished he would take up chess, or backgammon, and urged him in those cerebral directions. They were intellectuals, but had produced, by fluke, a son who was nothing of the kind.

Beryl Hayes had never viewed her attendance at sporting events as a necessary thing, and she had not rued the fact that her husband did not attend either – not until Robbie was gone, and she remembered him standing in the doorway with his skates over his shoulder.

"Come for a skate," he said to his father. "It's such a nice night. Come with me."

And Serge had laughed at the idea. "When ice freezes in the warmth of summer, my boy, that's when I'll come skating."

What he had meant was that he hated the cold, that the frigid winters here were something he would never get used to, but Beryl recalled his words exactly, and later equated them with "when hell freezes over." Though his answer had not been at all mean in spirit – at least, it had not been intended that way – her memory of it distorted the actual exchange and gave her reason, as time went on, to despise the only man she'd ever loved, the man who called her Berry.

As they rode to Ottawa, music filled the space that was empty of words. Beryl assumed they would be shopping for a new living-room carpet, something rich and Turkish, she imagined, but finally Serge said, without warning, and in that pigheaded, mannish way that assumes *I am boss*, "It's time to redo Robbie's room."

The sound of her son's name stunned her, and brought his pink, healthy face to life in her mind. She blinked rapidly, three times, but did not turn to look at her husband, whose white hair brushed the roof of the car. The music played on and his discordant voice sounded again among the violins.

"Now that I'm retired, I'll need an office at home."

Still she did not respond, having never heard anything so ludicrous. *Now that I'm retired, I'll need an office.* Selfish, idiotic man. She showed him the back of her head and looked out the window, but instead of seeing the trees and the farmers' fields, she saw the paradise-blue of Robbie's room, which in reality was dingy after years of disuse, but she did not envision the room now, she envisioned it then, his living self within it, his last day's clothes upon the floor.

"Berry," said Serge, with a gruff tenderness that punctured her anger and made her angrier still for the invasion. He put his hand, warm and familiar, on her arm, and she closed her eyes and listened to the violins. And Serge, turning toward her, to the back of her head, wished in his last breath that she would look at him, but he wished and looked for just an instant too long, lost in the dark curl of her hair, a vortex, as the car rounded a curve in the highway and drifted into the oncoming lane.

The collision that followed was spectacular.

⬤⬤⬤⬤⬤

Gus Devlin kept his head on the wheel, afraid to look up and discover the thing that could not now be undone. It was Wednesday, and he'd been in the greenhouse van, doing his weekly tour of the Valley. Nothing about the day had been much different than any other Wednesday until the car had careened into view. The last thing Gus had seen was a man's face turning toward him, eyes widening with the recognition of what was to come, and then blinking slowly, horribly slowly. Gus had never known anything to happen so slowly and so quickly at the same time. After the crash, he kept his head down for what seemed like hours, when mere seconds had passed – no longer than it had taken for another vehicle to fly into his own.

Gus looked up. Instead of blood, and debris, and bodies, four cows stared at him, their mouths moving in a circular motion. A field of lush grass, dotted with chicory, stretched toward a distant horizon. He took in the lump that rose like a hat between the cows' ears, and the way their ochre hides hung from their

308

spines. The cows had seen it all, which meant they knew more than he. They chewed and stared under the blue sky, just as they had before, just as they would every day, only the weather changing. How he longed to get out of the van and walk past them, right off the edge of the world, but even in his dazed state Gus knew that disappearing was not possible. He pulled on the door handle and stepped down.

The van must have spun when he braked, for the back of it was facing the road. The rear doors had flown open when the car had crashed into him, and the contents had spilled out onto the highway, where two twisted bodies lay among shards of glass. Water from the buckets of flowers wet the pavement and ran in pink rivulets away from the bodies, and Gus crouched among strewn petals, a smell like eucalyptus or gasoline rising off the pavement. He sat in the road between the man and the woman. He could see the woman's tiny face, pinched yet still intact, but the man's face was invisible behind a mask of blood. A cascade of orchids streamed across his back just as if it had been arranged there for mourning. Gus cried. He combed the man's wild hair with his fingers.

And around him, though he didn't see it, cars began to slow and pull onto the gravel shoulders. People rolled down their windows and ogled the scene with horrified, spellbound eyes.

⟨⟨⟨⟨⟨⟩⟩⟩⟩⟩

Kay, who had moved into the position of cook at her parents' restaurant, was frying eggs when the collision occurred. She couldn't have known what any of them were thinking the instant before the crash, and even after the crash had happened, she, of course, had gone on as normal, oblivious to the mess on the road, and the flowers.

When she found Gus in the hospital waiting room, she held his head to her chest as he told her of Serge's eyes locking with his own.

"I was the last person he saw," said Gus.

And Kay thought of Joe, and Robbie, and the staggering connections of fate and circumstance.

With the Hayes's demise, a line had died out. Kay didn't know it, but even Robbie's picture had disappeared from the high school's hall of fame, stolen by her own daughter and stashed in the cluttered half of the bedroom closet (the side that was Margar's), behind a copy of *Tales of the Arabian Nights*. Every trace of Robbie Hayes had vanished, due in part to the murky figure strolling by in the background of that photograph.

After the crash, Gus took a leave of absence from the greenhouse and moved in to 40 Huron Street. Whereas once Kay had been afraid to get too close to him, now she feared losing him forever – if not to a swift, cruel accident, then to guilt and self-loathing, the things that had stolen Joe months before the physical man had ambled away. She listened to Gus lament that he had not been sharp enough on the road that day, had been listening to the radio and singing, watching for hawks in the sky. And besides – his very presence on the road had been wrong, he said. If he hadn't laughed and chatted with the florists at each stop, he wouldn't have been behind schedule. If he'd taken his responsibilities more seriously, he wouldn't have been rounding the curve at that fatal moment. He would have sailed past a long while before, and never –

"It's not your fault," Kay told him. "You didn't do anything wrong." But she couldn't help thinking, *It's all my fault. I did everything wrong.* And though she hadn't been on the highway that day, she felt responsible for the death of two fine people. Friends, almost, who had been good to her. Surely life's coincidences came to remind her of her culpability, just when she thought she'd escaped blame.

Nevertheless, they began their life together. Bit by bit, Gus brought his belongings from Pembroke, and Kay made space in the house for him. The bedroom filled up with his things alongside hers, their socks intermingled, and on a bright September day as Gus weeded the carrot patch in the backyard, Kay dusted and rearranged the furniture to suit the man and the items that had arrived with him. This was the day she opened the jewellery box and saw the broken ballerina – which only annoyed her a little until she remembered the note she'd tucked into the lining so many years before, and had eventually stopped rereading. She dipped her finger into the tear, but the secret compartment was empty. Kay's blood quickened. Her head reeled as she recalled the words of the note, and what they might have given away. Only Margar could have broken the ballerina – but would she have found the note as well? She thought of Estelle, and her heart almost stopped beating. And then she sat on the bed and put her head in her hands. She spread her fingers and looked through them to Gus at work in the garden outside.

That night, she hung on to him as though the light of the moon might cut them apart. She felt so close to him, and was so sure that he loved her completely, that she considered telling him everything that had happened, right from the beginning, as a way of assuaging the guilt that gnawed at her, and the anxiety that had arisen from the missing note. She had convinced herself she must have thrown the note away years ago – she could almost remember doing it – but it was the persistence of her shame that haunted her. She had a hunch that she could be rid of it, once and for all, by confiding in someone who loved her, someone she loved enormously. But there was no telling how Gus would react. And he was suffering with his own demons, so wouldn't it be selfish to make him more miserable with confessions about age-old mistakes? For a moment it gave her some peace to think that she could stay quiet solely out of consideration for him – that she could be that strong. But she knew her true reason. She was terrified of losing him, just as she'd been terrified of losing Joe. To keep Joe, she'd kept on lying. Her happy years with him had been two, or four, no longer, and yet somehow he still held the pre-eminent title of husband. She reached out to touch Gus's face and saw his eyes find hers.

"Gus," she said. "I have something to tell you."

⦿⦿⦿⦿⦿

In autumn of 1977, after several unimportant exhibits, Edward Halliwell made a big splash in a tiny corner of the New York City art scene with a show of photographs called *Home*. It was a real accomplishment, despite the fact that no one outside of that tiny corner knew of him. His breakthrough show featured his abandoned houses series, a project he had been perfecting since he'd broken into his childhood home.

Viewers said the photographs were hard to look at, not only due to their forlorn content, but also because of the way they were pieced together again, forcing the eye to make sense of a kaleidoscope of despair. Only Edward knew that the fractured nature of the compositions had been inspired by the shattered lens of his childhood glasses. Each photograph was actually many shots of a room, taped into a collage and recaptured as a single image. The photomontages were then framed and placed on the gallery walls, and in front of each one, Edward recreated the original space by displaying relics from the actual houses he'd photographed – broken dolls, chipped dishes, rusty irons, kitchen chairs, sofas with the stuffing spilling out, tattered letters, greasy combs, family photos of a family gone missing. The result was a show that reeked of decay and brought the deadness of the abandoned places alive in a bright white setting. The work's beauty came from its brokenness: sunlight illuminating the blue that remained on a crumbling wall; the long feathered tails of the birds flaking away from the headboard.

Artists in their pseudo-bohemian outfits marvelled at the photos, and all the junk in front of them, and collectors who liked to buy off the beaten track came to suss out the young photographer, whose arrogance appealed to them. Edward felt a mixture of pride and disgust for himself and his chosen community. He wanted his work to be noticed and talked about. He wanted success. He had wanted it – and known it would come – since his Michelangelo phase, and later, in art school, he believed he was *better* than Michelangelo because the bodies he drew were less lumpy. Michelangelo had over-drawn, but Edward had known when to stop. And yet, now that success had happened in a semi-important way, the work itself seemed a sham and he, its maker, an imposter, for what was the purpose of pictures on a wall in a room? And since only fools would ogle and praise these pictures, what did that say about the person who made them? He had worked hard to come this far, and he knew he would work harder, despite his bleak recognition that the results were hollow and his life was no more meaningful than it had ever been. Less, perhaps, because as he got older, his ideas came from his brain rather than his heart and his gut, and, to him, his heart was unreachable. Regardless, he knew he could lose himself in the act of creating his work – that he could forget its eventual futility when he was engaged in the process of giving it life – and if he could just make it through the times between, then he knew he could go on indefinitely.

Weeks after the opening, his uneasiness began to subside. He even verged on being proud of himself, and days before the show came down, he sent a belated invitation to his mother. She wouldn't be able to see the work – he didn't want that – but she would know he had made it. She would have some idea of how far he had come. He also sent an article that had been written about the show, and after he dropped the package in the post box, he regretted it. He pictured his mother opening the package, and the fat ghost of him in his tennis clothes wanted to reach into the post box and pull the package out again. He thrust his hands into his pockets and carried on down the street in a gaggle of strangers who neither knew nor cared he existed.

By the end of the exhibit, every piece had sold for a decent price. The photographs of desolate interiors were shipped off to the fine homes of collectors. He thought about the spaces as he had originally seen them – the grit that had crunched underfoot, the scat and the animal tracks, the sparkly shoes, and the cereal boxes ripped open on the floor – and he marvelled at how bizarre it was that now those rooms were matted and framed, destined for the walls of rooms so unlike them. The show had been a greater success than he could have hoped for, and yet, again, he felt empty and raw.

All he had to remove from the gallery were the discarded personal possessions no one had wanted in the first place.

⊙⊙⊙⊙⊙

When Marie Halliwell received the envelope from New York City, her hands shook as she opened it. Instead of the ever hoped-for letter from her son, she received a postcard invitation showing a fractured photograph of a ruined home. Eddie's name – Edward Halliwell – ran across the bottom of the card, along with the words "*Home*, A Photographic Installation, October 15th to November 15th." Over and gone. She held the picture in her hands and thought of the camera that had gone missing from beneath the tree all those Christmases ago. He had put it to use.

There was another item in the envelope, folded behind the invitation. She opened it and read.

> Edward Halliwell drives around the outskirts of the city
> looking for sadness. He finds it in old, decaying houses, dis-
> creetly tucked behind clusters of trees, surrounded by

cornfields and the encroaching urban sprawl. If the door is locked, he'll enter anyway.

The houses Halliwell finds have been left behind for reasons unknown to him, and the recent absence of their inhabitants is palpable, like fresh history. One day these dwellings will be erased and forgotten, and surely replaced with sterile replicas, grouped together to form the ubiquitous cul-de-sacs and avenues that make up the city's ever-growing suburbs. *Tabula rasa*, the new buildings will in turn await their transformation into homes.

It is in this abandoned territory that Halliwell's photographs carefully tread, mindful not to disturb the residue of each room's former inhabitants. The homes Halliwell finds are like accidental museums, filled with clues and artifacts that only suggest what each place might have been to the families that once lived there; silently they acquiesce to a future without them.

Halliwell's project is to stockpile evidence of domestic transformation. Initially, he approaches this undertaking with an objective distance, dutifully adopting the role of historian or cataloguer: he enters, he photographs, he leaves. Of course he also loots, but the real chaos evident in many of the images is abuse inflicted on the houses prior to his entry. By whom no one can say. But the ghosts of these families come back to us through the installation process Halliwell creates within the gallery. By incorporating artifacts found within the homes, Halliwell deliberately reinvests these forgotten spaces with emotion, and suddenly his thoughtful "distance" is lost. His patchwork of photographs reveals gaps and distorts shapes, tracing paths for our eyes to follow. We are drawn to the sadness of these places, and their clues to a lived experience.

Marie Halliwell read and reread the article in the sterile tranquility of her home, trying to find some trace of Eddie in its words. As she touched the paper, she understood that he had touched it too. He had folded it in two and mailed it to her, and for that tiny offering, she was thankful. She placed the article in her dresser drawer along with the cards and letters she had previously received from him – a scant few.

As far as Marie knew, she had not seen her son since August of 1970, more than seven years ago, an appalling trench gouged out between mother and son. Just last year, she had asked if they could meet at the airport, for she was going to Seattle to see her mother and had a stopover in his city. To her surprise, he had agreed, and they had arranged a rendezvous at 3 p.m. at an airport bar. She sat alert, smoothing the pleats of her grey skirt as her eyes scanned the bar and the waiting area beyond. She checked her watch. She had until 5 p.m. to make her connecting flight. At three-thirty, and again at 4:45, she asked the man beside her to confirm the time. She watched his hand pull back his sleeve and listened for his answer. At 4:55 she left, despondent.

⬭⬭⬭⬭⬭

The man who had sat beside her all that time watched her go. He finished his drink, rose, and walked in the opposite direction.

He thought, maybe if she had been less distracted, if she had really paused and looked at his face. But no. The day had come when his own mother had failed to know him.

OOOOO

After his success with *Home*, Edward turned into a night walker, ambling in the glow of the streetlights, amid the neon signs and the billboards. He set up his tripod and attached a cable release to the shutter so that he could leave the lens open for as long as he wanted. And then he moved into the frame, lighting the scene with a collection of torches and electronic flashes that shone different colours of light at varying intensities. He lit his shadow and made his unrecognizable silhouette a part of the incandescent blur: he, a dark ghost on the streets of the city.

As an adult, he saw that photography had always been circling him, coming closer and closer, and culminating in the night he'd stolen his father's camera. Throughout his life, he had noticed that certain moments froze in his mind like snapshots. His mother lying still on the bed in her geranium dress. His father – viewed from Eddie's treetop hiding place – pulling closed the drapes of the upstairs window. It was as if he'd started taking pictures long before he had the camera in his hands. The photographs he eventually did take were of ruined houses unlike his, which in reality had never begun to decay, but in Edward's imagination the walls were licked black by fire and the ceiling was spotted with mould. This was how he saw the house whenever he revisited the night of his burglary, and he saw himself too, stepping carefully over sloped and caving floors.

After he'd robbed his parents, he'd pushed out into the black-and-white night, turned off Riverside to Poplar and then Huron, which was a slower route to the highway, and though he'd not admitted to having made any conscious decisions, his blood had pumped faster as he'd approached 40 Huron Street. At the house next door, he'd seen Olive asleep on a cushion in the picture window. He'd stood watching her for a moment, until she'd lifted her head and perked her ears in what had to be recognition. When he'd turned up the path to the LeBlanc household, he'd seen a man standing in the yard, still and misshapen as a scarecrow, and had already opened his mouth to shout out in fear when he'd realized it was a snowman with arms and legs and a pine-cone smile. He'd carried on.

And on the front porch where Serge and Beryl Hayes had invited Joe to Robbie's funeral, the same spot where a robed and bearded man had appeared to Margar, and where Gus Devlin had arrived beneath his striped umbrella, Edward Halliwell had stood with his hand on the doorknob. Had it been locked, he would have walked away. But he'd turned the handle and entered the house where his sister lived, not hearing the gasp of another little girl in the hallway, not seeing her shoot through the dark to her room, and of course never knowing the effect he'd had, given she believed he was her father.

⟨⟨⟨⟩⟩⟩

It was Christmas of 1977 before there were prowlers again at 40 Huron Street. As the bungalow's inhabitants fell soundly to sleep, a beam of light streamed through the window, cutting a

319

path through the living room to the empty sofa. There was no sound except for the intermittent buzz of the fridge from the kitchen, or the heat coming on too often. After all this time, heat still escaped through the walls and the roof and the poorly sealed windows, but the bodies snug in their beds were piled with blankets, and accustomed to the cool air. They didn't wake until morning. The mulled wine and rich food they had enjoyed for their Christmas Eve feast sunk them into a slumber so deep that not even Margar heard the front door creak open or the whispered voices of the men who entered. In the winter air, they were sweating beneath their plaid wool jackets as they carried Beryl Hayes's piano into the living room and set it down near the picture window.

They left without anyone knowing they had come, and the room returned to its former suspended state, waiting for morning, except that now the path of light that travelled across it caught the edge of the piano, and a section of the panel that covered the keys. Birds and chipmunks had been carved into the wood. A bow rested on the carvings, and attached to the ribbons that trailed down was a note that said, "For Margar. Merry Christmas."

⁙

Alphonse and Toussaint tried to deny sneaking the piano in, suggesting Santa existed after all, but everyone knew it had been they. There were special presents for each child that year. Louis got a set of woodworking tools and a box full of oak, chestnut, and cherry, and Estelle received a necklace with a tear-shaped amethyst pendant that had belonged to the uncles'

320

mother. Margar bristled as Kay fastened the delicate chain around Estelle's neck, for she knew great-great-grandmother Thérèse LeBlanc had been no relation to Estelle, and furthermore, she knew Kay knew it. She wished the necklace had resided in her mother's jewellery box all this time, instead of with her uncles, for then she could have pinched it, along with the note she'd stolen months before, and the precious heirloom would not have gone out of the family, to Estelle. No one would have known she'd taken it – not for a long time, if ever – because Kay rarely wore jewellery, and had no cause to go digging around inside the box. When Margar had scooped the note, early that summer, before Gus had come to stay, she'd seen the ballerina still lying broken on top of the chains and earrings. All she'd intended to do was check on the puzzling letter, to see if it was still there, but then her old recklessness had sent her finger dipping into the lining, and the note was hot in her pocket, destined for who knew where. She'd never been a girl to let a scab heal over, not when she knew where it was on her knee, not when she could feel the skin puckering around it, not when it lifted up at the edges, practically waving to call her to action.

⟨⟨⟨⟨⟨⟩⟩⟩⟩⟩

After his disheartening win at the provincial championships, Louis decided his time with gymnastics was over. His mother had always said she'd thrown away her chances for love, but maybe she'd never really been good enough, and Louis, despite his trophies, was no better. Because he had given up when he'd been given up on, he was a failure, and nowhere near an Olympian.

But over the Christmas holidays, he whittled an array of little men and buildings with the tools Alphonse and Toussaint had given him, and his obvious knack helped him come to terms with his disappointment. He still didn't know exactly who he would become now that he'd let go of his dream, but he felt closer to that man than ever, and less inclined to define him. With the stress of competing gone, a new calmness permeated his small body, and the fear that had always been with him began its slow transformation. He tried to see himself as berry picker, fisherman, carpenter, following in the footsteps of Alphonse and Toussaint. He even considered driving, like Gus, who had returned to work by the busy Christmas season, when the greenhouse had begged for his services. There was so much work that Gus had asked Louis to come along as a helper, and Louis had ridden beside him through the Petawawa Plains, thinking about the Hayeses and stealing glances at Gus, whose courage he suddenly (though secretly) admired. He suspected his mother would marry Gus, for he could see that they had grown closer since the accident, and while the idea of that marriage gave Louis a start, he couldn't see why it would feel different than now, since Gus was with them every day.

In the beginning, when Gus had been suffering from the trauma of the crash, Louis had detested the sight of him. He had been only a little boy in the Joe years, but he hadn't forgotten the haunted look his father had worn from January all the way to that day in August. Joe's face had seemed to grow in length, and the bones beneath his skin had jutted out more sharply. The smile, when it came, stretched his lips and turned them almost invisible. The worst part of the smile was that it used only the mouth; it showed in no other features, which made the smile something other than a smile altogether, something put on rather than let out. Louis found the man he had loved frightening, not a real man, but a bag of bones, and Joe had had to be pushed, shaken alive, to even notice Louis at all. Though Louis had never told a soul, he felt something like relief when a canoe swept Joe away, when the river swallowed him, when a bus took him to Montreal – or whatever.

After the accident, as Louis had come and gone from home, he'd seen Gus's gloomy head through the living-room window, the amber eyes clouded with misery. This told him that history moved back and forth in time, repeating itself, and that it also spread sideways, drawing threads through parallel lives, but he had yet to see the exercise as anything but futile. And then like a summer storm passing, Gus had recovered. It had taken time before he was ready to drive again, but he had worked in the yard and cooked fancy meals for the family, and in the evenings, he'd taught Louis chess and backgammon, games of skill, Gus said, and concentration, and to Louis's surprise, he – Louis – was good.

As the warm, summer smell of flowers rode with them through the barren winter landscape, past white fields and snow-laden conifers and the leafy trees that would be skeletons until spring, Louis thought again about Mr. and Mrs. Hayes and the quickness of accidents. At other times of year, deer stepped out from the woods and into the speeding traffic, and you could never know when it would happen. It was simply the way of things. He still remembered the bears swaying in the apple trees, and of course, in the ensuing years, there had been more of their kind coming out of the wild and into civilization, unaware of the border. He thought of Alphonse and Toussaint driving the bears back out of town in their pickup truck, year after year, and it seemed to him a more important duty than any roll or tumble could ever be. These were the men of Louis's family – Alphonse, Toussaint, and also Gus, in a way. He felt a mixture of pride and awe, a new ambition rising.

◌◌◌◌◌

Louis didn't know that the original Olympians had also been a family. When he thought of the word "Olympian," he'd always imagined a human hero on a podium, or bearing a torch, or himself with a medal around his neck, never a family of gods and goddesses descended from a race of giants.

Gaea, earth goddess and primordial mother, was the daughter of no one. She had the ability to procreate on her own, but once she'd given birth to him, she was unable to resist the temptation of her starry-eyed son, Uranus, god of the sky. It was their incestuous union that produced the enormous Titans, but Uranus – sky – pressed down on Gaea – earth – and would not allow the big babies to be born from her womb.

Being her own lover's mother meant Gaea was wiser than Uranus. She instructed their son, Cronos, still lodged inside her, to castrate his father the next time Uranus entered her. The sky went red with blood that day, and giants emerged from the earth. Cronos had been victorious, but he understood the notion of consequence. He knew instinctively that the sins of the father are visited on the son, and that someday he, too, would father children. By the time he mated with his sister Rhea, the brutality of his own act still haunted him, and hoping to break what was now becoming a cycle of patricide, he ate his children to prevent them from killing him. He was a giant, after all. Everything tasted good and his hunger was insatiable.

The thing about fate is that it's fated. Rhea was as horrified by her brother-husband's actions as Gaea had been by Uranus's. Each child she bore came out of her only to go into him. Finally, when Zeus was born, she hid him away and in his place fed Cronos a stone wrapped in swaddling clothes. The giant gobbled it whole, not knowing the difference. And Zeus grew. He became wily and strong. History was repeated.

After the defeat of Cronos and the disgorgement of Zeus's brothers and sisters, the Olympians settled into heaven. Zeus married his sister Hera. It was an everlasting, miserable pairing that produced only one child – Ares, god of war, who came to symbolize their combative relationship. Hera was the goddess of weddings, fidelity, wives, and family, which seemed a cruel joke because her own domestic life was in tatters from the beginning. Zeus was a roving, lascivious god. He changed into a swan, a bull, an ordinary woodsman, to have his way with mortal women, and babies who were half divine, half human, populated heaven and earth. Hera hated the sight of them. Humiliated, vindictive, she became known for her murderous rages against the victims of Zeus's lust.

No matter which mistress she drowned or burned alive, nothing changed. The insults to Hera's dignity continued, and she remained a bitter, lonely woman – a cold, pathetic queen – locked eternally in her futile war against infidelity. Life went on up there as scandalously as it did down below. And the people

325

paid homage to the childish gods on high, who were ultimately just as human.

The Olympic Games were one form of that homage. Louis knew nothing about that, but years ago Russell Halliwell had told the story to Kay in the mood-lit high-school gymnasium. Olympia was a little town in Greece, he said, and the Games took place there every four years from 776 BC on (this having come to him from Marie). No women were allowed to participate in, let alone watch, the Games, which Russell said was "a real shame, a waste, but understandable," because competitors performed naked. "How could anyone concentrate," he murmured, running his finger up the side of Kay's torso.

Buzzing with infatuation, Joe LeBlanc stood at the gymnasium door that night. He had met Kay mere days before, right here in the gymnasium, when she had more or less fallen into his arms. And that first evening, he'd walked her home, already knowing he'd walk her right to the moon if that was what she wanted. Now he was here to say so. Or at least, to ask her on a pre-moon date. He had his fist raised, ready to knock, but he could see that no light shone from the crack under the door, and he assumed that no one was inside. He turned, planning to look for Kay elsewhere, and as his shoe pivoted on the polished school floor, it squeaked and muffled Kay's giggle. Joe paused, sure then unsure he'd heard her. He smiled, thinking he was already so crazy about her that he heard her everywhere he went. As he left the building, pushing the school doors open and inhaling the fresh air of a spring evening, Russell Halliwell ejaculated into Kay Clancy. None of them knew that Estelle was conceived in that moment. Joe, the most oblivious of all, went on smiling, striding across the high-school parking lot with his thumbs in his belt loops.

Around the time that Margar had her eye-opening visit with Mrs. Halliwell, Margaret Trudeau had left Pierre, poking a hole in the great Canadian fairy tale. Thankful as Margar was for her more saintly but still beautiful namesake, she lamented the young mother they had seen in the streets of Ottawa, the dazzling smile and the delicate wave she had given for free. No matter how rich, no matter how powerful, families were fragile concoctions. Margar removed the photos from her wall – magazine pin-ups of Maggie and Pierre dancing, kissing, travelling all over the world. The one of Pierre on the camel, with the house caving in behind him, was still one of her favourites because he looked most like a king in it, high above the riff-raff. A king with his queen and his trio of princes. None of it was true any more. And once she'd taken them down, the rest of the collage seemed pointless, so she removed it too, and all that remained were the holes from the pushpins, a sloppy constellation that failed to shape itself into anything recognizable, like a hunter or a bear.

It was some time after Pierre and Maggie's split that poor Gus had collided with Serge and Beryl Hayes. Only later did Margar realize she'd sensed the tragedy as she'd rung the doorbell that Wednesday. At the time she hadn't quite known what she'd been sensing, but goosebumps climbed up over her scalp like a hood being pulled tight. Afterwards, she could only surmise that the Hayeses had been summoning her, Saint Margaret, goddess of dying people, but her useless flapper ears hadn't heard them. She was shaken. She'd been overwhelmed by the secret about Kay and Estelle, by life's sudden, terrible unwieldiness – but after the crash she was overwhelmed by the opposite, by life's smallness, by two lives gone in an afternoon.

Nevertheless, something good came out of it all when Gus moved in. She didn't know what would happen to him once Joe came home, but she was glad to have him around in the meantime. She had always felt sorry for Gus when she pictured Joe resuming his place in the household, and now she felt sorrier still, for Joe knew what Kay had done – it was obviously why he'd left – but Gus remained in the dark, of that there was no doubt. If anything, he seemed to love Kay more with every sun that rose and set. And the joy that brought Margar confused her. His very tenderness made Margar question which was the moral thing, to tell or to stay quiet? Both felt right, and both felt wrong. But she needed to do something with such sizzling, important information.

The answer came to her that Christmas, when the gift of Beryl Hayes's piano brought to mind Mrs. Halliwell's piano, and so, Mrs. Halliwell. As Margar watched her fingers pressing the keys, she imagined her boots in the white snow, taking her back to the Halliwell property, and before she could decide whether that would be saintly or evil, whether she was righting a wrong or making it more wrong, the note she had stolen months before was in her itchy mitten, folded small into an envelope that read *Marie H.* in disguised handwriting. Margar pulled it out and kneeled on the snowy porch. Lifting the lid of the mail slot, she spied on the sleepy interior of the Halliwell home. She wanted to see the boy walk by, or have him come face to face, eye to eye with her through this silent mouth in the door, but Eddie didn't come. No one did. She waited for plates to fly, but it was as if no one lived there.

Finally, Margar pushed the note through, holding on to its corner. She remembered her grandmother's expression, "opening a can of worms." She was sticking her whole hand in the can, into the wiggling pile, without knowing what the worms would do when she tipped them out. She felt the heat from the house warm her fingers. And when she let go of the note, it was as if she herself were falling, free-falling all the way home, and the dazzling ways things might change were raining down around her, now that the secret was out of her hands.

⦅⦅⦅⦅⦆⦆

From the second-storey window, Marie Halliwell watched Margar steal into the street. The poplars stood out against the dull sky like rows of stiff black lace, and Margar, wearing pink mittens, an orange hat, a red jacket she had long grown out of, raced by them, a speeding comet of colour. Marie Halliwell smiled, wishing her own boy was a child still, offering clues to himself. Given the chance, she would see them.

She stepped out of his room, and went downstairs to the door. The envelope lay face up, *Marie H.* in dramatic letters, and while she was surprised by its contents, and curious as to how a note so old had come into Margar's hands, Marie knew her place in the tragedy. Tucking the note back into the envelope, she slipped both into the woodstove. She poked at the fire. The stove was of the finest quality, and had saved their lives in the ice storm. Not once had they needed to step outside.

⟨⟨⟨⟨⟨⟩⟩⟩⟩⟩

News of Edward Halliwell's success had spread from New York City and eventually over to Halifax, where he'd begun his studies in earnest. They wanted him back now, by way of a solo exhibition held in the art school's gallery. They promised a prestigious affair, and said, "We would be honoured to have the opportunity to exhibit your work." Which made him laugh when he remembered how he had walked out on his life there, leaving his parents and the school to clean up after him.

For some time he had been putting together a series of photographs called *In Reverse*. The photos were not images he had shot himself, but ones he had collected over the years. Some of them were of people he knew — his mother and father kissing in an orange grove in Sorrento, his science partner Duncan Weir flying down Ridge Road on his bicycle. The common thread was that something had been scrawled on the back of each photograph. He'd always kept these snapshots with him and had added to his collection over the years. Now the bulk of the pictures were of strangers, each still with some defining script on the reverse. When these photos were held up to the light, the words showed backwards through the image.

One night he was sitting looking at them this way, as he often did, when it came to him that he could place the camera in a copy stand and recapture the images facedown on a light table. The result would be a new photograph, the image reversed, its

330

caption scribbled right-way-up across it: *Daddy and Estelle, January, 1961.*

This was the work he had chosen for the Halifax exhibit, but it was not until weeks before the show was scheduled to start that he began printing the first tests for his idea, because only the pressure of deadlines could motivate him to rise and dress and leave his dank apartment. For days, locked away in the dark-room, he printed the new versions of the snapshots at ten times their original size. He watched his parents come to life in the toxic fluid, and saw his father's hand resting on his mother's stomach, where Edward himself, a new life, was forming. He watched Joe LeBlanc and Estelle, his blood sister, floating in the bath of chemicals. After each long day, he fell into bed, exhausted, his mind swimming with all the things that needed to be done the next day and the day after that. But when he put the lights out and pushed the list of chores from his consciousness, his old despair arose to haunt him. *What is the point?* And each time he would fight with the feeling that alternately weighed on his chest or sank down to his bones and shook him.

By the time he'd printed the final images, framed them, and had them shipped in crates to Halifax, the stress of the last weeks had brought on a migraine. He should have been on his way to Halifax to oversee the hanging of the show, but for two days he lay in bed waiting for the pain to subside. In his lucid moments, he thought of the invitations going out – one to his mother – bearing the image of Joe and Estelle. How he had come to that decision he could no longer remember, but there was no turning it around now. He kept the room dark, and grew confused about whether it was noon or midnight, but if he held his arms up toward the window, he could still see how the veins and tendons stood out by the scant light that came in through the glass – noon, then.

In his periodic delirium, he imagined his skin was growing tighter on his body, strangling the workings inside. He used to get that feeling when he dissected the animals – a tightness that wouldn't let up until the blade had gone in. But he didn't want to think of that now. Instead he thought of clocks and watches, and how his own body was like those mechanisms. Under the glass, under the faceplate, was the intricate stuff of him, a million microscopic devices wound too tight but performing in unison.

His obsession with the workings under his skin had begun years before, when he'd shed the pounds he'd carried through childhood. His own fat had made his insides invisible to him, and once it was gone, he developed a fascination for the veins that carried the blood throughout his body.

As he lay in the dark with his arm in the air and his head pounding, he saw his skin tighten around his bones. He could feel that pressure in his whole body, as though his skin were growing smaller – or his skeleton larger. Somehow part of a day had passed. The clock read 5:50, but he had no idea which five. The faint glimmer of light through the blinds could mean morning or dusk. He thought of his mother riding on the train to Halifax, and wondered if he might go and meet her at the station. He could arrange for her to stay at the hotel where he would be, an old stone one near the harbour, and in the morning they would get up early and walk on the beach where there were washed-up pebbles and seashells, and bits of smooth coloured glass, and at lunch they would eat chips and fried clams.

Now he was very confused as to whether he was old or young. He believed he might not have left Halifax at all, and was standing at his dorm window, watching his parents drive away from him. The tail lights of the car stared at him like two red eyes. He waited, and held the curtain close, ready to hide if the figure in the passenger seat turned to wave goodbye, but no one looked back to find him. Just out in the hallway his roommates, Thomas and Nelson, were laughing, and all of his big shirts were hanging in the closet, undone, like the carcasses of animals that have been split up the middle and had their insides taken out. Across the street there was a lecture being delivered. Professor St. Clair would ask them if art was a means for survival, and if called upon, Edward would have to answer that he didn't know, and didn't understand the question.

The pressure of his own suffocating skin mounted. His head pounded, and he thought it was probably not caused by a migraine at all, but by the outside of him shrinking his inside. He pushed back the heavy covers of his bed and stood swaying in the dark, looking for his dresser. He pulled open the top drawer, where the little scalpel sat in its fancy case, and as he sliced the skin of one wrist and then the other, he felt the pressure release, and a cool rapturous breeze fluttered over him.

His last thought was of the boy Duncan Weir, captured in time as he speeds by on his bicycle, his legs pedalling so fast that they freeze into a blur of black and grey. He leans forward over his handlebars to go faster, as fast as he can. The hot August wind cools his blazing cheeks and stretches his mouth, forever, into the giddy smile of childhood.

⬤⬤⬤⬤⬤

That same day, Marie Halliwell boarded the train for Halifax alone. She'd told Russell about the exhibit, but had kept the invitation hidden. The picture on the front of it, *Daddy and Estelle*, had startled her, but it had also pushed her to action. Knowing Russell would have no interest in accompanying her, she announced one night at dinner that she was going on her own. Russell had pushed his plate away, as though the topic had put him off his food. He looked out the window to the river.

"Well?" she said.

"I don't know why you bother."

"Russell, it's been —"

"Too long, I know. Why should you be the one running to him?"

Marie looked down at her food.

"He's not our son, Marie. He stopped being our son years ago. He blew every chance he had. The airport, Marie, remember that? And we paid to put him through that school just to find out months later that he's not even going —"

"That was such a long time ago."

"So? Tell me where he's been lately. Tell me why we should support him now?"

Marie paused. Without looking up from her plate she said, "Because he *is* our son. Because he always will be."

It was not until the train pulled out of the station that her quiet anger began to subside. She imagined how she would hold

Eddie and tell him she still remembered the way he had smelled as a baby – though she knew she couldn't say it, too much had happened, it would be far too awkward, but she saw herself through the scene anyway, wrapping her arms easily around him and whispering, *You are my pride and joy. You will never stop being my baby.* She remembered how he had wailed in his first weeks of life, and how surprising it was to see first-hand that a baby is born crying but needs to learn how to laugh.

Marie leaned her head against the glass as the train sped through the wilderness. The white pines and the poplars stretched their arms out for her, as though trying to tell her something, but she was safe inside here, she could not be reached. In a matter of hours, all this bush would open into sky and ocean, and she would disembark, breathe the salty air, and walk without shoes in the water. She had a beautiful feeling of rejuvenation. She was not an old woman. Much of her life had passed in fear and despair, but it wasn't over yet. She had nothing with her but enough clothes for a long weekend, her toiletries, and an extra pair of shoes, but in the serenity of this moment, it seemed that she could easily leave the rest behind, that she would be lighter and happier without it. She turned to her reflection in the black window and smiled, and her hand rose shaking to her chest. The idea of not returning was both terrifying and exhilarating.

She thought of Sorrento, the steep cliffs and the seagulls screaming over the Bay of Naples below. She thought of the gardens, and of the music box Russell had given her. The song inside started blissfully and ended in sorrow, but neither she nor Russell had known that at the time, and even if they had, they would have believed their love to be the exception.

In her own garden, Marie had spent years turning wilderness into a botanical paradise. She had taken her cue from the rose-heavy, highly manicured gardens of Italy. There could be no orange trees, of course, as there'd been in Sorrento, but while she hadn't expected the plants that had grown in the Mediterranean to thrive in the Valley's starved, acidic soil, she'd learned to emulate their shape and design with others. She had loved her garden. How steadfast she'd been about weeding in the early days. The mint had been especially invasive. She'd dug it up and it had appeared in a hundred new places, sending its suckers beneath the soil so she never knew where it would sprout up until it did. She'd ripped it out by its roots and somehow it had come back stronger. Finally, she'd let it have its way. She saw now that she had let go of every fundamental passion she had found – art, the garden, her son. As if they were the feathers she'd collected as a child, one day she'd opened her hand and let the wind take them from her palm.

The train shunted east and Marie kept her eyes open, even though it had grown dark outside, and there was nothing to see. Wherever she went now, after Halifax, it would not be home, for she didn't need Russell's strength any more. In the pitch-dark she felt sure the road ahead was wide and smooth, that nothing could break her. She would go not to Seattle or Italy, but somewhere new, somewhere she'd never been, and begin again, in atonement. She would ask Eddie if he wanted to come with her, even for a while – if only to gain back a shadow of the time lost in the maze of her mistakes.

THE END

In the wee hours of a February night in 1984 – an Olympic year – Pierre Trudeau donned his fur coat over his pyjamas and prepared for a walk in a blizzard. His sons were snug in bed, his gorgeous estranged wife was on the brink of becoming his gorgeous ex-wife, and the country's economy was in a shambles. All he wanted was to go home. He was having a pool built at his house in Montreal, and he imagined himself safe from the blizzard, plunging into warm turquoise water. He walked until midnight in the storm, because walking and canoeing had always given him his clearest answers. Though he had resigned once before, and returned, he knew that this time if he left he would stay away for good. Many years ago he had announced, "I'm sure at some point I will feel I've done what I could, and I will find the appeal of private life irresistible. Then I know the party will go on without me – and so will the country." In the brisk winter air, he understood that day had come. But in order to be certain, he listened to his heart and looked for signs of destiny in the sky, and there were none — there were just snowflakes.

The next day he resigned as prime minister of Canada.

⬭⬭⬭⬭⬭

Though she adored Trudeau, Margar LeBlanc didn't trust him. Eighteen now, and wise beyond her years, she knew that he had resigned once before and returned, and down to her toes she believed he'd be back this time, too, no matter what he said, because 24 Sussex Drive was his home, and his children's home, and she had never known another prime minister, or at least not one who counted. So instead of languishing over the pictures of him in the newspaper, gushing over him, wishing her wish into the inky newsprint, she flipped past him and stopped at another photo buried in the back pages, of a man equally caught up in the storm that had helped Pierre make his decision. The photo showed a main street in rural Quebec, where the snow fell so heavily, and in such large flakes, that it veiled the lone, thin man passing by in the background. His feet were as big as snowshoes, and kicked up snowy clouds that rested just above the ground, frozen in time. Margar squinted at the picture. The man leaned into the wind with fierce determination, and his long legs scissored as though nothing could keep him from getting to wherever he was going. The snow piled up on him the way it did on the trees nearby. A hat with earflaps covered his hair and most of his face, but his nose protruded anyway, a large, hooked, Margar kind of nose, leading him out of the frame and into the eye of the storm. And maybe — finally — towards her.

ACKNOWLEDGEMENTS

Thank you to Jeff Winch, beloved man of integrity and belly laughs, and also my anchor during the growing of this novel and another baby not made of paper. Thanks too to Jeff the photographer, whose work inspired the *Home* and *Sleepwalk* series of Edward Halliwell. Thanks to Amy Satterthwaite, and to Gallery 44, Centre for Contemporary Photography, for allowing Amy's fine essay to be twisted into fiction. Thanks to Sara Angelucci for Edward's *In Reverse* series; for *Io sono molto bella*; and of course for Italians Love Love. Thank you Siobhan Maloney for the green dress dream; Julie Trimingham for her theories on kings and queens; Reed Russell for introducing me to the quiet dignity of perennial gardens; Jamie Sinclair for sharing memories of his art-school days; and Owen Wong, who, via Janet Hardy, let me in on the mournful stuffed animal secret. I must also extend my gratitude to the people of Deep River, and hope that they will forgive me for taking liberties with our town's history and geography. Thanks too to Jennifer Lambert, Ellen Seligman, and Denise Bukowski for showing such unfailing enthusiasm for this story, and for helping me find my way to the ending. And finally, thanks to my sisters for reading early versions, and to the rest of my ever-growing family – especially Nellie, who, big as she was, postponed her debut until the first draft was born.

Many books and Web sites were consulted in a quest for Olympic details both ancient and modern, but the statistics quoted at the start of each chapter come from www.olympic.org.

Again I am grateful to the Canada Council for the Arts, because a grant is more than survival money for a writer, it's encouragement and validation.